DEATH OF A THOUSAND CUTS

Barbara D'Amato

TOR®

A TOM DOHERTY ASSOCIATES BOOK
NEW YORK

This is a work of fiction. All the characters and events portrayed in this book are either products of the author's imagination or are used fictitiously.

DEATH OF A THOUSAND CUTS

A Tor Book
Published by Tom Doherty Associates, LLC
175 Fifth Avenue
New York, NY 10010

www.tor.com

Tor® is a registered trademark of Tom Doherty Associates, LLC.

ISBN 0-765-34257-X
EAN 978-0-765-34257-7

First edition: June 2004
First mass market edition: May 2006

Printed in the United States of America

0 9 8 7 6 5 4 3 2 1

To my wonderful writing companions,
Jeanne Dams and Mark Zubro.
Their talent, good taste, and unselfish care made every page
better than it would have been without them.

And to Emily and Adam, because they are people
who ask questions.

One

*The moment a man begins to question the meaning
and value of life, he is sick.*

—SIGMUND FREUD, 1937

CHAPTER *1*

JEFFREY CLIFFORD SAT in the passenger seat of his sister's Mazda, hesitating to open the door. He stared across the wide expanse of heat-seared lawn at Hawthorne House, the huge nineteenth-century mansion looming fifty yards away. Walls of bloodred brick rose from a stone substructure, with three stories of narrow arched windows like squeezed eyes. There were gable eyebrows over the third-story windows. On top of each gable was a sharp wrought-iron point. A steep roof of black slate rose from the third floor. Along its peak ran a wrought-iron railing crest topped with alternating spearpoints and balls. At the tip of the roof ends—there were four because the building was cross shaped like a cathedral—iron lightning rods rose up, each ten feet tall. The five brick chimneys that also shared the roof were funnel shaped, with the widest portion flaring out at the top. There were eighteen bedroom gables on the third floor.

Jeffrey liked to count. He always felt better when he knew just how much there was of everything.

As Jeffrey knew from experience, there were also four little servants' cells huddled up under the roof on the attic floor. Twelve bedrooms occupied the second floor, along with a gigantic ballroom in the center. Jeffrey had not seen the mansion in years, but he knew it by heart.

What sort of family would ever have believed themselves so important that they needed a pile like this for a home?

"I can not. Go in there," he said in his stiff, oddly patterned voice.

His sister, Catherine, said, "Then don't. You don't have to."

"I do. Though."

The mansion faced west. On this hot day in mid-July, the sun was still quite high at 6:00 P.M., but the light was taking on an orange tinge of late afternoon. The red brick burned in the light.

Maybe this would be the end of his life. It was going to destroy him in some way, he knew. It had damaged him before. Twenty-two years ago, he thought, this was a toxic place. Twenty-two years ago, when he was seven years old and terrified, his parents had left him here, and he was just as terrified now as he had been then.

"You've never been back since you were a child, have you, Jeffy?" Catherine asked.

"No."

"You've never even been driven by?"

"No."

With a rising note of hope in her voice, she said, "So you must see it now as a grown-up. It must look smaller. And less scary."

She paused. He said, "No."

He couldn't explain. He was never good at explaining himself, anyway. This hideous, dangerous, poisonous house of the sharp points and narrow windows—a facade like a headache—had only grown uglier over the years. The massive walls of meat-color bricks would crush him. The air inside would be foul. The rooms would be dark and the carpets dredged in dust. And inside, relishing the foulness, would be the toxic warlock who wanted to eat young children, bite by eager bite.

In his halting way, he said, "It was not. An ennobling idea to come here."

"Jeffy, I told you. You don't have to do this. We can go home."

"No. That is the difficulty. I do have. To do this."

He put the duffle bag on the curb and got out of the car. He slammed the door, which made a tinny, cheap-car thwack. The air conditioner hadn't worked in years, so Catherine kept all the windows rolled down. The temperature had reached a hundred and one degrees in Chicago today, the radio had told them, the third day in a row over a hundred.

Trembling, Jeffrey hung the duffle bag strap over the crook of his arm. His other arm was bent too, the elbow held next to his body. He said carefully, "Thank you for. Driving me."

"No problem."

"Mom always said you. Could never park anyplace within ten. Blocks of the University of Chicago."

"You're going to be hot in that tight vest."

He ran a hand over his chest. In addition to his shirt, he wore an old leather vest he'd owned for years. He liked familiar things, never wanted anything new. The vest strained at the seams even though Jeffrey was slender, and that, plus its scruffy appearance, bothered Catherine. She wanted him to look good, especially this weekend, seeing people he had not seen in years.

He said, "I like things. To be tight."

"Well—" Catherine paused. "Well, shall I pick you up on Sunday, then?"

He didn't dare look back at her. If he did, he'd turn right around and get in the car.

"That is the present plan."

JANE MACY WALKED SLOWLY toward Hawthorne House. She'd had to park five blocks away, but that didn't bother her. She liked hot weather, even really hot weather like this, and as she approached the building, she felt pleasantly warmed rather than uncomfortable.

Her little overnight case hung by its strap from her hand. She was rather proud of it. It was powder blue with stitching in a contrasting navy, soft-sided top-grain leather, round, like a huge pocket watch, and filled with thoughtfully designed compartments.

At the junction of the sidewalk and the Hawthorne House walkway, she paused.

The mansion rose up before her in the late afternoon light. It was so large that from her place on the walk it occupied almost all her visual field. The building wrapped its arms around her. The red brick glowed warm and inviting. Even the antique glass in its windows gave back a mellow amber shine.

She smiled at Hawthorne House.

It wasn't just the warmth of the old building that pleased her so much. She craned her head back and smiled at the whimsical pagoda points of the lightning rods, the funny wrought-iron decorative railing that ran along the roof peak. A wrought-iron fence, similar in style, surrounded the property on the sides and back. Then there were the gables, each with its own fancy little pagodalike peak, and the slate roof tiles, scalloped like cookies at the edges. And the tall brick chimneys, five of them, that flared out at the top, almost as if they were upside down. Whoever saw chimneys like that these days? The architect must have had such fun designing them.

Of course, she was well aware that her feelings toward the building were heavily colored by her warm feelings toward the six years of her life she had spent there. Psychiatric counseling had trained her to be conscious of the effect of emotion on perception. She was good at watching for these connections. Almost, she said to herself, doing it automatically by now.

With a little bounce in her step, swinging her overnight case in expectation of a delightful weekend, she sashayed up the walk to Hawthorne House.

⚔︎

A HAND-WAXED BLACK LIMO, longer than two Mazdas, slid to a stop in front of Hawthorne House, tires sighing on the pavement. The driver, wearing a two-piece gray uniform suit, got out and marched around to the right rear passenger door.

"Dr. Schermerhorn," he said, opening the door with a white-gloved hand. Although the limo was air-conditioned, the driver had started to sweat the instant he stepped out of it into the street.

The man who exited the passenger seat was tall, with silver hair and a neatly trimmed silver Van Dyke beard. He wore a light summer-weight three-piece English suit.

While the driver extracted the deerskin valises from the trunk, Dr. Schermerhorn studied the building before him.

Commanding, he thought. *Elegant. A wonderful example of midwestern faux Queen Anne. I knew the first moment I saw it that this was the place to establish my institute.*

Hawthorne House had been the home of the Cyrus Hawthornes. Built in 1881 by the Chicago architectural firm Treat and Foltz, it had been ahead of its time in conveniences—modern plumbing and steam heat—even if a bit excessive in design.

The Hawthornes lived at Hawthorne House through two and a half generations, until Frederick Hawthorne lost his fortune in the crash of 1929, and moved out of the house forever in 1931. A white elephant as a family home, it became a finishing school for young ladies in 1933, after lying empty for two years. Its nearness to the University of Chicago helped its recruiting efforts. Hawthorne House housed thirty young ladies at a time and graduated fifteen of them each year after a two-year course. They learned deportment, penmanship, sewing, how to speak properly, how to set a table properly, and how to entertain with grace.

But by 1960 young ladies did not want to be "finished." They wanted to be educated in a profession. Hawthorne House struggled along as a collection of offices. Several doctors practiced there, a few lawyers, and on the third floor were the editorial offices of a small but highly regarded academic press that turned out well-regarded but rarely read books.

Hawthorne House had not succeeded as offices. It was too far from the business district of the Hyde Park area of Chicago. When Dr. Schermerhorn saw it in 1968, only seven of a possible twenty office suites were occupied.

He knew the instant he laid eyes on it that it was perfect for his residential treatment center. Big enough for two dozen patient bedrooms, plus offices and schoolrooms, it was massive and therefore conveyed the solidity and respectability he wanted to express. The woodwork inside was elegant, despite some vandalism done by driving doors through several interior walls to produce office suites. There had been cheap remodeling performed on the beautiful ballroom to subdivide it into small office cubicles.

Hawthorne House would become Hawthorne House School, residential treatment for autistic children.

Wundershön, Schermerhorn thought as he looked at the building now, twenty-seven years later. *Those tall, stately windows. The assertive roof treatment. And that muscular brick, a wonderful masculine color as rich as aged mahogany. A building in charge of itself.*

There would be reporters here within an hour, an hour and a half at most. Time enough to get to his room and change into the new Brioni suit. His publisher had said Susan Somebody from *Time* magazine would be here. And early yesterday his office had received calls from *Dateline* NBC.

Good. Let them come. And confusion to my enemies.

CHAPTER 2

OLLIE AND I DROVE past Hawthorne House on our way back to the district station late that afternoon, heading over to Stony Island Avenue, but we paid no attention to the old mansion. I've been a detective several years now, Ollie a bit longer than I. It was hot, we were tired, there was no air-conditioning in the car, and we were both surly. My neck was sweaty. Thank goodness for short hair.

"I want a baked potato with sour cream and bacon bits," I said.

"Don't, Emily. That's five hundred calories."

"It'd be ninety without the cream and bacon, though."

"But would you eat it plain? You'll hate yourself in the morning."

"I want to be happy right now. I spend way too much time worrying about tomorrow."

"Besides, it's too hot for a baked potato."

"Potato salad, then. What are you, Emeril Lagasse?"

"It's supposed to be even hotter tomorrow. Hundred and two."

I groaned. "Maybe I'll phone in dead tomorrow." We were starting to see an increase in heat deaths already, and there was no end predicted to the heat wave. The patrol cops were spending their days trying to coax senior citizens out of apartments that didn't have air-conditioning, which meant carrying the old people down dozens of flights of stairs. But detectives like us saw the heat victims after heat had done its lethal work. I shuddered at the thought of coming to the job tomorrow.

The light changed. I paid attention to the road again. "Jeez! What we need. A fire in this heat!" We were at Fifty-fifth and Woodlawn. The smokies were pouring water on a large wooden house, just managing to keep the fire from spreading to other buildings, not even trying to save this one.

I said, "Looks like the place is gonna be totaled."

"Yeah. That house is engulped in flames."

I stole another glance at him. I never quite knew when Ollie was teasing me and when he really believed his malapropisms were words.

"Jeez," I grumbled. "Tomorrow will be hell."

Actually, for Ollie and me, tomorrow was going to get different, and not any better.

AT HAWTHORNE HOUSE, preparations were going forward.

"Look at him."

The three students hired to help in the kitchens this weekend swung their heads as one and stared at Karl Deemer. Deemer lounged in the pantry, his arms crossed, his long sandy hair pulled back with a rubber band into a stringy ponytail. He was thirty-six and had a bland, unworried face that looked twenty-two at most, as if no emotions had dwelled in it long enough to age it. Marcy Louis, the student who had spoken, was nineteen, pretty, and inclined to poke fun at people.

"Guess what he did? Just guess."

"Oh, go ahead and tell us, Marcy," said Peg Allesandro. "Don't make a drama of it."

Alexa Langmar nodded her head.

"Well, okay. Brian told him to make the margaritas." Brian was the caterer, now bustling around the ovens making sure the broilers didn't burn the spiced ground beef on toast. Brian had a staff of eight of his own people, plus three Hawthorne House regulars and five college student temps, of whom Marcy, Peg, and Alexa were three. With a hundred and fifty people expected, this was none too many, and Brian was rushed.

"*Well,* Brian gave him the pitchers of fresh margaritas—"

"I think it's from mix," Alexa said rather haughtily. "Not fresh."

Peg said, "Never mind that."

Marcy said, "I meant they just made it up. Anyway, Brian goes, 'You know what a margarita is?' Deemer goes, 'Sure thing.' Brian goes, 'Okay. Each glass should be filled no more than two-thirds of the way up and you know the glass gets frosted with salt around the edge?' He points at the plate of salt and the plate of I guess egg white. And Deemer goes, 'Sure thing.'"

"Sure thing," Peg said, mocking. Peg was twenty-one, tall, dark, and bored.

"So I wasn't watching, because I was supposed to assemble the crudités platters, but I heard Brian screaming 'What have you *done*?'"

"Well, what *had* he done?" Peg demanded.

Somebody dropped a baking sheet, with a clang like the last trump. Brian Travis of Brian Travis Catering frowned.

Marcy ignored it. "There was salt and margarita everyplace. On the floor, and just—everyplace. And Deemer goes, 'Well, I filled all the glasses two-thirds full. And then I sprinkled the salt on the edge, but it didn't stick and it all fell in the drink. And then I tipped the salt plate over the glasses, but the salt went all over the table. And then I tried tipping a glass into the salt, but the drink fell out.'"

"No!" Peg said.

"I don't *believe* it!" Alexa said.

"So Brian screams, 'Just go away, go away, go away and don't bother us!' and Deemer slinks away."

Travis, on the other side of the kitchen, said, "Kitchen staff will send all hot hors d'oeuvres upstairs *hot*. Hot-hot-hot. Particularly the spinach puffs, spiced beef, and the crab puffs."

"I've never *heard* of anything so stupid!" Alexa said.

Marcy said, "What an idiot."

"Hey, he is kind of an idiot, you know," Peg confided, "they say Deemer has been here since back in the days of the—you know." Seeing that Marcy and Alexa just looked at her blankly, she said, "The days when this was a home for crazy kids. Mrs. Kisilinski says Deemer was one of them, and he got too old to be in care here, like you had to be under sixteen or eighteen or whatever, so they hired him to work as a janitor and kitchen helper. And so he could still be, like, treated."

"Well, they didn't treat him enough, did they?" Alexa said.

Marcy said, "Now I feel really bad," but when the others laughed, so did she.

Brian Travis said, "Cold crudités and other cold appetizers will remain in the refrigerator until the *moment* you place them on the dumbwaiter. Cold-cold-cold! I will keep track of the order in which they are served, so that a variety is moved up constantly. Got it?"

Mumbles of "Yes," "Got it," and "Okay." Quietly, someone in the back said, "Duh!"

Someone else mumbled, "Yup-yup-yup."

While the girls giggled, they missed seeing Karl Deemer slip out of the pantry, where the plates and glassware were shelved, farther back into the dark rear vestibule. The garbage cans were stored in the vestibule before being taken out to the alley for pickup. Because the kitchen was in the basement, as in many old mansions, a short flight of cement steps ran up from the back basement door to ground level. Here in the dark, Karl Deemer smiled. He had heard most of what the girls said. Karl knew perfectly well how to salt a margarita glass. But he had developed his labor-saving dummy persona over the years and it had always stood him in good stead.

Karl sat on a garbage can and began to play with his hair.

CHAPTER 3

"WELL, OF *COURSE* SIGMUND Freud was a great man!" stated Professor Hansen.

The grad student blinked. Around them the packed crowd jostled and pushed. "But Professor! I thought you disagreed with everything Freud ever said."

The professor, Dr. Carol Hansen, said, "Freud was the greatest self-promoter of all time. Unfortunately, he was a crappy shrink. He didn't know shit about human psychology."

People nearby sent dark looks her way, but Hansen only smiled. "Let alone being a charlatan," she added in a clear voice. Now in her midforties, Hansen was a splendid greyhound of a woman, lean and lithe. Maturity had made her even more beautiful, the grad student thought admiringly, than the pictures he had seen of her as a young student. She was nearly six feet tall, with a face that was pointed but very attractive. People often said she had marvelous bone structure. Her coloring was splendid too. She had pale blue eyes and sleek blond hair, blunt cut to show off its gloss and straightness. Hansen's skin was an ivory shade, her arms lightly brushed with gold hairs. She had accentuated her Scandinavian coloring with a whipped-cream-color linen suit and an ice blue Jil Sander schoolgirl blouse.

Jeffrey stood just two feet in front of Professor Hansen. He heard every word; the professor made no attempt to be discreet. If anything, Jeffrey thought, Hansen wanted to be heard. Jeffrey had placed himself near Hansen intentionally. He had read every one of the professor's articles that were available on the Net, and owned every one of the five books Hansen had written. If he had a chance, he wanted to congratulate her. A woman in purple turned to Jeffrey, and said, "Who let *her* in?"

"Uh. Why would they—they not—" He pulled his elbows in closer to his body. Jeffrey was no good at chatting when suddenly confronted with a human he had never met. Fortunately, the woman had no awareness of his discomfort, or interest in it, for that matter. She wanted an ear, not a conversationalist.

"Why would they not let her in? Because she's against everything Dr. Schermerhorn believes in. She's a rabid anti-Freudian."

"Well, but—"

"Yes, I know what you're going to say. This is a university setting—a quasi-university setting anyway, I suppose—and we should be open to a variety of ideas. But a person who has done everything she can to destroy Schermerhorn's reputation ought to know she's not welcome. *Without being told.*"

Several people nearby tried to shush Dr. Hansen. Jeffrey had been taking lessons in how to conduct a social conversation, and said to the woman, "Are you a—"

"Therapist. Neo-Freudian, if you must have a label."

Jeffrey knew from his studies of how to make conversation that now she was supposed to say, "And what do you do, Mr.—?" To his puzzlement, she didn't. What good was learning the social rules if other people broke them?

A young woman came by with a tray of sherry in glasses shaped like tiny tulips. There were eight, and their spacing on the tray was utterly random and made Jeffrey cringe. Two rows of four would have been pleasing. Jeffrey didn't take any. Sherry might interfere with his medication.

"Dr. Schermerhorn is here, isn't he?" a man asked, rather breathlessly.

"Has to be," said a woman. "He's the main course."

"This is so exciting."

"Do you think he would talk with me?"

Quite a lot of press was on hand tonight. Jeffrey recognized Ann-Marie Garcia-Smith from CNN and on-screen TV reporters from local CBS, NBC, and ABC affiliates, as well as WGN and a couple of others who looked familiar, maybe Fox and CLTV. There would be print media people here, too, but he didn't know what any of them looked like. There were photographers, video and still, scattered around, and he noticed they stayed at some distance from each other.

It was hot. The window air conditioners were inadequate for the size of the building, and the packed bodies blocked the circulation of air.

The catering staff pushed through the crowd, bearing trays of food and drink. Even though a hundred and fifty people chatted and laughed, the noise level was moderate. The Hawthornes' architects had designed this room for musical events and they'd known something about acoustics. Sound carried but did not mix and muddle. When a man in his early sixties, pink faced, white haired, wearing a dark suit, stepped onto the low platform and clapped his hands for silence, it took only seconds before most of the people in the room had stopped talking. Those few who hadn't heard him clap quickly responded to the increasing hush and quieted also.

The man was cheerful, beaming proudly at the crowd.

"I'll only keep you a moment," he said, scarcely raising his voice. "I know those crab puffs are irresistible." There was a small amount of polite laughter. Jeffrey studied the man, aware that he had seen him years before. Jeffrey had a warm, good feeling about him. Oh, yes. Of course. He was—

"I'm Dr. Erik Emerson. We're here tonight to pay tribute to a pioneer in autism treatment. To a man who developed a residential treatment protocol for autistic children at a time when autism was itself a relatively new concept. To a man whose wonderful, evocative stories of the lives of children with psychological problems raised everybody's consciousness. Dr. Jay Schermerhorn!"

There was scattered applause in the room when he paused for breath.

"I first met Dr. Schermerhorn when I began my postdoc psych training. Dr. Schermerhorn was my teacher and mentor. He was charismatic. He was challenging. From then on, I signed up for all the courses he taught, which unfortunately was just one a semester. You know how med schools are." Laughter in the room. "He completely turned around my thinking, and I could see that plumbing the human psyche was the most exciting thing in the world. I'd been thinking of going into neurosurgery, but two courses from Dr. Schermerhorn and I was hooked. I owe my career and what I may call my life in psychoanalysis to this one man, a man who is like a father to me. I give you Jay Schermerhorn!"

Schermerhorn was in his seventies now, with silky hair even purer white than Emerson's, but he looked youthful and he took the step up to the platform with a brisk little jump. There was vigorous applause, roars of welcome throughout the room, and some cheers. The press pushed closer to the platform, elbowing other guests aside. Jeffrey growled softly in his throat.

"Thank you all," Dr. Schermerhorn said, inclining his head. Jeffrey, standing closer than he wished, saw that the doctor wore a three-piece suit of light summer-weight wool, a white silk shirt with a self-color stripe, and a red silk tie with tiny blue deer on it. A deep hush fell over the crowd. There was a push forward to get nearer the great man. "It's wonderful to be back here at Hawthorne House. The happiest years of my life were spent here. I was just out of the army, after serving in Korea. Army service is unpleasant in many, many ways and it makes you want to get out and do some good in the world. When I found this building and the children, I found myself. In the twelve years we worked here, I think the Hawthorne House School did much to reshape the treatment of autistic children. When we started, autism was very poorly understood and considered hopeless. We developed our full treatment protocol over several years and eventually our methods spread around the world. People everywhere began to believe that there was hope for children with this terrible problem."

Dozens of people applauded. Several cheered.

Jeffrey backed away.

"The cornerstone of our treatment was to *listen* to what the patients' words and behavior were telling us. Not the psychiatric theoreticians, not the parents, but the patients themselves. Some of the children did not even have words at first and could only speak to us with their actions. Of the seventy-nine patients who passed through our program, sixty-eight were able either to have a full normal life or were very substantially improved.

"We all know there are two schools of thought today in the treatment of autism. But for now I can only urge the continuation of the Hawthorne House School psychoanalytic-based approach, in which the psyches of the children are what we care about, as affording the best chance for these afflicted children. I am retired now, and I have nothing to gain by this suggestion, but I urge the continued study and development of my method.

"I'm reminded of a patient who came to me here at the age of six. I'll call her May T. She was one of our first autistic children. Her parents couldn't control her, nor could her school. Most of the time she would not speak. She made buzzing and flapping noises. Like this." Schermerhorn made a thwap-thwap-thwap sound with his tongue. "She twiddled her hands in circles. She did not relate to the other children at all. When food was placed on the table—as you may know, we ate family style at Hawthorne House—she would pull the plate of cheese slices, for example, toward herself, pick up every slice in turn and take one bite out of each, ruining them for anyone else. Over time, with patience, we traced her problems to a bad relationship with her mother. The mother, who was cold to her daughter, liked to cook, and ignored her child in favor of cake baking and so on. The mother appeared warm to outsiders because she was very involved in housewifely matters like baking and because she had a very pleasant manner, except with the child, to whom she was standoffish and uncaring. The buzzing noises poor May was making were the sounds of her mother's mixer and the flapping noises the sounds of her mother whipping batter. To make matters worse, her mother would not let May eat most of her baked creations, as she gave many to her church. Even the food the mother made for dinner could not be touched until dinnertime. The connection to May's behavior was obvious. Withholding food, withholding love. In addition, the centrifugal rotating, mixing motions that May constantly made symbolized not just the mixer but the child's feeling of hollowness at her core. Her mother's neglect left her bereft of love and reinforcement of her personhood. Naturally, the bizarre eating behaviors sprang from her reaction to the same neglect. She was trying to fill her emptiness. May was here with us for six years. At age thirteen she was well enough to leave us to attend a public high school near her family's home. She went on to the University of Illinois, and successfully completed a history major. She now teaches modern European history at a major university."

Applause spattered across the room. Light flashed from cameras, and video photographers shouldered people out of their way. Schermerhorn modestly ignored the furor.

Jeffrey was amazed to see that Schermerhorn looked only a little older than he remembered, and his voice was as young as ever. Jeffrey watched cautiously.

Dr. Schermerhorn said, "Now, I plan to have a delightful weekend in this wonderful old family home where so many good memories live, meeting again old friends who worked here with me in mutual eagerness to give these children a real future, and meeting for the first time healthy adults I knew only when they were troubled children. For me this is a time of splendid celebration. Thank you for coming to share it. And bon appetit!"

"Sir! Sir! Wait, Dr. Schermerhorn! Maddy Allencroft, CNN."

"All right. Just one question."

"Dr. Schermerhorn, two years ago you won the Henner Prize for Outstanding Contributions to the Treatment of Childhood Psychosis. Would you call that the height of your accomplishments?"

"Absolutely not! An award is just a committee's idea of whom they would like to honor. The outstanding accomplishment happens each time a child is raised to the highest level of functioning of which he or she is capable. And I think at Hawthorne House we have had dozens upon dozens of such accomplishments. Now, please, you all have my medical prescription. The doctor says, eat, drink, and be merry!"

"Just one more question—"

"Over here, Doctor!"

"Let me ask this—"

Schermerhorn pointed to one of the reporters, took his question, and responded pleasantly.

Jeffrey flicked his fingers while Schermerhorn spoke. He used only the right hand for this, cocking the index and middle fingers against his thumb, pushing hard until they sprang forward. He did this over and over at the rate of one flick every two seconds for the several minutes Dr. Schermerhorn spoke.

All the while, he backed slowly through the crowd, away from the sound of that voice.

That horrible voice.

Back up, back up. Can not see the floor. Too many people to see the floor. Do not stop to see the floor. The floor is for later.

In his teens, while living at Hawthorne House, Jeffrey had been fascinated by the building and determined to find out why it had been designed to look as it did. He read accounts of the early days of Hawthorne House and other Chicago mansions, many, like the Potter Palmer mansion, long since demolished. The library of old books in the Hawthorne mansion had been one of the few real delights of his time here. The former ballroom of the Hawthornes had gone through a lot of changes since the family had danced there.

Women in long gowns. Hems brushing the floor. Brushing the parquet, cherry and oak and lacewood. Ebony, teak. Long gowns with beads all over them. Bugle beads the books call them. Why bugle? They do not look like bugles. The men hold handkerchiefs. Right hand. Handkerchief in right hand. That is because their hands might. Perspire on the women's gowns. Why do the hands of men not perspire today? There is not a handkerchief in sight here. Kleenex? They do not hold Kleenex, either.

Jeffrey hadn't wanted to look at the floor; he'd made the decision to put that confrontation off. But now he pressed his elbows to his sides to hold in the fear and bent his head to look down.

He'd been building up to this during the whole reception, he now realized. Maybe longer. Maybe since he walked into the building. Maybe since he first heard about the Hawthorne House reunion.

From Jeffrey's present position he saw the beautiful parquet floor only in glimpses, small slivers between party guests who stood packed together, short wedges of view between their legs or a quick sight of a larger strip as people moved about.

But in Jeffrey's mind he saw it as he had seen it at the age of seven when he first crossed the hall to this huge room. It was his second day at Hawthorne House. The first day, he had been delivered here by his parents just before lunch. That first day had been a kaleidoscope of unfamiliar food eaten with unfamiliar, terrifying children making horrible noise around him. He cried in his unfamiliar room, unpacking his few possessions, mostly clothing, holding the clothes, stroking them, smelling them, the characteristic scent of the laundry detergent his mother used, as the one reminder of home. When a counselor came into Jeffrey's room that night and found him holding his Dr. Seuss T-shirt, rubbing it back and forth across his lips and nose, smelling and feeling familiarity, she had snatched it away from him.

"You have to break away from that," she said.

He had screamed then, but he had been so stressed all day by the changes in his life—he hated changes—and so tired by night that within twenty minutes he had screamed himself to sleep.

And yet that hadn't been as bad as the next day when he walked into the ballroom for the before-lunch calisthenics prescribed for everyone by Dr. Schermerhorn.

The huge room had been brutally divided when the building was used for offices. Then during the phase when the mansion became Dr. Schermerhorn's residential treatment center, the rooms near the ballroom windows had been retained as consulting rooms for the therapists and the dividers farther inside—nearer the door—removed, so that a large interior space was produced for group therapy and lectures. When seven-year-old Jeffrey entered the ballroom for the first time, he saw only half of the elaborate parquet design. The beautiful chrysanthemum-and-leaves pattern, with an ebony rosette in what once had been the center of the room, was sliced across by walls. Only part of the original design was visible, the vines and flowers on the sides and the rosette of concentric circles of petals in the middle simply cut across by the dividers.

Little Jeffrey had frozen on the spot. Staring at the cut-up design, he moaned. Then his paralysis ended and he ran to the wall, falling to his knees at the join of wall and floor. He ran his hands over the parquet, following the design to the spot where a flowing curving vine disappeared under the wall. Into the wall? Into nothingness? He scrabbled at the place with his fingers, trying to claw the vine out from beneath the plasterboard. He clawed and clawed, the tips of his fingers quickly rubbed raw, then bleeding, his fingernails breaking. In a minute or so the counselors dragged him away.

Now Jeffrey tried to puzzle together the floor that had so frightened him as a child. Living in Hawthorne House, he had come to tolerate the broken design by the sheer repetition of seeing it every day, but he had never liked it. It was a wrong thing.

Now he had a chance to see the floor whole, even though under the feet of a hundred people. His eyes discovered the scars on the inlaid wood where supports for the temporary walls of the office cubicles had been screwed to the floor. A little recent Internet research—he had a lifelong obsessive need to understand Hawthorne House—had told him that after Dr. Schermerhorn's treatment facility closed in 1980, the mansion had become a popular preschool, which was in fact its current use. The preschool, a going concern, must have had all the dividers removed, because the ballroom had now returned to its original size. *Miracle, a phenomenal miracle. The fluted columns are all there. Ringing the ballroom. Survived the alterations. Ballroom filled with preschool children. A play space, a gymnasium for rainy or snowy days. An auditorium maybe for little children performing music and dance. To show parents how well their children were doing.* The reunion invitations had explained that the preschool closed during the summer, making this weekend's event possible.

"Dr. Schermerhorn!" a reporter called out. "Are you planning a new book?"

"Yes. Just finishing one."

"What is it about?"

"The title is *The Heart of a Child*. You know the Kurt Weill song that begins 'How many miles to the heart of a child?' The song says 'thousands of miles.' But it's not so far as that if you watch what the child's actions are telling about his inner life. You can work back to his earliest years and decode what went wrong. You can reach out and touch the heart of a child. We have advance reading copies available now and a pub date of November twenty. My publisher has the information on his fall list."

The WGN reporter said, "We heard you might come on WGN regularly as an on-camera psych resource. Is there any truth to that?"

"Yes. But the negotiations are in its early stages."

Several other reporters clamored for Schermerhorn's attention and he, laughing, took them one at a time.

"No. No. Nonono," came a low, desperate voice. Jeffrey tried to see who it was, but the crowd was too thick.

Then an area opened around a man of about thirty, wearing a yellow shirt and purple pants, who was spinning in place, around and around, mumbling "No." He wasn't shouting; he was mumbling to himself. An older man spoke firmly to him. "It's all right. That's okay."

The younger man spun faster.

"It's all right, Henry. Come on, now," the older man said.

Henry. Henry Rollins! I know him. He is not a boy anymore. How strange. Henry Rollins. And that must be his father.

The spinning man lost his balance and fell. He hit his head on a chair. The scalp above his ear started to bleed. He slapped his hands wildly on the cut place, splattering blood. Dr. Emerson appeared, putting his arm around Henry before Jeffrey even saw Emerson move. "It looks worse than it is, folks," Emerson said.

Henry's father got a white handkerchief out of his pocket. Emerson pressed it on the cut. The two older men got Henry to straighten up and they walked him over to a bench next to the wall not far from Jeffrey and sat him down. "Cuts on the head always bleed a lot at first," Emerson said to the people nearby.

"Maybe coming here wasn't the best idea," Henry's father said.

"The bleeding is stopping already," Emerson said. Then he added, "I think you're going to have a good time this weekend, Mr. Rollins."

"I'm just not sure if Henry can deal with it. He doesn't like—you don't like change much, do you Henry?"

Henry didn't answer. He was rocking back and forth.

Emerson said, "No, I know, Henry. Change is hard. How have you been doing, Henry?"

Henry stared at his hands. He said, "Hideous. Hideous."

Jeffrey backed up until he was out of the ballroom and in the main hall where arches on either end led from the hall to the upstairs. The memory of the parquet floor was painful to him still. Now, as an adult he knew, of course, that it had simply been built as a full design and cut across by dividers later, not a dreadful fragment designed by an insane jokester. But the poisonous aura of it hung over him nevertheless. In any case he could study it tomorrow when no one was here. Maybe seeing it in its entirety would take the toxins out of it for him. He turned around and came face-to-face with a woman of about forty, on duty at a table near the door.

"Wonderful reception, isn't it?" she asked.

"Oh, yes, it is. Yes, it is, yes," Jeffrey said, looking at the wall sconce and sidling toward the north hall. He hurried to get away from her.

There were accordion-fold gates—folded back for now—at the stairway that led from the second to the third floor, and for a moment this afternoon he had stopped dead still at the sight.

They will lock me away. On the third floor forever! No, certainly that can not be. The reunion is. Not an elaborate hoax to trap us here and eat us alive. Maybe it is, though. How would I know? Yes, it is a trap! No, think. This is a preschool now. The gates are to keep little preschoolers from climbing up. To the third and fourth floors and getting lost or hurt. Therefore, it is a good thing. It is nice, in fact. Keep the children safe. Nice. Nice.

His room for the weekend was in the south end of the third floor. He knew exactly where, despite two branching corridors. This afternoon, when he had gone to his room to leave his duffle bag there, he'd run his hand along the wall of the corridor, feeling as well as seeing the way to his old room several doors farther along, the one he had lived in for his last three years at Hawthorne House, after he graduated from the two-person dorm room. Often as a child he had felt his way along this wall with his eyes closed because he didn't want to see that he was still here.

When Jeffrey got to his room, he shut the door. It had a bolt on the inside, which pleased him very much. None of these rooms had bolts on the inside when he had lived here as a child. They must have been installed when the building went through the stage of being law offices and publishing businesses. The bolt moved smoothly into place. The sound was very reassuring. He bolted it and unbolted it half a dozen times. Snick-snick-snick. Then a dozen times more. He looked at his watch.

Dread. Dread. Have to go down to dinner soon.

Jeffrey sat on his bed and began to flick his fingers.

CHAPTER **4**

NOT COUNTING THE BASEMENT and attic, there were three complete floors in Hawthorne House, but on the third floor the ceilings of most of the eighteen bedrooms, former servants' rooms, were hunched under the roof slope as if ashamed. However, four of the third-floor bedrooms were much prized—the end rooms. Since the mansion was built like a huge cross, each of the four end rooms had three windows, an end window and two side windows. Living in one of those rooms was like being in a magic boat sailing over Hyde Park, the gliding of clouds making the rooms appear to move. Those facing east could even see Lake Michigan, just a few blocks away. Jeffrey had "graduated" to one of these rooms for his last year as a resident at Hawthorne House.

There were also four rooms on the fourth floor. They peeked out of the ends of the roof, two at the north end and two at the south end of the cross shape, with a vast dark attic in between. Servants' back stairs ran all the way up from the basement to the fourth floor at each end, and in the 1900s, in these four rooms, the least important of the servants used to live. The gardener's "boy" and the groom who assisted in the care of the horses—which meant cleaning manure from the barn and keeping the tack in order—lived at one end. A kitchen girl and a scullery maid lived in the two at the other end. The rooms were about the size of an elevator, with low, sloping ceilings, and were hot in the summer, cold in the winter.

Running down the middle of the attic was a huge open space. During the tenure of the three generations of Hawthornes, it had been used by the household staff for storage, including out-of-season clothing, extra china, dressmaking dummies, and even wooden stacking racks for some vegetables and fruits being dried for winter use. Small hooks for hanging herbs to dry still remained on several rafters.

No subsequent tenant had found any use at all for this space. When Dr. Schermerhorn opened his residential facility here, it already contained discards from previous tenants. Nobody had the time or the energy to throw out the accumulation. The discards had not been touched in decades.

Most of the boxes of papers and other detritus lined the sides of the long attic storage space front to back. But there was an area on the east side, the back of the mansion, where the boxes and trunks had not been pushed all the way to the edge where the sloping roof met the floor. Here, quite far from the nearest hanging lightbulb, was a wedge-shaped void that could be reached by crawling between a pile of broken suit-cases and several stacks of 1930s newspapers tied with twine.

In this dark, hot crevice at 11:00 P.M. sat Jeffrey Clifford, folded up with his arms around his knees.

Dinner had been hell for Jeffrey. After the many reception guests had left, all the weekend residents here for the reunion went down to the first floor to dine in Cyrus Hawthorne's din-ing room.

Twenty-nine people were going to spend the weekend at the reunion. In addition to Dr. Schermerhorn and Dr. Emerson, there were five therapists, all of whom had been associated with Hawthorne House at one time or another in the old days. Therapists at Hawthorne House were all M.D.'s—psychiatrists who had their own practices and did not live in the mansion—coming in by appointment to treat the children. There were seven members of the counseling staff here to-night. Most of them were women—only one was a man—who had been undergraduates when the school was running and who had worked at the Hawthorne House School for college credit. Some were simply hired on from the community as ex-tra help. Most of them had lived in the mansion to help super-vise, since the children needed twenty-four-hour care. One reunion guest had been a cook in the old days, another the school nurse for several years. The rest were several patients, now grown to adulthood, and the parents of a few of them.

The Hawthornes' dining room had originally seated two dozen around a huge dining table. But that table had been sold decades ago, along with its thirty chairs and a twelve-foot sideboard. The current dining room furniture ordinarily con-sisted of several low tables designed for the preschoolers' lunches, tables now stacked to one side with their legs folded; and the room was still faintly redolent of peanut butter and jelly, incongruous with the paneled walls and heavy gilded chandelier hanging overhead. The chandelier was four-tiered, like an inverted wedding cake, and held dozens of etched-glass chimneys, each with a small bulb inside. It looked as if it had been wired for electricity from gas in the 1890s, had not been dusted since 1910 and had not been turned on since 1950. Light for the big room was shed by hanging fluorescent fixtures. Folding tables had been brought in for the weekend. Each could seat four diners.

Jeffrey ate with the former Hawthorne House School cook—Jeffrey remembered him fondly and thought his name was Chaz or Chuck—and Dr. Emerson, and a former patient whom he had never met. Her name was Rita. Rita said not one word all through dinner. Dr. Emerson started off talking about psychoanalysis, claiming that it had changed the world. He discussed Freud and Jung and the treachery of Sandor Ferenczi. Jeffrey was as quiet as Rita for nearly half an hour until the former cook, thoroughly fed up with Emerson, said, "Just look what they did to this chicken!"

"It's chicken tetrazzini," Emerson said. "I suggested it. They always serve chicken at events like this, but it doesn't need to be baked to rubber."

"They've used peas! And pimientos. Any decent chef knows better. This may be chicken with *stuff*, but it isn't chicken tetrazzini"

Never good in social situations, nevertheless this discussion was Jeffrey's metier and triggered his quirky memory.

"Chicken tetrazzini, named for Luisa Tetrazzini, the great opera singer."

The chef said, "She cannot *possibly* have had pimiento and American cheese in hers. It is *not* made this way."

Jeffrey said, "Bacon pieces, minced onion, green pepper, American cheese, pimiento, almonds, peas, and chicken. *Betty Crocker's Picture Cookbook,* 1956."

Chaz said, "Gah! That's disgusting!"

Dr. Emerson was staring at Jeffrey. Head cocked, the doctor

had diagnosis in his eyes. Jeffrey knew Emerson had him pegged, but he could not help himself.

"Chicken, thin-sliced mushrooms, unsalted butter, spaghetti, flour, heavy cream, sherry, nutmeg, grated parmesan, *Gourmet Magazine,* 1991," Jeffrey said.

"Much better," said Chaz.

"Chicken, spaghetti, nutmeg, velouté sauce, butter, mushrooms, Romano or Parmesan cheese, salt, pepper, *Fannie Farmer Cookbook,* 1990."

"Do you cook, Mr. Clifford?" Emerson asked.

"Ah—I—ah—no—" He had to stop this list making. Jeffrey fixed his gaze on Emerson's purple-and-blue tie. "I am a computer engineer."

"Oh, yes," Emerson said. "I think I read that." He hesitated. For a moment, Jeffrey believed Emerson was embarrassed. He could only have read what Jeffrey's job was in a summary of the present condition of former patients. In which case, he would know that computers were all that Jeffrey did. He still lived at home, never went anywhere except work, had no children, had no friends—

"Well, computers, that's admirable," Emerson said gently.

"Shredded boiled chicken," Jeffrey said. "Macaroni, mushrooms, butter or chicken fat, flour, broth, heavy cream, sherry—" He couldn't stop.

How ridiculous! All I have to do is. Shut my mouth and keep it closed. Now. Now I will stop. I will. I will. Right now. "Parmesan cheese—"

Emerson nodded sagely.

"Shredded almonds. *The Joy of Cooking,* 1953," Jeffrey said, and then he could feel it. The itchy pressure evaporated. He could stop. And he did. He sat silent through the rest of the meal.

By the time he got back to his room he was not only flicking his fingers, his head was bobbing up and down in time with the fingers. He turned immediately and went to the attic.

Now in his special place, he felt at peace. There was a sort of long alleyway between the row of boxes and the place where the roof met the floor. He squeezed into this space, as far to the end of it as he could go, his back against a pile of newspapers left at the very end. With the boxes pressing in on him on one side, the roof on the other, an adult in a child-size space, he was calmed.

Jeffrey had always known he was different from other people. He'd have to be a lot dumber than he was to miss that. When he was little, there were the visits to his pediatrician, then the visits to psychologists and psychiatrists, play therapy that was really, he knew, play diagnosis, then talk therapy, medications, times that he was in school with regular children, times that he was not in school, times that he was in remedial school. If that hadn't been enough to tell him he was different, there were the times the doctors talked to his mother about his problems right in front of him, as if being different meant he couldn't hear. He'd had a variety of diagnoses over the years, but it had all kind of settled down into Asperger's syndrome, considered by some to be a less-severe variant of autism, or maybe a similar entity. The good note in all this was that he was "high functioning." He was intelligent, but so were many patients called Kanner's autistics. Kanner's were supposed to be more "damaged," he knew.

Jeffrey puzzled a lot, when he met other autistics, about whether the ones with Kanner's were actually more damaged, as one of his teachers had explained, or whether they were just different kinds of people.

Because he knew that was what he was. A different kind of person. Over the years, even before he reached his twenties, he had figured out that one of the things that troubled the "normal" people about autistics and near autistics like himself was that they—*we*, he thought—didn't know how to make the faces that regular people did. Making the faces and understanding faces. It was like learning to read. Regular people went by facial expression. They would say, "Look at that man. He's sad." Jeffrey could look at the same man and be puzzled. He could look at the man just like the "normals" did, as far as he knew—*I have excellent eyesight*—and see the downturned mouth, but how could he be sure the man was sad? Maybe he was pretending to be sad. Maybe he had a stomachache. Maybe his face was just naturally droopy.

"Happy" was even worse. In Jeffrey's experience, people made happy faces all the time, pointlessly, meaninglessly, even when they couldn't possibly be especially happy. Like the nurse in the doctor's office smiling just before she was going to give you a shot. Unless she really *was* happy to stab you, which was not so nice, either. Or the lady at the bank when she gave out money. She couldn't possibly want the money to leave the bank, could she? Sonia, who worked in his computer company's office doing payroll, smiled all the time. Could she possibly be happy all the time?

And what about people who were lying? If you were supposed to be able to read people's faces, why didn't people who could read faces know when other people were lying?

And why did normals have to be so loud?

He remembered thinking these things even as a child. At exactly what age, he wasn't sure. He was at Hawthorne House by then, he thought. A lot of what happened at Hawthorne House blurred in his mind, because the days were so much the same.

All his life people told him he didn't look people in the eye. *Why? Why look people. In the eye? It is embarrassing. Prying, too, very prying. Not precisely the problem. The problem is, there is no point. Why eyes? What is it that makes the normal's world so. Interested in eyes? People lie with their eyes just as much as with their smile. Normals don't believe that.*

But he worked hard at faking it. He could look people in the eye if he remembered to do it. *He really could!* It just made him feel uncomfortable, scratchy and restless.

How do normal people think? Are they really a different species? he wondered for maybe the hundred-thousandth time in his life. They kept asking him about things like whether he had empathy. *Why do they ask that? Do they really believe that I do not know other people have feelings?*

Big problem. Some of the feelings the normals had. Very puzzling. Arrogance, for one. Normals. Pushing themselves forward all the time. As if the recognition of themselves as individuals who. Were better than other individuals was vitally important. Why does that help? You were who you were—were you not?

And were these not the very same people who talked constantly about empathizing?

He also puzzled about clothing. So often as a teenager, when he made a major effort on a visit home to dress in a suit and tie, which he thought was stupid, and the clothes didn't feel right, either, not worn into comfort, he would come downstairs and his mother would say, "Oh! You look so nice!"

He would thank her. He knew he was supposed to. *When somebody gives you a compliment. You say "thank you." Always do that. Always. Always.* But he never understood why it was a compliment. Didn't he look exactly the same as he ever had? He hadn't had plastic surgery or anything. Maybe she should have said the *suit* looks nice. She seemed to really mean that *he* looked better, and he couldn't understand that, since it was just a suit hanging over the same old body underneath.

Jeffrey had settled very comfortably into his hot den between the boxes when he became aware something was different. The lightbulb was so far away that the light here was the color of maple syrup and he certainly had not seen a shadow move.

There is no change in the night sounds—cars make a hiss

going by in the street. What is that creaking? It is only the old house; it moves and groans and sighs.

Two of his therapists had told him that he preferred diagnosing the world through touch and smell over sight and hearing. When he got older, he realized that was characteristic of autistics. Smell and touch were "closer" senses, the doctors said. He had never understood this, because while he didn't like being touched, noises bothered him more than they bothered the regular people, and that was paying attention to hearing, wasn't it?

But he realized that he smelled a change in the attic. He smelled a human.

CHAPTER 5

DR. SCHERMERHORN TIPPED UP the bottle and a ribbon of cognac ran into the balloon glass. Deliberately, he tilted the bottle down only enough so that the amber fluid stopped running, moved the neck of the bottle over to an adjoining glass, and poured an inch and a half into that as well.

Dr. Emerson said, "Thank you, Jay. Your new book?"

Copies of Dr. Schermerhorn's most recent book, *The Heart of a Child,* were stacked on the coffee table along with several ARCs, advance reading copies of his next book, a thick collection of stories about "his kids." "I brought them for the reporters. I've found over the years that they'll read books but they won't buy them."

Schermerhorn glanced at the room around them as he settled back more comfortably in his chair. He crossed one long leg over the other gracefully. "You know I never lived in the mansion. In all the years I directed the institute, I never slept here in the mansion overnight."

"I thought not. This was the nurse's room, wasn't it?" Emerson was shorter than Schermerhorn, pink and rounded. He wasn't plump, but while Schermerhorn had an elegant, long head with a dominant nose and intensely blue eyes, Emerson's bony structure did not show so much. His face was gentle rather than assertive. He was ten years younger than Schermerhorn, but despite being well enough padded to erase wrinkles, with his white hair he looked about Schermerhorn's age.

"Nurses' rooms, plural," Schermerhorn said. "There's a bathroom en suite, as they call it on the Continent. And a separate bedroom. Two nurses in residence was all the turnover we had in all those years."

"That's quite a record. School nurses usually change jobs pretty frequently."

"Yes. They use the credit for their résumé and move up to something that pays better. But this is really comfortable living."

"Your house is comfortable, too, Jay." Dr. Schermerhorn lived in a large, stately Hyde Park house on the other side of the University of Chicago campus. While it was a roomy and elegantly constructed Georgian-style brick house, bought with some of the considerable money Schermerhorn had made from his books, and was more modern—better heating system, much better air-conditioning—and therefore probably more comfortable, it was no mansion as Hawthorne House was. Emerson had been invited to Schermerhorn's house for dinner several times back in the '70s, when Schermerhorn's wife, Hilda, was still alive. The two had no children and entertained quite a bit.

"How long has it been since we got together like this?" Dr. Schermerhorn asked.

"More that five years, I guess."

"Wie schade. A pity, Erik. But I know how busy life can be."

Reverting to the earlier topic, Schermerhorn said, "It was important for me to have a break from the school, at least to go home for the night. Get perspective." Schermerhorn had walked to work at Hawthorne House every day, home for dinner, then back to work, and walked home again late in the evening.

Emerson said, "Dealing with disturbed children takes it out of you."

"The thing about disturbed children is that they're disturbed all the time. You can't turn them off on weekends or holidays."

"I suppose that's one reason why I went into treating adults when I finished training. They come in for their appointment and then they go home. They go about their lives."

"I wondered, you know."

"Why I didn't follow in your footsteps?"

"Oh, not that exactly—"

"Well, they would have been hard footsteps to follow. Your lectures were a great inspiration to me, Jay. The mystery of the human mind and the way it reveals itself in psychotherapy. Your insight into the psyche. Your lectures on the meaning of myths was one of the most thrilling courses of my grad years."

"You embarrass me."

"Oh, surely not. You must have known how charismatic the students found you."

"Ach—whoever knows what students think?"

"So, Jay, what is this about being an on-camera resource for WGN?"

"They need a commentator for psychology-related stories. Medical advances, trials involving psychiatrists as witnesses for mental competence. You know the kind of thing."

"Nice! You can reach a whole new audience."

"Maybe. There's also going to be a *Time* magazine article."

"What's the theme?"

"Apparently the cover article is going to headlined 'A Hundred Years Since Freud.'"

"Dating from *Studies on Hysteria,* I suppose."

"Exactly. Which he wrote with Breuer. It would make more sense to wait for the hundredth anniversary of *The Interpretation of Dreams,* since it's a great deal better known, but they are determined to do it now. The piece will be subtitled 'Psychotherapy Comes of Age.' It seems I will represent the development of psychoanalysis for treating young children."

"Wonderful! And well deserved."

"Thank you, Eric. Will you be contributing to the Festschrift Cambridge is putting together about me?"

A Festschrift, a collection of essays in honor of an important person, was a particular distinction, Emerson knew. "I'm not sure I'm prominent enough, Jay."

"Nonsense. You are very well known. A touch more brandy?"

"Just a whiff. It's late. I'd better get to bed soon. There's the symposium to go to at the college tomorrow. And you have that plus a lot to do here."

"Yes, and *Time* magazine is coming during the afternoon to take some pictures in situ."

"That's nice."

"You seem tired, Erik."

"Oh, I haven't been sleeping well."

"Bad dreams?"

"Now, don't start that," Emerson said, chuckling. "Maybe a few, though. Dreams of being closed up in a box. It's dark. I can't move."

"Fear of birth trauma, Jay."

"Actually, I was wondering whether it was prophetic."

"Oh, please. There's no such thing as being able to see the future. But the past is always with us."

"Well, Jay. I hope you're right."

⚔

SOFT, VERY SOFT FOOTFALLS. A sound of cloth on something—something—cloth brushing along the side of a cardboard box? Wait, there's a pause. Maybe it's nothing. Nothing. More of the cloth sound . . .

Most important, Jeffrey smelled a human scent. It wasn't sweaty or perfumy or hair oily or anything even more disgusting. It was as if body warmth was a scent. Human metabolism. Jeffrey held very, very still. He stopped breathing. He held his eyes wide open.

He waited.

A woman shrieked.

She was crouching right in front of him. He saw a round moon face and a round frightened mouth. She said, "What doing here?" as she tried to turn around in the confined space.

"Do not be afraid."

"Afraid."

"I am not dangerous."

Very carefully, in a monotone, she said, "This-is-April's-place."

"This is my place, too." He watched her relax, judging not by her eyes but by the set of her shoulders, which had been held high and now slowly settled. "Please. Sit down."

Carefully, she sat. She looked at his foot, and said, "April can use pronouns. April knows—I know what pronouns are. I. Me. You. When I get flustered, April doesn't use pronouns."

"I used to do that too."

Now that he had a chance to study her, taking glancing

looks at her hair, her arms, her jawline, but not her eyes, Jeffrey realized that she was older than he was, possibly by five years. She was probably forty. The round pale face was haloed by wispy, pinkish hair. Her body looked soft but her skin looked healthy. The two of them were silent for several minutes, a long time, he thought, for normals to be quiet in a social situation. Then, worried that she would feel she ought to leave, he said, "This was your special place, too."

"Yes."

"I think I may. Remember you. You came to Hawthorne House earlier than I did." He let pauses go on quite a long time, which, unlike the effect on normals, made her more comfortable.

"Left in 1974."

"I got here in 1972," Jeffrey said. "But I didn't. Find this place right away. Here we must. Have just—"

"Missed each other?" Her voice was too loud for the space, for how close together they were. Jeffrey knew this because he had been taught to watch his vocal volume.

"Yes."

There was another long silence. Jeffrey finally said, not looking at her, "I needed a place. Like this. To get away from everything."

"Everything."

She sighed a deep, satisfied sigh, as if just the agreement from Jeffrey validated her feelings. "Why come here?" she asked.

"Up here?"

She shook her head.

Jeffrey said, "Now? To this reunion? My therapist said I should."

"April's therapist did so too?"

"She said I should find out. That I could put it behind me."

"Me, mine too."

Jeffrey said nothing and in a few seconds she added very carefully, "Still an evil man."

"You are right about that."

"Will tell you a secret?"

"Certainly. Go ahead." Jeffrey wanted to say "I would be honored," but he thought it might be too forward. There were some social conventions that were hard to master. It was almost always better to leave out personal remarks.

"The story he told? That girl?"

Jeffrey nodded. Hearing her speak in sentences with a rise at the end like questions reminded him that that particular vocal pattern was one of the voice habits diagnostic of autistic children. He had been laboriously taught not to do it. And now, ironically, it was very popular among normals. They called it up-talk. He wondered whether teachers these days still taught their autistic students not to do it. Possibly it no longer sounded so abnormal.

"May T?" she said. "Who ate all the cheese, would not talk? That was me."

"Really? You are May T?"

"Yes. He made up a name? I am April Tausche."

"You are the person who teaches history now? That is wonderful."

"No."

"No?"

"Me, April can never keep a job. Ap—I live at home with my mother? Dr. S lied about that part."

THEY SAT FOR HALF an hour in a silence the ease of which surprised both of them. They weren't used to finding human company comfortable, and to be relaxed with a stranger was even more unusual.

It was quite late when they heard another person approaching across the wood floor of the attic. Whoever it was had less tentative footsteps than April. Jeffrey deduced that it was a man or an administrator. Administrators, male or female, walked with authority, as if it were okay for everyone to hear their feet strike the floor. Twice during his childhood at Hawthorne House he had been discovered in the attic. Someone had noticed that he was not in his room—there were no door locks then, so that the staff could look into their bedrooms at any time—and when he was found to be missing there was a great hue and cry. He had been punished and afterward he had waited several months before going to his special place again. The great peace of the place, the sense of being enfolded, of being safe—he had put aside all that until the two staff members who had found him there had left the school. One graduated from the University of Chicago, one got a higher-paying job at university counseling, and at last Jeffrey was able to go back. It was more than a year before his visits to his refuge were again found out.

The fear of being caught here came back to him now. He turned to look at April and saw that for the first time she was looking him in the face. She too felt fear.

The footsteps drew closer. The opening to the special place darkened.

"I knew it!" a shrill voice said.

April squeaked. Jeffrey kept silent, but was dismayed.

"Jane!" he finally said.

Jane said, "Both of you! I might have known it! I saw that April was gone from her room. If you want to sneak out, you know, you have to use more of your brain. Don't leave your door wide open." She added with a sneer that distorted her face, "You always were a stupid person, April."

Jeffrey remembered Jane had been a patient—*we're supposed to say resident, not patient*—at Hawthorne House when he arrived. She was probably two years older than he was. She must have overlapped April's time here and his. Thinking back, he was quite sure she'd left before he did. He could vividly remember being glad she was gone.

"We have every right. To be here, Jane."

"Jeffrey. You are such a little turd."

He looked at her shoulder. He couldn't bear to stare into her eyes.

"You never liked him. You always had to fight back."

Jeffrey knew that by "him" she meant Dr. Schermerhorn. "Fight *back*," he said slowly, "carries the. Implication that I was. Being fought with."

"Oh, you always have to be so stubborn. You couldn't be grateful for anything. I remember the day you smeared your own shit on the hall floor. And Dr. S was so patient with you."

"I was seven. He made me clean it up. With a single rag. Back and forth to the sink. Back and forth."

"How else were you going to learn? And this dumb one here"— she stuck out her foot and nudged April. "Whiny, whiny, whiny. Dr. S gave you every opportunity to become a mature person, but you couldn't thank him. Oh, no. Not even by just getting better. Like I did. I was a mess when I came here. See—I can admit it. I hid under my bed for the first three weeks. I was scared and really, really angry with the world. But he coaxed me out and gave me love and support and took away the anger—Look at me now. I have a good job. I supervise a whole travel bureau for a major cruise line. I'm a success!"

"I suppose that you are, Jane," Jeffrey said. "You know we all are. Grown-up now. We can be in the attic. If we like."

"You can't! You owe it to him to act normal and show how well you are."

"Are we well?"

"Of course you are. And so am I."

He said, "But if you are well, why are you so angry with us?"

CHAPTER **6**

HAWTHORNE HOUSE SLEPT. AT two o'clock in the morning, even the elderly water pipes were quiet. Faint air-conditioning sighs scarcely disturbed the silence. After the hot day, the roof had creaked and popped as the slates contracted with the comparative coolness of evening, but finally that, too, had stilled.

In the rooms set aside for reunion guests, there was no talking and the sibilance of whispered gossip between old friends had long since ended. The caterers had gone home and the kitchens in the basement had fallen silent after the last of the dishwashers ended their cycles.

The fourth, third, second, and first floors were quiet. There were sounds in one part of the basement, but except for the two people present, no one noticed.

Two

It must be admitted that women have
but little sense of justice, and this is no doubt connected with
the preponderance of envy in their mental life.

—SIGMUND FREUD, 1932

CHAPTER 7

9:02 A.M.

Officer Bissell stepped outside of Hawthorne House to use his radio. He had debated using a phone in the building, but you never knew whether phones had recording devices, especially business systems. Or extensions where people could listen in. He had also debated walking to a store with a pay phone, but the nearest were at least three blocks away, and he didn't want to take the time.

The disadvantage of using his radio was that the media monitored police zones for news items. There was a way around that, though. He keyed the radio.

"Two-thirty-three," he said, his mouth close to the mike. He noticed his hand was trembling. Funny he hadn't been aware of it before.

"Go ahead, thirty-three."

"Give me a supervisor on zone twelve." They switched around the numbers for the closed zone, kept mostly to use during drug raids. The drug dealers monitored the police radio just as avidly as reporters lying in wait for a scoop.

"Go ahead, thirty-three."

"I need a supervisor at fifty-one-sixty South Prairie."

"Nature of the problem?"

"Possible homicide. We need somebody heavy over here. This thing might go kinda hot." Even on the confidential zone he wanted to say as little as possible. The supervisor picked up on this at once.

"*I'm on it.*"

"Thanks, squad."

Bissell went back to zone two, leaving his radio just loud enough so that he could hear the traffic in the district.

As he walked back to Hawthorne House, a picture of the scene he'd just witnessed flashed again in his mind. His knees went weak and his body felt cold.

⋈

"ISN'T IT TOO EARLY in the day for snack food?" I said. At nine-fifteen, we were on a call to Hawthorne House in our un-marked and un-air-conditioned car. I was driving. Ollie was fiddling with a shiny bag.

It was already hot, even though the day was young. With no air-conditioning and the sun coming in at a low angle, I was baking. Unlike Chicago's winter cold, which just chills you until your bones ache, heat is the kind of weather that is way too personal. It invades your armpits and gets under your bra and in your crotch. It makes tickling rivers of sweat run down into private places.

I squirmed in the seat, trying to obliterate an icky little river of wetness in the small of my back that was making its way down between the cheeks of my rump like an intrusive finger.

"Didn't get breakfast." Detective Oliver Park pulled apart the top of the small bag of onion-garlic-barbecue-flavored corn chips. I wouldn't let him bring potato chips into the car, because I couldn't resist them. The potato is the queen of vegetables—potato chips, french fried, baked, or best of all, mashed with turkey gravy. Opening the bag, he tried to be careful, but several chips sprayed around his knees.

I said, "Plus you were gonna take off ten pounds."

"These are only a hundred calories a serving. See?" He

pointed at the bannered words "100 Calories Per Serving" on the front, right under the word "Pow!"

"I see. But how many servings in the bag?"

"Uh, let's look. Wait a minute! Twelve? *Twelve servings!* How can they *say* that? The whole bag is about one serving, tops! Skimpy at that."

"So every handful is what? Two hundred and fifty calories?"

"It's fraud, that's what it is. Consumer fraud!"

"So what's the address?" I asked as we pulled up to a light on Hyde Park Avenue.

"Fifty-one-sixty South Prairie."

I liked Ollie. We'd been partners for two years now and got along well. Ollie was Korean-American, but seemed to have no interest in Asian-American police associations. Once he had admitted to me that his mother complained that he was not Korean enough. At forty-one he was six years older than I. He was a lot bigger and heavier than I was, too, bigger than Koreans were generally thought to be, and, while I was trying not to gain, he spent a lot of effort trying to lose weight. Then a hunger fit would come on him, and he'd gain back all he had lost. Ollie was strong yet somehow cuddly looking. If you crossed a duffle bag with a Scottish terrier, you'd have Oliver Park.

Since the CPD doesn't have grades of detectives—unlike New York, for instance, which has detective first and so on, which some folks cheerily call dick one and dick two, and I think L.A. even has detective threes—the fact that I haven't been a detective as long as Ollie doesn't matter much. And Ollie was anything but the kind of guy who stood on his dignity. No sweat, that was Ollie.

As we rolled over to Hawthorne House, Oliver said, "I told Jason maybe I could take him to the beach tonight."

"Depends on what we find here, doesn't it?" Jason was Oliver's son, who lived most of the year with Oliver's divorced wife in Memphis, but stayed with his father during the summers.

"Get cooled off, you know."

What we were both not talking about was what we'd spent the last three days doing. There had been several heat deaths in Chicago, three in our district up to Wednesday. On Thursday the heat index in Chicago had reached a hundred and six degrees. Today was the fourth day with a heat index over a hundred. The city sent workmen out to spray water on the drawbridges over the river so that they wouldn't expand shut and close the river to boat traffic. Or for that matter, expand when they were up and then not lower into place. Transformers, overstressed by heavy air-conditioning demands, had burned out, leaving part of the city without electricity. Patrol cops and firefighters carried disabled and elderly people out of high-rise buildings where the elevators didn't work because the electric power was down, and where the indoor temperature often exceeded a hundred and twenty.

Thursday there were fifteen "excess deaths" in Chicago. Yesterday, the third day over a hundred degrees in actual temperature, there were a hundred and fifteen excess deaths. And today, Saturday, we'd heard predictions at the station that the death toll would surely go over two hundred.

Every death not attended by a physician had to be investigated. Even if a death really looked heat-related, it could be a disguised homicide. A full investigation by detectives was required. By people like Ollie and me. In hot rooms where the victim had been dead for hours or days, this was very unpleasant. So Ollie and I were glad when we were dispatched to Hawthorne House.

"Whatever this turns out to be, it's gotta be better than the heat patrol," Park said.

Two deaths yesterday had been ours, elderly men found alone in single rooms. No air-conditioning. The windows closed and locked. Both men had been dead at least twenty-four hours, lying in rooms that had not gone under ninety degrees even at night.

"Poor old guys," Park had said to the patrol sergeant as we passed through the lobby of the Second District.

Pekach, the sergeant, who was hot, irritated, and not of the best temper even when he wasn't hot, said, "Hey, Park. How much am I supposed to feel sorry for people who don't do anything to help themselves?"

I said, "These guys were old!"

"Bullshit. One was sixty-eight and the other was seventy-one. Seventy-one ain't old. They can at least open their windows, can't they? For that matter they could walk over to the beach and stand in Lake Michigan. Can't they do that? I see people in their eighties standing in Lake Michigan, splashing their wrinkled old torsos."

"If they're too scared of crime to open their windows, how can they go to the beach?" Park asked.

"In the daytime. Those streets are full of people in the daytime."

"That one guy, the younger one, had a bad leg," I said. "He had a walker and all. His canes were in the closet, so he must have got to the point where he couldn't use a cane anymore."

"Okay, I'll give you that guy, but not the other one. They said he's hidden up in his room like a miser, with his lifetime possessions."

I said, "Little single room with all his worldly goods and no air conditioner. That's sad."

"Wait a minute, Folkestone. If he wanted to get cool, all he needed to do is go to the library. The branch couldn't've been more than two blocks away. Am I right?"

"Sit in the library all day?"

"Well, yeah. Hell. Why not? If he's that hot, let him go there and read a book. But you know what else he could do?"

"I'm sure you'll tell me, Pekach."

"The library has these story programs for kids during the summer. People read to groups of kids, different age groups, different times of day. Always need readers. You don't have to be a teacher or have any qualifications, except you can read. How about if that guy just went there to read to children? Do a good deed and get cool at the same time. But no. He's going to sit in his room with his possessions."

"Maybe he's depressed."

"He's depressed me, that's for sure."

"I still think you can feel sorry for somebody who has so little in his life."

"Look, I'm not a monster, you know? I feel sorry for those kids, the ones yesterday."

Yesterday the operator of a day-care service had taken her charges to an air-conditioned movie. When they got back to the day-care center, she took the children inside for a nap. It was not until she went out to her car an hour later that she realized she had left two of the children inside it. She called paramedics immediately, but both children were dead, their body temperatures over a hundred and eight.

"You know, Pekach," I said, "it doesn't take any longer to feel sorry for four people than for two."

CHAPTER 8

THE BASEMENT WALLS WERE dark red brick with drippings of dried effluvium, and the floor was ancient, stained slate. Overhead a single twenty-five-watt lightbulb dangled from an elderly, fiber-wrapped cord. Hawthorne House was a century and a quarter old, but the basement could have dated to the 1700s. Lake Michigan lay just eight blocks away, and the subsoil was damp. Decades of rain and snow had trickled down the exterior walls, carrying lead from paint, nitrogen in rainwater, and calcium in groundwater, the chemical mix percolating into the cellars.

The cellar smelled musty, but the odor of age and moisture was swamped by the smell of death. Blood, coppery and warm. Urine, feces, and terror-sweat.

In the center of the floor was a naked, white body, lying on its back. Its arms were stretched out to the sides, its legs straight, very much as if, had it been standing upright, it might have been directing traffic.

Dr. Jay Schermerhorn, lecturer and writer, had died with a gag stuffed in his mouth. His clothes were neatly folded and lay near the wall, complete except for his red silk necktie with tiny blue deer, which had been rolled up and used to gag him. His wrists and ankles were tied with ropes. The two ropes that ran from his wrists had been tied to pipes on the right and left walls of the room. The rope tied to his left ankle ran to the lower hinge in the inward-opening door, where it had been pushed through the gap and tied around the hinge itself. The killer had had a harder time finding a place to attach the rope from Schermerhorn's right ankle, since there were no pipes or fixtures on that side of the room. The killer had settled for wrapping the end of the rope around and around a sack of cement. The cement, apparently very old, had long since hardened into a pillow shape. It was heavy, but the thrashings of the dying man had dragged it several inches toward the body. Sometime after death, the victim's two legs had been straightened and placed next to each other.

Schermerhorn's white body was covered with several dozen cuts, each about an inch long. While they looked like slices, the amount of blood that had run from them told me they were deep. There were so many that the ME's man had as yet made no effort to count them. From most of them ran rivulets of blood. The lines of blood and lines of cuts gave the body, in places, the look of red-and-white plaid fabric.

The rivers of blood had run down Dr. Schermerhorn's body

and the blood was now pooled around it. There was a large pond of blood near the left thigh. Both arms had thrashed in blood, as much as the ropes would allow. The pattern around them made me think of a snow angel, in red. From the side of his nose near the right nostril snaked a thick worm of now-clotted blood. The cut into the nose must have bled a long time, as the snake ran down his cheek, across his earlobe, into a long Z-shaped crack in the cellar floor, filling the crack and creating a lightning bolt of blood over two feet long.

I thought, *A doctor, a teacher, a writer, a healer of children, and somebody hated him this much? Why?*

It was now 9:45 Saturday morning. The young doc from the medical examiner's office stood up, accidentally brushing his head on the hanging lightbulb. It swung back and forth, the pendulum-light making the corpse appear to lean left-right-left, as if struggling to get away from the ropes that bound it.

The young ME said, "Damn! How low is this stupid ceiling?"

"Six feet maybe," I guessed.

The ME, whose name was Haskell Czerba, backed away from the body. "He's got at least five hours of cooling off in him. Could be more. We'll narrow it down when we get him on the table." Czerba picked up his laptop from the doorway. He and I and Ollie all carried laptops, modern-day cops that we were. They were much more cumbersome than the old notebooks.

Czerba was already starting to walk away to find someplace to sit and make notes. I stopped him with an upraised hand. "There's a lot of press out there in front of the building, Haskell. Not a word."

Haskell zipped his lip, then spoiled the effect by immediately opening his mouth, and saying, "Anybody know when he last ate?"

"Dinner, all we know now," I said. "I'll get you the details."

Detective Park and I contemplated the corpse from a distance so that we wouldn't contaminate the crime scene. I said sourly, "Would've been nice if they'd tried not to walk in the blood."

"Always happens," Ollie said. "You gotta expect civilians'll do that. Anyhow, the guy who found him had to see if he was dead."

"Looking like that?"

"Even looking like that."

Ollie heard distant noises from the kitchen two corridors away, raised his finger in a "back in a minute" gesture, and left.

I studied the body, staying far back. The dusty slate floor between here and the kitchen had showed no footprints, because the killer had dragged a broom over his trail as he left. The broom lay near the entrance into the kitchen.

AFTER ELEVEN YEARS in the police department, I still have trouble with man's inhumanity to man. After the first visual examination, I was averting my eyes from the victim's penis. Not out of ladylike delicacy but from horror. There were half a dozen slices in the organ. The cuts were hard to see, because the organ had retreated as far as it could and now appeared as a small purple acorn with red stripes. Judging by the amount of blood on the thighs and pooled between his legs, the slashes had been made before death. I wondered whether they had been made early in the cutting process or the last thing the killer did before the victim expired.

"Death of a thousand cuts," I said to Czerba.

He raised his eyebrows.

"Schermerhorn was an internationally known psychoanalyst," Czerba said. "It's a pity for him to end up this way. In a dirty basement with stained brick walls. Slate floors! Give me clean concrete any day."

"It's my understanding, Czerba, that concrete as we know it wasn't used in residential construction until early in the

1900s. And this building dates from twenty years before that."

"Very 'Cask of Amontillado,' " Czerba said.

"More like 'The Pit and the Pendulum,' " I said. I thought, *Take that, Doc,* and then felt doubly guilty—for reacting to the ME and for doing it in the presence of death. The man on the floor had been alive and accepting honors last night, living, breathing, and probably in good health. This was a nasty murder, and we'd do well to remember we were looking for a very nasty killer.

My cell phone rang. A cold male voice said, "Detective Folkestone? Hold for Chief of Detectives Kelly."

Yikes. Chief of Detectives South Polly Kelly was my boss's boss.

"Folkestone?" she asked. She spoke fast and very, very clearly.

"Yes, boss."

"Dr. Shermerhorn is a heater case. Dot every i and cross every t. Don't let any VIPs there pressure you to move the body before you have everything you need."

"Yes, boss."

"People in the mansion there will ask you to move the body. For dignity's sake. As if you honor the deceased by getting him into the morgue wagon fast. They'll imply that an important person should not be left lying on a basement floor. Don't fall for it. Don't let them rush you."

"Right, boss."

"Dr. Schermerhorn was a man who gave a lot to the world, Detective. He was a giant in his field, and a great man."

"Yes, boss."

"This murder is not going to be lost in the flood of heat-related deaths, understand me?"

I said, "Yes, ma'am."

Kelly hung up.

Oliver Park came back, bringing with him a stocky, solid

man with a boyish face topped by a burst of red hair, his face too young for the apparent middle age signaled by his spreading waistline and the little bit of graying at the temples. "Tech is here," Park said. "We ready for him?"

I said, "Yes, Park. But I want him to take all the time he wants."

Park nodded.

"One good thing," I added.

"What?"

"With all this blood, the killer's gonna have stained clothes. Bloody shoes."

"I hope so. We can check the people who were in the mansion last night. We can ask to see their shoes without a warrant."

I nodded. I already knew that. "But of course they don't have to agree."

"Everybody who was here last night is still here, Emily," Park said. "The first uniforms on the scene buttoned up the house real good."

"That's right. Nobody's left the building."

"Since the cops got here," Czerba said. "Bet you in the night this place was like a sieve."

CHAPTER *9*

CHIEF OF DETECTIVES KELLY picked up the phone and asked her ADS to track down Emily Folkestone's area commander, Tommy Hasseen, a buddy of Kelly's, from way back when they had been at the academy together.

"Hey, boss!" Hasseen's voice was deep and decisive. The kind of voice born to be used for command.

"Hi, Tommy. Wanta thank you for the fast heads-up on the Hawthorne House thing."

"Hardly do otherwise. Dr. Schermerhorn himself! I can't believe it! He's more famous than God. Even the building is famous. It's gonna be a mob scene."

"Already is. Patrol has six units there on crowd control."

Dr. Schermerhorn was extremely well respected and there would soon be people crying out for the blood of his killer. In addition, if word of how he was killed got out, the press coverage would be deafening. Kelly wasn't at all sure that Folkestone was the right person for the job.

As chief, Kelly could micromanage the choices made by the area commanders, if she wanted. Chicago has twenty-five police districts and six area centers. Patrol works out of district stations. Detectives work out of area centers. In practice, these can be in the same buildings, but when patrol and detectives occupy the same building, they are usually on different floors and each has its own command structure.

Kelly was chief of detectives south. There was also her opposite number on the North Side, Fred Baumann, chief of detectives north. Kelly ran everything south of Adams Street, in other words from the central Loop south, which involved Detective Division Areas 1, 2 and 4. This included the whole University of Chicago, as well as such landmarks as the Museum of Science and Industry, Comisky Park, the Adler Planetarium, and the Field Museum.

Hasseen said, "I bet you're not calling just to give me an attaboy."

Polly Kelly laughed. "You've been in the business too long, Tommy. What I need to know—is Folkestone up to it?"

"If she wasn't—"

"You wouldn't have sent her. I know that, Tommy, but I also know we work with the people we've got. And we're strained right now. This is a big case. Does she need help?"

Hasseen considered for a few seconds. "Ollie Park's with

her. They've been partners maybe a year and a half, two years now. Work well together. Folkestone is a real smart cookie. Got her masters—"

"In what?"

"Medieval church architecture, of all things. But she's not an academic. Seven years of patrol. Four as a detective. She's a real up-and-comer."

Kelly understood what Hasseen was saying. Chicago was a young department, generally. Four years as detective after a strong stint as a patrol officer counted as experienced. When you first came on, you were considered green. After a couple of years you hit your stride and were considered at the top of your game. Sometime around the age of fifty the seesaw started to swing down and you began to be viewed as having lost a step, gotten a little outmoded. When you got near sixty you were believed to be "just putting in your time." Forced retirement was at sixty-two. Folkestone, at thirty-five, with eleven years on the department, was a good choice, at least on paper. And Hasseen had teamed her with Park, who was forty-something and was probably very experienced. Hasseen had probably put Folkestone in as the brains of the team and Park as the brake, the guy who would make sure nothing hideously ill-advised got done.

Kelly had heard Folkestone's name, too, which was unusual in a department with thirteen thousand cops. "She's had a couple of high-profile commendations, Tommy. I can't quite remember for what."

"That shooting last February? She shot the asshole after the guy shot Park."

"That was her, huh? She's okay about it?"

"She's very okay. Didn't seem to lose a minute's sleep over it." Hasseen chuckled. "She's hell on bad guys."

"We're saying she's a rising star, right?"

"Right."

The question was not, of course, whether she was ambitious. Obviously she was. The question was whether she was too ambitious and would overreach somewhere. This was the kind of case that could make a name for a detective. "Well, it sounds good to me," Kelly said. "I'm gonna check in on them, though, Tommy. This one's complicated."

"Your job to do," Hasseen answered. Kelly could tell Hasseen was slightly insulted, but she could live with that. The buck stopped here. Every murder in her part of the city was her case. And this was an ugly murder. Of a man revered all over the world.

How, she wondered, could anybody hate a healer like Dr. Jay Schermerhorn that much?

⚶⛧⚶

PARK AND I STOOD in the Hawthorne House kitchens with the evidence tech. My arms were folded across my chest, but lightly. I was trying not to wrinkle my clean linen blazer, which was just as crisp as my sharply creased navy pants. It was important in the department not just to be efficient but to look as if you were efficient. Unfortunately these clothes would look like dishrags by tonight. And I hate to iron.

Park, who cared little for clothes, was in a tan Penny's jacket and wrinkled chinos. I've told him and *told* him. He just says, "You take things too seriously, Emily."

"You have to look promotable to be promoted," I say.

He says, "Maybe I don't want to be promoted."

"Someday you might."

"Emily, when you get to be superintendent of police, you can promote me."

Oh, well.

The tech, Bernie Hagopian, gestured at the oven and said, "The kitchen staff noticed this was on. I turned it off as soon as I realized what was happening. But it'll take a while to cool down."

Park and I said nothing.

Bernie said, a little louder, "I figured you'd rather have me do that than wait until I could ask you."

"Oh, hell, Bernie, don't sweat it," I said. "You did the right thing." Bernie wouldn't ordinarily be so eager for my approval. Maybe he was aware this was going to be a case that got media attention—which meant attention of the bosses.

"Naturally I printed the latch and the controls first. Actually printed the turn-off dial first, then turned it off, then did the other stuff."

"Wonderful. And?"

"Clean as a whistle, I'm afraid."

"Wiped. Damn."

I tried to peek through the glass window, but the interior heat-shield was in the way. I said in a strangled tone, "Maybe there was nothing important in there."

"Somebody turned this on in the wee small hours, way before any of the cooks arrived—for no reason at all?"

"Shit. What do you think you can save?"

"Not much. You realize it was on the self-cleaning cycle."

"Shit!"

⚔

THE OVEN WAS too hot to handle. "We can't open it until it gets down to its preprogrammed release temp," Hagopian said.

I sighed loudly enough to convey that my patience was at an end. I was in no mood to cater to inanimate equipment. "Force it open."

"Can't. The latch is fail-safe."

Park said, "Liability-claims prevention. Consumer protection in action."

"Plus," Hagopian said, "even if we could, we don't want to. You slam a sudden blast of room-temp air into a five-hundred-degree oven, you blow ash around and demolish the evidence."

There was nothing to do but wait while it cooled. Hagopian said, "I'm gonna spend the time collecting trace evidence in the basement. That place is fulla crud and dust."

Park said, "Well at least you don't have to test everything that's down here. Except for the trail between the body and the kitchen, the dust on the floor is unbroken."

Hagopian said, "Duh!"

Park and I climbed two flights of stairs to the ballroom.

"By the way," I said to Ollie while we were still by ourselves on the stairs, "Chief Kelly called my cell while you were out getting Hagopian."

"Oh, hell. What did she want?"

"Basically to tell us not to screw up."

"Aaack! We're dead."

All the people who had been staying the weekend in Hawthorne House were now in the ballroom, plus the building manager, Mrs. Kisilinksi, a slender, middle-aged woman with nut brown hair, who had not stayed overnight. The kitchen staff was penned up in the west parlor, and not happy about it, but I thought the tech would declare the kitchen finished and free in an hour or so. Since none of the catering staff had stayed here overnight, they were probably not involved, but two uniforms were out at their addresses, inquiring whether they had spent the hours between midnight and 5:00 A.M. at home.

This morning, as soon as the patrol cops confirmed that there actually had been a killing and not a false alarm, they sealed off the entrances to the mansion and waited for the evidence techs, the doctor, and us detectives. The front door had a spring lock that was functioning. You could let yourself out from inside, but the door would lock behind you so you couldn't get back in. Outsiders would not have been able to get in that way, unless they had a key. Mrs. Kisilinski swore that only she, the head of the day care, one teacher, and the janitor, Karl Deemer, had keys to the front door.

While I got the techs going on the victim's bedroom, four cops under the direction of Detective Park had gone through the mansion visiting each bedroom. They told whatever guests were still in their rooms that there had been an accident, asked the guests to show them their shoes. Then they politely asked to "borrow" those with stains that looked like they could possibly be blood. They had explained that the accident involved a death, but they didn't say who was dead. Details would have to wait a little while, they said. Most of the guests complied willingly, but Park told me there'd for sure be objections soon. He did what he could now, quickly, while they had not yet got their defenses up. Some, Park said, simply wouldn't give up their shoes. Some claimed to have only one pair. There was no way we could confiscate all the shoes at this point without a warrant for each room, so Park and I decided to take what we could get. Then we asked everybody to leave their bedrooms and assemble in the ballroom.

By now the crowd had been milling around for an hour. Two patrol cops had stayed with them, keeping gossip to a minimum. One of the kitchen helpers named Karl Deemer had found Schermerhorn's body. I had had the uniforms keep him isolated in the dining room downstairs. I had been uneasy about him, alerted by his manner, which was the kind of excited, gleeful interest cops saw quite often in people who came near murders or disasters. It wasn't suspicious, exactly, or even very unusual, but I made a mental note of it. Dr. Erik Emerson had been second on the scene. I let him stay with the others in the ballroom, because I trusted him more than Deemer not to brag about it, but I specifically asked him not to talk about the murder to anyone. Still, Park and I knew that rumor would be rife. When we reached the ballroom, we were shouted at by several people who thought their rights were being violated. Guests who had been eager to help an hour ago, in the first flush of shock and horror, were getting irritated.

"They think we should have explained everything by now," I mumbled at Ollie.

"Well, you want to talk to them or do I?" he asked.

"I'll do it."

I had commanded a coffeemaker and rolls to be carried up to the ballroom—carried, not sent by the dumbwaiter, since it might contain evidence—but I was not surprised to discover that nobody thanked me.

Straightening the back of my jacket, I strode to the low dais, which was still in place from some reception held last evening.

"Please, everyone," I said firmly. They quieted immediately, except for one woman who hummed softly to herself. "I am Detective Emily Folkestone. I have some very sad and serious news." That had a good ring, sad and serious. "Dr. Jay Schermerhorn has been killed."

A murmur rose from the crowd. A few gasps. I heard some high-pitched shrieks. A woman sobbed.

"At the present, there is every indication that Dr. Schermerhorn was murdered. Now, I'm sure you all understand that it will take us some little time to search the building, and we need you to be patient. In addition we will need to interview every one of you as to what you may have noticed during the night. You've already given the officers your names and addresses but we will need to ask you for greater detail shortly. I am having more coffee, some cold drinks, and a few more comfortable chairs brought here so that you can all be as comfortable as possible. I hope you will give us your cooperation. Dr. Schermerhorn was a beloved man; you will all want us to find his killer as expeditiously as possible."

"When did this happen?"

"How was he killed?"

"I want to go home."

"Can't keep us—"

I said, "Please. Let me finish. You are absolutely correct.

We certainly can't hold anyone here who wishes to leave. I want to be perfectly clear about that. I'm asking you to stay in the interest of justice and out of respect for Dr. Schermerhorn. Everyone here was planning to remain through tomorrow— Sunday—afternoon, so we know you don't have pressing engagements at home." I was skirting a threat, not quite saying that it would be suspicious to leave.

"Where was he killed?"

"What happened to him?"

"We're trying to figure out exactly what happened to him. I can tell you he was found in the basement." There were gasps from several people. I cut in before they could all start talking and asking each other questions. "Please, folks. The uncertainty we all feel at this time is really my point. We need to find out what each of you saw or heard, if anything. We'll all feel better when we know what happened. To keep your information uncontaminated, I'm going to ask you all not to talk with each other about it, until we can interview each of you in depth. And we'll get started on that process right away."

"Can't you just tell—"

"This is scary."

"I want to go home!"

I said, "The police officers here will make sure everybody is safe. We'll tell you more very soon. For now, I'd like you all to get coffee and rolls and relax. We will be taking you one by one for further interviews."

"Wait a minute!" A woman in a blue-and-white striped dress stood up. She was very thin, but looked healthy, like a runner or a gymnast.

"Yes, ma'am?"

"Dr. Harriet Garner. I need a clarification."

"Yes, ma'am."

"Several of us came here for the reunion *plus* the symposium over at the U of C. There are papers being given all day, and there are two of them I really want to hear. I have no objection to staying here to help you out, but I want to be at the symposium for an eleven o'clock talk and another one at three."

"Ma'am, as I said, you are not under arrest. Would you give your name to Officer Cannon there, who is making a list? Maybe I can schedule an interview with you in between the events you want to attend, say at twelve-thirty?"

The woman nodded crossly, as if she was disappointed not to have to make a fight of it.

⁂

PARK WATCHED EMILY FOLKESTONE field questions. She looked so good to him, cool in this horribly hot weather. He could feel the sweat starting to collect in his armpits and on his back between the shoulder blades, even though it was still morning. But Folkestone's eyes were bright and alert. She stood straight and responded to each question with a brisk attentive move of her head and a clear answer. She had fine, expressive hands and crisp, dark hair. Wine-dark hair, he thought, like that phrase "wine-dark sea." Where was the wine-dark sea? Someplace near Greece? His mind was wandering.

And he knew why. He was ducking the fear that had hung over him since Wednesday.

Emily Folkestone stepped down off the low dais.

"Good job," he said. Up close he could see that, while she was alert, she was a little too alert. She was tense. She surprised him, though, when she studied him for a few seconds, and said, "Oliver? What's the trouble?"

⁂

OLIVER PARK, THE TECH, Hagopian, and I stood in front of the warm oven. The latch-lock light had gone off. "Well?" Hagopian demanded.

I reflected that evidence techs did not have the respect for detectives that they should. They considered themselves a separate branch of the department, subject to their own rules.

"Sure. Go ahead and open it," I said.

Hagopian slid the latch back, unlocking the oven. "I think we should close the kitchen door before I open it."

"Why? Nobody's watching."

"Drafts. If we have ash—*since* we'll probably have ash—we don't want it blown around."

I stepped back and closed the door, being careful not to show my annoyance by slamming it. I should have thought of that myself.

Hagopian had laid evidence envelopes, evidence buttons, scrapers, tweezers, and so on out on the kitchen table, on top of a white paper sheet. In one hand he held a camera. Gently, he eased open the oven door.

The oven light came on. I leaned forward to peer inside.

"Don't *breathe* in there, dammit!" Hagopian snapped.

I kept my temper. I always blame myself if anything goes wrong when I am in charge, but then I react with annoyance when anybody else gives me advice that could avoid trouble. Got to get over that.

Hagopian ran off three photos, leaned a little closer, and took three more pictures.

In the oven was a blanket of varied ash—white, gray, and black. Much of it lay in wrinkled drifts, like the ghost of dead, folded fabric. There were also discolored brassy rings.

"What are those?" I asked.

"Don't *breathe* at them!" Hagopian snapped again. He was several inches farther back than I was, careful not to let his breath ruffle the ashes. I stepped back a full pace. Hagopian pointed at the wall opposite the ovens. On a row of pegs hung towels, pot holders—and aprons with yellow metal grommets.

"Oh, no," I said.

"Look." Hagopian pointed at a silver triangle protruding from a wrinkle of pale ash. It was the point of a knife.

"Why would the killer roast the knife? All he had to do was wipe his fingerprints off. Plenty of rags around here."

"DNA maybe."

Park said, "What's that stuff that looks like rat brains?" Light tan curls lay in two small lumps.

"The leftovers of two of these, I would guess," Hagopian said, picking up a rubber glove from the sink.

"Jeez."

"He covered his hands," I said, "but he may have stepped in the blood."

"And those"—from where he stood, still a foot away from the oven, Hagopian pointed at some blackened crumbly mushroom shapes on the oven floor—"I would bet are what's left of plastic garbage bags."

All three of us, as one, looked down at our feet.

CHAPTER 10

JEFFREY CLIFFORD HUNCHED on a folding chair in the ballroom of Hawthorne House. His chair had silver-color metal legs and frame and a pink molded one-piece plastic seat and back. Of the thirty-five chairs in the place, he noted, twenty-one had baby blue seats, three were light green, and the rest, eleven, were pink. Jeffrey wondered if you felt more comfortable in the pink ones. Did the body sense the color it sat on? People never seemed to care about issues like that.

Numbers came easily to Jeffrey, people not so much so.

Last night at their private reunion dinner, he had counted twenty-nine people, carefully including himself. Counting them was easy, and very reassuring. You knew where you were with counting. Then he tried to figure out which people were which. If he was right, there were seven former counselors, all but one of them women, who had been little more than undergraduate hired help at Hawthorne House. There were five former therapists, plus Dr. Schermerhorn and Dr. Emerson, plus the longtime cook, and one nurse. He thought he could tell the counselors by their body language, which was more relaxed than that of former patients, but not quite as arrogant as the therapists.

Which would leave thirteen former patients. Twelve besides himself. But some of them looked too old. He didn't know why. That puzzled him until he realized that some former patients had probably come with a parent.

For safety.

There were now thirty-one people in the ballroom. Two were police officers. One was a woman he had not seen before, but she had the look of an administrator about her.

Well, that helped him to know where he stood.

Scared.

According to his watch, it took Jeffrey twenty-five minutes of thinking about standing up before he actually did it. Reflecting that he was much improved at social interaction—he *was,* he *was!* he had practiced at home and was now able to handle water-cooler conversations at work—he walked slowly but purposefully to the coffee machine. He poured two Styrofoam cups just barely half-full, not anywhere near the top, in case he got really nervous and twitchy. Then still with purpose but a little bit slower, he crossed the room.

April raised her head as he approached.

"Hello," he said.

Staring at the hall door, she said, "Hello."

"How are you doing? Doing? Doing?" He quickly used one of his three personal methods for breaking out of repetition— he bit the tip of his tongue—not terribly hard, but hard enough to stop it from moving. He'd read about it in a book, where somebody had said, "Bite your tongue!"

"O-kay," April said, accenting both syllables equally.

"Well, that is good. I was worried. About you."

He could see she didn't know how to deal with that. *Should I not have said that? Was that a too-personal remark? I am supposed to be careful of too-personal remarks.*

She responded loudly, "Worried about you?"

"You. April." He wondered whether he should tell her to lower her voice. He quite often said personal things that embarrassed people, despite trying not to, so he'd learned to stop and think before speaking.

April said loudly, "What do you think what—"

"Will happen? I do not know what will happen." Jeffrey saw Jane Macy get up and walk toward them. One of the cops, a skinny guy with a red face and noticeable Adam's apple, fell in behind her, reaching him and April the same instant Jane did.

"Sir? Ma'am," the officer said.

Jeffrey knew the tone of voice. People used it when they were pretending to be polite and respectful but really were bossing you around. Teachers used that voice sometimes. Administrators. People like that.

Jane said, "Yes?" to the officer.

"We're asking everybody not to confer at this time," the cop said.

"We're not conferring," Jane said. "We're talking."

"Well, we're asking people not to do that, too."

Jeffrey was going to say "Asking, or telling?" but he thought that would cause trouble. It might embarrass April, which he didn't want to do. He knew she was more fragile than he was. He hoped he wasn't being cowardly in not objecting to the cop's bossiness, but quite often it was hard to tell what your very own real motives were.

One thing is certainly true. The police will not blame the normals. Normals can talk their way. Out of problems. They have charm. They deploy charm when they like. Normals are slick talkers. The cops are already figuring out. Who in this group were patients. If they cannot tell, the records will soon be available. We are the weird ones. We are not normal. We do not have the. Normal amount of human empathy. That means at any moment we. Might impulsively kill. That is what they will think. They always think like that.

Under the eye of the skinny cop, Jeffrey held out one of the cups of coffee. "I brought you this," he said to April, keeping his eyes on the cup, not her face.

"O-kay," April said, taking it.

Jeffrey patted April's shoulder awkwardly, ignored Jane, and with his elbows pressed into his sides, walked haltingly back to his seat.

IT IS 1968. April Tausche, age seven, is sitting on the floor of the kitchen. Her mother is making raisin cinnamon scones and little April is eating raisins, one at a time. She has taken them from a big pile that her mother has on the wooden kitchen table, pulled away a fistful while her mother was busy turning on the oven. Now she lines them up in a perfectly straight row on the floor, each raisin one inch from the next, and starts eating, first a raisin from the left end, then a raisin from the right end, so as to keep the center of the long row in front of her until the last raisin is eaten.

Suddenly, her mother catches sight of what April is doing. "Oh, honey!" she says in dismay.

April looks up, but at the back of the chair, not at her mother.

"April, sweetheart, those are dirty. You can't eat off the floor, honey."

Her mother lifts April up in her arms, then, shifting her to the crook of the left arm, sweeps the raisins from the floor and throws them in the sink. She places April gently in a chair in front of the pile of raisins.

"Have some of these, honey." April looks at the pile, which is all jumbled and ugly.

Her mother is now aware that in the few seconds it took to lift April and put her in the chair the little girl has drawn in a huge breath. She begins to scream, shrill, piercing screams, one after another. April is turning purple with the effort of getting out her rage and fear. Her arms stick out from her sides.

"April! April! Oh, honey," her mother says. "It's okay. Oh, April, my poor little thing."

April, at the age of seven, should be in school, not sitting on the floor arranging raisins. But her parents have tried several schools and each one has enrolled her for a couple of months, then called her parents in and explained that they can't keep her.

"We don't seem to be able to reach her," the teacher at her last school said.

April's mother said, "But you're a school for special needs children. Helping difficult children is your job—that's what you *do*."

"April won't talk. Or listen to us. She hits the other children and she steals—I mean, takes—their food and eats part of it and throws the rest at them."

"When I met with the principal in January, he assured me you'd dealt with children exactly like April."

"We can't keep her. We just can't. For the sake of the other children."

Now April's mother holds her screaming child. The mother is wearing a long cotton dress, white with little sprigs of green, a granny dress. She sits on the chair and puts April in her lap, picking up the skirt and wrapping it around the child for warmth. In a while, April quiets. But she doesn't hug her mother back. She is as stiff as a wooden doll.

"April? Honey?" her mother says. But April doesn't speak. She has not spoken more than a few words at a time since she was two-and-a-half, although up to then she was learning words very well.

"April? We have to do something."

The child doesn't move.

"You can't go on like this. Honey? We have to find someone who can help you."

April is still rigid and silent.

"April. You need—" For a minute April's mother doesn't quite know what it is that April needs. Then she says, "You need to have a future."

OLLIE AND I STOOD in the second floor hall, outside the ballroom doors and far enough down the hall so that no one in the ballroom could see us. Dr. Schermerhorn's room was right behind us.

Ollie hadn't told me what was bothering him when I asked. He had said, "Oh, jeez, Emily. Just the crap life throws at you." Which was no answer at all, of course. Probably, I thought, that teenaged kid of his, Jason, was acting up, but that had happened over and over and Park never behaved exactly this way. When the kid was making trouble, Ollie reacted with a sort of half-amused cranky exasperation. This seemed more like fear or apprehension. But if he wasn't going to answer, I certainly didn't have time to pester him about it now. The suits downtown were watching my results on this one. Unfortunately, unlike the last major case we had, a complex financial scam that we drew shortly after Ollie came back on the job after being wounded in the arm, this one looked difficult and high profile. The last one had turned out to require a lot of detail work and precision but no special brilliance. In this case I knew all too well that I didn't understand our prime suspects, the autistic former patients, and the lack of knowledge unnerved me.

Anyway, there were too many people around to have a long discussion with Ollie right now.

"We need to get over to Schermerhorn's house pretty soon," I said. "It's possible the killer might go there to dispose—"

"Sent a guard."

"You did?"

"I sent a uniform to sit on the place until you or I could get there. In case there was something the killer wanted to get rid of."

"You're a genius, Ollie."

"Just because I think of the same thing you do?" He grinned at me. "But yeah. I'm a genius. Let's get started. Then I'll jump over to Schermerhorn's house and take a quick look around."

"I told Cannon to get two teams of canvassers out in the neighborhood. Find out if anybody was seen coming in or out in the night."

"Ordinarily, I'd say the chances in this neighborhood late at night were zilch."

"But?"

"This hot, who knows? People might've been lying on their front porches fanning themselves."

"We can hope. Let's pace this off," I said.

The small suite Dr. Schermerhorn had used had formerly been assigned to the staff nurse and was near the main stairs, in other words quite centrally located in the second floor, diagonally facing the ballroom doors, which were in the very middle. The ballroom doors directly faced the wide sweep of elegant staircase.

"I suppose," I said, "they put the nurse here in the old days so she could be got hold of quickly when anything went wrong."

"Which with this bunch I'll bet it did every two minutes," Ollie said.

He and I entered the nurse's room, where Dr. Schermerhorn had spent his last night on earth. The main room had a small sitting area and a folding screen to one side shutting out an alcove where patients might have been examined, and for that matter preschoolers possibly still were. In the central part of the room, a wooden chair and an easy chair flanked a small coffee table. On the table stood several copies of books written by Dr. Schermerhorn, including three fat paper-bound advance reading copies of *The Heart of a Child*, and near the books a bottle of cognac and two glasses. Off to the left was a door to a bedroom with a bed, a dresser, a closet, and a second doorway into a bathroom. Dr. Schermerhorn's belongings were spread around the bedroom. I walked in, trailed by Park. A pair of pants lay over the back of a chair near the bed. The dresser held Schermerhorn's hairbrush and, I noted, no comb. I have known several men, including my father, who preferred to brush their hair rather than comb it as their hair became thinner and finer with age and their scalps more tender. Schermerhorn had a good head of hair, though. When I saw him dead in the basement, his white hair had looked well cared for and silky despite the blood and sweat in it. *Does that tell me anything important about him? He was vain? People don't get killed for being conscious of their appearance. I need to know what Schermerhorn was really like.*

"Bed's still made," I said.

"Hadn't been to bed, then."

I studied the bedroom, trying to read from it who Dr. Schermerhorn was. Two deerskin suitcases stood upright next to the wall. There was fingerprint powder on the latches—black powder, since the latches were bright brass. The dresser top held a pair of cufflinks. The round white china pulls on the dresser drawers were lightly dusted with black fingerprint powder. I opened the drawers one by one. Park opened the suitcases.

"Three white shirts," I said to Park, closing the top drawer. "A blue cardigan sweater and a tattersall sweater vest," I said, closing the second drawer. "In this weather, how was he gonna need them?" The bottom drawer held socks and underwear. "Silk boxer shorts." Four pairs for just two days. *Takes good care of himself.*

Park said, "Both suitcases are empty. Now, me, when I travel, I leave practically everything in the suitcases."

"Does that make you a slob?"

"Naw. Makes me ready to bolt if there's a catastrophe."

I checked the bathroom. A toothbrush with a dark blue handle stood in a water glass. The toothbrush was powdered with white fingerprint powder, the glass with black, smudged in such a way that I could see tape lifters had been used.

Park said, "Then again, the real reason I do it is I'm lazy."

On the flat back of the sink were a bottle of bay rum aftershave, Tom's spearmint toothpaste, an ivory-handled straight razor, an old-style shaving brush and wood container of shaving soap, and powder for dusting the cheeks after shaving. Looking at the brush and the powder, I couldn't help imagining Schermerhorn fingerprinting his cheeks.

I opened the medicine cabinet and found it empty.

"No," Park said. "I'm lying. The real reason I do it is I'm afraid if I unpack everything I'll forget something when I leave."

"Schermerhorn was definitely not afraid he was going to leave something. Spread his stuff all over the room." *He's arrogant. Or maybe he's territorial.*

"Marking his territory," Park said, reading my mind.

"Well put."

"Tech's coming back to take the bedsheets."

I said, "No blood in this room?"

"Not that anybody could see. But when they get back they're going to Luminal it."

"Are the techs testing all the other bathrooms in the mansion for blood?"

"Yes, but I'll double-check." Park made some notes on his laptop, holding it in one hand and hunting and pecking with his index finger. If he was making notes, I wouldn't duplicate the effort right now. When he finished, he said, "So let's walk the thing for timing."

I said, "Okay. Two ways this could work. Number one, the killer comes to the room here. Says, 'Dr. Schermerhorn! There's a problem in the basement.'"

"Says somebody's sick or dead in the kitchen, I would bet. I mean, this has got to be past midnight."

"Right. Schermerhorn's not going to go down there just because the oatmeal wasn't delivered for breakfast."

Ollie said, "Sure. Killer says 'I think your old patient Mr. X is having a heart attack in the kitchen. Mr. X went down there to get something to eat because he was feeling faint, and I heard him calling for help.'"

I said, "Works for me so far."

"But it's cumbersome. What if he's not convinced? Or what if he says 'I'll call nine-one-one first.'"

"True."

"So maybe instead of that, the killer knocks on Schermerhorn's door, says, 'I got to talk to you, Doctor.' The doctor lets him in. Schermerhorn's a healer, right? A troubled person needs to talk."

"Yeah. Schermerhorn is maybe a guy who thinks he always knows what to do."

"You don't want to have preconceptions about our victim, do you, Emily? Anyhow, the killer gets in here and either knocks Schermerhorn out or has a drink with him and slips him a sedative. There's the cognac bottle on the table. And two glasses."

"Why did the techs leave this stuff?"

"For us to see it where it was," Ollie said. "They're bringing back a box and paper envelopes."

"Okay. Anyhow, Dr. Emerson already told us he was Schermerhorn's guest up here last night. They drank cognac."

"That doesn't mean Schermerhorn can't have had another guest later."

I said, "Of course. And if the killer doesn't give him a sedative, but knocks Schermerhorn out right here with some blunt weapon, there oughta be blood around."

"The pathologist is supposed to phone us about whether his scalp was broken. With all the smeared blood on him, I couldn't tell, could you?"

I shook my head. Park went on. "They're gonna let us know if he was hit on the head. I mean they'll do that right away."

"The pathologist is going to do something *right now*? Oh, my, the world has turned on its axis."

"Don't get too excited. They're just gonna eyeball the scalp. They got the message from downtown it's important. Press's hanging around the CPD, too, not just here, asking about Dr. Schermerhorn."

"Aren't they logging a lot of heat deaths?"

"Hundreds, I hear."

"So—let's say he was struck on the head."

Park said, "Or maybe drugged, but I still think that's unlikely. Not too many things act really fast and don't taste terrible."

"The lab'll find that out."

"Eventually."

I said, "Okay, the killer doesn't call the doc to the basement. Somehow Dr. Schermerhorn is knocked out here in this room, probably by a physical blow. So somebody's here on the second floor with a limp body he wants to get to the basement."

"Why?"

"Why to the basement? For the privacy to torture him. It's too dangerous to do it here."

"Right. Let's go."

We left the nurse's suite and walked into the hall. I carried a stopwatch. Park paced the distance to the grand double doors of the ballroom where the reunion guests were unhappily penned up.

"Only twenty feet to here," Park said.

"You can do this part in under twenty seconds. Couldn't take half a minute, even carrying Schermerhorn. He was tall, but he wasn't heavy."

"I wish we could go through the ballroom."

"Forget it. We'd be mobbed," I said. "Anyway, we don't have to. The distance from here on is the same whether you go through the ballroom or down the main hall into the north wing, give or take five feet at most."

We turned left, walked down the main hall, then turned right into a second hall that ran along the side of the ballroom's back wall, pacing and timing as we went.

"So here we are," Park said.

We had arrived at a paneled door three feet by three feet. We opened it and stared across the intervening space at the back of an identical door, which if open would have looked directly into the service area of the ballroom.

"You could get in from either side, see?" I said. "Perfect elevator for bodies."

It was the door to the dumbwaiter.

I SAT BEHIND the scarred desk belonging to the play-school administrator. At last, a place to set down my laptop. I was in a square room that had once been part of some sort of long east-facing parlor. Because of its position facing the rising sun, I figured the Hawthornes would have called it the morning room. Possibly ladies sat here to write their thank-you notes. They used to be called bread-and-butter notes, I thought.

Right now it was unbearably hot. A window air conditioner puttered away with little effect, and I could hear plops as it drooled into the garden outside. Double-glazed windows would have helped a little. But I suppose the present owners wanted to keep the effect of the original mullions. I had been told it was owned by a consortium connected with the University of Chicago that wanted to preserve Hyde Park landmarks.

The original long rectangular parlor had been subdivided into two squares, this office and another square room with big square cubbyholes along two sides for the preschoolers to store their jackets and hats and mittens and boots and so on. Weather cool enough to require even a light jacket seemed an illusion today. Did it ever really snow in this oven of a town? Right now the cubbies held a few empty vases and some notebooks, but were mostly bare. You entered through the cubby room to get to the office.

The office I sat in was jam-packed with equipment. The back wall was entirely filing cabinets. The facing wall was obscured by stacks of boxes, some of them labeled "Legos," some of them with labels of paper-manufacturing companies. At first, coming from the record-keeping culture of the police department, I naturally figured they were boxes of forms and printer paper. But looking closer, I saw that three cartons were marked "Construction Paper—Yellow." A glance told me the rest were purple, red, blue, green, white, and black. No brown? Maybe it all got used up making turkeys at Thanksgiving. Two other cartons were from finger-paint companies and one was marked "Crayolas" in green felt-tip pen. Since the room was not large to begin with, the supplies made it claustrophobic. The roasting heat only made it more so. The sun must hit this side of the house first thing in the morning and by now the accumulated heat had soaked deep into the boxes and walls.

Ollie had taken Dr. Schermerhorn's keys and gone to double-check the buttoning up of the doctor's house, just half a mile away. He'd decided to leave a uniform to sit inside the house to make sure nobody broke in—the killer or the press—even if it turned out that the place could be quite securely locked.

Officer Cannon brought me my first interviewee. Dr. Emerson had been briefly interviewed by the first officers on the scene, of course. It was time now for a fuller story.

As I went to the door to greet Dr. Emerson, I stepped on a blue crayon that had been hiding near the only other chair in the room. One foot slid out from under me.

"Careful!" Emerson said, reaching for my arm.

I grabbed the edge of the desk instead. "Come in," I said, straightening up. "I almost did a triple klutz."

Emerson smiled.

"I want to extend my sympathy to you," I said as we both sat down. "I know Dr. Schermerhorn was your friend."

"He was more than a friend. He was my teacher and my mentor, more like a father to me. My inspiration. And of course, a huge figure in his field. When it came to writing about the world of troubled children, there was no one like him. I think I have to say he was irreplaceable."

"I'm sorry for your loss."

"Thank you."

"Does Dr. Schermerhorn have any relatives we should get in touch with?"

"Not that I know of. His wife died several years ago and they had no children. I don't know of any siblings of either Jay or his wife."

"Do you have any idea whether he made a will?"

"I'm sure he must have. He was very particular. I'm sure you've thought of checking the office in his home first. Then his lawyer, I suppose, but I don't know the name."

I studied Emerson openly. He'd have to put up with my professional interest. If shrinks studied people and got paid for it, so did I. But my pay was a lot less. Emerson was a gentle-voiced man of medium height, and not quite pudgy. He made me think of an Episcopalian minister. He appeared to be in his early sixties and wore a three-piece suit, despite the hot weather. I wondered whether the suit was a psychiatrist's uniform. At least it was very light wool, and Emerson, as we sat here cooking, looked cool. Then I thought: *He's cool because he's calm.*

He had a round, pink face, high forehead, and once must have had a full head of dark brown hair, now mostly white with just a fleck of dark brown at the crown. He folded his hands together, and said, "You didn't ask me in to hear my woes. Do you want me to tell you what happened this morning? I explained to the first officer who arrived, and then to Officer Cannon."

"Thank you. I will want you to do that. I know it's repetitious, but—"

"But I might remember something new. No doubt I will. People do, even though they hate to admit it. My patients go over things and over things and they get more out of their memories pretty much every time."

"Do you mind if I record you? We keep everything accurate that way."

"Not at all. Go ahead."

I punched on my tape recorder, identified myself and Dr. Emerson, the time and place, and then said, "Dr. Emerson, what I'd like you to do first is explain to me what this weekend event is all about. People all say it's the Hawthorne House School reunion, but what was Hawthorne House, exactly?"

"Let's see where to start. Hawthorne House School functioned here from 1968 to 1980, treating children with emotional problems, especially autism."

"So I've been told. But what is autism?"

"It's a developmental problem that ordinarily begins by the time a child is three. In a typical case—and let me say there really isn't any typical case—the child seems normal at birth and develops pretty normally for the first couple of years. He may not like to cuddle, but he starts learning and using language, and so on. Then the parents notice that he isn't playing with other children. He's clumsy. He has strange repetitive behaviors. He doesn't look people in the eye. Stranger yet, he may behave as if other people aren't there, or treat them the way you would treat furniture, as objects rather than something special. Actually as objects that aren't very interesting."

"What happens as he gets older?"

"I should have mentioned that language, whatever language he's developed, starts to deteriorate. The child may become more and more withdrawn and isolated. There's a whole spectrum of how seriously affected the child may be. Almost half of autistic children never speak. At the high-functioning end, there are some who are just awkward with people, and maybe a little physically clumsy, and prefer to have non-people-person jobs, but are pretty much able to function in society. They're not what used to be called retarded, necessarily. Most autistics have average or above-average intelligence. They just can't express it. Some of them are what used to be called idiot savants, people who could instantly calculate what day September 12, 1277, fell on, for instance."

"And what did Hawthorne House do for them?"

"Dr. Schermerhorn kept them in a protected, cheerful environment. He concentrated on teaching them coping skills and working with how early conflicts between them and their parents had damaged them."

"So this reunion—?"

"Well, after Hawthorne House closed, the staff went other places to work, most of the children went on to high school and in some cases college, and Dr. Schermerhorn went on to teach and to write several very successful books."

"I'd sort of got the gist of that."

"So the people who had been at Hawthorne House didn't see each other after it closed. Most of them had never met again until yesterday. Their experience here was very intense. Intense for the children, of course, since they were away from their homes and families and this became their real home, with Dr. Schermerhorn effectively their father. Except for a few who never settled in, or were dangers to the others, most of these children stayed several years. One was here all twelve years."

"Lord! I didn't know that. I'd pictured a treatment period of a few months."

"Well, psychiatric treatment isn't like rehab after a broken leg, you know. The idea was to get the children entirely away from their earlier family influences and develop their potential from a new base."

"As you say, this became their home."

"Exactly. Which is why I say it was intense. It was a total experience. We were in loco parentis, virtually became these children's parents. But life here was an intense experience for the staff, too. The live-in counselors were mostly young and inexperienced and it was very important to them, very involving. The therapists, of course, were M.D.'s with a specialty in psychiatry. For example, I had my M.D. and had then gone to Korea as a kind of MASH-like doctor. When I came back to do my specialization, I took up a residency in psychiatry. I needed a job to pay my way through school. I had Dr. Schermerhorn as a lecturer in some classes and even though I didn't have any experience with autistics, he took me on as one of the therapists. I worked weekends and some nights, so I could still go to all my classes. Even when I opened my own practice, I continued to do therapy here. I was entranced by Dr. Schermerhorn and his ideas. We therapists were *all* afire with Dr. Schermerhorn's ideas. We were going to cure these poor children and send them out into the world to live a useful and satisfying life."

"And did you?"

"Yes and no. We were very young. I know now you can't cure everybody. But we did pretty well, I think. Of course there's a tremendous emotional toll in dealing with children so troubled. We therapists didn't live in, and we were older than the counselors, and more experienced, but we were excited about doing something new with autism." He grinned. "I'm being long-winded. To answer your question, Jay thought that having a reunion after fifteen years would give anybody who wanted to come back a chance to revisit an important part of their lives. Sometimes that kind of thing can help you put your memories in perspective, too. He approached me about it and I agreed."

"But obviously not everybody who was ever here came back."

"No. The weekend was sold out by early May. There were several people who decided later that they wanted to come who couldn't. Space here in the mansion is limited. The idea was to charge just enough to cover the basic cost of renting the place for the weekend, plus food, catering, and housekeeping staff, and a small cushion in case of cost overruns. We were planning some group discussions, and a party on Saturday night—oh, good heavens! Saturday—that's today—that's tonight. What will we—? Well. Anyway, we held the reunion now because this is also the weekend of a major psychiatry symposium at the University of Chicago, so some of our therapists who had moved away would have a double reason to come back. Several of the people at our reunion planned to go to hear papers given at the symposium. Plus a lot of the media wanted to get hold of the famous Jay Schermerhorn, since he was going to be honored by the association, and anyway he was a giant in his field."

"I see. How many patients did Hawthorne House treat?"

"About three dozen."

"Over all twelve years?"

"Yes. With so many of them staying several years, that was pretty much a capacity crowd."

"I heard that at the sherry reception last night Dr. Schermerhorn talked about seventy-nine patients."

"Well, yes, he did. I don't know why. Sometimes Jay, uh, embroidered a little bit."

I studied Emerson.

"Altogether," he said somberly, "the reunion should have been a triumph."

Emerson fished around in his pocket for a minute, finally pulling out a prescription bottle. He dumped a tablet into his hand and swallowed it. "Bursitis. I'm supposed to give up tennis, which was my one athletic outlet. What can you do that doesn't use your right shoulder?"

"Detective Park tells me you had drinks with Dr. Schermerhorn after all the ceremonies were over last night."

"That may make me the last person to see Jay alive. Except for his killer."

Was he being disarming because he was guilty? Was he just cutting to the heart of things like the therapist for the police department who prided himself on being up-front? I said, "Yes. Exactly. Can you tell me what you all did after the dinner broke up?"

"People sat around and gossiped for a couple of hours. After all, they hadn't seen each other in years, and everybody wanted to know what had happened to everybody else in the meantime."

"Did you all stay up late?"

"No, some drifted away. In fact, most of the former counselors and therapists stayed around to talk but a lot of the former residents didn't. They probably go to bed on a fixed schedule at home. Autistics like regular scheduling and just being here would be as much change as most of them could handle. You have no idea how *brave* it is of them to come at all."

"Who exactly left early?"

"Jeffrey Clifford, as I remember, left almost the minute dinner was over. April Tausche and Ben Goodspeed and Ben's mother I think left pretty soon. Henry Rollins and his father left. Jane Macy left after an hour or so."

"Then what did you do?"

"Jay felt he had to talk with people, to be courteous, of course. But we hadn't seen each other in several years, either. So when it got to be about ten-thirty, he invited me up to his room. He had a bottle of cognac, and we chatted for maybe an hour."

"How did he seem?"

"Very much as usual. He's a self-confident, generally optimistic person. Was. If you're asking whether he was worried, as if he'd had threats or believed somebody was out to get him, he didn't say and I surely didn't see it in his manner."

"And you're an expert in observing people's demeanors, I think."

"Well, maybe. But therapists, like Jay, are experts in concealing their feelings, too. You have to be; you just can't react facially to some of the things patients tell you."

"And you left at what time?"

"Eleven-thirty to eleven-forty-five. I looked at the time around then, because I remember saying something about Jay having a big day tomorrow. Today." He stopped suddenly, possibly realizing what he had just said. I waited, in case there was more he would add. But he simply stared into space.

"Did you see anybody hanging around when you left his room?"

"Not a soul."

"Tell me what happened this morning."

"Right. There was a major talk scheduled, with a panel of commentators, at the symposium at nine A.M. Jay wanted to be around here most of the day. After all, it was his Hawthorne House reunion. But he had to put in an appearance on the panel. The panel was on autism, and naturally he had to be there. He was going to spend the rest of the day here."

"When did people realize he was missing?"

"It happened like this. The kitchen staff started serving breakfast at seven-thirty. They probably arrived about six-thirty. Mrs. Kisilinsky would know. They were to go on serving until nine. There wasn't continuous service all day, you know; after all, this isn't a hotel. The play school just serves midmorning snacks and lunch, so there's not even much kitchen equipment here. Which is why we had everything catered. Anyway, we expected Jay to turn up in the dining room about seven-thirty, as soon as they started serving. He had to go to the early panel, plus he was always an early riser in the old days. Even though he usually stayed at Hawthorne House until late in the evening, he was always here by eight A.M. Pretty much of a workaholic. Devoted to his kids.

"When it got to be eight o'clock, one or two of the therapists and I got worried. A guy named Morton Haseltine and a woman named—uh—Sandra Hall I think. He had told them they'd have a chance to chat over breakfast."

"You thought something had happened to him?"

"Oh, Lord, no. I thought he'd brought a traveling alarm clock and it hadn't worked and he'd miss his symposium. He liked to take time shaving just right, and eat his breakfast without rushing—you know."

"So . . . "

"I went up to his room to call him, and of course he wasn't there. When I knocked and knocked and didn't get an answer, *then* I got worried and went in. You know the second-floor doors don't lock, because of the preschool?"

"Why is that?"

"I think it's a city code requirement for schools. You can't have a situation where a child could accidentally or on purpose lock himself in. So, even though the third-floor doors lock, the second-floor bedroom doors don't bolt on the inside or even spring-lock when you go out."

"Yes, I'd noticed that."

Emerson smiled, probably suspecting that locks would be one of the first things the police would check out. "So we went looking for him. We weren't terribly worried. There hadn't been any disruption to his room."

"Had he been to bed?"

"I didn't look in the bedroom. I just called his name."

I knew, of course, that the bed was still made. "No blood? No signs of struggle?"

"I certainly didn't see any. But I didn't look carefully. I had no idea there was any serious trouble. Why do you ask? Did you find any?"

"No, but somebody could have slipped in and tidied away evidence while you were searching downstairs for Schermerhorn."

"I didn't search downstairs at first. And upstairs we couldn't run around shouting. Some people were still sleeping, you see. But I checked the obvious places on the second floor. There are six hall bathrooms. Jay had a bathroom in his suite, but there might have been something wrong with the plumbing that forced him to use one of the others. It's an old place, and you never know. Back when the Hawthorne House School was here, the toilets were always backing up. We had plumbers in constantly. I checked the bathrooms and then the ballroom. He could have been chatting with an old friend in the ballroom."

"Was anyone in the ballroom?"

"Nooody at all. There wasn't any sign that anybody had been there this morning—coffee cups or things like that. The staff had pretty well cleaned up after the reception the night before."

"No sign of a struggle in the ballroom?"

"I wasn't exactly looking for—no. No, I think I would have

noticed. So I went back to the dining room. The two therapists had gone outdoors to see if Jay was in the garden in back. The grounds are pretty large for a city lot, and there's play equipment and benches and so on out there. But they hadn't found him, of course."

"Go on." I preferred to let people ramble. They tended to edit themselves if you asked them direct questions.

"Well, we met in the kitchen. Who knows, he might have been getting himself coffee, although there was coffee on the sideboard in the dining room. Jay didn't cook, but maybe he wanted the caterer to make him something different. The staff said they hadn't seen him. One of them asked us whether we'd turned one of the ovens on to self-clean."

I ignored that comment, not wanting to give away any information I didn't have to. "Who was down there?"

"Three people. A cook and an assistant, I don't know the names of either of them, and the general gofer, Karl Deemer."

"You know him."

"He was a resident here years ago."

"And he's still here?"

"He got too old to stay on as a patient. Jay only treated children. Ordinarily, they had to leave when they got to the age of eighteen. Karl was nineteen when they asked him to leave, but he didn't have anywhere to go. I think his father was dead and his mother in alcohol rehab at the time. Or the other way around. Jay tried to get him a job nearby, so as not to shake him up too much. He was—quite fragile. But if Karl wanted a specific job, the job didn't want him. And if the job wanted him, Karl didn't want the job. He was always strange. I'm sure you think all our patients were strange, but he was more manipulative—and defensive at the same time. The others weren't like that. Anyhow, finally they hired him to work here as a janitor. He lives at home and comes in by the day."

"You know a lot about Karl."

"Sure. I was his therapist for several years."

I kept quiet. In a few seconds Emerson went on. "So we decided that Morton and Sandra would go up and check the attic and Karl and I went looking around the basement. It's a full basement under the whole house, so you can imagine how huge it is."

"I've seen it."

"Oh, yes. Of course you have. That was silly of me. We went beyond the kitchen part, where some lights had been left on. But a lot of the bulbs were burned out. It was like being in the catacombs. I blundered into something that had once been a large wine cellar. It smelled like vinegar. There were some bottles still in the shelves, but most of them had started to leak. Rotten corks, I guess. It was like a scene out of Edgar Allan Poe. And then I heard Karl yell."

"And?"

"He'd found Jay. Found him after about three minutes of looking."

CHAPTER *11*

BORN IN 1960, Jeffrey Clifford had been a beautiful baby, plump, with pink cheeks and a lot of fluffy pale hair. He ate well, slept well, and grew well, but his mother, Nancy, worried because he didn't like to be hugged. His older brother, Anthony, had loved to be hugged and cuddled and tickled, but when she hugged Jeffrey he stiffened and his arms and legs stuck out like a starfish. When she tickled him he screamed with fury or fear, she couldn't tell which, but it certainly was not laughter. He was a very good, quiet baby otherwise, and when he talked early, even speaking in short sentences by his first birthday, she and her husband, Edward, thought they had a quiet, reflective genius on their hands.

Jeffrey's mother and father, Edward and Nancy Clifford, had met in college at the University of Michigan in the mid 1950s. They were children of their generation, a little rebellious, joining sit-ins and marches, but thought they were a lot more rebellious than they really were. Edward majored in physics. When he was admitted to the graduate school at Princeton, he and Nancy married. She wore a white wedding dress, and in the interests of asserting that she was still a flower child, wore a headband with a jade stone that centered in the middle of her forehead. She followed Edward to Princeton and set up house in a modest apartment. She had had only three years of undergraduate work. It was very difficult to transfer from one school to another in those days, so she let college go. In a year, she was pregnant with Anthony. Two years later, when Edward got a teaching fellowship at the University of Chicago, she was pregnant with Jeffrey. After three years of living in Chicago, Catherine, their third and last child, was born.

At four years old, Jeffrey was reading, having decoded language from the picture books that were read to him and from his older brother's comic books. At five, he read the entire series of Oz books to himself and soon after graduated to Narnia and the Hobbit, but could not tie his shoes. He spoke less and less. He spent hours of his day reading and hours more opening and closing the closet door in his room. His parents put him in a play school, hoping that playing with other children would "bring him out of himself." He sat in a corner and watched, and solved and re-solved a wooden puzzle. They put him in a smaller, very structured play school. Here he did better and seemed to enjoy the experience, but he didn't play with other children; he would play near them, but not with them. And he spoke very little, often repeating the same word over and over. He'd develop a fad for a word and use it constantly for months on end.

In first grade, when the other children were starting to print well-drawn letters of the alphabet, Jeffrey's lines were wobbly and crossed each other in such wacky places that it was hard to tell which letter he was trying to make. *H* looked like two *L*s, one upside down. *K* was completely beyond him. When other children were drawing primitive but rounded pictures of people, he could produce stick figures at best.

He still didn't play with the other children. He rarely talked, and when he did he made remarks that even six-year-olds knew were socially unacceptable, questions like how did they know for sure when they had to do pee-pee.

Jeffrey was peculiar.

He walked stiffly, with his elbows held far back and his forearms parallel to the floor.

Nancy had two other children to compare Jeffrey with and she knew something was very wrong. His younger sister could do ordinary things that were beyond him, like buttering bread. Nancy took Jeffrey to their pediatrician, who said Jeffrey was a late developer and a little awkward, but that time would straighten the problems out.

Time only made him worse.

His teacher told his parents that Jeffrey's problems had been caused by their urging him to learn to read before he was ready.

They had never asked him to learn to read; it had just happened.

In second grade, his penmanship was worse than it had been in kindergarten.

He knew he was different, too. Jeffrey stayed in his room unless he was forced to go outside to play. In his room, he played checkers over and over and over, the board set up near a wall where he had propped a mirror to pretend there was another player, even though he played both sides. He still couldn't tie his shoes and didn't know how to take a shower. He would turn the light switch in his room on and off hundreds of times in a row, and had broken it several times.

Every day, every item in his routine had to be exactly the same, all the furniture and toys in precisely the same place. Nancy joked once that Jeffrey would like a chalk outline on the floor to show where each toy lived. She came back later to find that he had outlined each one on the floor in red crayon.

If a plate fell and broke, he would jump at the sharp sound and then scream for hours.

His second grade teacher told his parents he was only doing all this for attention.

Nancy Clifford knew they couldn't just let the situation go on. For one thing, Jeffrey was getting worse. He had more frequent periods of rage, when he'd be so furious he would destroy anything breakable within reach, then fall on the floor and curl into a ball. While he was curled up, he refused to speak. No, she thought, maybe he wasn't refusing to speak; maybe he couldn't speak. He was a child trapped inside himself and the carapace that surrounded him was hardening day by day. It was a horrible, unremitting, discouraging tragedy that played out over and over, hour after hour, and sucked the joy out of their lives. Their intelligent, promising son had a mind that was wasting away. And their gnawing misery damaged their other son and daughter.

Having struck out with the medical profession, Nancy tried several counterculture methods of improving Jeffrey's thinking. She put him on a gluten-free diet. Unfortunately, most of the foods he loved were on the prohibited list—jam sandwiches, soft peanut butter cookies, and spaghetti. Gamely, she tried rice bread, rice noodles, bean-flour peanut butter cookies. She slaved over yeast-raised corn breads without gluten. Anthony and Catherine hated the food. And after all, it was wrong to punish them for Jeffrey's problem. But it was worse when she gave them bread for their sandwiches and restricted Jeffrey to his special diet. He threw tantrums at most of the meals they ate in those days. Also, the diet wasn't making him any better.

She took him to an allergist who put him through a three-month course of desensitization injections for house mites and a couple of other allergens. The injections didn't do a bit of good.

Desperate, she invited a healer to the house, who placed a small pyramid and two crystals under Jeffrey's bed and charged a lot of money. Nothing changed.

She and Jeffrey spent four months taking lessons in *pranayama* breathing; then they joined a breathing group. She and Jeffrey quickly advanced to the second level of the alternate-nostril technique. Nancy felt less anxious as a result, and Jeffrey liked the sessions himself, possibly, Nancy thought, because his breathing was a function he could control. But between sessions Jeffrey was no better. Alternate-nostril breathing was not a cure.

Weekly visits to a psychiatrist, Dr. Sydney Lambert, made Jeffrey frustrated and in a few months made the psychiatrist frustrated too.

Nancy, of course, blamed herself. If Jeffrey had some sort of organic brain damage, maybe it had happened because she didn't eat the right things while she was pregnant with him. Or maybe she ate the wrong things and damaged him. But she hadn't drunk alcohol while she was pregnant and she had never smoked cigarettes. She had smoked marijuana during her hippie period, and maybe smoked some early in her pregnancy with Anthony, before she realized she was pregnant, but not at all when she was pregnant with Jeffrey.

Maybe, she thought, it wasn't organic brain damage but psychological trauma. Had she treated him differently from the way she treated Anthony, who continued to develop perfectly normally, if a little hyper at times when his brother acted up? And his sister, Catherine, was fine, cheerful, easy-going, and, magically, well able to tune out Jeffrey's tantrums.

Had she been too busy after Catherine was born, with three children to take care of? Had she neglected Jeffrey? Could a middle child easily be overlooked in the tumult of raising three children? Had he been pushed aside?

Had she allowed him too much sugar? Too much white flour? Should she have called the doctor sooner when he had that high fever as a toddler, the illness that had turned out to be a bad ear infection? When he was an infant, should she have put him to bed on his back instead of his stomach? In those days doctors told you to put the baby to sleep on his stomach, so that if he spit up he wouldn't choke.

Maybe he had been terribly traumatized the time she and Edward left the children with her mother for a weekend and went to New York to see a play and a musical. Her mother had reported that Jeffrey had cried for hours.

Had she this—?

Had she that—?

Should she have—?

Should she not have—?

How could she make amends?

In her own way Nancy Clifford was suffering as much as Jeffrey. Edward worried about them both, but knowing what to do about it was another thing entirely.

Edward taught in the physics department at the University of Chicago. He loved numbers. Edward was a somewhat aloof man who had few friends. He was very much wrapped up in his work, close to his family, and regarded them as all the friends he needed. He chatted with his colleagues, though, and at one point described Jeffrey's problems. One of his colleagues had a friend in the history department who had a cousin whose child was in a wonderful residential school for children with emotional problems. The school was located in

Hyde Park, just a few blocks from the campus. This particular child, an eight-year-old girl, had been nearly without speech since early childhood. The school, Hawthorne House, had drawn her out. Her parents reported that in two years she had made more progress than in the previous six.

Edward and Nancy did not rush blindly into the idea of sending Jeffrey to the school. It was very expensive, and besides they wanted him to grow up with his family. They asked friends, especially people in the education world, and discovered that Hawthorne House was well known. It had an excellent reputation. The director, Dr. Jay Schermerhorn, had written several books on the treatment of disturbed children. Nancy bought two of his books on a Friday morning, read them in an all-day, all-night blitz attack, finishing on Saturday morning. Schermerhorn's humanity and concern for the children glowed from the pages.

"He has such wonderful stories, Edward," she said. "He really cares."

"All right. I'll read them too." He finished them by Sunday night.

They were convinced. For the first time in years they had hope. First thing Monday morning they made an appointment to see Dr. Schermerhorn at his next available opening, which was Thursday morning, and they could hardly stand to wait that long.

⋈

DR. JAY SCHERMERHORN'S OFFICE was just inside the front doors of Hawthorne House. Directed to the office by a young woman counselor, Nancy and Edward Clifford entered cautiously. They had no idea whether Jeffrey would be accepted at the school and both believed that this might be Jeffrey's last chance.

They found a tall, scholarly-looking man, who held out his hand to shake theirs but stayed behind his desk. This made it necessary for Nancy, then Edward, to lean over the desk to take the man's hand. His cheeks were pink, glossy, and freshly shaved. His hair was a lush chestnut brown, thick, and worn full, brushed back with no part.

Dr. Schermerhorn gestured toward two low chairs opposite the desk, then sat in his own chair behind the desk. He was tall, and his chair seat was set higher than theirs. Nancy felt at a disadvantage and was sure Edward did, too.

"Now, what is it you think I can do for you?" Schermerhorn asked.

"You—ah—I assume you received our application. For our son Jeffrey," Nancy said.

"Indeed I did. I have the report from his pediatrician, and from Dr. Lambert. All his medical records, in fact, from birth."

Nancy, thinking he was complimenting them for thoroughness, said, "Yes, we wanted you to have—"

"Jeffrey is a very sick boy."

It was a blow. She knew Jeffrey was sick; why else were they here? But it hurt to hear it.

"We know we need—"

"It's not a question of what you need. It's what Jeffrey needs. Jeffrey has deteriorated steadily over the last four years. If this continues, he will end up a vegetable."

Nancy heard Edward cough. She thought he was covering a sob.

"Jeffrey appears to be autistic. You have heard of it? As you may know, autism is considered incurable. Hopeless." Dr. Schermerhorn paused but the Cliffords didn't speak. Schermerhorn continued.

"You are fortunate that I am deeply involved in studying the treatment of childhood autism. This is an ongoing program of several years' standing, and in my opinion the work here is beginning to show promise. I am willing to take Jeffrey on."

Nancy heard Edward let out a breath.

Dr. Schermerhorn said, "He will report to my school on Monday. This is a list of the clothing and personal items he will need. You will drop him off before noon."

"Thank you," Nancy said.

Dr. Schermerhorn stood.

"May we tour the school now?" Edward asked.

Schermerhorn walked to his office door, herding them out. "No."

"No? But we're going to leave our son here," Edward said.

"My patients are not zoo animals to be shown off to parents."

Nancy said, "Well, I can understand that. I admire that. But I'd like to see where he'll live. How long will he stay? How often can we visit him?" Nancy was horrified at the thought of leaving Jeffrey. At the same time, she was desperate to have him start the treatment.

"He will stay, I hope, until he is better. You may not visit. I wish to wean him as completely as possible from the home influences. If we are going to change him, we must change everything."

"That could be months!"

"Probably more."

Nancy was aghast. "He'll think we're abandoning him!"

"He will think what he will think. Hawthorne House will be his total environment." Relenting slightly, Schermerhorn said, "When I believe his improvement is sufficient to make it harmless, he may spend a weekend at home."

Harmless? What was he talking about? They had harmed Jeffrey, that was what the doctor was saying, and only by being removed from their care, their influence, would Jeffrey get better. It was Nancy's constant nightmare come true.

She said, "All right."

CHAPTER 12

"MR. DEEMER, I'm Detective Folkestone."

"Oh, you are, huh?" he drawled. Deemer pulled his pony-tail from behind his shoulder, moved it to the front of his neck, and slouched lower in his chair.

I definitely did not expect men to jump to their feet when I entered a room. In fact, it bugged me when they did. There was something a little condescending about it. But if you were slouched when a person enters a room, it was only a show of courteous attention to sit up straighter.

I said, "Yes, I am." Deemer chewed his gum with his mouth half open. I reminded myself that he had been a disturbed or autistic child and was probably not a normal adult—although that might not be the politically correct way to think of him.

"I'm sorry to have asked you to stay in here so long, Mr. Deemer. I wanted to keep the details about Dr. Schermer-horn's death just between you and Dr. Emerson and the police for now."

"To see if somebody knows more than they're supposed to?"

"Maybe." He didn't sound stupid. Maybe he was just plain weird. Weird? I was going to have to absorb some of the technical terms or I'd sound bigoted. "At any rate, Mr. Deemer—"

"Emerson ain't here, though."

"What?"

"He's not here. Have you got him in a different room? Or did you let *him* mix with the rest of the gang?"

I felt heat rising in my face and hoped I wasn't visibly blushing. I didn't want to tell him I just plain didn't trust him.

I could pretend I'd kept Dr. Emerson apart in another room, but I refused to lie just to pacify the little twit. "No, he's with the others. We thought we needed a doctor there. He told us he wouldn't talk about the crime scene."

"Hansen's there."

"What?"

"Hansen's a doctor."

I drew a breath. "And in addition to you not being a doctor, I thought your attitude was odd. I wasn't sure whether I could trust you not to say anything."

Deemer smiled broadly and wriggled his hips in the chair. I could have sworn he was thinking "Got you, cop."

"Mr. Deemer, let's just get down to business so you can leave here as fast as possible."

"Sure thing."

"All right. Let's take this morning. What time did you arrive?"

"Six-thirty."

"Who let you in?"

"Ah—I have a key. To the front door. 'Cause I'm supposed to clean up whether anybody's here or not."

I knew that, but I was pleased he was honest about it. Probably thought he'd better be, because Mrs. Kisilinski would be sure to tell us. "Was there anything out of place in the kitchen?"

"Nope."

"Help me out here. Think back. Anything at all missing?"

"Ahh, maybe an apron. You know we got caterers, which we usually ain't got. Who knows where they leave stuff?"

"Did you notice that the oven was on self-clean?" When he shrugged, I said, "You didn't think that was odd?"

"Who knows? We had that Brian caterer guy around and some of the people here for the weekend were loonies. Who knows?"

"Weren't some of those loony people residents you had been here in the school with when you were a child?"

"Yeah. Plus counselors and shrinks and shit."

"Weren't they friends of yours in the old days? Weren't you happy to see them again?"

"Didn't even go upstairs, did I? Never were friends then, aren't now."

"Even some that were your age when you were here? Jeffrey or April or Henry?"

"They were nuts, lady."

"But weren't—um—"

"Wasn't I nuts, too? That's for me to know and you to find out."

I gritted my teeth. "Dr. Schermerhorn accepted you as a resident at this school for a reason. You must have had problems. You stayed here several years."

"Yeah, I was pissed off at the world. I got arrested over at the college, once, breaking windows and shit. Then I did some bad stuff to some cab horses in the park."

I shuddered. "How old were you?"

"Eleven."

"So what did Dr. Schermerhorn do for you?"

"Ahh. He talked to me. He liked to hear about my ma. See, my ma was pretty rotten, the way she behaved with all these men and all. Dr. S liked to hear about how rotten she was. He had ideas about how all that made me real mad. And my dad dying right in front of me, like, when I was five. He had a stomach thing from drinking all the time and he threw up a whole lot of blood, all red and globs and all, on the living room rug and died, and Dr. S thought that made me mad at life."

"A hemorrhage?"

"You bet," Deemer said with another smile, and I felt I'd been set up again somehow. I was unsettled, also, by the fact that he was meeting my eyes.

"All right. This morning—when did you first know Dr. Schermerhorn was missing?"

"When Dr. E came down looking."

"Who suggested searching the basement?"

"Dr. E."

"But you went along."

"Oh, sure. Beats loading dishwashers."

"How did you happen to find the body so quickly?"

"Well, ma'am, I guess I'm just naturally lucky."

———

"CANNON!" I YELLED on my way back to the school office. Officer Cannon appeared at the end of the first-floor south corridor and walked quickly toward me.

"I need you to run a guy."

"Sure, boss."

I led him into the office, where we wouldn't be overheard. "I need everything you can get on Karl Deemer."

"The thirty-five-year-old teenager?"

"That's the one. But I also need his parents' histories. The father is dead. I'm not so sure about the mother. She could be in jail. Get the parents' old arrest data. I need it sooner rather than later."

"Will do."

After Cannon left, I made notes about Deemer on my laptop. It wasn't long ago that we took notes on actual paper and then at the end of the day had to translate them onto forms using an antiquated typewriter. I think I preferred that.

Done with my notes, I studied the list of reunion attendees. Twenty-nine people had slept in Hawthorne House last night, but it looked like only seven were former patients. For a moment I wondered about the fact that, out of maybe three dozen patients who had "graduated" from Hawthorne House, so few had come to the reunion. The ratio of staff to patients seemed larger than it should be.

But I had no time to worry about that. I had to get as much

detail from the people here as I could before everybody recovered from the shock and started to demand to leave. Once a couple of them left, the exodus would grow.

Park had come back from Dr. Schermerhorn's house.

"Let's split the list between us," I said. Cannon and another uniform had finished the preliminary interviews—home address, occupation, age, where each person's room was, whether he or she had heard anything suspicious, and whether anybody else could vouch for their whereabouts in the night. That last was a major problem.

I said, "Literally nobody in the entire group is firmly alibied."

"But why should they be? If the murder happened between, say, midnight and three or four A.M., in a group of unrelated people, most of them sleeping in separate rooms—I mean, nobody was watching anybody else."

"I suppose. But even the parent-child combinations are inconclusive. They're sleeping in the same rooms. And every one of the parents swore they would have known had the child—well, adult offspring—"

"But you don't believe them. Neither do I."

I assigned Cannon to draw up a floor plan of the house. He sat down on a chair in the cubby room to make a preliminary sketch. I studied the attendee list Cannon had put together.

Ollie said, "Okay. I'll interview two of the therapists, Dr. Sandra Hall and Dr. Andrew Pastucci, four of the counselors, and the school nurse, Serena Simms. Did you see Cannon's notes? He says that Simms was the nurse here from 1968 to 1977, and she 'refuses to give her age.'"

"Will you take Henry Rollins and his father, and that other former patient who came alone?"

"Probably means he functions fairly well."

Maybe he could answer questions adequately. On the other hand, the parent-child combinations gave us somebody, the parent, to talk with who was . . . I didn't know how to phrase it, even in my head. Somebody normal? That sounded terrible. Somebody who—well, it didn't matter. The point was to get on with the work.

I scanned the list twice and made a mental note to have Cannon or another officer put the names in alphabetical order when he typed up the preliminary statements, or use "sort" if he worked on a computer. But later. Busywork could be done anytime.

Then my eyes went back to one name on the list whose data raised my suspicions.

"Cannon," I said. The cop sprang forward. "Get me Mr. Bettleby."

FORMER HAWTHORNE HOUSE patient Shawn Bettleby was what I thought of as a pleasant-looking man. Certainly not handsome. Neither tall nor short, he was stubby bodied without being fat, and his hair was middling graying tan. The tan hair was thinning on top, but Bettleby made no effort to comb the remaining side strands over the dome as so many men did, hoping for a camouflage that never worked. I liked him for that.

Nevertheless, there was something wrong about Mr. Bettleby. Despite his thick body, his cheeks were sunken. His mild green eyes were pinkish all the way around the rims. He seemed preoccupied. I had to ask him twice to please sit down before he did so.

I got his agreement to tape the interview.

"I'm Detective Folkestone, Mr. Bettleby."

"Yes. How long do I have to stay here?"

"You don't *have* to stay at all. You're not under arrest. You're not even under suspicion. You can leave at any time. But I'm sure you want to help us find whoever killed Dr. Schermerhorn."

Bettleby just stared.

"So, Mr. Bettleby, I have the basic data you gave the officer. You're a CPA. Live in Northbrook. Have your own company, says here you employ thirty accountants. That's very impressive, sir. Especially for a person who previously had problems as a child."

Still Bettleby said nothing. His eyes were as expressionless as if they had been green grapes.

"So, Mr. Bettleby, why did you come here this weekend?"

Bettleby blinked. "For the reunion."

"Of course. But why did you want to come to the reunion?"

"Well, to see, ah, old friends. The house, Hawthorne House."

"Nostalgia?"

Bettleby pursed his lips. "I guess so."

"But you were never a patient here, Mr. Bettleby."

Bettleby stopped breathing. Then, after a few seconds he took in some air, and said, "What makes you think that?"

"You're too old. Hawthorne House accepted children only. You're a full generation too old. You gave your age to Officer Cannon as fifty-eight. Come on, Mr. Bettleby," I said when it looked like the man would stonewall, "we can get the patient records quite easily."

"It—my son was a patient."

"I see." I waited. Nothing happened. "Is your name really Shawn Bettleby?"

"I'm Frank. Shawn is my son."

"So you kept his name—which you had used to make your reservation—when you talked to my officer, but gave your correct age because you couldn't fake the way you look."

Bettleby said nothing.

"Why didn't Shawn come?"

"He didn't want to."

"If he didn't, why should you?"

"I wanted to."

I sighed. I didn't like the answers or the feeling I was getting from Bettleby, but strangely enough I liked Bettleby. I felt a sense of vulnerability about him. The fact that he was too old to have been the Shawn Bettleby, former patient, that he claimed had made me interview him first. It made me wonder about his motives, but not necessarily think he was a murderer.

"So, Mrs. Bettleby didn't want to come with you, either?"

Bettleby shifted his feet noisily, large boots clunking. "My wife wasn't interested in coming."

"I'll ask again. Why did you want to come?"

"Well, it was the first chance any of us parents ever got to see the inside of the place."

The first chance to get close to Dr. Schermerhorn?

"And that was your only reason for coming?"

He just shrugged.

I steepled my fingers. "You want to help me with this, don't you, sir?"

"I can't help you."

"Mr. Bettleby, what is it you're not telling me?"

Bettleby stood up. "I think I'll go back to the ballroom now. Don't be alarmed, Detective. I'll stay in the building."

⚔️

AFTER A FEW MORE INTERVIEWS, I decided it was time to smooth over the feelings of the people in the ballroom again. As I had told them, there was no way I could hold them here. But I hated having to say it and really wanted them to stay. I knew my chance of solving this murder was much better if I had the most likely suspects right at hand. If there was a "golden hour" in trauma treatment, there was also a golden day in murder investigations. The most important evidence was that collected immediately, before memories faded, or trace evidence got stepped on or blown away by wind or washed away by the actions of people.

I glanced out the front windows as I crossed the hall. The street was full of media vans.

⋈

BE CONVINCING! BE CONVINCING!

I climbed the wide stairs to the second-floor ballroom. "Listen up, everybody! I know the first thing you want to ask me is when you can get out of here."

A couple of people laughed, but there was some angry muttering, too.

"Look. It's almost lunchtime. The reunion committee has planned a good lunch, and it will be brought up here in"—I made a show of glancing at my watch—"fifteen minutes. Meanwhile, you all already know where the bathrooms are." Some more laughs.

"Detective Park and I have interviewed quite a few of you and will talk to the rest of you over the next couple of hours. I think I've made it clear that you are free to leave anytime you want to go. However, we'll certainly appreciate cooperation. And we will have to come to your house to reinterview you if we can't finish it off here. You would probably waste less time staying. And there is that free lunch." This time I got mostly chuckles.

"Those of you who are not from Chicago will be interviewed more extensively right away." They seemed to be in an agreeable mood, so I said, "I do have something more to ask. We need to examine the guest rooms now—"

I was scarcely into the next word when the reactions erupted.

"Not my room!"

"There's nothing in my room you need to—"

"You can't do that."

"You need a warrant!"

"Absolutely not!"

"Un-uh. Nope."

"Wait! Wait a minute!" I shouted. "Hold it!" When they wouldn't quiet, I yelled, "I'm not your enemy!"

A large, middle-aged man wearing a bright red T-shirt stood up. No doubt he was the parent of the younger copy of himself who sat huddled in the next chair. The younger man wore a yellow shirt and purple pants. They were Henry Rollins and his father, whom Ollie was going to interview. "You've probably been searching our rooms while you kept us here," Rollins Sr. said.

"Please. Hear me out. I assure you, we have *not* searched your rooms. We asked you to stay here for a while just so that people wouldn't be wandering all over the building confusing whatever evidence there may be in the bathrooms, halls, or public rooms. We are not *allowed* to search your rooms without your permission. A room in a lodging like a hotel or rooming house is in law exactly like your own home. We can search it only with your permission or a warrant. What I *am* doing is asking you to give us permission. After all, you've only been here one night. Your room here isn't really your personal space. We need to look, in case the killer has hidden evidence in a guest room."

Mr. Rollins said, "The killer would be pretty damn stupid to let you search his room and find evidence against him."

Mr. Bettleby said, "A smart killer would throw a weapon into somebody else's room. And let the innocent person get blamed."

"That's right!" Mr. Rollins said.

"Believe me," I said firmly, "we know that a guilty person could hide evidence in somebody else's room. Even if we found a bloodstained shirt in a room, the person who stayed there is not necessarily guilty." Bloodstained shirtsleeves were exactly what I was hoping for, a vision of a wadded-up shirt in the back of a closet flashing into my mind. That damned apron hadn't covered the whole body of the murderer, had it? It left the arms free. And there may have been blood splatter, if I was lucky. I hoped the killer had not thrown his shirt in the oven along with everything else. He wouldn't have wanted to go back to his room bare chested. Still, if he planned thoroughly, he might have taken an extra shirt with him. Or, worse, put a plastic trash bag over his upper body and let his head stick out. And how terrifying that butcherlike apparition would have been to Dr. Schermerhorn! I stopped my tumbling thoughts there and turned my mind back to the group. "I promise that you won't be automatically blamed if we find something incriminating in your room. Evidence analysis can tell a lot about who really wore a garment, for instance. If you have nothing to hide, you have nothing to worry about."

When there was no response to this only half-true platitude I went on. "Don't you owe it to the doctor to help find who killed him?" There was a murmur of agreement, and a couple of people said, "You can search my room," but there was less support than I would have expected. That was odd.

"Folks," I went on, "I didn't want to come right out and say this, but it's going to look suspicious for the people who are afraid to have their rooms searched."

Silence. Then Jane Macy said, "You can search mine."

Mr. Rollins said, "Oh, hell, go ahead. We don't have anything much there, anyway."

"Detective Park has consent-to-search forms. He's going to bring them around. Please print your name as well as signing it, and tell us which floor and which hall your room is on."

I WAS BACK in my temporary interview room in the office on the first floor. The woman sitting in front of me was small and plump, like a blond cocker spaniel puppy. Her hair was a pinkish tan. She had a round face and pale eyes and appeared to be in her early forties.

The woman patted her hands together soundlessly several times. I thought for a second or two that she was mocking me. But that wasn't it; she was just doing it for the sake of doing it.

"Ms. Tausche, you're very important to this investigation because your room is on the second floor two doors down from Dr. Schermerhorn's."

"Are they on the floor?" she said loudly.

"What?"

"The doors?"

Puzzled, I said, "They're both on the second floor."

"They are flat?"

Something clicked for me. "No, when I said your room was two doors down, I didn't mean the doors were down flat. I meant you are staying in a room near Dr. Schermerhorn's."

"A room near? Staying. You are here."

"I'm here? You mean you? Yes, you're here. You're not there now, I know. You're here."

April hummed. She said, in a monotone, "You are here." She hummed and patted her hands together, not in time to the humming.

I closed my eyes for a couple of seconds and opened them again. I didn't want to insult the woman, didn't want to talk down to her, but I sure didn't know how to talk with her. "Ms. Tausche. Can you tell me when you went to bed last night?"

"Went to bed last night. Ten-twenty-two."

I blinked mentally, startled that Tausche was so precise when she had seemed so fuzzy.

"Did you hear any strange noises during the night?"

"During the night. In a strange place all noises are strange."

"So you heard noises? People walking in the hall? Arguing? Banging doors?"

"Matilda does not like strange noises."

"Who is Matilda?"

"Who is Matilda? Matilda is a Manx." April Tausche nodded her head several times. "Or baths either."

I felt my impatience growing into sharp annoyance. On the other hand, I was *not* going to let myself get angry at a "mentally challenged" woman. "Did you see Dr. Schermerhorn at all after—ah—ten-twenty-two?"

"Your nose is too pointy."

"It seems to do its job."

"Do its job. Is it at work now? Manx cats have no tails."

April Tausche was wearing a lacy white shirt and Levi's. The sleeves ended in lacy edging, and I now noticed brownish stains on the left cuff.

"Ms. Tausche?"

"Mmm-hmm."

"May I take a sample of the stain, there, on your sleeve?"

"On your sleeve?" She raised her arms curiously and studied the spots. Then she nodded her head.

I rose and went to the door. "Cannon?" I called, loudly enough for Cannon to hear, but not so loudly as to alarm April Tausche. Cannon appeared immediately. He had been standing in the center of the entry hall, sketching painstakingly at his floor plan.

"We're just going to take a washing of Ms. Tausche's sleeve."

Cannon realized immediately that he was here as a witness. He proceeded, though, to act as if he was needed to do the actual work. He took a piece of paper similar to an envelope, called a pharmacist's fold, some sterile gauze, and a small bottle of sterile water from my evidence briefcase. Meanwhile I removed a permission form from the case and asked April Tausche to sign it, handing her a pen. If it ever came to a trial with April Tausche as defendant, there would certainly be questions about whether Tausche was competent to sign the form, but for now the woman was an adult, and here on her own. She could be treated as compos mentis.

"After this, when you have a minute—" Cannon said to me.

"Sure. Let's just get this done."

Cannon snapped on a pair of gloves. He soaked the end of April's sleeve with a few drops of sterile water, then opened two packages of sterile gauze. He pressed the two pieces together, one on each side of the fabric, carrying some of the stain onto the gauze. Then he slipped both pieces into the paper, where they would dry. He wrote the day, time, place, Tausche's name, and his name and mine on the outside edge. I initialed it. He sealed the paper, which was porous enough to let the water evaporate.

I picked up the permission form I had laid in front of April. It was signed with big, scrawly, unreadable letters.

"Thank you, Ms. Tausche," I said. Cannon took out a Polaroid camera and, with April's permission, photographed her sleeve.

I had left the door of the office halfway open. These days you just did not shut yourself up with a civilian in a room, ever. There was no point in inviting lawsuits.

A huge crash came from upstairs. I heard shouting and bumping on the floor above my head. Then I heard feet pounding down the stairs. I got up fast, as the half-open door bashed back hard against the wall. Bettleby came in at a run. "You'd better get yourself to the ballroom," he said. There was a police officer close behind him.

"Why?" I started moving. "What's happening?"

"We've got a problem," the cop said.

Bettleby said, "You just don't have a clue, do you? You've left a bunch of people who can't stand change and can't make friends easily and took a great risk from their point of view just to come here—" He stopped to wave his hands. "You've penned them up with complete strangers in an unfamiliar place and an unstructured environment and a threat of murder—"

I said, "Ms. Tausche, I think I have to cut our interview short."

"Cut the interview short." She made scissoring motions with the fingers of one hand.

CHAPTER *13*

I HURRIED UP THE STAIRS, Bettleby at my side, the cop running on ahead. "It's not like they're rioting," Bettleby yelled as we ran. "They're *suffering*."

In the ballroom one of the plastic chairs was overturned and a group of half a dozen people clustered around a young man on the floor who was making strange gulping sounds. Their bodies blocked me from seeing exactly what was happening. But since Officer Cannon was with that group, kneeling on the floor, I turned from them to a sound of screaming.

A man with dark hair and the profile of a hawk was screaming, "I'm scared. I'm scared!" He had a pale, bony face, attractive in an austere way. He held his abdomen with both hands and screamed. Two women in their late forties, which put them possibly ten years older than the screaming man, stood next to him, stroking his arm, saying, "It's all right, Cameron. We're all friends here," in a persistent counterpoint to the words he screamed.

I recognized the two women with relief. Both had been pointed out to me as former staff. One was a former counselor at Hawthorne House, Beth Pollie, and one was the therapist,

Dr. Sandra Hall. They had evidently known Cameron when he was a patient here and they were far more qualified to talk him out of a panic attack than I was.

I scanned the room, glancing at Cannon's group again, again deciding that with several former aides and therapists, there were plenty of people present who knew what to do. Someone had thrown that chair against the wall. But no blood had been spilled. No fights were happening. There was no immediate emergency.

Jeffrey Clifford sat on a chair, hunched over, his hands in his lap, left hand gripping his right wrist. He said "I'm *not* scared! I'm *not* scared. I'm *not* scared." Whether as a response to Cameron or his own idea, the mantra appeared to be working fairly well. He repeatedly flicked his first and second fingers of his free hand against his thumb.

I circled the room. The only person who caused me serious worry was the young man on the floor.

It's a bias in myself, and I'm not proud of it, but seeing men sobbing repels me, while seeing a woman crying her heart out would have awakened pity and sympathy. Henry Rollins was now being helped into a sitting position, his knees up, arms wrapped around his legs. His father hovered over him. When I first entered the room, I had heard the younger man gulping loudly but he had stopped that now. His upper body swayed back and forth as regularly as a metronome while he gasped for breath. On the back sway he gasped and on the front motion he moaned.

Dr. Emerson was among the people near Henry. To my surprise, he was on his knees next to the young man. My impression of Dr. Emerson was of a gentle older man who might be kindly and yet valued his clothing and dignity. But I could see the dust being mashed onto the knees of his navy slacks, and the creases being stretched out by the strain of kneeling. He had one arm around Henry's shoulders. He rocked forward and back with him.

"That's okay, Henry, that's okay," he said. "There's no danger."

I held still, intrigued by the evident kindness in Dr. Emerson's face. A couple of minutes went by. Mr. Rollins, in his red T-shirt, stopped wringing his hands and the younger man quieted and stopped rocking.

Emerson looked around.

Seeing me, he took his arm from Henry's shoulders, but paused as he did so to make sure no reaction was forthcoming. Then he struggled to his feet. He touched Henry on the shoulder, as if to reassure himself that the young man would be okay. Then he said to the group around, "Let him sway if he wants to. It calms him."

Henry's father appeared with a plate on which were three pieces of cake and three cookies. Emerson came over to me.

I said, "Dr. Emerson. What happened here?"

"Some kind of social kindling, I guess you'd call it."

"Kindling? What are you talking about?"

"Oh, in psychiatry kindling is a condition where electrical impulses in the brain amplify themselves. You get a progressively bigger response to the same size stimulus. Basically, it means that once things go bad they get worse and worse. What happened here was that Henry"—he gestured at the young man, now sitting fairly calmly on the floor—"got into a nervous attack. He threw his chair. And that pushed several other people over the edge."

"But weren't they all peacefully having lunch?" There were sandwiches on the sideboard, potato salad, soda pop in cans and urns of coffee and hot water on a table, along with buckets of ice. A chocolate cake, a pie, and a large pile of cookies looked very inviting. A couple of the former patients sat calmly eating lunch, ignoring the trouble as completely as if it were not taking place.

"It happens this way sometimes. Everything's fine and

then bam. Autistics don't take well to having their routines disrupted."

"Then why did they come here at all?"

"I think in most cases their therapists told them it would be helpful. I'm not sure I agree. It's okay for some, I suppose. But they're very apt to get frightened. Of course, to be fair, their therapists certainly didn't know a murder would happen."

"No."

"Listen, Detective, these people need to get out of here and go home."

"I'm working as fast as I can. Doctor, if you actually think there's a risk to any specific person, send him home. Get him a cab or get somebody to drive him —"

Emerson said, "Oh, I guess I can deal with this for now. Some of them don't even want to leave. But they think police are scary. You've got to bring the active questioning to a close."

"I'm doing my best!"

"Otherwise, I'm just going to advise *all* the autistics to go home."

⚔️

I SURVEYED THE ROOM, trying to decide whether things were stable. One of the former counselors approached the mansion's administrator, Mrs. Kisilinski, who had been hovering around the proceedings this morning. I couldn't hear what they said, but they went off together down the stairs. April Tausche took half of a sandwich from the buffet table. The sandwiches had all been cut across diagonally, making triangles. She looked slyly to right and left, then took three other half sandwiches from a tray, bit off a point from each, put them back on the tray, and poked dents in a few more with her index finger. Apparently satisfied, she found a chair and sat down with her paper plate of food in her lap.

Henry Rollins lay back flat on the floor.

Cameron, the man who had screamed that he was scared, was laughing at something a middle-aged man, one of the former Hawthorne House therapists, had said to him. I remembered the therapist's name was Dr. Morton Haseltine. Cameron now seemed as happy as he had previously been frightened.

Mrs. Kisilinski and the counselor came back up the stairs and into the ballroom. They were carrying two piles of boxes—a chess set, two checkers sets, and several containers of Legos. Good idea.

I walked over to a mother-son combination I had not yet met. I said, "Ms.—?"

"Mrs. Goodspeed." She nodded at me, and said, "This is Ben."

"How do you do, Mr. Goodspeed," I said. To call him Ben seemed like treating him as a child. "How are you doing?"

He didn't speak. His mother said, "I'm sorry. Ben doesn't talk."

He was a nice-looking young man, kewpie-doll chubby, a person who probably didn't exercise. His face was sunny. He had been smiling when I first walked over to them, one of those smiles that makes the cheeks bunch into pink apples, and he smiled more widely when I spoke.

"One of us will interview you soon, Ms. Goodspeed, Mr. Goodspeed. Meanwhile, there should be plenty of food. Please let one of the officers know if you need anything."

The mother said, "It's all right. Don't worry about us."

I smiled at her and started to turn around to head toward the door.

"You're in real trouble," said a voice right behind my shoulder, unfortunately echoing my thoughts.

"Mr. Bettelby."

"You have no idea what you're doing, Detective. This is just like a cop. The Chicago Police Department at its most ham-handed. Blundering around completely uninformed."

I silently gestured to Bettleby to follow me and was careful to say "Please" aloud, however much I didn't feel like it. Then I walked to the far corner of the ballroom. With a couple of dozen people in a space that could hold two hundred, I had plenty of room to get out of earshot of the guests. "We don't need to get the, ah . . . the . . . everybody all riled up again." I smiled at Bettleby. "If you're going to yell at me, do it here."

"What were you going to say? Get the *what* riled up?"

He had the manner of the teacher I had most disliked in high school, bullying students, thinking he was being Socratic, when in fact he was just plain rude. But he also might know something. I said, "I was going to say 'the patients.' But they're not necessarily patients anymore."

"Patients, like sick?"

"They were, weren't they? Otherwise they wouldn't have been sent to Hawthorne House for treatment."

"Treatment for what?"

"What do you mean for what?"

"For being crazy?"

I was worried enough already, pressed by the need to solve this case, and fearful that I'd never be able to understand the autistics. Bettleby wasn't helping. "Listen, you're angry at somebody, but it isn't me. Who is it, Mr. Bettleby?"

"I'm trying to help you, whether you realize it or not."

I reflected that I'd learned things from far less appetizing people than Bettleby.

"These autistic people are not crazy. Look at Jeffrey Clifford over there."

I searched the group for a couple of seconds and then remembered who Clifford was—the blond man who was rocking back and forth saying, "I'm not afraid."

"He's a good-looking guy," I said.

"And brilliant. Even speaks well. But not conversational. He's a computer engineer who's developed programs for important accounting and inventory-handling problems. In his spare time, he makes inlaid furniture. Handmade, you understand."

"He sounds very accomplished."

"He's had photographs of his furniture in several magazines. A table he inlaid with rosewood and white ash and ebony was on the cover of *Woodworker*. He used the natural colors of the wood for the design of leaves and vines. His stuff sells for thousands of dollars."

"Well, why—"

"And he can't tie his own shoes. His sister has to figure out what the customers owe him and send out the bills."

I digested that for a minute. Without wanting to say it, I thought, *I don't understand these people!*

"He can hardly maintain a casual conversation with another human being," Bettleby said, "although he's very verbal and can make clear statements. It looks like he's had some training in social interaction since he was here. He's very high functioning."

"Which means?"

"Some high-functioning autistics are said to have Asperger's syndrome. They can lead pretty normal lives. A lot of people think Einstein was autistic. He didn't talk until the age of three, and was compulsively focused on one area of math, and all his life could hardly find his way home. He was a poor husband and a negligent father. Thomas Jefferson, too. Brilliant in a lot of ways. Political writings, farming, architecture. But he was never any good at getting along with people."

"And your point is—?"

"These are autistics, not crazy people, and they're not mentally deficient, either. You're frightening them by penning them up in here, which is bad enough. They don't like change."

"I didn't invite them here, Mr. Bettleby. And I didn't kill Dr. Schermerhorn. Don't blame me for it!"

"If your goal is to learn something from them, you can't do it with interviews. They don't *converse*."

"Listen, I know you mean well. But I don't have a lot of time and I need to—"

"And as a result you're going to draw the wrong conclusions and mess up."

I called on all my patience to produce a talking-with-the-public voice.

"I appreciate your input, Mr. Bettleby, and I'll be happy to chat again later. Anything you can explain to me will be a help. Right now I need to get to work."

Just then April Tausche stood up and screamed. I started to go to her, but Dr. Emerson got there in two seconds, so there was no need. Anyway, I didn't feel especially competent to deal with Tausche, and Emerson certainly was.

"April is lower functioning than Jeffrey," Bettleby said. "She spends most of the day spinning around and around. That's called stimming. Self-stimulation. People think autistics do it to block out excessive confusing stimulation. In other words, the real world. April has eating problems, obviously. At that, she's pretty high functioning, for an autistic."

April had begun to spin slowly in place. The action must be calming to her; her face was now serene, almost euphoric.

Bettleby said, "Look at Henry."

"Henry Rollins?"

"He wants everything in his life to be always the same. He *always* wears purple and yellow. He doesn't speak in sentences at all, just single words, but his speech was normal until the age of three and a half. Then he basically stopped talking forever. He doesn't relate to people. Hardly looks at them. He likes machinery. He's a genius at fixing electric motors."

"How do you know?"

"I've been talking with his father."

"Why is he here?"

"Oh, his father says his therapist said he should come here to confront it."

"Confront what?"

"The past."

"What about the past?"

No reply.

I stared at Bettleby for several seconds, but he didn't answer. I hate it when people make cryptic comments and then won't explain.

I said, "What is the cause of autism?"

"Nobody knows for sure. It's at least four times as common in boys as in girls. If one identical twin is autistic, the other is likely to be. So it's pretty clear there's a genetic component. There may be prenatal influences, too, like maybe a virus."

"If these kids were so dysfunctional when they were here as patients, it's pretty amazing they can come here now, some of them by themselves, and spend the night and get to meals and so on."

"It certainly would be."

"So they have all been cured? Partly cured, anyway?"

"Hell, no."

"But Dr. Schermerhorn treated them for autism."

"Not exactly. Most of his patients were either run-of-the-mill disturbed children or had Asperger's syndrome. The lowest-functioning person here is Ben and he's not as bad as some autistics are, plus he may not even be autistic."

I thought about that a few seconds, but wasn't sure how it could help me. I said, "How do you know so much about autism?"

"Don't be disappointing, Detective Folkestone."

"Your son."

"My son. Exactly. I've made it my job to find out what was wrong with him. No, I put that badly. It's been a *necessity* of my life to find out."

I folded my arms. "It's not that I don't sympathize. I do. But I've got to get to work. You were making a point about this investigation—?"

"I want you to have a feel for autistics so that you won't talk down to them, but especially so you won't blame them because you interpret their behavior wrongly. They're not basically violent people. They got a bad rap because they do fly into rages—"

"That sounds violent to me." Thank goodness, something to go on. It sounds cold, but there had been a murder, and *somebody* did it.

"No, I don't think so. Autistics can't communicate well. When they get angry it's because they're frustrated by not being able to make themselves understood. Let me give you an example. With an ordinary child, you never have to teach him to look at the person he's talking to. That just comes naturally. Autistics don't automatically know they should do that. An autistic could be standing here right now, talking with me but looking at you, or looking out the window. If he were looking at you, I might not answer him because I didn't know he was talking to me and you might not get what he meant because what he was saying was never intended for you in the first place."

"All right."

"So he might fly into a frustrated rage."

"And hit you or me?"

"Not likely, but if I'm being honest, yes, it's possible. My point is this: You have a *planned* murder here. Right? This isn't a case of somebody flying into a brief rage. Whatever happened, somebody had to get Dr. Schermerhorn to the basement without a big, noisy struggle. This killing did *not* happen because somebody stopped to talk with Dr. Schermerhorn and felt misunderstood and lashed out. The killer planned ahead. I deduce from the fact that you haven't arrested anybody that the killer also removed evidence and covered up well. That's *not* autistic, Detective Folkestone."

I nodded, feeling grim. "All right. You've made your point."

"Let me make one more. As I said, these former patients aren't all autistic. But as to the ones who are, don't start thinking they're behaving suspiciously just because they don't answer your questions or won't look you in the eye. You'll think they look 'shifty.' They're behaving normally for them and are really doing quite well."

"I hear you." Damn.

"So take it easy on them. They're *not* your killer. Okay?"

"I can't go quite that far, Mr. Bettleby. You do want me to find out who killed Schermerhorn, don't you?"

"Whatever."

CHAPTER *14*

"I INSIST THAT you interview me right now," the woman said. Her feet were planted wide, her arms crossed over her chest. She had very curly hair and the corkscrew shapes bobbed angrily, as if they were all positively electrically charged and repelling each other.

I said, "Your name is . . ." I held my list in my hand.

"Cassie Garibaldi."

"Ah, Ms. Garibaldi," I said, hoping for the soft word that turneth away wrath. "I'm glad you came up to me. The officer doing the preliminary interviews said your room was near to Dr. Schermerhorn's."

"You should have talked to me yourself. Immediately."

"Do you have information about the murder?" Ms. Garibaldi had told Cannon she didn't know anything, but if she had changed her mind, the last thing I wanted to do was turn her off now.

"No, Detective. But you'd learn more if you listened for a minute."

"Certainly. Go ahead, Ms. Garibaldi."

To my amazement, the vigorous little face crumpled into sadness. The anger had steamed off Garibaldi, leaving her wan and watery eyed. She said breathily, "I want to apologize for everybody here."

"What?"

"This is so wrong. The way they're acting."

"Would you explain, please?"

"Didn't you notice? They're practically ignoring Dr. S! I mean, he's dead, *murdered*, and they're all just worrying about themselves."

"Specifically who?"

"Most of them! That nasty Mr. Bettleby and Mrs. Goodspeed. Dr. Emerson feels sad about Dr. Schermerhorn, I think. And a couple of the counselors. I just want to tell you they're being *ungrateful*. It's horrible. He did so much for all of them!"

"The patients, you mean?"

"Sure, but the counselors, too, people like me. Most of us had no special training at all when we came here, and he hired us and trained us. I came to Chicago from Minnesota. I was looking all over *everywhere* for a job. Somebody told me about Hawthorne House, and I came and interviewed with Dr. S."

"When was this?"

"Fall of 1976."

"So you didn't come to attend the university?"

"No. I had two years of junior college back home, but I didn't really do much with it. I didn't like school all that much. So he asked me questions, like did I have experience with children, and I told him I'd been a camp counselor every summer back home. Well, of course I'd done baby-sitting for-*ever*, but camp was the main structured thing."

"So he hired you here on that basis?" I tried to keep the surprise out of my voice. Up to this minute I had thought that all the staff at Hawthorne House had been professionals or at least students in psychology.

"Well, sure. The counselors were a lot like camp counselors, you see. Look. Here's a picture of three of us in the old days."

She held out a color photo of three young women. It was not well focused, and the colors had begun to change, getting more orange. But I could pick out Cassie, in 1975 clothing and hair. She looked rather fierce even then.

"He trained us himself. In fact, he said he wanted people who didn't have preconceptions. He was looking for people who could empathize with the children, and play with them, but be firm about rules."

"You weren't junior therapists?"

"Oh, my God, no. You wouldn't even *suggest* such a thing if you knew! The therapists would have a fit! They're highly trained professionals. And they never let you forget it. But, see, when I left Hawthorne House, it was such a great credit, I could practically walk into any other job. I had worked with the great Dr. Jay Schermerhorn."

"You took the credit and left?"

"No, no. Not the way you just expressed it. I didn't leave until the school closed down in 1980."

"Why did it close?"

"I guess it just got too expensive to run."

"So you left."

"Only because it closed! I wouldn't have left Dr. S. You never met him, did you?"

"No, but I've read about him."

"It's not the same thing. He was so charismatic. We all just loved him. He could talk about the children and make you see what was going on inside them. The problems they were having, the difficult homes they came from—I don't know—it was like he knew exactly what to do for each one. He had a sense about how cruelly they'd been raised, and how to fix it. He was here all day, every day, even though he and his wife had their own home. Late at night you'd find him in his office. Or he'd stay to counsel one of us, the staff I mean, talk about our fears and our own upbringings and what baggage we carried with us, psychologically speaking. He could make you understand yourself. Dr. S was *wonderful.*"

A tear crawled down the woman's cheek.

"I'm very sorry, Ms. Garibaldi. This must be a very difficult time for you. If you feel you need to go home, you may, you know."

"Oh, no." Some of her fierceness returned. "I'm going to stay right here as long as there's a single person left! Somebody has to be here to stand up for Dr. S. Now that he can't speak for himself."

Were you in love with him? I wondered. He certainly entranced a lot of people. If he wanted to, he could have taken advantage of that hero-worship.

⚔️

DETECTIVE PARK CAME STRIDING into the office as Ms. Garibaldi left. Garibaldi gave him a fierce stare, having reverted to anger.

"What'd I do?" he asked me as Garibaldi flapped the door closed in a motion that was not quite a slam.

"You are associated with me. Although I didn't do anything either, except listen to the people here. She's mad at them for not grieving more. How'd your interviews go?"

"Nobody knows anything. But that's not the big deal," he said portentously.

"What've you got?"

Park lifted his left foot onto a stack of wrapped blocks of yellow construction paper. He leaned his arm on his knee, building suspense.

"The stain from April Tausche's shirt?" he said.

"Yes?"

"Hagopian says the Hemastix say it's blood all right."

"Human blood?"

"You know Hemastix won't tell you that. The techs ran the Hemastix test here, 'cause they figured we'd want to know right away whether to pursue it at all. They'll do the test for human blood back at the lab."

"Which is gonna take longer. And if it's human, they ABO type it."

Park said, "Which by itself doesn't take long, but—"

"It's the paperwork," we said together. We smiled at each other wryly, in mutual understanding of the department we worked for.

Park said, "We probably won't hear about that until late today or early tomorrow morning. And then if it matches Dr. Schermerhorn's type, they'll DNA it, which will take yea long."

I remembered when DNA typing took literally months. It was still many weeks. The most advanced labs were just changing over to RFLP, restriction fragment length polymorphism techniques, which will cut the time down a lot. The time is coming when the test will take just a day or two. The problem was, the more DNA was used in making cases, the greater the backlog in the labs. But you do what you can with what you have. I hoped it wouldn't be long. Possibly the suits downtown could force the lab to schedule us first. DNA could tell us exactly whose blood was on whom. And I was in the hot seat right now.

I said, "Let's face it. April's shirt was nice and clean except for that one stain. It must have been washed and freshly ironed at home before April came here to the reunion. So the bloodstain's fairly fresh. And I don't think she was butchering chickens in the kitchen for dinner last night."

CHAPTER *15*

"OKAY, CANNON," I SAID. "Tell me what you have, and then I want you to get Jeffrey Clifford for me." Cannon had entered with a face as meaningful as Park's had been five minutes earlier. Park was in the dining room interviewing one of the therapists.

"Yeah, boss. It's that guy Deemer."

"What about him?"

"Well, you said his father was dead. He's not dead. The kid lives with his father."

"He *does?* That sure isn't what he told me."

"Plus, his mother lived with them both until about six months ago." When I nodded at him impatiently he went on. "She's in prison. Been in and out over the years, but when she's out she lives with the husband and Karl."

"What does Daddy Deemer do?"

"He's some kind of small-time con man and general all-around chiseler, to use an old-fashioned term."

"Very old-fashioned. I didn't know you went so far back, Cannon." The kid looked about twelve.

"I don't. I just love old movies. *Double Indemnity. The Thin Man. Laura. Mr. and Mrs. North.* Like that."

"Give me an example of what Daddy Deemer does for a living."

"Okay. You know these sidewalk salesmen you see around. They set up a bunch of merchandise maybe on a card table. Watches, sometimes. Gloves in the winter. CDs. Like that. They sell until the cops come along and move 'em out. And everybody knows it probably fell off the back of a truck. But how'd it get from the truck to the sidewalk guy? Well, Deemer Sr. is a middleman. He takes stolen goods to people he knows who'll sell the stuff in the street."

"And they pay Deemer a low price for the goods, and they sell it for a little bit more, but less than the customer would pay in a legit store, just like a good capitalist?"

"Of course. But. Deemer is recently out of the business because he wasn't really selling good stuff some thief boosted, he was selling damaged stuff. Not thinking ahead. This Deemer is maybe not the sharpest tack in the box. His latest deal was DVD players and such that were in a store for repairs. The robber, some guy Deemer knows for years I guess, who maybe isn't so terribly bright either, cleaned the store out of this practically useless crap, no good without major repair, and Deemer Sr. gives it to his guys to flog, so to speak. And since most of them sell in neighborhood areas, not on the corner of Michigan Ave and Adams, their customers know who they are and now their customers are pissed and coming back to them wanting their money back. So the street salesmen are angry at Deemer. So Deemer is hiding in his apartment. He goes through this kind of thing off and on. I mean, he's a crook, but he's just plain crappy at it."

"What's the mother in for?"

"Passing bad checks. She has to go pretty far from her own neighborhood to do it, too. They're *so* on to her locally."

"Hmm. Well, thanks."

My beeper went off just as I was about to call Jeffrey Clifford in to interview him. I glanced at the number and groaned. No need to call and find out who it was. I stopped by the dining room.

"Ollie," I said, "I've got to take an hour for lunch." He looked at me funny, knowing I wouldn't ordinarily leave. I said, "Is that okay? When I get back, you can get your lunch break?"

⚔︎

I PULLED UP in front of my parents' house. They lived in a narrow wooden Chicago-style bungalow northwest of the Loop. The house had tall narrow windows, a narrow door like a startled mouth, and a tiny porch like a scrubby goatee. There was never any parking around here. I muscled in front of a motorcycle, the front of my Jeep half into a space blocked out with a bright yellow curb, fire hydrant perched on the edge. Thank goodness for my red flasher, which I left turned off, but placed on the dashboard where it could be seen easily from outside. I added a ticket book for good measure. I hadn't been in patrol, giving out tickets, for a couple of years, but the book still worked like a charm.

I slipped into the back of the car and reached into a brown sack. From it I pulled a ratty blue sweatshirt and sweatpants. Keeping my body below the level of the car windows, I took off my shoes, then wriggled out of my blue dress pants and pulled the sweatpants on. I removed my blue blazer, under which I wore only a short-sleeved but immaculately clean white T-shirt. It was so hot the shirt would have been more than enough clothing, but over the shirt I dragged the grungy sweatshirt.

I folded my good clothes, placed them carefully on the backseat, put my shoes back on, then left and locked the car.

❧

"EMILY!" MY MOTHER STOOD on the porch and shrieked at me. "Oh, thank God!"

"What's happened?" I was less than panicked. I'd been through scenes like this before.

"In here." My mother ran into the house, hyperventilating and flapping her hands.

In the living room were several children under eight, the oldest one of them bleeding freely all over his mouth, neck, and shirt. He was screeching at the top of his lungs—even louder than my mother. "Petey fell and knocked out his tooth!" my mother said. She picked up Poppy, the baby, and pointed at Petey.

"Where's the tooth?"

"The tooth? Oh, I don't know. Around here. It must be," my mother said, staring wildly about, as if it could be on the ceiling, in a vase, or on the top of the upright piano that stood against the far wall, its keys dabbed with peanut butter. "I mean, it has to be someplace, doesn't it?"

I studied the situation a little more closely. On the sofa lay my sister Helen's husband, Carlton, dead to the world and from the smell of him, dreaming of beer. He was Petey's father.

"Where's Helen?"

"Uh—out someplace."

My mother covered up for Helen's long absences, which I suspected were related to gambling. Small stakes, thank God. Helen was mad about bingo, the lottery, and the new riverboat casinos, but so far, to my knowledge at least, she hadn't lost big amounts of money. Of course, she didn't *have* big amounts of money.

Petey, who was seven years old, now attached himself to my leg and wiped blood on my sweatpants. He looked up at me and smiled. There was a gap in the front of his mouth. An upper front tooth, then. He clutched my pants and buried his head against my body, spreading blood on my leg. But the actual flow of fresh blood from the tooth had pretty much stopped. Seeing him getting this attention, his little sister, Brendatha, grabbed my other leg, spreading raspberry jam down the knee. Mom cooed at Poppy.

"Mom, listen up! Where's the tooth? They can put them back in, you know. It was a new permanent tooth. You can't just let it go missing."

"I was changing Poppy, dear. I didn't see."

"Well, where was he when—look, how did it happen?"

"Riding the Big Wheel," Petey mumbled, spattering blood.

"Outdoors?"

"Mmm—"

I am one of seven children. I'm the oldest, followed by Paul, who is thirty-three and in the navy. He comes home very infrequently. Helen the gambler is thirty-one, a secretary with the Board of Health. Nella is twenty-eight, and lives at home, except that she's currently staying with a new boyfriend. Harold is twenty-four, away at art school. Ruth is twenty-one, and lives at home because she hasn't found herself yet. Louise is seventeen and lives at home because she's seventeen. My mother has a heart of gold. She also has her hands full. My goal was not to be like her.

I walked into the kitchen, both children dragging along on my pantlegs. I knew my father would be reading the paper. He was.

"Dad, did you see Petey's tooth?"

"No, dear," he said mildly, "isn't it in his mouth?" and went back to his paper. I made no attempt to ask him to help. Petey had run, bleeding, right past him and he hadn't noticed.

"I t'ink Margaret ate it," said Brendatha. Chubby Margaret was two, and I had seen her in the living room, rubbing peanut butter on the drapes, which fortunately were beige and brown. I doubted that the little butterball would find the tooth tastier than peanut butter, although, given the fact that Margaret was always eating, the idea was a very reasonable one, quite smart for a child as young as Brendatha to come up with.

I caught a glimpse of purple and fuchsia slipping by behind me. I spun around. It was my sister, Louise.

"Louise, give me a hand, here. Petey's lost a tooth." Louise wore a purple tube top and magenta-and-fuchsia striped skirt that ended just below the fold of her rump.

"Don't know anything about it."

"Well, take Brendatha, then, while I look." I lifted Petey up into my arms to quiet his crying, but the little girl still clung.

"Can't!" Louise said, backing away, flashing lavender talons. "Nails aren't dry yet." She was gone.

I peeled Brendatha's sticky hands off my legs and went out the back door. I set Petey down on the step. In the unkempt grass and weeds, there was an overturned Big Wheel. The front end was on the cement driveway.

There was no tooth on the driveway; that much I could see just glancing at it. I dropped to my knees on the grass and crawled, quartering the area around the Big Wheel, working methodically back and forth in best evidence-tech fashion. Brendatha crawled around near me, imitating me, and I worried that the child might step on the tooth and mash it into the earth, but I didn't have the heart to move the little girl. Petey wandered back and forth whimpering. He stepped on my hand twice. Fortunately, he was not heavy and the grass was a cushion.

I found the pearly tooth six inches from an anthill. The ants, amazingly, had not yet discovered it.

"Up, Carlton. You're coming with us."

"Watzzat?" he said.

"Mom, do you still use Dr. Westerfeldt?" I asked.

"Why, of course, dear. Whyever not?"

I found Dr. Westerfeldt's number in the phone book. It was Saturday, and he wasn't in his office. The service said they would contact him.

"We have an emergency," I said, using my best cop voice. And I described the situation. Westerfeldt, the service said, was in a group practice, therefore they would call somebody, but not necessarily Westerfeldt. Dr. Somebody would meet us at the office.

"In the car, Carlton," I said.

"Why? Why do I have to go?"

"You're Petey's father. You're gonna sit in the back and console him."

"Can't Ma go?"

I sighed. "You must be kidding."

I thought I had read that you should put a knocked-out tooth in milk to take to be replanted. Or was it water? Salt water? One of the cops had told me that replacing it in the socket to take to the dentist was the very best method. That might work for adults, but it was out of the question here. Petey was still moaning, pausing only long enough to gulp a lot. If I put the tooth in his mouth it certainly *would* be swallowed.

I wrapped it in a damp paper towel along with a couple of ice cubes, put that inside a plastic bag, and put the whole thing in my pocket. It felt quite nice in the sweltering heat.

"Out to the car."

I carried Petey and gave Carlton such a fierce look that he followed obediently.

"You will sit in the back and hug him," I said. Thank goodness Petey was technically tall enough—just—to ride without a child seat, as long as he was in the back and belted in. I belted him in firmly, told Carlton to fasten his own seat belt or I'd shoot him, and we were off.

⚓

"JUST AS WELL you did it this way," Dr. Olney said. He was on call today and would fill in for Dr. Westerfeldt. "The latest research on avulsed teeth is that they don't do so well if you put them back in the mouth. Saliva isn't so good for the root."

"I heard milk was good."

"Cold fresh milk is all right."

"I guess I should have tried that."

"No, no. This looks fine. The main point is to keep the tooth moist. How long has the tooth been out of his mouth?"

"Um—Carlton, did Mom call me right away?"

Carlton shrugged. "Dunno. I didn't see it happen."

I tried to figure it—my mother probably had called as soon as Petey came running in bleeding. It sure didn't look like she'd done anything else, like clean him up, for instance. So five minutes before the call, ten minutes for me to drive over, ten minutes in the house, fifteen to get here, add another five or ten for the fact that all this was an estimate—? "Under an hour," I said.

"Good!" He dropped the tooth in a little basket inside a container filled with fluid. The contraption hummed.

Carlton was leaning sleepily on me, so I gave him a shove in order to keep my arm over Petey's shoulders. The little boy was sniffling but not crying. Now he slid around to try to hide, standing half behind me. He knew this was not going to be fun.

"Let's get him in the chair and see what we can do."

Petey whimpered.

"Come on, big guy," I said. "I think this really isn't going to be so bad."

"It's not," the doctor said gently. He used a very soft, quiet voice, which I could tell reassured the child somewhat. At least, Petey's face said, the doctor wasn't a scary guy.

I eased Petey into the chair. Carlton propped himself against the doorway.

"Let's just see what we've got here, young Peter. Been doing a bit of big wheeling, I guess." The doctor had taken the tooth from the basket and dropped it as he spoke into a shallow bowl containing a clear solution. "We call this stuff reconstituting solution, Peter. It kind of makes the tooth cleaner and happier. Its name is Hank's solution, but I don't have a clue who Hank is." This earned a small smile from the boy. "Shall I call you Peter or Mr. Peter?"

Petey giggled. "Petey."

"Petey it is. Let me explain what we're going to do, Petey. You know about planting seeds to make things grow?"

Petey mumbled something about bean plants at school.

"That's right." Dr. Olney cleaned Petey's mouth with a gauze pad and fluid. "Now we have to look for what we call PDL cells, which have to do with your periodontal ligaments. Think of those as kind of like the roots on plants. They're on the part of the tooth that grows into your jaw."

I was fascinated to see that Petey had stopped crying. Dr. Olney pointed to the part of the tooth he was describing, and Petey stared at it with wide eyes.

"It's a nice healthy tooth, Petey. Well worth keeping. Now, you see I'm not touching the root," Dr. Olney said. "We're keeping it clean. I'm going to just swab out your mouth a little more while the tooth takes its bath. I really don't think this will hurt. Knocking it out hurt, though, didn't it?"

"Mmmm-hmm!" Petey said.

"You were very brave to come here. And you're going to have a really, really great story to tell the kids at school."

I pushed Carlton, who smelled of beer, nearer to Petey, where the child could see his father if he needed support. Then I edged away and stepped into the waiting room. "You have any coffee?" I asked the woman at the admitting desk.

"Oh, honey! Are you kidding? Life can't go on without caffeine."

"Could I have a cup for my brother-in-law?"

The woman at the desk could scarcely have missed the beer smell, but I was not in any frame of mind to apologize for Carlton. And the woman may have sympathized with me; she poured a Styrofoam cup full and didn't mention Carlton's behavior.

I went back to the treatment room, where Carlton had leaned against the wall and closed his eyes. "Wake up, Carlton," I said, kicking his foot hard.

"Why are you hitting me?"

"Take this and drink it. You're going to stand next to Petey while the dentist finishes. Move."

I placed Carlton back within Petey's line of vision. Dr. Olney was saying, "Then we'll just drop the tooth in your jaw gently, and tape it in place with a thing we call a splint."

"Carlton," I said. "You will stand here. When they're done, you will get the after-care instructions, and then take Petey home in a cab. You have taxi money?"

"Yeah. Why can't you drive us?"

"I have to work. I love Petey, but this is now *your* problem. It's eaten up my lunch hour already."

CHAPTER **16**

"MR. CLIFFORD, PLEASE SIT DOWN," I said. Jeffrey stared past my ear, looking somewhere in the direction of the boxes of Legos. There was an Eiffel Tower composed of yellow Legos on top of the top box, a construction the preschool teachers must have found too good to dismantle. Clifford raised his eyes and stared fixedly at it. "Please," I repeated more firmly. He sat.

I observed him for a few seconds. His whole body language was disconcerting. For one thing, his posture, though stiff, showed none of the usual hallmarks of uneasiness, no fear of me. Now, I've never believed in terrifying my witnesses. Usually. Unlike a lot of cops, I didn't think scaring people helped open them up. But in my experience witnesses usually either cringed or blustered nervously to some degree. The crabby ones were annoyed to be asked to take time out of their busy lives to be questioned by cops. Or they were indignant that a person so obviously guiltless as themselves should be suspected of a crime. The self-important ones were swelled up with the idea that their testimony might be valuable. Some of the self-important types invented details to be impressive, to show how closely they paid attention to what was going on around them; they colored up the small details they had noticed, or declared themselves much more certain of what they had seen than they could possibly really be. I have long since learned to be alert to that sort of person and cautious about accepting any witness statements as gospel. Sometimes the witness was actually guilty of the crime himself and therefore eager to be deceptively charming. Other guilty ones covered their guilt with belligerence.

Jeffrey Clifford didn't show any of these signs. He simply sat and waited for me to ask him questions. To do whatever I was going to do. I felt another rush of self-doubt. I knew nothing about autism, really next to nothing about mental illness in general, except the depression that stalked my father's family. I could accept that mental illness was real, that the person was not behaving peculiarly just to be difficult, but I knew I accepted it intellectually, not emotionally. I still wanted to tell my father to pull himself together. Get the hell up and *do* something. Take a walk! Help with the kids!

Adding to my awareness of my own ignorance was the fact that I had now heard, from several people who ought to know, that autism wasn't really a mental illness. It was more like a developmental wiring glitch, more like a physical illness, more like a brain injury than a mental illness. My ignorance might be added to my bias—what a killer combination! *Damn it! How am I supposed to evaluate a person like this?*

Folding my hands, I resolved to be patient with Jeffrey Clifford.

He was wearing a tight leather vest, made of glossy chestnut-color hide, closed by snaps. It was so tight that it pulled at the snaps, opening little wedges down the front, showing the shirt underneath. The vest troubled me. The day was unbearably hot and this room on the east side of the house was stifling. There were beads of sweat along Clifford's blond hairline. What could he possibly be covering up with a garment so inappropriate? Bloodstains?

"Aren't you hot, Mr. Clifford?"

"No."

"Wouldn't you like to take off your vest?"

"No, thank you." His voice was normal pitch, but with no inflection.

"Well, I would like to ask you to remove it, if you're willing, so that we can look at your shirt."

He just stared at me.

I reviewed the way I had phrased the request. It had not been a request, I realized. "Mr. Clifford, I need you to do this of your own free will, since you aren't a suspect. Please take off your vest."

With no sign of resentment, he stood and unsnapped the vest. There was no visible blood on his yellow-green shirt. Maybe wearing the damn vest was just a peculiarity of his. Let him keep the shirt. I could get a scientific investigation of it done later, if there was any serious reason to suspect him.

"You can sit back down, Mr. Clifford." Then I revised the sentence to a clear request. "Please sit down."

He sat woodenly, clutching his vest in one hand. His elbows

were held close to his body, but the pose, while awkward, didn't telegraph fear. Just weirdness.

"Where do you work, Mr. Clifford?"

"CCCH Systems."

"What do you do there?"

"I am a computer engineer."

"Really?" I was impressed. "How long have you worked there?"

"Nine years."

Most people would have expanded on that, maybe bragged a bit, or at least explained what they did. I was getting no sense of what Clifford was proud of and what he wasn't, or what sort of question would make him get chatty. Maybe he didn't feel pride. Who knew? I simply couldn't get a handle on him at all. He was like a black hole. This frightened me. I could screw up, out of ignorance, if I wasn't careful.

"Mr. Clifford, let's go back to last evening. After dinner, what did you do?"

"Do. I went up the stairs."

"What time?"

"I went to my room. At exactly nine-seventeen. Seventeen is a prime number. The other primes before it are two, three, five, seven, eleven, and thirteen."

"Uh—huh. Good. So. After nine-seventeen, did you hear any sounds?" It wasn't just the content and cadence of his speech that was weird, his phrasing was clunky.

"Of course. How could any person who was not deaf. Not hear sounds? The pillowcase rustles when. You put your head on it." He stared with wide eyes at a pile of boxes to my left. "You can hear yourself breathe. Do you listen to. Yourself breathe, Detective Folkestone? I do. Also there are water pipes. Water gurgles in pipes. I believe I heard a police siren. Or it may have been an ambulance. It can be quite difficult to tell a police car siren apart from an. Ambulance siren, if they are not familiar to you. That is, from your own municipality. With which you are familiar."

I pressed my palms together. I could feel my impatience rising, fizzing through my body. The only foolproof way I had ever found to damp down my irritation at life's frustrations was jogging. And obviously this was not a situation in which I could run around.

"In the night," I said. "Late in the night, did you hear any arguments? Shouting?"

"No." Jeffrey twisted his body back and forth but looked more uncomfortable than guilty.

"Thumping? Doors slamming?" If people on the second floor didn't hear anything suspicious, it was unlikely that Jeffrey Clifford would have, in his room on the third floor. But you never knew with the acoustics of these old houses. Also, his room was right above Dr. Schermerhorn's.

"No," he said.

"Footsteps on the stairs, maybe around two A.M.?"

"Two A.M. I deduce I was asleep at two A.M. One is not conscious. Of being asleep."

"Mr. Clifford, did you hear any strange sounds from the room below yours?"

"No." Now he was staring fixedly at the wall behind my left shoulder. His stare was so intense that I half believed there was an attacker standing behind me, and I wanted to turn around and look. But I resisted, knowing I would feel ridiculous if I did.

"All right. Mr. Clifford, tell me about Dr. Schermerhorn."

"What should I tell?"

"What was Dr. Schermerhorn like?"

"Like a crow."

"In what way?"

"Very avid."

Oy! Did the doctor have a sharp beak? Was he a scavenger?

"You were a—a student, a resident here. Did he help you?"

"I do not believe he did."

"Why not?"

Clifford blinked. He looked like he was thinking about the question, looking up at the ceiling, looking for inspiration, but he didn't answer. Time passed. A lot of time. "Mr. Clifford?" I said.

He began to flick his fingers again. "He did not care," he said.

JEFFREY COULDN'T UNDERSTAND this strange woman. He twisted his body to the left and to the right as he sat, back and forth, a motion he sometimes found consoling. It helped him to release his extra fidgety energy. Throughout his life Jeffrey had been told to look at people, look in their eyes, don't fidget, don't flick your fingers while you talk with people. And he understood that he ought to follow that advice. It was stuff the normals got fixated on, just as if it was important. He could do it if he had to, but he didn't like it and he didn't see why he had to.

Her hair was fluffier on the right side than on the left.

She was so tedious! Her questions were silly. What could it possibly matter what he *thought* of Dr. S? The actions people took were real; thoughts weren't. People could think all kinds of things. They could think about murder, they could think they could fly, for that matter, couldn't they? They could think about turning themselves green, then purple, then back to pink again. And they surely could lie about what they were thinking. Instead of thoughts, she should be looking for evidence. Were there fingerprints to find, if this police person really wanted to know who had killed Dr. S? What about DNA? Was there DNA at the scene? The police probably were looking for DNA. When Detective Folkestone asked him how he felt about Dr. S, she was probably trying to trap him somehow. Which meant he needed to think about how he appeared to her. He was absolutely no good at figuring out how he appeared to other people. There was no point in trying.

Now that he thought about it, he really wondered whether there had been any DNA left at the scene.

⚔

I SAT FORWARD in my chair, leaning toward Jeffrey Clifford. One technique that detectives use in the interrogation of suspects is to go back over the same questions again, just as if the suspect had never answered them. You would be watching, of course, for changes in the answers and changes in physical responses to the questions. Quite often the suspect became annoyed by being asked the same thing twice and blurted out a piece of information he hadn't intended to. Clifford was not, strictly speaking, a suspect. Yet. If he were, I would have to caution him. But I sure as the devil wasn't happy with his answers.

"Did you hear anything unusual in the night?"

"All sounds are unusual. In a strange place," Jeffrey responded, with no apparent impatience. He snapped the fingers of his right hand, pressing them against the thumb, as if cocking a trigger, then snapping forward.

"Tell me about them."

He did: Sirens, cars, water pipes.

"You heard no footsteps whatsoever?"

"Footsteps, indeed, yes. In the hall."

"You didn't say that before. Whose footsteps?"

"There was the dinner. People remained after the dinner. To talk with each other, I would assume. People went to the hall bathrooms. I would assume. Yes, of course they would."

His voice was bland. But that infernal finger snapping went on. It was virtually soundless, but immensely irritating just the same.

What did he think of Dr. Schermerhorn? What did other people think of Dr. Schermerhorn?

"I do not know."

"Why don't you know?" I was increasingly impatient. This *outrageous person* was toying with me. Or if he wasn't doing it on purpose and wasn't hiding something, he was just stupid. And if so, I was wasting precious time.

He said, "Because you never. Know what anybody. Is thinking."

There was a lot of truth to that. Hoping to relax him, I said, "Well, tell me how you first came to Hawthorne House."

"By car."

I gritted my teeth. "How old were you then?"

"Seven years, three months, and twenty-three days. Twenty-three is a prime number too, you know."

Holy *shit*! I thought. Maybe he was just so defective, he wasn't fully human. But he looked okay. Change his clothes, take off that idiotic yellow-green shirt, get rid of that stupid vest; give him maybe ivory chinos instead of the Willy-off-the-pickle-boat too-short pants, and a decent haircut and he'd actually look pretty great.

"How long did you live here?"

"Six years, four months, and—"

I thought, by God, he looks like Brad Pitt. He's actually a handsome young man, and you don't see it because he talks like such a loser! If he'd just stop acting like this!

"—twenty-one days. Twenty-one is not—"

"Is not a prime number! I know that! It's three times seven! Will you just the hell *look* at me for a minute! Damn it! This isn't a goddamn game!"

CHAPTER 17

ALL THAT AFTERNOON, I felt like a person trying to walk up the down escalator. I pushed myself through exasperating interviews with counselors, parents, therapists, and former patients, being as thorough as possible in the time available, but I had the sense that I really needed to take twice as long with each as the twenty minutes I allowed. Even so, there went nearly four hours, I noted uneasily. Several of the therapists, staff, counselors, former patients, and their parents had decided to leave Hawthorne House and not stay overnight. Once they left, following up on them would be much more difficult.

Mr. Bettleby had called his lawyer, barking orders into the phone, and the lawyer had arrived and was hovering over his client. The lawyer wanted to explain that if we suspected his client of murder, we had to caution him. No amount of repeating that we knew that did a bit of good.

"I have counseled Mr. Bettelby to sue, Detective," he told me, rubbing the bald spot on top of his head as if a genie might pop out.

"Sue who?" I sounded like a vaudeville act. "For what?"

"The owners of Hawthorne House. For inadequate protection of the visitors. I'm going to go very carefully into the question of locking the exterior doors. And as far as having no interior locks on the bedrooms, that is utterly unacceptable."

"My understanding is that there can't be interior locks in an area where small children are schooled."

"Even if that proves to be so, some should have been installed temporarily for this event."

"Well, we have no objection to your suing," I said.

"And the Chicago Police Department for false imprisonment. That means keeping people—"

"I know. We haven't," I said, half closing my tired eyes. Opened them thirty seconds later; time to get back to work.

Cameron Blount, a quiet young man except for his earlier crying jag, a former patient whose room had been on the third floor and who claimed to have admired Dr. Schermerhorn, waited in the hall for his father. The man eventually arrived to take him home. Ben Goodspeed's mother packed his small overnight bag and hers and let Ben, the chubby cherub with the happy smile of a child, carry the bags down to the lobby. I had run into her just as she was shepherding him across the hall. "Oh, I'm sorry!" she said, even though she had not bumped me.

Ollie had interviewed her, and I didn't have much sense of what she was like, even though I had spoken to her once.

"I may want to talk with you later this week, Mrs. Goodspeed," I said.

"Oh. Should we have waited? I'm sorry if I'm upsetting things. But Ben would really like to go home."

"You're free to leave."

"Thank you. We don't mean to be any trouble."

As the hour drew close to five o'clock, Ollie Park and I tallied up how many were staying and how many going. Park said, "Five of them have left already—"

"Detective?"

I turned and found Miss Simms, the former Hawthorne House nurse, standing behind me, holding a small, tailored suitcase.

"I'm leaving," she said. "I only came for the fun of it, and it's not so much fun now."

"No, I wouldn't think so."

"It's all right to leave, then?"

"We have your address. I'll probably come and talk with you once more in the next couple of days."

"I don't know anything more. Didn't know anything in the first place. I slept like a log."

I thought, *How nice for you.* I said, "I understand. Maybe we'll have different questions later on, when we know more." I surely hoped we would. There was way too little to go on so far, and I was more and more worried that we might not be able to make an arrest.

By four o'clock, when the caterers came to the office to tell me they would roll in the predinner drinks cart as soon as I gave them the go-ahead, I had lost ten of the original twenty-nine weekend guests. In addition to Miss Simms, two of the therapists left, waiting until the end of the day so that they could attend the day's symposium events at the college. Three stayed, planning to go to the other lectures tomorrow. Three counselors left, sad and frightened. Dr. Erik Emerson stayed. I figured he felt an obligation to protect the former patients who remained and bring the reunion to its finish in some kind of order. There were eighteen for dinner, where the night before there had been twenty-nine, counting Dr. Schermerhorn.

Some of them probably stayed the night because they were just plain curious, some to please their therapists, some to prove something to themselves, some because their ride couldn't get here until tomorrow. Some of the counselors may have stayed out of camaraderie, possibly thinking of themselves as being helpful to the others. Some, like Cassie Garibaldi, may have stayed to push the idea that Dr. Schermerhorn was wonderful.

Some stayed because they had paid for it and by God they were going to get their money's worth.

I said, "Roll the drinks in at six. I want to cover just a couple of things first."

Park waited with a sheaf of papers. There was a rough stack about an inch thick that he held between thumb and first finger, but I noticed a sheaf of just a few sheets isolated between his second and third fingers.

"Tell me," I said, gesturing at the papers.

"Wait'll you hear this." Park set the thicker stack on the desk and retained the others.

"No, *don't* make me wait."

"First," he said, ignoring my response and picking one sheet of paper out, "Schermerhorn was knocked out, but his scalp wasn't broken. He was hit by something heavy and flat."

"So we're not going to find his blood in his bedroom even if he was knocked out there."

"Right. Second, bigger news. The footprint in blood on the floor near Schermerhorn? The tread matches the shoes Jeffrey Clifford gave us. And the lab says there's blood on the sole of his shoe, mostly in the cracks between the treads."

"Well, good. We're getting somewhere." I was surprised, though. Jeffrey had struck me as more fidgety than guilty. But I realized once again how little I understood him.

"And . . ." Park said, building suspense, shuffling papers. "And they've typed some of the blood already, believe it or not."

"Somebody pulled rank."

"I guess. The blood on April Tausche's shirt is human and the same type as Schermerhorn's."

"No kidding!"

"We'll have to ask her for the shirt. The blood on it will have dried by now, which is good for preserving the DNA." He shuffled that sheet to the back. "*And*—there was blood on the side of the pants leg and side of one shoe, the upper part, of Henry Rollins. Same blood type as Schermerhorn's."

"No shit!"

"*And*—on the wall near the bed in Ben Goodspeed's room is a thin red smear. The lab says it's human blood, and the same type as—"

"Dr. Schermerhorn? Jeez!" I was totally amazed at this one. Park said nothing.

I said. "All four samples are Schermerhorn's blood type?" Hot dog! We were getting somewhere at last! "Kind of Agatha Christie," I said.

"Yup. Now, you realize, Emily, this is just blood *typing*. It's not DNA matching."

"I understand that. And Schermerhorn's blood type is what?"

"Type A," he said unhappily.

"Which is very common."

"Right. That's the bad news. Forty percent of the population is type A. The good news is they're gonna start on the subtyping and the DNA right away."

"Meanwhile, we've got four people with what may be Schermerhorn's blood on them."

Ollie said, "Ain't it excellent? Still, DNA'll take weeks."

But I felt a surge of hope. If four of them ganged up to kill Dr. Schermerhorn, I didn't really have to understand the suspects, did I? Didn't have to know how an autistic person thinks. I could solve this thing.

CHAPTER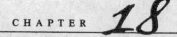

September 21, 1972

AT THE AGE OF SEVEN, Jeffrey Clifford was a thin, nervous child. His hair was blond and stiffly straight, as if a brush had been fixed to his head. His hands and feet were large for his body, and his joints were big, made more noticeable by the way he moved, much like a clumsily articulated wooden puppet. He held his elbows close to his body, his forearms parallel to the floor and his hands slightly raised, as if in preparation for falling down. He walked with his legs stiff. His toes hit the ground before his heels.

At that, he was an attractive child, his blond hair contrasting with dark eyes and long dark eyelashes. Unlike his arms and legs, which looked poorly assembled, his facial features blended into a strikingly handsome whole.

His mother and father stood on either side of him in the entry hall of Hawthorne House. They were about to hand him over to a counselor, with no idea of when they would see him again. Two tan suitcases flanked Mr. Clifford closely, as if guarding his ankles.

"I really want to see his room," Nancy Clifford said in a thick voice.

Miss Garibaldi said, "I've checked with Dr. Schermerhorn, and he says you may."

Nancy and Edward Clifford glanced at each other. Edward muttered, "Good of him." Nancy elbowed him in the side and took Jeffrey's hand. Jeffrey's fingers were cold, but did not clutch at hers. It was terribly difficult to know what Jeffrey was thinking at any time. And asking wouldn't do any good.

She squeezed his hand, and said, "We'll see your new room." They followed Edward, who was following Miss Garibaldi. They climbed to the second floor, passing a girl who looked about twelve and a tall boy who must have been at least fifteen years old. "How old are your oldest pa-students?" Nancy asked.

"We don't talk about our residents," said Miss Garibaldi.

Blinking, Nancy followed as Garibaldi turned left past double doors to a large open room. They continued past several open doors. Inside one room was a bed festooned with wheels and an antenna and what looked like windshield wipers. Nancy didn't have time to look more closely. The other bed in the room was austere, with a navy bedspread and no decorations except a pile of books. The next room held a blond girl of about eight or nine, lying on the floor on her stomach, kicking at the floor with her toes. There were three beds visible, two of them laden with teddy bears and other plush dolls. The room was full of reds and blues.

The next room was Jeffrey's.

The four of them clumped up together in the doorway. Miss Garibaldi stepped back to let Jeffrey and his mother go first, but Jeffrey didn't budge. He stood with his arms close to his body, the elbows pressed into his sides. Finally Edward entered the room. "Come on, Jeff," he said.

Nancy Clifford put her arm around Jeffrey's waist and drew him in.

It was an ordinary room, about twelve by twelve feet. There were two pine beds with a window in between. Two pine dressers with five drawers and two small pine tables flanked the door. The bed on the right was draped with at least a dozen catcher's mitts. Game schedules were tacked to a corkboard, arranged in perfect, tidy order, so tightly packed that Nancy could see almost no board underneath. The bed on the left was bare. Both beds stood a bit away from the wall.

"Oh," Nancy said. "Can we push that bed over? He's used to having the side against the wall."

"No, Dr. S wouldn't like that."

"Why not? Jeffrey gets upset when things aren't the same. We brought his bedspread so he could have something familiar."

"You'll have to take it away with you."

"He would settle in better if we could make this look a little bit like his room at home."

"We can't do that."

"Why not?"

"We're giving him a different world from the one that created his problem."

Nancy stepped back a few inches. Trembling, she hugged Jeffrey as hard as she could. He hugged back a little bit. Then she stumbled from the room, catching her shoulder on the doorjamb, blinded by tears.

CHAPTER *19*

Saturday July 15, 1995

DETECTIVE OLIVER PARK STIFLED a snarl and repeated his question. He was hot, he was tired, he had his own worries to deal with, and he was *not* amused at civilians who were more worried about themselves being criticized than finding a killer.

"I am not blaming you, Mrs. Kisilinski," he said. "I just want to know who was supposed to lock the basement door last night."

"And I told you it was already locked."

"Except it wasn't. And it still isn't."

"Well, it may not be now. Maybe you people left it open when you came in this morning."

"It wasn't *open* then and it's not now. It was just unlocked. When we got here."

"I'll go look for myself."

"Let's do exactly that."

They marched from the first-floor office through the grand dining room, down the stairs to the kitchen, Mrs. Kisilinski's thin little back as straight as an ironing board. Oliver mentally berated himself for being sharp with her. She probably desperately needed this manager's job. She was fifty-five or so, and would have a hard time finding another job as good at her age. But the back door was important, since the front door had been on snap-lock. People could let themselves out the front door, but they couldn't get back in without a key.

The back door of the kitchen opened onto a cement stairwell big enough to store six plastic garbage cans on wheels. Two were bulging with garbage bags holding the remains of today's lunch. Oliver gave thanks that the techs, not he, had searched the trash and the garbage from last night's dinner and today's breakfast. The garbage had marinated in the overnight heat, and must have been utterly disgusting.

The door was sturdy oak, three inches thick. "They sure don't build them like this anymore," he said. The spring-lock was solid but old, and its tongue could be loided, he thought, with a credit card. There was a separate auxiliary bolt above it. The lock itself was controlled by two buttons in the edge of the door. If the top button was pushed in, the door automatically locked when it closed. With the bottom button pushed in, it stayed unlocked and could be opened from outside.

Mrs. Kisilinski tried the outside knob. The door was unlocked.

"Well!" she said.

"It was unlocked when the first officers arrived."

"I suppose the caterers unlocked it while they were working down here last night. They were supposed to close up. It's part of their job. It would be my job at any other time. I admit that."

"I understand—"

"But I had no idea how long they would take to clean up. So I asked them to lock the door when they finished. I don't live in, you know."

"It would sure be easier to keep taking trash out during the evening if you didn't have to get somebody to let you back in every time."

"Well, it's a black mark against Brian Travis Catering in my book, I can tell you."

Oliver sighed again. People who were afraid to take responsibility were bad enough; people who then blamed the next guy pissed him off very, very seriously.

"Who let the Travis caterers in this morning?" he said.

"Uh—I did."

"Which door did you come in?"

"The front. I wouldn't ordinarily. I know they're not—not guests. But I was coming up the walk as they were coming in. There were only three of them. All the food had been brought in yesterday—"

"Mrs. Kisilinski, please. I really am not going to be upset that you let them in the front."

"Well!"

"Thank you, Mrs. Kisilinski."

"I APPRECIATE YOUR STAYING ON," I said to one of the therapists, a man named Max Buller.

"Hey, I paid for the weekend and I'm getting the weekend," Buller said.

"Very self-sacrificing of you," Dr. Emerson said, earning a dark look from Dr. Buller. We were picking up cocktails from the cart, waiting for the dinner announcement. Buller edged away from Dr. Emerson, turning his back to him as he neared the drinks cart.

Buller said to me, "Not my problem what happened here. I didn't kill anybody. Plus I came in from Denver, and I'm not changing my ticket and paying whatever penalties the damned airlines charge."

"You must be very sorry Dr. Schermerhorn is dead," I said.

"Well, of course. But I hadn't seen him in fifteen years. He was a great man, though."

Professor Hansen, seated nearby, said, "Bullshit."

I had decided to stay at Hawthorne House for dinner. Tension had been building even before cocktails, but I had an uneasy feeling that it was getting worse now that the guests were faced with the issue of who would sit near whom at dinner. I had urged Oliver to go home after his report on the unlocked back door. He had a teenager depending on him, plus it would be nice if one of our team was fresh and rested next morning.

In addition to the interviews, the afternoon had involved phone calls from relatives of two of those former patients who were here alone. When I answered Jeffrey Clifford's father's call, he said to me, "No, I want the officer in *charge*."

"That's me, Mr. Clifford."

After a slight pause, he said, "I want to know whether I should come and get Jeffrey."

"That's a decision I have to leave up to you."

"I know *that*. Of course I'll make the decision. What I need from you is your opinion on whether it's safe there."

"I am going to post an officer in each of the halls tonight, sir. And we have no reason to think the attack was directed at anybody but Dr. Schermerhorn."

"So you know who killed him?"

"Not yet, sir."

"Then how can you know he's the only target?"

Spare me. Set me free of the civilians. Or is he right? Should I advise all the guests to leave? Is it dangerous here? Am I making a terrible mistake?

"I can't possibly know that for certain, sir. I am only saying that we've had no indication otherwise."

"Jeffrey's therapist thought this would be good for him."

"I take it that's true of several of the former residents who came to the reunion." *The ones whose therapists didn't think so aren't here.*

"Well, this experience *can't* have been good for him."

Forbearing to mention that it was worse for Dr. Schermer-horn, I said, "Shall I put Jeffrey on the phone so you and he can make a decision?"

"No. Just tell him I said to stay."

CHAPTER 20

THE DINNER CROWD bunched up at the drinks cart.

"Is this alcohol okay for the former patients—the former residents? If they're on medication?" I asked Dr. Emerson as we stood at the drinks cart, each holding a small sherry.

"Well, that's one of the reasons I'm standing here."

"To keep an eye on them?"

"Yes. No, maybe just to exercise moral suasion. You under-stand, Detective Folkestone, that they're adults. I can't give them orders, or even advice, really, anymore."

"Did you in the old days? Give them advice?"

"A psychotherapist doesn't so much give advice as draw out the patient. Ideally, the patient describes himself and his life, over a period of sessions. And over time he sees why he's behaving the way he habitually does. With knowledge should come some ability to change the behaviors that aren't working for him."

"He gains insight."

"Exactly."

"So that's a therapist. What did the counselors do?"

Emerson looked around to see if any former counselors were within earshot. We sidled a bit away from the others. "They were like camp counselors. They rode herd on the kids all day, or all night, depending on which shift they were on. They mostly lived in, you know. There was a lot of riding herd, because these were sick kids. They'd throw shoes, and tear books, and defecate on the floor. And worse things I don't want to go into because it's dinnertime. Elimination was a problem for almost all of them. They also had obsessive behaviors, like spinning in place or pulling their hair out one strand at a time. They'd produce bald patches and the only way we could deal with it was cut the hair so short they couldn't get hold of it. There was a lot of stimming, self-stimulating. Counselors helped them dress and eat. Several times a week they took the kids who could deal with it to the park."

"And helped with lessons?"

"Most of the kids went to public school, although some were in special classes. Some could only deal with half days and we supplemented here."

"So you're a psychiatrist. Your role here was just like Dr. Schermerhorn's?"

"Well, not just like. I came in three times a week. Nobody was like Dr. Schermerhorn. Jay did the lion's share of the therapy. He had a one-hour session with every single child at least once a week. He took his job very seriously."

"All those kids once every week—"

"Well, there were only about twelve to fifteen children in residence at any one time. It was very personal attention they all got."

"But you were doing essentially the same thing."

"Basically, yes. I was here longer than any of the other therapists."

"So—is it possible that whoever harbored such fury at Dr. Schermerhorn is filled with just as much anger at you?"

He looked stunned.

The dinner gong sounded. Since I was chatting with Dr. Emerson, I took a seat at his table. Jane Macy and Chaz, the former cook, came into the room just after Emerson, and asked if they could sit with us.

Jane, I remembered from my notes, had been a patient—resident—at Hawthorne House for quite a few years, six years if the data was right. Despite the neediness that length of time suggested, she was obviously a success story, well-spoken, well dressed, and with a good job, too.

Unobtrusively, or so I hoped, I cast a glance at the former patients whose clothes or room had had blood on them, blood I assumed was Dr. Schermerhorn's. Of the four, three were still here, Jeffrey Clifford, April Tausche, and Henry Rollins. Only Jeffrey, though, was directly linked to the death site by his footprint in the blood.

If only they weren't so hard to understand!

There were salad plates in place already. Avocado, hearts of palm, and orange slices lay on the plates, in what looked like a raspberry vinaigrette dressing. Personally, I've never understood hearts of palm. They don't taste like much, and I've always wondered, do you have to kill a whole palm tree to get it? Nevertheless, this salad certainly was a lot better than limp mixed greens. It was cool and good on a hot night.

Jane said, "Well, at least there isn't going to be any shortage of food. Half the people have left. More for the rest of us."

"Oh, Jane," Emerson said, "you haven't really changed much."

"You mean I'm too honest? It's insensitive to say that other people leaving means lots of food?"

"Too—I don't know. You're forthright, and I guess that's healthy. Still, it's Jay's death that caused everyone to leave, you know."

Trying to be gracious, I said, "From all I've heard, there was plenty of food last night, too." For a split second I glimpsed myself in high school reading *All Quiet on the Western Front*. World War I. The soldier was thrilled that there would be ample rations that night; the reason was that several of his company had been killed. How weird the human mind was! I couldn't have given one thought to that book in fifteen years. Suddenly I realized how difficult it must be to be a psychiatrist. The mind darted this way and that so fast, and it had so many layers—how did you ever know what was relevant?

I tuned back in to the conversation and found Jane just a few words further into her sentence. "—not only a friend of yours, Dr. Emerson, but a person who probably saved my life. I'm every bit as sad as you are."

"I understand, Jane."

Chaz said, "Do you know who did it, Detective Forts-uh—"

"Folkestone, Mr. Tortola. No, not yet."

"You ought to take a look at that kid, Deemer."

"Why is that?"

"There's something not right about him. He was a patient here when I worked here. Wasn't right then, either."

"Resident," Jane said.

Chaz stared at her for a second and went on. "And he's still here. That's weird too."

Emerson said, "They hired him on when he got too old to be treated at the school. Dr. Schermerhorn limited the school to people under eighteen."

Chaz said, "I know that."

Finishing my last piece of avocado, I said, "But why work here?"

Emerson said, "He couldn't get a job outside. And he was used to this building."

"But surely the building was closed for a while. Didn't I hear—"

"No, it was only empty for a while before Dr. Schermerhorn established the school. After his school closed, it became a preschool pretty much right away."

"What does Deemer do here?"

"Caretaker, janitor, general gofer."

"He's no gofer," Chaz said.

I said, "What do you mean?"

"He doesn't do the 'go' part. He does the 'sit' part. He does the 'duck-the-work' part. He's not a gofer; he's a sitter. Plus, I don't think he ever respected Dr. S."

"Oh, Chaz, he's just slow," Emerson said. "He doesn't think or move as fast as you or I do."

"He could. He just doesn't."

Emerson sighed. I could almost read Dr. Emerson's mind. He was thinking that people like Chaz, who were not psychiatrists, were habitually unsympathetic to people with mental problems. Actually, when it came to Deemer, I pretty much agreed with Chaz.

"Plus," Chaz said, "there's something *funny* about him."

Dr. Emerson said, "Well, of course there is, Chaz, he's mildly autistic."

I said, "I appreciate the input, Mr. Tortola. I'll check into him."

Emerson said, "I don't want the poor man frightened, Ms. Folkestone."

I looked more closely at Emerson and saw real worry there. It was obvious he cared about his former patients, which Deemer must have been. I'd seen his concern for Jane. And Henry earlier today. I said, "Please don't think I'm going to threaten him. But you understand I do have to get details from people about where they were last night?"

"Yes, I understand," Emerson said sadly.

Two waiters removed the salad plates—Jane had eaten only the avocados and palm, not the orange slices, despite her talk about liking lots of food—and a staffer unloaded the dinner plates from the dumbwaiter onto a cart to wheel them to the tables. I had released the dumbwaiter for use at 5:00 P.M., but was a little surprised to see it back in service so soon, the caterers using it so casually. Then I reflected that as far as the staff knew, it was just one of many areas of the house that had been under scrutiny, so they wouldn't have had any particular squeamishness about it. Only I and the other officers knew it had probably been used to transport the unconscious or tied body of Dr. Schermerhorn. Only I, the other officers, and the killer.

It wasn't surprising the techs hadn't found blood in it, either, if Schermerhorn's scalp wasn't broken.

Trying to lighten the mood, I said to Jane, "Ms. Macy, you said Dr. Schermerhorn may have saved your life. What did you mean, exactly?"

A plate of pasta appeared before me, and a second one in front of Jane, who was staring down at the table. The waiter placed plates for Dr. Emerson and Chaz Tortola. I realized that the whole day I hadn't seen Jane at a loss for words, or looking away from the person she was talking with until now. Ordinarily Jane stared right at you and told you what she thought you should know. In no uncertain terms. Before meeting with the other autistics, I would not have thought of this as something unusual.

Jane looked up and smiled like a child thinking about cotton candy. "It was just—when I came here—ah, it was just magical."

"Hawthorne House?" I asked.

"Yes. Don't get me wrong. I didn't act like it was. I was terrible. I was a mess inside, see? I was just so angry I was ready to hit anybody who got in my way."

"How old were you?"

"Six. My mom was a roaring, raging alcoholic, you know? My dad we never saw, hardly. When he came around, he hit both of us. I mean, this wasn't one of those child sexual abuse things you hear about. Thank God. Although Dr. S thought for a long time that it was. He kept asking me about being 'touched.' My parents were just plain terrible parents. They'd go out to party and lock me in the house. And when Dad wasn't in town—as a matter fact, I don't know whether he was in town these times or not. He could've been right next door for all I knew, but that was the way Mom always put it. 'Your Dad is out of town, so I'm going out with Uncle Jack.' Whatever. Uncle Fred. Uncle Jim. Anyway, they'd go out and party and lock me in the house. So it wasn't a whole lot better when Dad was gone."

"Lock you in the house?" Dr. Emerson said, gently.

"Mmm." She paused a couple of seconds. "Well. They'd lock me in the closet, actually. Mom'd drop a package of Oreos or Twinkies in the closet and turn the key in the lock."

"And go away for how long?" I asked, horrified.

"A day or two."

Dr. Emerson said, "A day or two?" I figured that Emerson knew the story already.

"Three at the very most."

"But you'd need water," I said.

"See, she usually left a few bottles of Nehi orange soda."

I said, "And you'd also need—uh—"

"Don't want to say it, do you? A bathroom? She left a pail."

"Oy!" I said.

There was a period of silence. Finally, I pushed her a bit. "So you were saying Hawthorne House was wonderful."

"I said *magical*. And it was. The front door was this gorgeous glossy bright blue. Inside, there were pictures of flowers everywhere. There were these huge Raggedy Ann dolls sitting in the hall. Just sitting there in chairs like they were funny people."

Dr. Emerson said, "Whimsical. Jay liked the children to feel they could play."

"The bedrooms," Jane Macy said, "had bright red or yellow or blue bedspreads. You got your *choice*." When she emphasized the word "choice" by saying it almost in a whisper, I had a glimpse of the home the girl had come from.

"Lovely meals, right on time," Jane said. "All you wanted to eat."

Chaz said, "I am a *very* good cook."

I said, "It must have been nice, Ms. Macy." Obviously, it was more than nice to her, but I wanted to keep her talking.

"And this building itself—well, you can see how beautiful it is. The woodwork, all carved and inlaid. I love the marble in the main hall. And look at this chandelier. I wish they could light it now. It must have been so glorious in the old days. I had *never* seen anything like it."

"Most people haven't," said Tortola, a bit sourly.

I said, "So when you got here, you were a mess, you said. . . ."

"Hitting things. Throwing the Raggedy Anns on the floor and kicking them."

"Which was one of the things they were there for," Dr. Emerson said.

"Having tantrums. Lying on the floor and kicking my toes into the floor."

Dr. Emerson said nothing. Although he knew Jane's history, I suspected he wouldn't talk about it because that would violate patient confidentiality. He smiled at her, though, and nodded, and she continued.

"I broke things. Dr. S was so wonderful. Meals were served family style, with big bowls of potatoes and gravy and meatballs, or whatever we were having. There was one time I just swept the whole bowl of gravy onto the floor. Broke the bowl. Gravy went everyplace."

"I remember that," Dr. Emerson said.

"Me too," said Chaz.

"See, Dr. S was so patient. He said it was all right. Can you imagine! He had me and another kid mop it up—the other kid had splashed his feet in it—but he didn't yell or send me to my room, or whatever."

"Whatever" meant "put me in the closet," I thought.

Suddenly, Jane Macy said to Dr. Emerson, "You can talk about me if you want, Dr. E. I don't care. I want her to know how great Dr. S really was."

Emerson said, "Thank you, Jane." He turned to me. "Jane's always been very up-front about her experiences here. When she came she was deeply angry. She took it out on everybody around her. We even had to watch her near the other students."

"I'd haul off and swat them," Jane said.

"Or trip them up. Or call them horrible names. But slowly she learned to trust us." He looked at Jane and smiled again. I asked myself just exactly what that expression reminded me of, and then I got it. Pride. One of my teachers had exactly that same look on her face when a failing student in her class began to do A-level work.

Emerson said, "Jane became less and less angry. You could actually *see* it happening, in her stance, her body language, and her facial expression. She looked like a pint-sized prizefighter when she first got here. It took a long time, at least the first two years she was with us, but little by little you could see the anger go. It was the effect of consistency and a good environment. Day after day, regular meals, support from the counselors, Dr. Schermerhorn talking with her, taking her feelings seriously. No one in her family had ever really talked with her before. They just plain didn't care."

Jane lifted her chin. "See? That's what I mean. I don't know what would have happened to me otherwise. Dr. Schermerhorn saved my life."

Emerson nodded, smiling. To my amazement, I believed I saw the glisten of unshed tears in Dr. Emerson's eyes.

CHAPTER 21

JEFFREY CLIFFORD KNEW he was not especially alert to how other people felt. But he was usually painfully aware of his surroundings—when he could override the excess buzz. A great many background sounds grated on him—chairs scraping, feet shuffling, silverware tinging on plates. He especially hated the sound of knives scraping plates. Too much input upset him and made him try to drown it out by humming or flicking his fingers. Right now he was intentionally paying attention to everything around him, as much as he could stand to. It was easier tonight. Last night there had been twenty-nine people in this room. Tonight there were fourteen. He had counted twice to be certain, even though he never ever made mistakes in counting.

Twenty-nine people would make lots more noise. That meant you could hardly make a fair comparison. Tonight was a night after a murder was done. That should make a difference, but what?

Jeffrey had spent a lifetime learning that he had to discount his impressions of other people's emotions, because they were no better than guesswork; he just wasn't good at emotional stuff. On the other hand, he had spent the most recent years laboriously learning how to decode how other people felt, learning the "mind reading" that came naturally to most people but not to autistics. His therapist had trained him with a series of videotapes that illustrated emotions—you looked at posture, facial expressions, hand gestures, and so on. After a while he had graduated to decoding emotions in movies and TV with the sound turned off. It would never be automatic, but at least he could do it.

April, sitting on his right, had her head low, studying the food. There were three freckles on the left side of her nose. None on the right side. How awkward for her. She hadn't said a word all during dinner. He tried to read her mood from her face. It was neutral, as far as he could tell. But if he watched her body language, rocking slowly back and forth as she rubbed a piece of bread between her fingers, rolling it into a ball, he knew that she, too, was trying to limit input. When she ate, it was in little pounces at her food.

Dinner was good. Avocados were quiet foods. Pasta was quiet too.

The other two people at his table were a former counselor named John Thatcher and Dr. Carol Hansen. He remembered both from back when he was a resident. Thatcher, whose head was held high and alert, had been a weekend fill-in and had taken the kids to the park every Saturday and Sunday. He also filled in for the live-in counselors if one of them was sick or on vacation. He had a white, untanned band around the ring finger on his left hand. Dr. Hansen, who was now salting her food even before tasting it, had been really quite young, he realized now, although she had seemed old to him then.

"Were you really young back when you were here?" he asked her. She laughed, and then of course he realized that normals wouldn't have asked that question, or maybe not asked it that way. Normals were peculiar about age. But he couldn't see why. It was just factual, wasn't it? Everybody got one year older every year. Saying you thought somebody looked younger than they really were got a "Thank you." That was peculiar.

"I was twenty-seven when I started here," she said.

"Oh."

"And what about you? I remember you, but not how long you were here."

"I was a resident. For seven years."

"You were still"—she paused, thinking, then went on—"very uncomfortable with social interactions when you left. And yet you're here now. On your own. How did you learn to do this? Or did you just—um—mature?"

"I have had training. Dr. Spofford instructs me on how people respond. We even do movies and. Watch them and then I tell her. Why the people are behaving the way they do."

"That's wonderful. That's exactly right."

"But I am not always right."

"I mean the approach is right. And does Dr. Spofford ask questions about how mailboxes make you feel or what you think about bananas?"

"What do you. Mean?" Jeffrey suspected he was being made fun of, but he didn't quite understand how.

As if she read his mind, the way normals so often did, Dr. Hansen said, "I'm not making fun of you, Jeffrey. I'm making fun of Dr. Schermerhorn."

"But Dr. Schermerhorn is dead."

"I know."

BETWEEN COURSES, Jeffrey studied the room around him. Dr. Hansen twiddled her thumbs when she was bored. He had never noticed that before. At the next table he could see Dr. Emerson's back. Apparently when Dr. Emerson got his hair cut the barber shaved his neck. Emerson was leaning toward Jane Macy. Even in the days when Jeffrey had lived in Hawthorne House, he had known that Emerson had approved of Jane. You could see it now as plain as day, from the slow nodding of his head and neck as Jane spoke and the slight lean toward her. You didn't need to see his face.

Dr. Emerson was a good man.

Jane herself was readable too. *Left hand moves back and forth. Like waving smoke. Slowly. Speaking at the same time. Jane is explaining something. Something. It is important to her. Her face is like it always is. I do not have to try to read the face. The hand gesture is good enough.*

The former cook, Chaz, was so obvious it was kind of funny. When the main course arrived, he pulled apart the elements of his pasta, isolating mushrooms, onions, bits of broccoli, and shrimp, then taking up one at a time and tasting them. His eyebrows went up and down. Up and down. Now and then he would nod or tip his head to one side. *The nod means yes. Of course. The tip means so-so.* A quick jerk of his head to the side as he tasted the shrimp. Not so good? Jeffrey tasted a shrimp. It was dry.

The last person at that table was the police officer, Detective Folkestone. Here was an altogether harder problem of analysis. She sat quite still, only nodding her head from time to time. There were many kinds of nods in human language. *Fast means hurry up. Slow—like this—?* This was the kind of nod that meant "Go on talking" and didn't tell anything much about her actual response to what she was hearing. Jeffrey studied Folkestone's hands. Hands often were very revealing. She was eating, which meant that a lot of time her left hand was in her lap and the right hand was wielding her fork. But when she put the fork down on her plate, which she occasionally did, probably to listen better to what Jane was saying, she did a strange thing. She folded both her hands together, fingers interlaced but the thumbs up, the pads of the thumbs pressed together. What did that mean? You would think somebody taking a break while eating would just drop her hand in her lap, or even rest it near her water glass. This particular gesture looked to him judgmental. He looked back at her face. It was pretty much expressionless.

Judgmental makes sense for. A police officer. Yes. Bet she does not know she is doing it. Bet she thinks she is just. Looking pleasantly interested.

Should he feel scared of her? She was trying to find out who killed Dr. Schermerhorn. Maybe he ought to be worried about that. He did not feel worried. At least he did not think he felt worried.

Wait. That buzzing in his head was starting up. Too much data coming in. Too much. Small wonder with all these people and all these—these problems. A person really should not have to deal with so much at once. It was not fair. Now he did feel something. He felt angry. Probably he should not have come here this weekend.

Stop focusing on the people.

I wish I had my laptop.

First, staring fixedly at the table, Jeffrey counted quietly to himself. If there were fourteen people here and each had a three-tined salad fork, a four-tined dinner fork, and a four-tined dessert fork, there were 154 tines in this room. Except that the salad plates had been removed with the forks on them, which left 112. But if—

This wasn't helping enough. It was too easy. Refocus on the sounds. White out the individuals and think of them as a group, a swarm. Making sounds. So what did the room sound like?

Nervous. Nervous. Tink—tink—tink!

How did the room smell? Jeffrey had told his therapist that he could smell things at a great distance, but Dr. Spofford probably didn't believe it. Thatcher smelled of smoke. Dr. Hansen smelled of flowers. Chaz smelled of either sweat or cumin. Cumin and sweat smelled the same.

DR. HANSEN LEANED FORWARD, her pale coloring enhanced by an ivory linen dress, exactly the shade of her silky hair, and asked John Thatcher, "How long did you work here?"

"Five years. I teach junior high English now."

"Do you feel you wasted your time here?"

"Uh—not really. Of course not. Why would I?"

"You're a teacher. So I imagine you were interested in children even back then." Thatcher nodded. "So I imagine you expected to learn something from Dr. Schermerhorn."

"I guess so."

"Did you?"

"I think so."

Dr. Hansen raised her eyebrows, implying that Thatcher was being evasive. "Did you learn about the psychology of the child from Dr. S?"

"Well, I—possibly what he was teaching—his approach may have been—a little outmoded. I mean, seen from today's perspective."

"His approach was outmoded then. Or put another way, there was never the least foundation for his treatment methods. He spent his time psychoanalyzing children whose problems were not in their psyches. He was wrong."

Dr. Emerson was sitting at the next table, with his back to Dr. Hansen, but her voice carried to him. He went rigid. The people at his table, Chaz Tortola, Emily Folkestone, and Jane Macy, became quiet as Dr. Emerson slowly turned around, his chair scraping on the floor. His face was that of a stern biblical father, and he said, "That's quite enough. Dr. Schermerhorn died here less than a day ago. Your nasty talk is inappropriate."

"I'm speaking the truth," Hansen said. "Tell truth to power. Is that ever inappropriate? Dr. S didn't know his job."

Jane Macy jumped to her feet. "He did. He *did!* He helped *me!*" She ran out of the room with her hands over her mouth.

Emerson rose too. "See what you've done?"

Dr. Hansen stood up slowly and gracefully, as if anything

she were to say was so obvious her opposition was just being irrationally stubborn.

"Dr. S was a con man. He foisted his untested and undigested Freudian claptrap on us and on harmless children. And heaven help us, their sad, desperate parents. He had a sweet deal here, with a great income, a beautiful building, and God knows he was a genius at fund-raising. But he didn't know anything about autism, and he didn't make it go away."

Emerson said, "Autistics get better. But we all know that doesn't mean it goes away."

"Ours *didn't* get better, beyond the 'better' most high-functioning autistics get just by getting older."

"He worked day and night with them. He practically lived here. Plus, his writings alone helped other—"

"Helped him make money, that's what. He held those poor children prisoner here, away from their families, for virtually their entire childhoods. On the *fiction* that he could cure them with Freudian blather."

"Freud was one of the prime movers of the twentieth century."

"Look, Dr. Emerson, I realize you can't say anything else at this stage of your career. Schermerhorn really sucked you in, didn't he? He was a smooth talker, all right. I got sucked in for a while myself. But I started to see that nothing was happening with most of our patients. Dr. S was putting out his books and making money and a big name for himself, but he wasn't putting out healthy graduates. There were at least half a dozen poor kids who were quietly moved from here to permanent care facilities. They've been there ever since."

"I could say a lot about that, Carol, but we can't talk here in front of—"

"In front of the children? They're adults, and they can make up their own minds. Which you should have done too, years ago."

But Dr. Emerson was already leaving the dining room. Dr. Hansen stalked after him. I rose and followed both of them. Dr. Emerson stood in the hall, arms crossed, unperturbed that I was listening. He said to Dr. Hansen, "I approve of Dr. Schermerhorn's approach entirely. With some updating, of course."

"Your problem, Erik, is you can't back down now. You're stuck. You have written so damned much on the psychoanalytic approach that if you changed now, you think you'd be a laughingstock. Actually, I feel sorry for you. You must know you're wrong, but you still have to pretend that the emperor has clothes on, no matter how butt naked he looks."

"Freud explained the human psyche. Without him, we wouldn't have modern psychiatry."

"Oh, please! That's bilge. The ancient Greeks knew more than Freud. Where we've made progress is in brain metabolism and neural wiring."

"You treat the symptoms, not the disease."

"The symptoms *are* the disease."

"You can't cure the human spirit with drugs."

"You can cure biochemical brain problems with medication. You can help decrease the problems that come from structural brain problems with medication. And it was perfectly obvious, even twenty years ago—even forty years ago—that autism was a physical brain problem."

"Are we all just chemicals, then?"

"Not *just* chemicals. But entirely chemical."

"If you're so angry at Dr. Schermerhorn, why did you bother to come here this weekend?"

Dr. Hansen ran her hands down her sides, then placed them on her hips, elbows sticking out. For a moment, I thought Hansen didn't have an answer. I waited and watched.

But then she said, "I came here to see if he was sorry."

CHAPTER 22

I CAUGHT DR. HANSEN as she stalked away. "Dr. Hansen, wait! Jane Macy really *did* get better. Dramatically better, if you believe her. And I do believe her."

"I believe her too. But was she autistic?"

"Well, of course. Dr. Schermerhorn said all his—oh, I see what you mean. We have only Dr. Schermerhorn's word that she was autistic."

"More than that. You heard her explain her symptoms. Did you hear any autistic symptoms?"

"What do you mean?"

"You've been told enough here today to understand a little about autism. Did Jane say anything about having language problems? Trouble meeting other people's gaze? Did she have any trouble looking into your eyes today?"

"Pretty much the opposite. I noticed that."

Hansen smiled. "She is kind of in your face, isn't she?"

"But maybe she used to, and she's gotten better."

"I can assure you she didn't *used to* either. Besides, they don't get over it that completely. They have to fight it all their lives. Like Jeffrey does. Does she prefer solitude to social interaction?"

"Not as far as I can see."

"Have clumsy movements?"

"No."

"Use inappropriate words? Show lack of awareness of social cues and manners?"

"Disdain for them, maybe."

"Okay. But you see what I mean. Jane was never autistic. She was a neglected, physically abused child who was furiously angry."

"And after a few years here, she got better."

"She did. One of the few. It was a much more pleasant atmosphere than her home. But the point, Detective, is that Dr. Schermerhorn claimed he had a wonderful new treatment system for autistics. He got funding by curing them, and he sold books about curing them."

"You mean he would have claimed Jane was autistic?"

"I mean he *did* claim Jane was autistic."

"Oh."

"And that she'd been cured by the psychotherapeutic environment here, and his exploration of her psyche by Freudian methods. He may even have convinced her she was autistic."

I said nothing. Dr. Hansen took that as approval and went on.

"Basically, Detective Folkestone, he was trying to talk the children out of their autism. You might as well try to talk somebody out of appendicitis!"

CHAPTER 23

TIRED AND VERY HOT, even though it was 10:00 P.M. and the mansion's inadequate air conditioners were running with less opposition from the outdoor heat, I trudged up several flights of steep stairs to the third floor. I wanted to be absolutely sure that I had made all possible arrangements for the safety of the remaining overnight guests. I would work my way down from the top, checking everything.

The third floor was the hottest of all. There were only a

couple of guests still up here, including Jeffrey Clifford, in the north wing. Officer Hal Perkins sat in a folding chair in the hall, between their bedrooms and the south wing's hall bathroom.

He struggled to his very large feet when he saw me.

"No sleeping, Hal," I said.

Hal pointed at a thermos. "Iced coffee."

"Good. Somebody will relieve you at eleven."

I glanced down the south wing, which was equally well lighted but had no guard, as no one was rooming there. This seemed like enough.

On the second floor, where most of the remaining guests had their rooms, I had stationed an officer in each hall, plus one in the ballroom. The dumbwaiter was locked down. "You need to listen for it anyway," I said to Mark Dams, the cop in the ballroom.

"Why?"

"I don't think there's going to be a problem. But if the killer used the dumbwaiter last night, we'd look like idiots to let him use it again tonight."

"That's for damn sure."

As if this killer is stupid enough to use it a second time. Criminals are mostly stupid and they're creatures of habit. But not this one. I'm locking the barn door after the horse is stolen. It wasn't my fault the horse was stolen, but it sure would be my fault if somebody took a second chance at it.

All the wall sconces were lit throughout the halls and up and down the stairs.

On the first floor, the front door was locked tight and under observation, while the servants' door and French doors to the backyard hadn't been opened in years but were both locked tight, and an officer was near enough to have each one in view.

In the basement, the kitchen door was locked and bolted and an officer sat at the kitchen table. The coal chute door, unused for decades and chained shut, had been double-checked.

It was clotted with rust. Nobody was getting in that way. Prying it open would make enough noise to wake the whole house.

Finally, just before leaving, I stood in the front hall. Grand marble pillars rose up from a green-and-white marble floor, a five-tier crystal chandelier soared overhead, and incongruously a police officer sat under it on a cheap folding chair.

The Hawthornes had really known how to live, I thought.

I pictured myself sleeping in one of those elegant bedrooms, possibly in a huge canopied feather bed with cool, crisp, pure linen sheets put on fresh every day. In the morning a maid in a gray uniform and white apron and white cap would enter with coffee, a perfect soft-boiled egg, toast triangles with a little dish of orange marmalade, and a single rosebud in a vase, all on a pretty white wicker tray. The maid (her hair would be in a bun and her hands would be pink from scrubbing things) would place the tray on my lap and say "Good morning, miss," 1880s style.

What was I *thinking*? None of that would make up for the lack of air- conditioning.

Or for that matter, independence.

I nodded good night at the cop watching the front door. I struggled out onto the street. It had been a fifteen-hour workday. My feet dragged on the walk.

⚘

I LET MYSELF in to my apartment with a great feeling of relief. Just flicking on the light and seeing my few possessions in their usual places was a delight. This was the great benefit of living alone. Nothing had moved. Nothing had become dirty while I was gone. Nothing was broken. There was no crud in the sink. Nobody made demands on me to *do* anything. What bliss!

Glad I wasn't married.

Glad I wasn't at my mother's fertile, fecund, fermenting, festering house.

I poured myself a glass of sparkling water from a bottle I kept in the refrigerator and sat down on the couch to drink it. Slowly I sipped and slowly I unwound.

My carpet was light blue, although I had considered white when I was looking at samples. White was going a little too far toward the austere, I decided, even for me. I had enough self-awareness to know that I would have white everywhere if I wasn't careful. This was a very pale blue, ice blue. In the sense of being icy, it was whiter than white. The sofa was denim blue. My only upholstered chair was white. Three walls were white and one was blue-and-white vertical stripes. Okay, it isn't everybody's taste, but it's mine.

I slipped my shoes off.

I looked around. Was the simplicity here an effort to limit distractions, like Jeffrey? Lower input and think better, relax better? Was I more like Jeffrey than I thought?

Dealing with the people at Hawthorne House had wiped me out. The former patients were just god-awfully incomprehensible! But I had better learn to understand them. The therapists and former counselors were stressful, too. There wasn't one of them who didn't seem to have an ax to grind, a polarized view of Schermerhorn, even a way of looking at me that made me feel under a microscope. The parents of the former patients were the worst of all, with their big, wounded eyes, as if I should have cured their children. They acted like everything was my fault.

Well, that was ridiculous. That was just my exhaustion talking.

I was very uneasy about letting people leave Hawthorne House, knowing I might have let the killer go home, but what else could I do? I had no authority to hold anybody.

On the other hand, I would know more about them when I saw them in their own homes. Hawthorne House was not their home and didn't display their interests and personalities the way their own lairs would.

Okay, okay. I leaned back and closed my eyes, clicking on the television with the remote. A few minutes to unwind, then bed.

Late baseball scores came first. Then a piece on the heat wave. Shows our priorities, I suppose. Then the newscasters said:

"The dean of child psychiatry, Dr. Jay Schermerorn, died this morning in the building where he spent many years treating ill children. Spokesmen at the Chicago Police Department say Schermerhorn most probably was murdered. The assault took place in Hawthorne House in Hyde Park on the city's South Side, where Schermerhorn's treatment facility was located. Police decline to give further details.

"Dr. Jay Schermerhorn was a pioneer in the treatment of autistic children. His many books were perennial best-sellers in the field of—"

I clicked it off.

Had the killer left the Hawthorne House building or was he still there, sleeping among the innocent? Or lying awake, listening? Listening to the distant breathing of the innocent around him? That was a silly idea. But would he be planning a second attack? Man, I had to admit I didn't think he—or she—had left. I didn't think he wanted to leave.

And if so, what the bloody hell am I doing here at home? It had seemed like such a great idea to get away, get perspective, get some peace. It was a terrible idea. Cripes! I pulled on my pants and shoved my feet back into shoes that had shrunk two sizes smaller. The place I had to be was Hawthorne House.

CHAPTER **24**

I**T WAS JUST** past midnight. The tours of duty for cops changed at eleven. There was a different uniformed cop outside the front door when I got back to Hawthorne House, a tall, rangy blond woman whom I didn't recognize and who didn't recognize me, either. But the cop knew my name and gave a welcome when I displayed my credentials. Her name was Jeanne Zubro.

"Has anybody come in since you've been on?" I asked.

"Nobody in or out. Except that it's a hundred degrees out here, this is easy duty."

"Grumble, grumble, grumble. It can't be one degree over ninety-eight," I said.

"So you say."

Inside Hawthorne House, the temperature was not much cooler. I nodded at a new cop in the downstairs hall, a graying man named Giorgio-something who was marking time until retirement in a year or so. He sat on the cheap folding chair placed directly at the foot of the curving staircase. His face was impassive, his body in that slumped-vertical posture you get after being on stakeout or guard duty for hours. He would see and hear anything that happened—he nodded at me—but his brain was basically turned off.

I stood absolutely still and listened. Aside from the resigned putter and sigh of an air conditioner trying to catch up with the heat—it seemed to be saying that too much was being expected of it *never catch up never catch up never catch up*—no sounds came to my ear.

Now that I was here, I realized how tired I was. I could easily enough lie down in one of the bedrooms vacated by the
guests who had decided to cut the weekend short and go
home. Between the pressure I felt of having to solve this murder and the sheer exhaustion of working a double tour in this
heat, lying down and giving up consciousness for a while
would be wonderful.

Nope!

This case was either my downfall or the best chance for
promotion I ever had.

I took a deep breath and strode through the dining room to
the kitchen stairs. In half a minute I was in front of the ovens.
The killer had stood here, right here, shoving in the apron, the
garbage bags he had put over his feet, the knife, and the rubber
gloves. Plus we had not identified shirt buttons or fabric in the
ash. Did he take off his shirt and do his butcher's work bare
chested? Or did he put a garbage bag over his shirt? Poking a
hole for his head and arms wouldn't take more than seconds.

Why roast the knife? Was the tech right that the killer could
have wiped off fingerprints and still been afraid that traces of
his DNA might remain? That would argue a very sophisti-
cated killer. And anyway he had worn those rubber gloves.
Unless he had touched the knife without the gloves on—
before or after he killed Schermerhorn. Or—what? Inadvertently let it brush past his arm or his face? Coughed on it? Got
his own blood on it in the crack between the handle and the
blade? Sweated on it? Sweated in the hot night as he cut and
cut and cut.

Had he drooled on it? Had he licked it? I was starting to
disgust myself with my thoughts.

Roasting the knife showed him to be extremely careful.
What intelligent person wouldn't be careful, after committing
a murder? It showed him careful and coolheaded.

The killer? Or were there four killers? Jeffrey? April? Ben
Goodspeed? Henry Rollins? Could all four of them have acted

together? The little bit I had learned about autistics made me think they wouldn't cooperate very well. The most likely scenario was that Jeffrey Clifford did it all and the other three, so much less competent, at most stood by and watched.

Why would they hate Dr. Schermerhorn that much?

The back kitchen door to the alleyway and garbage cans was locked. Looking out, I saw a uniformed cop sitting on the concrete edging around the stairwell. He seemed bored, but was clearly awake.

Turning on lights as I went, I paced into the long, dreary basement. The bulbs were dim and several were burned out. The floor was made of slate, stained with the silt of more than a hundred years. There had been flooding; I could see a whitish high-water line on the brick two feet up from the floor. Possibly there had been a sewer backup; a wide area of the brick on the south wall was discolored an orangish shade. There had been more than one burst pipe leaking from upstairs; the wooden walls that roughly subdivided the huge basement into rooms had drip marks in several different places and some of the later-addition plywood dividers were warped.

There was a doughnut-shaped patch in the dust where the coil of extra dumbwaiter rope had lain. The lab had the rope now.

The room where Schermerhorn's body had lain, where he had been tortured, was the seventh walled-off space along a corridor leading at right angles from the main central corridor. Like the mansion above, the basement was shaped like a huge cross. This put the death room at least two hundred feet from the kitchen. But it was not only the distance that I noticed now; it was the fact that a person had to make his way in semi-darkness down one corridor and choose one of three branches where the arms of the cross converged. This argued that the killer was familiar with the building. I supposed a visitor might choose a room down here randomly, and anybody would know that the building must have a large basement. But on the whole, familiarity with Hawthorne House was most likely. What was even more interesting was what Dr. Emerson had mentioned—that the young man, Kurt Deemer, had discovered Dr. Schermerhorn's body very quickly. After just a few minutes of searching.

That was improbable, if he didn't already know where it was. Deemer? Or Jeffrey Clifford?

Now I stood at the death site. Who would have heard sounds from here? Dr. Schermerhorn would not have screamed, of course, with the gag in his mouth. Or to put it another way, he might have screamed, but almost soundlessly. A gag left a person able only to whimper and groan. What first-floor room was above this one? My guess was the morning room, one end of which was currently my office. Nobody would have been there in the small hours of the night. No one would have heard Dr. Schermerhorn, even without the gag.

But the killer was very careful, and gagged him just in case.

I tried to picture his actions:

The killer goes to Dr. Schermerhorn's room. Does he pause outside the door? Does he consider going away and letting the doctor live? Does he tap on the door, and does Schermerhorn let him in? He knocks the doctor out—with what? We haven't found a weapon. Now he's got a body, a living, unconscious body lying on the floor. He could kill him right now, smother him with a pillow, but he doesn't want to do that. He isn't finished with Schermerhorn. He carries the limp body to the dumbwaiter. Does this mean the killer is strong? Maybe not all that strong. Dr. Schermerhorn was tall but lean.

Unless it was four people. Each holding one limb?

But suppose it's one man alone. What if somebody had seen the killer as he carried Dr. Schermerhorn along the hall? Had he planned for that possibility?

What would I do if it were me? I'd say, "Help me get the doctor to bed! I found him unconscious in the hall!" But then, when Dr. Schermerhorn woke up, he would report who hit him, wouldn't he? Maybe not. I've heard that most people don't remember what happened just before a head injury. Is that called retrograde amnesia? I'd better ask an expert.

It's taking a terrible risk! Wait—not so very much risk. He hasn't killed anybody yet. At worst it's aggravated battery. Maybe he's willing to take that much risk. It's worth it to him, isn't it, if he's terribly angry? As he must be, judging from the way he butchered Schermerhorn.

But nobody comes along; nobody sees him, and he gets Dr. Schermerhorn to the dumbwaiter. Lowers the box with the doctor in it to the kitchen and goes down there and gets him out.

How does he know that there isn't somebody in the kitchen, making a cup of tea or something? Imagine the dumbwaiter coming down, the person in the kitchen thinks "What's this?" and opens it and there's an unconscious body!

Oh, I know. He lowers it to the dining room level on the first floor, where it's in the serving pantry. Nobody would be in the dining room anyway at night. Then he goes down to the kitchen and if that's clear, he lowers the dumbwaiter the rest of the way.

He carries the unconscious man from the kitchen along the basement corridor to the basement room. There he ties him up. Gags him. Did he know that rope was in the basement?

He goes back to the kitchen and gets the knife, apron, garbage bags, and gloves. Does he cover his clothes while in the kitchen or go back to the basement room and put on his butchering gear there?

I think he gags Schermerhorn and waits for him to wake up, so Schermerhorn can watch his killer put on his killing gear, knowing he was going to die.

If it is Jeffrey, does he go get the other three, April, Ben, and Henry, and let each of them take a turn at pushing the knife into Dr. Schermerhorn?

Assume it's one person.

When he finishes his butchery, the apron, gloves, knife, and garbage bags are bloody. Does he step out of the garbage bags in the basement room, in which case he might get blood on his shoes, or does he wear them to the kitchen and take them off there? Even then, if he wears them to the kitchen, if blood got on the kitchen floor from the bloodied garbage bags, it might have stained his shoes.

He drags the broom over his trail in the dust.

Did the tech examine the kitchen floor for blood? The catering staff making breakfast had walked all over the place before the body was discovered or even searched for. They made breakfast before anybody noticed that Dr. Schermerhorn was missing.

Anyway—the bloody gear goes into the oven and the killer sets the oven to self-clean. And the cloth, plastic, rubber, and blood all vaporize. And here Dr. Schermerhorn's body lies for the rest of the night, cooling and stiffening in a sticky swamp of blood.

Quite suddenly I was aware of the length and darkness of the ancient, deteriorated basement at my back. It seemed an old, old darkness. The air was damp, and because of the long, deadly heat wave, it was a blood-warm, clinging dampness.

The very air felt slimy.

I hurried back upstairs, not even stopping to turn out all the lights.

Ten minutes later, I was in Dr. Schermerhorn's bedroom, much relieved to be out of the cellar. I've never been a nervous or fearful person, and probably wouldn't have joined the police department if I were. However, that basement was unpleasant.

I let myself into Dr. Schermerhorn's rooms.

Had I missed anything when I was here with Ollie?

Dr. Schermerhorn's possessions were still distributed around the bedroom and bathroom as he had left them. All except the brandy and the two glasses, which the techs had now picked up and taken to the lab. Dr. Schermerhorn's shaving lotion, his hairbrush, and his toothbrush were in the bathroom. His shirts, his extra jacket, his books in the sitting room.

His books. The advance reading copies of his most recent publication, three heavy copies of it.

I punched my cell phone and left a message for Hagopian, the tech. "Pick up the books from Dr. Schermerhorn's room at Hawthorne House. See if you can get hair or scalp cells from any of them. And anybody's fingerprints besides the doctor's."

A nice heavy book could knock a man out quite easily.

The room of a dead man is spooky. Even though this wasn't his home, this was where the process of his death began. Added to the unpleasantness of the basement, the night gave me a shiver of unreasoning fear.

I walked into the ballroom.

"Snap out of it," I whispered as I stood, hands on my hips, studying the door to the dumbwaiter. Opening the door, I hooked its latch back against the wall, holding it in the open position.

The dumbwaiter was not in sight. The counterweight, a flattened arrangement of what looked like lead bars, hung against the side of the shaft. A wheel on the right-hand side of the opening could be turned, pulling the rope that brought up the dumbwaiter box. The wheel geared into a second smaller wheel that actually carried the rope over a pulley, giving you a mechanical advantage so that you didn't have to work as hard.

I turned the wheel. Even with the gears, it was quite stiff, and I smiled to myself a little grimly, realizing that making housework easier for the servants was not a major goal of late-Victorian stately home design.

Here came the dumbwaiter. The box rose up the dark shaft into view. As I continued to crank the wheel, it came fully into position and stopped, filling the opening.

It had its own door also, which I now opened. Inside, the wooden box displayed careful cabinetry, even though it wasn't ornate, as was the rest of the mansion. It was a little over two and a half feet wide and two feet deep and three feet tall. Plenty of room for a body. The techs had finished with it, so I could study it as much as I liked.

I leaned into the box, running my hands over its floor. I wouldn't find any new evidence, of course. The techs had searched every inch of it, including the cracks between the boards, for blood and anything else they could find. There had been fibers from Schermerhorn's jacket, which confirmed my belief that he was still clothed at this point, plus a few hairs they expected would turn out to be his. Other than that, no blood, nothing. No evidence of who had put him in there.

I'd fit in the dumbwaiter easily. Fold up my legs, cross my arms over my chest. There was room even for tall Dr. Schermerhorn—

A hand touched my shoulder and I jumped, hitting my head on the top of the dumbwaiter. "Ack! Damn!"

"I'm sorry. I thought if I spoke to you it would scare you."

I lurched backward out of the dumbwaiter. Dr. Emerson stood behind me, both hands raised in apology.

I said, "Why are you sneaking up on me?"

"I'm sorry," he said.

"What are you doing here?"

"I heard somebody moving around and thought I'd check."

"Check on what?" I demanded. "See if it was the killer? Did it ever occur to you that if I were the killer you might get *dead*?"

"You're angry. I don't blame you."

I thought I heard the psychiatrist in this remark, so I just looked at him.

He said, "Actually, my first thought was that one of the guests was having nightmares. One of our former residents. This isn't easy for some of them—being away from home."

"All right. All right. Next time say something. Don't tap my shoulder. Not that there's going to be a next time."

Dr. Emerson glanced from me to the dumbwaiter. "You think Jay was carried down to the basement in this?"

"Maybe. What do you think?"

"I think it makes a lot more sense than what I had been assuming."

"Which is—?"

"That the murderer invited him down to the kitchen for some reason. Jay wouldn't have been likely to go to the kitchen unless there was some extremely urgent reason and I just can't think of one."

"Why wouldn't he go to the kitchen? What about getting a midnight snack?"

"Jay wasn't really into snacks. He liked meals to be rather formal. And he didn't cook for himself or make food, really."

"How did he get along at home?"

"He has a housekeeper."

"Oh." I hoped that Ollie had told the housekeeper to take a couple of days off. But he would have; Ollie was absolutely solid.

I said, "Can't you sleep, Dr. Emerson?"

"No. I haven't been sleeping so well lately. And also I keep thinking of Jay." He drew a deep breath. "To you I'm sure he seemed an elderly man, but he had a lot to look forward to. The TV work was exciting to him, so he was looking forward to being a commentator, and the Festschrift honoring him would be coming out next year. And did you know that *Time* magazine was interviewing him for an article?"

I said, "Come and sit over here." I led Emerson to a group of plastic chairs and when I sat down he did too. "What was Dr. Schermerhorn really like?"

"That's not easy. He was a complex person, Detective."

"People say that when they mean the person had good and bad qualities."

"We all have good and bad qualities. But Jay was a good person. Brilliant, creative, hardworking. It's no accident he became famous."

"Was he humble?"

"Well, no."

"Flexible? Willing to allow another person's point of view, even if he disagreed?"

"Ms. Folkestone, Detective Folkestone, he was doing *his* thing, and a person can be allowed to do that. He was very focused. You don't make progress without following through on an idea."

"This is getting too abstract. What kind of shrink was he?"

"He was a psychotherapist. A psychotherapist is a kind of facilitator. He helps a person take responsibility for his actions, and second, to take responsibility for changing his life."

"Does this technique work with children?"

"When you do it in a way that's appropriate to their age, yes, it works for children. Yes. If they're troubled, if their families have damaged them, yes. Yes, yes. You help them to grow. They're more adaptable than adults, so in some ways you make progress faster. Look, a medically oriented psychiatrist like Dr. Hansen is acting on a disease model of mental disorders. A disease is something that happens *to* you. The doctor tries to find the right combination of medication to fix you. A psychotherapist has an interactive approach. Your interaction with the patient makes it possible for him to understand himself better and see what it is in his thinking that has led him to be unhappy. It's very hopeful, in a way. You act on the belief that your exchange with the patient helps the patient to heal himself."

"I would think that would make you get angry with them when they don't manage to help themselves."

"Very good, Ms. Folkestone. That's certainly a trap you could fall into. But the therapist has to be aware of the possibility and not let himself react like that."

"What do you do? You personally. I mean, literally, what do you do all day?"

"That's a fair question. I spend about three-quarters of my time in private practice. The rest is teaching and writing."

"Private practice means what? Having an office? Where people lie down on a couch?"

"Well, some do, actually. That's called psychoanalysis. I have three patients in analysis—"

"Only *three*?"

"Yes. Because in analysis you see patients four or five days a week. I'm a training analyst and one of those patients is a candidate, which means he's in training to become an analyst. I also have psychotherapy patients. They come in once a week and sit in a chair. That's called 'psychodynamic psychotherapy.' I have an office with my chair, two patient chairs, a desk, and a couch. The office is soundproof so that patients can be comfortable knowing no one outside can hear them. And it has two doors so that patients exiting don't see the ones arriving. If I have a patient in psychoanalysis, the analysand—the patient in analysis—lies on the couch and I sit in a chair slightly behind the head of the couch, so that he doesn't see me and I don't see his face. Does that answer your questions?"

"I guess so. So do you still have children as patients?"

"No. Just adults."

"Why no children?"

"Child psychiatry is a specialty. I just never went in that direction."

"But you had experience here with children."

"That's true. But a person has to make choices."

"Do you treat autistics? Adult autistics?"

"No."

"Why not?"

Dr. Emerson shifted, as if uneasy. "The treatment of autism has changed a lot. Autistics, especially the higher-functioning people among them, do engage in psychotherapy sometimes to help them adjust to dealing with the expectations of a world filled with people who are different from them. But primarily these days they get a lot of basic training in how to do things."

"Such as?"

"Such as when to say 'How do you do?' How to look people in the eye. When to smile. How to talk in vocal cadences like other people, not in a monotone. And not too loud."

"Which was not what Dr. Schermerhorn was offering here, was it?"

"What he offered was very good life training in a very pleasant atmosphere. Each child had a specific primary counselor who lived in and bonded with the child. Jay and this person replaced the parents. It's true Dr. Schermerhorn believed that autism was caused by bad parenting, in most cases by a cold mother. We don't really think of that as causal today, although the parents' reactions may contribute to the child's problems."

"Are we saying that Dr. Schermerhorn's treatment was wrong?"

Dr. Emerson sat more rigidly in his chair. "It was excellent treatment for the time."

I nodded, deciding not to pursue that.

"So tell me, Dr. Emerson, could an autistic person have killed Dr. Schermerhorn? Mr. Bettleby has been telling me quite vehemently that it's not possible. Or at least it's very unlikely."

Cautiously, Emerson said, "I'd agree it's unlikely."

I waited, but he didn't go on. "What are you not saying? Bettleby's argument is that an autistic person might react with anger when they're frustrated, but none of them would have planned this elaborate a killing."

"I think that's right."

"You're not cooperating with me, Doctor."

Dr. Emerson simply shrugged, an out-of-character, almost rude gesture, foreign to such a courteous man.

I said, "Let me guess, then. There's quite a wide range of abilities among the former patients who are here this weekend. You would probably say some of them are less affected by their autism than others. Some of them, in other words, would be better able to plan a murderous attack than others."

"I can't say."

"Jeffrey Clifford, for example. He's quite capable."

"I'm simply not going to respond to that."

"And the reason that you don't want to talk about it is that you worked with most of them and you view them as former patients. So you feel you have some sort of confidentiality problem involved."

"You're very astute, Detective Folkestone."

"But—?"

"But even if you make good guesses, I won't talk about them, not individually and not as a group."

"Would you talk about them if I told you that at least one of them had blood on—let's say his or her—his or her shoe?"

Dr. Emerson's mouth fell open. He realized right away that he had reacted to my news and resumed a face of professional detachment. After a few seconds he said, "I can't believe that. And no, I still wouldn't talk about them. Blood or no blood, I would still say it's unlikely that any of them killed Jay."

"And if I tell you it's the same blood type as Dr. Schermerhorn's?"

Again Dr. Emerson kept silence for a few seconds. He appeared extremely troubled, and trying to hide it. Then his face lightened, and he said, "You weren't here Friday night, last night, of course."

"Of course not. Why?"

"Henry Rollins fell down during the opening sherry reception. He had a reaction to all the unusual input, actually. He got overloaded on too much input and freaked out, you might say, and fell and cut his head."

"Where did this take place?"

"Right over here." Dr. Emerson got up and walked to the center front of the ballroom, just inside the big doors. "Right here exactly." There were a few dark streaks still on the floor. He said, "Blood always leaves a stain."

I had followed him. I stared at the spots, dismayed. "Oh, hell. Right where everybody tracked through it on the way out."

This was disaster to my best theory of the murder. My mind made a note: C*all Hagopian back again and leave a second message. Come and get a scraping of this blood.*

"Yes, Detective. I suppose you'd better type the blood from these spots, or from Henry himself, before you rush to judgment."

CHAPTER 25

I SAGGED ONTO A BENCH.

"You look awful," Emerson said. "I didn't mean to be snide about it."

"I'm okay. Long day, that's all." I had stomped over over to the bench and sat myself down, devastated. Was I back to square one? Emerson came over and sat next to me.

"That's not all that's bothering you."

"Don't analyze me, Doctor," I snapped. When Emerson seemed not to have taken offense, I said, "Did anybody touch the blood?"

"With their hands? Not that I remember. Do you mean one of them had blood on their hands? You won't tell me, will you?" He sighed. "I hate to make you feel worse, but Henry sat down on this bench for a while, and people came over trying to help him. Then after he got up, I'm pretty sure other people used the bench." I jumped up, studied where I had been sitting, and seeing nothing sat back down. He said, "Listen, I'm sorry, Detective Folkestone, but there could be a number of people with blood on them. That's if we're talking about a very small amount of blood."

"That's what we're talking about."

"I know you're trying to do your job. I'm sorry."

I nodded. I wasn't feeling happy.

"But you'll have DNA results to fall back on, won't you?"

"Yes. But not for quite some time."

"It doesn't take weeks and weeks anymore, does it?"

"Not weeks and weeks, but a couple of weeks at least."

"A long time to be left hanging. You're young for this amount of responsibility."

"What's that supposed to mean?"

"Jay was a famous man. His death was reported on all the major networks this evening. With long profiles of him. He had the kind of fame that meant the media had his obituary all ready to run. The media is swarming over this. When they learn *how* he died, the furor will be even worse. You and Detective Park are in the crosshairs. You have a mansion full of people with varying motives, and some of the suspects are incomprehensible to you. Your usual way of assessing people doesn't work on autistics. Even to psychiatrists, it's a puzzle how autistics think. The autistics can't tell us, of course. So you're dealing with that problem, too, and the awareness that you can't be seen to be unkind to them. It's no wonder you're stressed."

"I'm *not* stressed!"

Emerson smiled. "Don't you mean 'I'm not stressed, *dammit*!'"

I smiled too. "Okay, so I'm a little stressed. Stress is good for me."

"No, it isn't," he said gently. "A challenge is good. Stress isn't good for anybody."

"I can't worry about that now. I have a job to do."

"You can only do your best. You don't have to be perfect."

"No, Dr. Emerson. There's no excuse for sloppiness. Of *course* I have to be perfect."

AFTER TEN MINUTES MORE TALK, I was drooping from weariness. I got up, said, "Good night, Doctor. I've got to get some sleep."

"I suppose I should too."

A thought hit me. "Listen, Doctor. Your door doesn't lock, does it?"

"I don't think any of them do on this floor. Somebody told me the third-floor doors have bolts. Why do you ask?"

"Do me a favor. Shove a chair under your doorknob."

He cocked his head and looked at me as if I were nuts. "You have guards in the halls. And why would anybody come after me, anyway?"

"Guards can fall asleep. They'd better not, but they can. They also take bathroom breaks."

"I haven't any enemies here."

"You probably would have told me yesterday that Dr. Schermerhorn didn't, either. Right?" Emerson stared at me. "If one of these former patients is viciously angry at Schermerhorn about the way he was treated here, he could be angry at you, too. You were part of it."

"I'm sorry, but I just don't buy that! We did our best and we helped these people."

"So Dr. Schermerhorn isn't dead?"

"That's not fair. We don't know why he was killed."

"I don't want to argue whether you helped the patients. Not everybody may agree with you. Schermerhorn was murdered. Who do you think killed him?"

"An—an intruder."

"An intruder from where? Why? This wasn't a random murder. The front door was locked. The back door may have been locked. No burglar is going to walk into a mansion like this and wander up the stairs to the second floor and randomly enter one bedroom among thirty bedrooms. If they do anything, they go for silverware in the dining room."

He was silent. I said, "And then take Dr. Schermerhorn to the basement? Please!"

I went on. "Why are we arguing about this, anyway? How hard is it for you to just shove a chair firmly under your doorknob? I give you permission to call me a blithering paranoid idiot while you do it."

He smiled wanly at this. "It's the principle of the thing."

"Promise me you will. Humor me."

"Oh, all right. Gee, Folkestone, you're so bossy you ought to be a cop."

Three

Sadism is all right in its place,
but it should be directed to proper ends.

—SIGMUND FREUD

THE SUN ROSE OVER Lake Michigan at 5:29 A.M. into a day that was already ninety degrees. A street-cleaning truck had passed through at dawn and the pavement in front of Hawthorne House steamed. Everything else was bone dry. There was dust on the grass, dust on the bushes, and a copper shimmer in the air. Now at six-thirty the sun had had an hour to cook the city. Garbage cans along the street smelled like old soup.

I watched from the front hall as Karl Deemer let himself in the front door with his key. He slouched into the hall, not seeing me at first, and he all but bumped into me. He lurched back. "Yow! Dammit—what the hell do you want?"

"Come with me."

There were people in the dining room drinking coffee. A couple of other guests milled about the parlor and side halls, gazing at the ornate walls. I headed down the stairs to the kitchen.

The catering staff was firing up the oven for biscuits and laying out trays of little milk and cream pitchers. One of them draped rashers of bacon onto a wire grid set in a pan for baking in the oven.

"Keep following me."

Deemer mumbled objections, but as I stomped along the basement corridor away from the kitchen, he followed. "Are we going to the—you know?" he asked.

"No, we are not going to the death scene. We're stopping right here. I just don't need the caterers to hear this." I leaned against a stained brick wall.

Deemer shifted feet uneasily.

"First, I'm planning to take you downtown as a murder suspect."

"You can't do that."

"Of course I can. Second, I will give the Schermerhorn estate all they need to sue your parents for fraud. They defrauded the Hawthorne House School out of nine years of tuition, room, and board." I was on thin ice here. What the Deemers had done was fraudulent, yes, but a good defense attorney could make the case that Dr. Schermerhorn should have been able to tell what was going on. Plus I hadn't had a chance to look up the statute of limitations on fraud. However, I was counting on Deemer knowing less that I did.

He said, "You don't have anything against me."

"There may be criminal charges. If so, your parents will be jailed—your father, that is. Your mother is pretty much where she belongs already, right? And while you're in custody, before we pick up your dad—who by the way is *not* dead, as you well know, Karl—I might just let everybody in the area know where he lives. He's always kept his home address kind of quiet, and we both know why. Some people might get a little testy, huh?"

"You can't do that!"

"Oh, yes, I can. Probably what happens next is that your dad, assuming he's still able to walk and talk after his 'friends' visit, can't pay the rent. Which I'm sure he always keeps a month or two behind on. . . ."

I studied him. Right so far. "So while your parents are guests of the taxpaying public, you lose your apartment and you lose your job here and even if we don't keep you in jail, you can't get a new job because what other place is going to let you *pretend* to work?"

"Ahhh, shit!"

"So you'll have no home, no job, no money, and that's if I can't get you indicted for murder. But I think I can. Of all the people who were here this weekend, you're the only person who knows the building *since* the school for autistics closed. You knew where to find the items used in the murder"—I paused, making sure not to tell him anything I didn't want him to know, but he'd seen the body, so—"that there was the old dumbwaiter rope in the basement, and what equipment could be found in the kitchen, and where that basement room was, and whether it was under a first-floor room that people might be in, or hear noises from, or not. You knew everything the killer needed to know. Yes, I think we can get you indicted for murder."

Deemer sagged as I spoke. I stopped and stared him in the eyes. Abruptly, he straightened, and like an experienced con, said, "So what do you want from me?"

"Aha. Very good. I want you to tell me the truth. It'll be hard for you to be honest, of course, out of practice as you are," I said as the sly expression crept back over his face. "But I'll know if you aren't. I'm short of patience on this and I'll fudge evidence if I have to." Actually, I wouldn't. But if there was one thing sure about dishonest people it was that they thought everybody else was crooked too.

"Yeah, shit. Go ahead. Ask."

"Did you kill Dr. Schermerhorn?"

"Shit, no." He glanced at me to check out the effects of his words.

"Why not?"

"Why not? He was my buddy."

"No, he was your dupe, wasn't he?" I said. Deemer smiled at me, big-eyed, with the look of total honesty I'd seen on any number of con men. And not, by the way, on the autistics I had met this weekend. "Come on, Karl. What did you do? It's 1971. Your dad's in prison someplace. Your mom has maybe lost her apartment and she's planning to run some sort of elaborate con on a guy and doesn't need a little kid around."

"She loved me. She wanted me to be cared for."

I almost stopped right there, because of a rush of sympathy. I had a strong feeling that this statement was true. On Deemer's part at least. His mother had told him she loved him and he believed it.

I said, "So your mother had heard there was a scholarship for some underprivileged, autistic, or disturbed Hyde Park–area child. Room and board and treatment."

"Mmm-hmm."

"That's a yes?" He nodded, and I went on. "You had been picked up a couple of times for petty theft, shoplifting, like that. Hardly surprising, considering your parents. And a record at school—you were in sixth grade, I think—for fighting with kids. And vandalism, sabotaging class projects, like tearing up other kids' paintings and ripping down work on the bulletin boards, huh? Small stuff. But you and your mom worked it out that she would tell the do-gooders looking for a few bad children that she was afraid you sometimes tortured horses. Which you hadn't done."

"Yeah, fuck. Who cares about stupid horses!"

"Maybe DCFS looked into the case and confirmed you were in a bad home situation. Your mother had done a little research into Dr. Schermerhorn—trust a con man, or woman, to research the mark—and she gave you a few hints. And lo and behold you got into Hawthorne House. Nobody thought to ask whether there actually were any injured horses, I bet. Right?"

"Yeah. Shit." He cocked his head back. "He was just so glad to get me."

"And your mama takes off to Nevada with some poor rich schmuck who thinks she's wonderful and doesn't realize she's gonna take him for everything he's got. We pick up her trail out there pretty clearly. She shouldn't've chosen the nephew of an FBI agent."

"If a guy can't take care of his shit, he deserves to lose it."

"Ah, the ethics of crooks the world over. And meanwhile, you were set up here, in clover."

"Yeah, jeez, good food, much as you wanted, too, second helpings. My own room. Just share with one other kid. We hadda go to school, but I would've had to go to school anyway. Yeah."

Good food and his own room. I pictured Karl as a twelve-year-old boy. His father was off in prison, and he was living with his neglectful mother in a small apartment, with her "men friends" coming by all the time and staying overnight. And meals whenever the mother got herself together enough to buy potato chips and Coke. The food at Hawthorne House had been very good. Well worth running a con for.

"Besides going to school, of course, Karl, you paid for your room and board in other ways?"

"Oh, yeah. But hey, that was kind of fun. He wanted what he wanted so bad."

"Tell me."

"He wanted my mother to be a real witch. Took me a while to figure out what to say exactly. But, like, I told him she beat me if I didn't wash the dishes."

"And she didn't?"

"Hell, no. The fuck she care about dishes? We got takeout. Or eat chips out of the bag. He loved hearing how bad she was. Then he kept on about—you know—about toilet training when I was little. I didn't remember shit about it. That's a pretty good joke, huh? Didn't remember shit about it? But after a while I got onto what he wanted and I told him about how she'd beat on me if I wet the bed, and how she'd hit me on the—uh—the—"

For a crook, I thought, he was a shy crook.

"On my dick, you know, and I'd scream. So he asked me about the horses. I figured out he wanted me to say I hurt the horses because horses have a big, long schlong if they get excited. So once I figured out he wanted to hear about this I eased into it. See what I mean? Give him a little hint and then take it back and then a little more later, next week's session, and finally it's 'Oh, Wow!' Like cowabunga! Right? And then I told him how much better I felt after talking about it, and he just creamed he was so happy." Deemer laughed until he choked.

"So you fed him what he wanted to hear." Deemer kept on laughing.

"I studied the weirdos, too. Imitated 'em."

I watched, slightly sickened, as Deemer looked away from me, avoided eye contact, held his arms awkwardly near his sides and said in a loud mono-tone, "And talk like this."

I said, "Why did he believe you?"

"He *wanted* to believe me, man. You get that, don't you?"

"Of course. But he was in the business of analyzing young people. I would think he'd see through you."

"Old saying. The easiest person to con is a con man."

"That's true."

"He had this test. Oh, man, I don't get it why these shrinks think they're so cool, like nobody's going to get what they're after."

"Such as?"

"There was this one he called a soundy. Don't know why. It was so stupid, and I mean obvious. He shows me a bunch of pictures, seven or eight at a time. They show people, you know. Photographs of people. And, like, in each set you're supposed to pick two pictures you like best and two you don't like. I mean, get real! I'm going to pick the ickiest, right? Convince him I really need help!" He laughed a high-pitched giggle.

"Why are you telling me this?"

"Well, this place was basically bullshit, wasn't it? All these different kids and you treat 'em all the same way. And you're going to make them better by talking to them."

"That and having them in a safe environment."

"Yeah, yeah."

"How did you manage to stay here—what was it, eight or nine years?"

"Well, I guess, Officer, that I was just so traumatized and so stupid that I just couldn't manage on the outside." He dropped his jaw and made a stupid face.

I switched subjects on him abruptly. "How did you find the body so fast?" But he hardly blinked.

He said, "Oh, come on. You're a detective. You tell me. Hey—you think it's 'cause I put him there, right? You think I killed him?"

I said, "If you didn't, then how'd you find him?"

"By smell, Ms. Detective. You ever been at a crime scene? Know what it smells like?"

I nodded. I did know, of course, and the moment he said it, I believed him. In fact, he was right; I should have thought of it myself. I nodded again, but he made it explicit anyway.

"Shit and blood, Detective. Smell it a mile away."

"THE LITTLE SLEAZE DIDN'T strike me as violent," I said to Ollie when he arrived a few minutes later.

"Yeah, but Emily, what if sometime Friday evening he talked with Dr. Schermerhorn, and what if Schermerhorn realized then, for the first time that Deemer had been conning him all along?"

"Not impossible, I suppose."

"And what if the doctor threatened to expose him? Call the police or file a lawsuit?"

"Would Schermerhorn do that, exposing his own gullibility? I doubt it. He was very protective of his public image."

"But maybe Deemer discovered that Schermerhorn had other ways of getting even."

"That's possible. I'm beginning to think that Schermerhorn was capable of being pretty devious himself."

CHAPTER **27**

By 9:30 A.M., most of the guests were leaving the Hawthorne House reunion.

Ollie Park had watched the first two go. They were April Tausche and her mother. Ollie was not happy to see the suspects leave. It seemed to him he was missing a bet not keeping a closer eye on the departures. He decided to hang around outside the Hawthorne House front door. He said to Emily Folkestone, "I just had an idea."

"Glad to hear it's happened at last."

"As they leave, you stay inside in the hall, chat 'em up, ask parting questions, tell 'em you're going to visit them at home, basically talk a lot."

"Meanwhile you will be . . . ?"

"Standing right outside the front door, silently observing, see if they look relieved or scared when they leave. Doing my inscrutable thing."

"You're about as inscrutable as an open-face tuna melt."

"Watch me." He looked blankly in Emily's face.

"You're thinking about a quarter pounder with cheese."

"Oh, blast. Got me again."

"However, I think it's a good idea."

"A quarter pounder with cheese?"

Emily snorted and walked from the Hawthorne House front door to a place well inside the large marble vestibule. Park watched as she started chatting with Dr. Emerson. April Tausche's mother had arrived to pick her up right after breakfast. She'd gone to April's room, and, Park assumed, helped her pack. Then they'd come hustling down the stairs, the mother's hand on April's elbow, hurrying her along. Park's impression was that her mother had barely managed to stay away the whole weekend and had been nervous about April's being away from home on her own. Couldn't wait to get her out of here. To him, April seemed no different from yesterday, or in other words, strange. But of course he had not known her before the murder.

Two women came down the stairs now, one carrying a small overnight bag and one dragging a huge suitcase with two small wheels in the back. As they crossed the great hall, the suitcase made a sound like a car going over a railroad track as the little wheels dipped into the spaces between the marble slabs.

Oliver Park observed them with what he hoped was an analytical eye, but he was not sure how the guilty person would look as he or she left the scene of the murder. He thought to himself that he was far more accustomed to stupid murders and stupid murderers—drug dealers, abusive husbands, teenagers who didn't quite get the idea that people really died if you shot them. Killers, in other words, who were so obvious you just about had to put out your hand and pick them like a peach.

Whoever killed Dr. Schermerhorn differed from Park's garden-variety killer in at least two ways. He or she would not be used to violence. He or she would not be used to deceiving the police. Unless the killer was Kurt Deemer. And while Kurt was used to deceiving the police, there was nothing in his record that suggested he was violent. Sneaky, dishonest, opportunistic, weaselly, even nasty, but not violent.

So would the murderer leave Hawthorne House with a sigh of relief? A smile of triumph? Would he feel he had killed Dr. Schermerhorn untraceably and was getting away clean? Would Oliver see that glow of relief and know who the killer was?

Or would the killer, not used to murder, leave in fear?

Would his fear be increasing; might the murderer even think that once he left he wouldn't be able to keep track of what the police were up to, and might that be harder for him to bear?

Could Ollie watch for a face shadowed with anxiety, and find a killer?

Ollie was interested in people, anyhow, and he would watch the faces.

A third woman came hurrying down the stairs after the first two, calling, "I'm here! I told you I was a fast packer."

They were Cassie Garibaldi, Sally Dear, and Beth Pollie, all former counselors, who before Friday had not seen each other in fifteen years. Ollie had interviewed Pollie and Dear, and Folkestone had interviewed Garibaldi. Two had very positive attitudes toward Dr. Schermerhorn, and one of them only lukewarm. Skeptical as Ollie tried to be about their self-descriptions of having been happy to come back to visit and having no resentment toward Schermerhorn, he could not imagine any reason for one of them to kill him. One of them now lived in Iowa, one in South Bend, Indiana, and one in Niles, a Chicago suburb.

They stopped in front of Dr. Emerson and Folkestone, although they did not come quite as close to Folkestone. They were all in their mid to late forties, all dressed in light summer dresses. Beth Pollie, who was given to flowered pastel dresses, said to Dr. Emerson, "It was very nice, uh,—" She so badly wanted to say, "Thank you. I had a lovely time," that Park felt sorry for her. She half giggled, and finished awkwardly, "Nice seeing you, um, anyway—"

Cassie Garibaldi was made of sterner stuff. And tighter clothes. "We enjoyed the chance to see the old place again, Dr. Emerson. I'm sorry it had to end this way. But we all feel it was very good for us to have come."

"Yes, we did," said Sally.

"Cassie, Sally, Beth," Dr. Emerson said. "There's no need

to feel awkward. We'll all have to deal with Jay's death in our own way."

"But it was wonderful to see you, Dr. Emerson."

"And to see Miss Simms," Sally said.

"And Chaz, everybody's answer to Julia Child," Beth said, laughing.

There was a crowd of media people on the lawn and sidewalk, and the street was clogged with TV vans. Microwave masts bristled on vans like fishing rods on charter boats. Two reporters were doing stand-ups with the mansion as a backdrop. Others were talking with their offices on two-ways. Eight uniformed police officers from the district held back the media pack. The cops were keeping a path clear for guests to leave Hawthorne House, but once the guests got to the street, they were fair game.

By now two other people were approaching from the stairs and the women said their good-byes. As they passed Park, he heard them say, "Do you think the Mellow Yellow deli is still here?"

"Or the Agora. I could really enjoy a Greek Sunday dinner right now."

"Oh, yes!"

"Or the Medici."

"With all the art on the walls!"

"The University Tap!" Pollie exclaimed.

"That's a beer joint," said Cassie Garibaldi. I want something solid. Sunday dinnerlike. Even if it's expensive."

"You're right," said Sally Dear. "We deserve it after what we've been through."

"Well, we'll have to organize this," said Garibaldi, obviously the practical one in the group. "We all have cars. Do we want to go in one car and then come back and pick the others up later . . . ?"

They started down the walk. Park had watched them for

signs of guilt, and seen none. Now he was amused at the way they sailed past the media with their chins in the air. Cassie Garibaldi even said, "No comment! No comment!"

Her voice faded, and from inside the house Park heard Henry Rollins and his father. Henry was mumbling unintelligibly, then bursting out with "Arrividerci!" The father said to Folkestone, "Hey. Sorry if I was crabby. I know this whole goddamn thing wasn't your fault."

"Thanks, Mr. Rollins. Henry, I hope you're okay."

Henry said, "Lavish."

"What with all that happened. It must have been hard for you."

Henry was looking over Folkestone's shoulder at the hallway. "Arachnida, arachnida, arachnida," he said. "Duplication."

Henry's father said, "Four words at once, Henry. That's very good."

"Well," Folkestone said.

Henry's father said, "Well . . ."

He gave Henry a gentle push toward the door. They headed down the walk as a young woman strode up. She was very attractive, Park thought. Plus she reminded him of somebody. She spoke to Park. "Do you know if Jeffrey Clifford is ready to leave?" she asked.

That was who she looked like—Jeffrey Clifford.

Park heard Mr. Rollins, now approaching the news media, yell, "Get out of my way, you bloodsuckers!"

Park answered the young woman. "I think he's getting ready. He ought to be downstairs any minute. But you could ask Dr. Emerson."

She looked in the door at Emerson and Folkestone and frowned. "I don't think I will," she said.

"Are you Jeffrey Clifford's sister?"

"Yes."

"You heard about Dr. Schermerhorn's death."

"Yes," she replied in an abrupt tone, as if she wanted no more said.

"Mr. Clifford's room is on the third floor. You could go up and see."

Park then witnessed her behave in a way he thought very strange. Mr. Bettleby had come down the stairs and was talking with great emphasis, gesturing at Folkestone and Emerson. Park was pretty sure Folkestone didn't see Jeffrey's sister, who was still with him on the large flagstone area just outside the front door. The young woman glanced inside the door, looking to the right and left. The she put one foot in the building and peered into the front hall. Then she cautiously stepped inside and stood stiffly just inside the door, as if afraid.

"We have police officers in the house, ma'am," Park said to her. "Whoever killed Dr. Schermerhorn isn't any danger to you."

She spun around and stared him in the eye. "Schermerhorn *was* the danger," she said.

She backed out the door, obviously unwilling to roam around inside Hawthorne House looking for Jeffrey. Park decided that looking for Jeffrey was not his job, either. Clifford would be down soon enough. Besides, he wanted to overhear what Chaz, who had just arrived in the lobby, was telling Emily.

Chaz said, "I know how you cops eat. Doughnut shops. Fast food."

"No, really. It isn't like that anymore."

"I've seen the TV."

"TV shows are way behind the times. All the cops I know eat yogurt and go to health clubs."

"That's not good either. You need a full sit-down dinner. *Attend* to your food. Relax and enjoy well-chosen ingredients well prepared."

Dr. Emerson, who had just bidden good-bye to Dr. Sandra Hall and Dr. Morton Haseltine, said, "He's right, you know."

Chaz Tortola hefted his old-fashioned canvas bag. "The only reason anybody ever got better here," he said, "was my good food!" And he strode off down the path.

As Ollie Park watched, Folkestone and Emerson blinked in surprise. Folkestone said, "What was *that* about?"

Jane Macy appeared on the beautiful marble stairs. She posed, her round, powder blue overnight case in her hand. Catching the gaze of Folkestone and Dr. Emerson, she descended the last few steps.

Park suspected Jane Macy briefly had pictured herself as one of the Hawthornes, the lady of the manse, strolling down the marble stairs to greet her guests. He could see her change, step by step, as she reentered reality. She still stood straight but her shoulders sagged and her little blue suitcase actually looked heavier. Park knew about her childhood, how she had been rescued by her time at Hawthorne House, and he felt a deep pity for her.

Jane hurried to Dr. Emerson and threw her arms around him. "You take care of yourself, now, you hear, Dr. E?" she said.

"You too, Jane. I can't tell you how good it is to see you doing so well."

"I *am* doing well. And it's partly because of you."

"You're wonderful, Jane. God bless."

Behind Jane, Park saw Dr. Carol Hansen descending the stairs. Wearing a creamy silk suit, and carrying an understated alligator suitcase, she had all the elegance that Jane Macy wished for. Hansen gazed at the three people a few steps below her in the hall, Folkestone, Macy, and Emerson, then descended the remainder of the stairs briskly, and, speaking to no one, passed through the door, nodded at Park, and walked away down the path.

Jane came out the door and Ollie, feeling sorry for her, gave her a smile. "We may come and talk with you later this week, Ms. Macy," he said.

She grabbed his arm and stood close. "Whenever you want. When you interview April and Jeffrey, will you pass on something for me?"

"Of course." She produced a sly smile.

"Tell them the way Dr. Schermerhorn found out about their secret hiding place was that I told him. They'll know what that means."

Ollie didn't know what it meant, but he didn't feel quite so sorry for Jane Macy anymore.

Meanwhile, Jane made her way down the path, walking slowly, gathering the stares of the media. She swung her little suitcase just a bit. Dr. Hansen slipped away easily while Jane paused right in the middle of the media mob.

The reporters shouted questions, and videocameras homed in on her. Park wished he could hear what the reporters were asking. Even more, he wished he could hear what Macy answered. He saw her gesture with her hand toward Hawthorne House. He saw her place her suitcase on the sidewalk to talk better, and saw her put both hands to her cheeks in the age-old gesture of amazement. He saw her swivel her head back and forth, as if at the unkindness of fate.

She mourned Dr. Schermerhorn, Park believed, but she was having a wonderful time.

All the while, Jeffrey Clifford's sister had been standing rigid on the broad porch, outside the door, peering into the building. Park picked up on it the instant she paradoxically relaxed her stance but heightened her alertness.

Jeffrey Clifford emerged from the gloom inside, coming up behind Emerson and Folkestone. He carried his duffle bag in a peculiar grip, hugging it to his chest with his left arm. The other arm was held, elbow in, forearm parallel with the ground. In this posture, he worked his way around Folkestone and Emerson.

Emerson was facing away from him, but Folkestone, seeing him, said, "We'll try to interview you tomorrow, Mr. Clifford. I'll call."

Jeffrey ducked his head up and down, possibly nodding, and kept moving. Dr. Emerson turned around in time to see Jeffrey's back.

Jeffrey reached his sister, who grabbed his free arm. They started across the porch. Park thought: Jeffrey Clifford is leaving Hawthorne House forever, and glad of it.

Just before they started down the porch steps, he heard the sister say to Clifford, "You did it, Jeffie. I'm proud of you. You went right in there and did it."

※※

THE FRONT DOOR WAS heavily grained dark oak with raised paneling and a glass window guarded by three vertical and three horizontal bars of wrought iron.

Oliver Park and I let ourselves into Dr. Schermerhorn's house with the engraved silver key on his key chain. The chain itself was unusual, made of flat silver links, alternate links pierced by threaded posts, very much like the posts used to hold earrings to pierced ears. The keys slipped over the posts and a small silver bead screwed down to hold them in place. Among them was a hand-hammered Phi Beta Kappa key, with its square body and three stars in the upper left. Like the rest of the keys and chain, it was freshly polished.

"Thought pretty well of himself, didn't he?" Oliver said.

"Well, maybe he had a right to."

"I don't like this place." He pushed the heavy door closed behind them.

"If the house were a car," I said, "you'd tell me that door had a good, solid sound."

"Yeah, well, if this house was a car, it'd be a hearse."

We found ourselves in a large vestibule. The walls were

beige plaster framed by dark wooden beams. The floor, tiled in mud-colored glazed terra-cotta, sounded a steely note under our heels as we stepped forward.

Like many houses in the Hyde Park section of Chicago, the Schermerhorn house was old and very solid. Despite the hot day and the dead air, the feel of the house was chilly. Ollie didn't like it. I didn't like it either.

In the living room, mullioned windows were composed of small chunks of thick glass. I looked out on the back lawn as if through the faceted eyes of an insect, a slightly different view from each. Dark, Germanic furniture blocked our way. Beyond a heavy sofa with carved arms, giant brass andirons guarded an empty fireplace. Above the mantel was the head of a large deer with great branching antlers. "Do you call that a ten-point buck?" I said.

"When they say that, is it ten points altogether or ten points on each side?"

"Beats me. I hate it, though."

"Me too." Unlike most game trophies mounted in the United States, this one had no glass eyes or deerskin. It was a bare skull, with empty eye sockets.

The rest of the room was as cold as a skull.

"No plants," Park said.

I touched the sofa fabric. It was thick brocade, which looked rich and felt stiff as vinyl. I followed Oliver through the dining room—upright chairs with narrow backs and heavily carved dark wood, plus a gigantic sideboard—and into the kitchen.

Here everything was quite different, at least in the sense that it was very modern. A Subzero refrigerator and a separate freezer stood next to each other. Gaggenau ovens shouldered up to a double sink with a tap attachment that would produce boiling water instantly.

"Hmm," Oliver said.

"Well, it certainly is clean. I hope this doesn't mean the

housekeeper tidied up and threw anything personal away after he died."

"Couldn't have. When I got here yesterday, she hadn't even heard he was dead. In fact, I had quite a time persuading her to leave. It was like she thought he'd come back and ask why she wasn't hard at work. And dock her pay. We went out together and locked the door behind us."

"Well, if so, she certainly kept things up on a daily basis."

I ran my finger across the countertop, finding no dust, then looked under the counters. Nothing but bins with a few potatoes and onions in one, detergent, silver polish, spot remover, scouring powder, window cleaner, and so on in another.

A side door next to a pantry led into a small room with a single bed, dresser, white lace curtains, and a minuscule bathroom, floored in the small hexagonal tiles popular in the 1920s. A closet contained several black uniforms, four pairs of black low-heel shoes, each left shoe with a bulge on the outside where the little toe would press, a dozen crisply ironed white high-necked shirts, and very little else.

"There's nothing suspicious here. Let's find his office."

The hall that led into the kitchen also led the other way, past the living room arch into the back part of the downstairs. Here was a side room with desk and files and past it stairs to the second floor. "You want to do the office and I'll try the bedrooms?" Oliver asked.

"Yup."

The hall was half-timbered just as the living room was, with vertical, heavy hewn beams at intervals interspersed with cream-colored plaster. In the center of each plastered space was an old-looking print of an antlered deer. One print showed the buck standing on top of a rocky crag. Another pictured him leaping a stream. In a third, he was rearing on hind legs.

"Jeez," Oliver said. "It's kind of Germanic, isn't it?"

"My guess is it's Austrian."

"What's the difference?"

"Well, don't ask me. To the Austrians quite a lot, I imagine. But I'm no expert. I just think it's Austrian because I think he was trying for Viennese. It think it's an homage to Freud."

~⋈⊱~

TWO HOURS LATER, Park came downstairs and into the office. By then I'd been through easily a hundred patient files, just skimming. The whole bunch would take hundreds of hours to read thoroughly, which I hoped would not be necessary. Maybe we only needed to read about the people who had been at the reunion.

Besides the files on paper, I had found a humongous cache of little minicassette audiotapes, the small kind used in hand-held tape recorders popular twenty years ago. They were carefully filed in wide, shallow drawers. Since there was no player here that I could find, I had not listened to them.

There were no threatening letters or threatening phone messages. There was a will, however, in a file labeled, as well it might be, "Last Will and Testament." At a brief glance, it confirmed Dr. Emerson's belief that Dr. Schermerhorn had no close relatives. Everything was left to fund a scholarship for postdoc students in psychiatry. It was to be called the Jay Schermerhorn Scholarship in Child Psychiatry. It surely was not a motive for murder.

As Ollie came in the door, I started reading aloud an early page from one of the patient files:

" 'Jeffrey Clifford presents as a seven-year-old male with a history of school problems and difficulties at home. His parents report many enrollments in public school and in schools for problem children, none successful.

" 'History of normal delivery and apparently normal development [pediatrician's report appended] until age three, when according to parents he began to withdraw. Parents report accelerated reading skills up to age five. During this period, Jeffrey did not make friends and withdrew further from family as well.

" 'Pt. has two siblings, m. nine and f. five. Father employed as professor, mother housewife.

" 'In first interview, pt. appears well nourished, and medical report confirms good physical health. Pt. uncommunicative, refusing to make eye contact, flapping hands. Utters occasional nonsense words but can speak sense when he wants to.

" 'Posture unconventional, elbows held close to sides. Gait awkward. Axis of body bent forward from waist.

" 'Note to self: Father cold and perhaps resigned. Sits still and does not agitate or ask many questions. Mother attempts to show concern for J. but despite fidgeting wants to get rid of the child. Eager to have him enrolled at HH. Sat straighter and leaned forward ready to do combat whenever I suggested other possible approaches.

" 'Intake diagnosis: Autism consequent on maternal rejection.' "

After I finished, I waited for Ollie's reaction.

First he said, "Jeez."

Then he said, "Um, those records are probably protected by confidentiality rules."

"Probably."

"And therefore—?"

"Therefore I'll read the whole lot of them. Or whichever ones I damn well want."

"Now?"

"No. I've got to go to the autopsy. I'm due there in half an hour. Dr. Choudhary scheduled it for four o'clock."

"And the files?"

"I'll come back tomorrow and read the ones about our suspects, at least."

⋊⋉

I SMELLED THE MORGUE four blocks away as I got out of my car. I was glad I had told Ollie to give the autopsy a miss. He'd had only half a day off in the last eight days, and he should go to the beach with Jason. In fact, I had made him promise that he would. He was worried about Jason, I believed.

About seventy people die in Chicago each day. On Friday the number had been a hundred fifteen. On Saturday, projected to go over two hundred, it was three hundred sixty-five. Of the seventy deaths on an average day, only seventeen or eighteen go to the medical examiner for determination of death. The rest are explainable, unsuspicious deaths, most of them in a hospital or while "under a doctor's care." All of the heat deaths, by now over five hundred, had to be autopsied. One dozen pathologists were working double shifts and still the backlog of bodies increased.

The Cook County Medical Examiner's Office at 2121 West Harrison, due west of the Loop, was a new building with— unlike the old building—adequate parking. Today the parking lot was filled with refrigerated trucks, and a long line of police cars snaked around the block. The police cars were there with bodies the officers had picked up; their wait for a morgue worker simply to take delivery of the body was now several hours. The fifty-foot-long refrigerated trucks had been donated by a meat-packing company to hold the hundreds of incoming bodies. When I arrived, I made my way between trucks, squad cars, squadrols, fire department vans, television vans, media automobiles, and private-company hearses.

The morgue could hold two hundred bodies. It was now hundreds over capacity. Body bags are manufactured to be strong and tight, but they aren't space-suit tight. The refrigerated trucks were closed, but they weren't airtight, either. The stench of death was everywhere in the still, hot afternoon.

Inside, the air was cooler and felt quite cold after the heat outdoors, but it smelled worse. Gurneys with the dead lined the corridors. When I asked at the desk for the Schermerhorn autopsy, the secretary snapped, "Well, at least you know the name!" She was overworked, overtired, and from her response apparently frustrated that many of the dead were unidentified.

When I found Dr. Choudhary, I mentioned it to him.

"We got in a bunch of forensic dentists to try to identify people," he said.

"Why? Cops know when we pick them up who lives in that room."

"But do you know the body is actually the person who lived there?"

"Well—"

"And they aren't all coming from apartments, either. We got people from underpasses, and lower Wacker Drive, and shelters."

I sighed.

Dr. Schermerhorn's body had been found naked, so the usual process of removing and labeling the clothing wasn't needed. The autopsy suite was a long, narrow room, with several procedures going on at once, each at its own table with its own pathologist and diener, or morgue assistant. I had attended several autopsies as the detective in various cases, but I recognized only a couple of the dieners by sight, including the short, chubby one we had today. I greeted him, saying, "How're you doing?" and hoped he wouldn't realize I didn't know his name. He nodded back at me. I recalled that he was always too jokey, although, giving him the benefit of the doubt, he had to keep the grimness at bay.

Dr. Choudhary's eyes looked sunken. I said, "How long a shift have you been on, Doctor?"

"Twenty hours."

The diener said, "See the kids?"

I thought in horror that he meant children's bodies until I realized he had jerked his chin at the other autopsies. Some of the people doing the dieners' jobs were surprisingly young. "Yes, I do. Who are they?"

"Students."

"Students from where?"

"Some school of mortuary science," the diener said. "Got a bunch of them in to lend a hand. Although I can't say they're worth much."

Choudhary said, "They are *very* helpful. We'll be working triple shifts into the middle of next week, even if the heat wave ends now. Which it won't."

The diener said, "We already got slimers, poppers, and bursters."

"Philip!" Choudhary said. "That's quite enough!"

I said, "All this makes me feel guilty about pushing you to get to Dr. Schermerhorn. Everybody at Hawthorne House thinks Schermerhorn's so important but over here he's one body among hundreds."

"No, you're right to push it. Most of these"— he waved his hand at the rest of the room—"are natural deaths. Preventable, maybe," he added grimly, "but natural. Dr. Schermerhorn was clearly murdered. And *that* we need to do something about."

"Right."

"He's been dead, what, thirty-plus hours? I don't like to leave them unautopsied that long."

"But it's pretty clear what killed him, isn't it?" the diener said.

With that, we all looked at the body. After detailed photography of the wounds, the diener had washed the blood from the skin. I could see more clearly now how very white Dr. Schermerhorn was.

"Exsanguination, blood loss," said the diener.

"I'll be the judge of that," said Dr. Choudhary, in a repressive tone. The diener shut up.

Schermerhorn's wrists and ankles were deeply abraded,

where he had struggled against the ropes that tied him. His tongue was swollen. Inside his mouth was a large amount of blood, which Dr. Choudhary swabbed up and inserted, swab and all, in a vial. With tweezers, which he called pickups, Choudhary removed small reddish threads from Dr. Schermerhorn's teeth. The threads were probably from the necktie that had been tamped into his mouth. He had chewed on it.

Choudhary palpated the head wound. It had not bled, at least to the naked eye, but hey, what do I know? "Our Dr. Czerba looked at it when he first came in," Choudhary said. "I agree with him. It didn't bleed."

"If he was knocked out in one place and killed later in another, would that blow to the head have left any evidence?"

"You could probably find hair and maybe scalp cells on whatever he was hit with. Something flat. It had no sharp edges, of course, at least none that struck the head, or it would have bled."

"Something flat like a heavy book?"

"Could very well be."

He had the diener give him small paper labels with numbers on them, which he placed on the body, one next to each wound. He rephotographed each of the wounds, now numbered, with a Polaroid CU-5. He measured all the wounds and then, speaking into the pedal-activated mike, recorded his observations of the length, depth, and location of each wound by number.

"Thirty-seven cuts," he said. "None on the back."

While he had gently probed the wounds for depth, he double-checked by dissecting into them.

I had come into the morgue feeling tense. Now, as Choudhary with meticulous care went about his work, paradoxically I started to relax. The methodical persistence of his gloved hands was soothing. My urgency melted away in the face of Choudhary's unhurried precision. He had a reverence for the human body that many people would have found surprising.

They would believe, since his job required him to cut up bodies, that he was disrespecting them. But I knew he had a deep admiration for the human machine, and I'd come to feel like he did. I was not repelled by an autopsy any longer but awed, filled with amazement at the complex body that usually worked so well.

I had noticed that Choudhary himself looked very tired. His dark skin was gray. He was slender and his wrists were thin. He was the kind of thin person who was not weak, though, rather stripped down to muscle and sinew, with no fat. I had seen him turn large cadavers himself when his diener was busy; he was very strong. For him to be so exhausted, he must not only have worked many hours but also be emotionally affected by what was happening—as he had said, the "preventable" deaths. Here was a doctor who had no living patients, and yet had deep compassion.

The opening of the body continued. Dr. Choudhary freed the whole front of the rib cage and lifted it off the body. The organs underneath were exposed like an anatomy textbook, except that there were gelatinous clots of blood in several places. Choudhary began to rummage in the entrails.

How horrified Schermerhorn would have been at this indignity!

The heart was intact, unwounded, and according to Choudhary quite healthy.

Choudhary slit the aorta lengthwise and showed me the inside. Stripes of fatty deposits were clearly visible. "But that's not bad for a man of his age," Choudhary said. "I see fat in the arteries of twenty-year-olds." Of the lungs he said, "This man took very good care of himself."

That's everybody else's observation, too.

I had long since blocked the smells of the room from my mind. Also, sheer exhaustion of the sense of smell took over and was a blessing. After a while you simply didn't notice the odors anymore. It was harder to block the sounds. There was less casual chatter today than usual. The comments, the requests, "Get that tray over here," "Where's my methylene blue?" "Somebody plug in the saw," were more somber than I remembered. There were the sounds of the bone saws, metal clanks as instruments dropped into basins, the repeated surflike sigh of rubber wheels as a gurney went out or another came in. Possibly the worst were the wet sounds: the constant gargle of running water carrying fluids down the table gutters, the squashy slap of organs dropped into scales for weighing, and the liquid sucking of flesh as organs deeply nestled were pulled out of body cavities.

None of the autopsies I had witnessed before had been of famous people. None in fact had been of people I had known or even known of before they died. I hadn't known Dr. Schermerhorn in person, but I'd seen pictures of him over the years and in a couple of interviews on television. That made his corpse, emptied of organs by Dr. Choudhary, all the more poignant. Like everybody, I always wondered at an autopsy where the spark of life had gone—where was that human spirit? The eternal mystery was more mysterious today, when I knew of the man and had heard his ideas.

And the mystery of Dr. Schermerhorn himself had not been solved. Saint or sinner? When Dr. Choudhary finished and turned away to let the diener close up, I felt even more emphatically how little I understood the man.

"Blood loss," Choudhary said, with a small smile at the diener, who was now holding a curved sewing needle with a yard of thick black thread attached.

I said, "I'm sorry, Doctor, but the wounds all look so small—are they really enough to kill him?"

"Amply. They are indeed small individually. You're looking for a knife with a blade not more than three-quarters of an inch wide. About four inches long. Like a paring knife."

"I'm afraid we've already found it, Doctor."

"Afraid?"

"It was right there at the scene and doesn't have any physical evidence left on it. It was in a self-cleaning oven. Tell me more about the blood loss."

"A few of these cuts have severed small arteries. When I say small arteries, I mean like this one on the nose, the lateral nasal." He pointed. I winced, thinking how much that cut, right into the side of the nose, must have hurt. Choudhary went on. "The frontal, over the eye here. And the digital." He showed me the hand, with two cuts deep enough to go all the way through.

"The killer got the anterior tibial, which must have bled a lot. And of course he cut lots of veins."

"The arteries would have bled more than veins?"

"Arteries are under more pressure than veins. An artery the same size as a vein will bleed more. They spurt with each heartbeat."

"But these were small arteries?"

"They would have bled a lot but a smaller quantity than large ones naturally. They would have bled and bled and not stopped bleeding."

"So the killer could have cut larger arteries that would have bled faster if he had wanted to?"

"Of course. The femoral, for instance. Here, the brachial under the arm. Or he could have cut Dr. Schermerhorn's throat and got the carotid."

"Which would have killed him swiftly."

"Yes."

I said, "Therefore, Schermerhorn's death—was it quick, do you think?"

"No."

"How long?"

"Possibly as much as an hour."

"Intentionally long?"

"I would certainly say so."

I shivered. "Would this, uh, careful process, making it take a long time, have required medical knowledge?"

"Not much. Most people have an idea where the biggest arteries are. Not exactly, maybe, but if they wanted to draw the death out, they'd know not to cut the throat, or slash the wrists, or stab the heart, of course."

"When do you think he died?"

"There is cognac still in his stomach. The stomach empties in two to five hours. Some peas—the skins—are still visible in the stomach, but most of the dinner has moved on. He was about five or six hours into the digestion process."

"All right. He ate dinner at eight o'clock."

"Then between one and two A.M. perhaps."

Dr. Choudhary threw his gloves into the discard bin with a sharp flap, which I recognized as typical of doctors. *Do they teach that in med school?*

Dr. Choudhary's hands were delicate. They didn't show his strength. They were very clean and damp looking. The hands of pathologists resemble the hands of dishwashers in restaurants.

"Dr. Choudhary, tell me something about these heat deaths. If an elderly person in a hot apartment took a cold shower several times a day, would it help?"

"It would probably save his life."

"I thought so. It would cool him down—"

"Especially if he did not dry off afterward. The evaporation cools the skin."

"And they don't do it," I said, "because we've all been told by our elders that if we get wet and don't dry off we'll get pneumonia."

"Very likely. And they're old and more afraid of pneumonia than the young would be."

"I've been thinking a lot about the voice of authority lately."

"It can be quite pernicious," said Choudhary dryly.

Choudhary walked me to the door of the autopsy suite. The hall was jammed with cops, gurneys, and MEs. I said,

"Thanks for getting to him now. I know you've been rushed off your feet."

"No problem. I am sorry about the crowd."

"I don't mind the crowd. I do mind the smell."

"Oh, this is nothing. Most of these bodies have been dead a day or two. There are a great many human beings out there in our beautiful Chicago, Detective Folkestone, who have nobody worrying about why they haven't been heard from. Nobody is asking why they haven't been seen since Friday. Think about how it will be here on Monday or Tuesday when the police start bringing in people who've been dead four or five days."

Four

I have found little that is "good" about human beings on the whole. In my experience most of them are trash, no matter whether they publicly subscribe to this or that ethical doctrine or to none at all.

— SIGMUND FREUD

CHAPTER 28

I HAD ALL the car windows rolled down, having climbed over to the passenger side and pushed that one down manually. It was a quarter of nine in the morning and already eighty-seven degrees. The city air blowing in through the windows made me hotter instead of cooler. I might as well have been in a clothes dryer with a load of hot wet washing. Besides, I was driving under the El and dust kept sifting into the car. If I chomped my teeth down they gritted. But rolling the windows up was not an option. I'd tried that and could hardly breathe.

As I slid toward the curb at State and Lake, Ollie Park was waiting for me, head bent over something, looking like a woodchuck eating a root. When I stopped, I could see he had his cell phone held close to his mouth and was speaking into it urgently. Predictably, he was wearing his wrinkled tan chinos and a white polo shirt. Mr. Average. What was it with him, this antagonistic relationship with clothing? Was it intentional? Then again, what business was it of mine?

I heard him say to the phone, "I don't see why it should take so long. In surgery, they'd get it back in a few minutes."

Then he looked up, caught sight of me, said, "Yeah, I'll call back later," and slammed his phone closed.

I watched him slouch over and slip sideways into the car. "Trouble?" I asked.

"What? No, just life." He shrugged and pulled the car door shut.

⚒

"DETECTIVES FOLKESTONE AND PARK, ma'am," I said. The small, eager little woman opened the front door wide.

"Oh, yes! Come in! I'm Henry's mother."

Henry Rollins stood behind the woman, tall enough to look right over her fluffy hair, his big head moving back and forth as if he were denying everything anybody could ask him. But I had seen him doing that at Hawthorne House, too, the head ticking metronomically for an hour at a time, so I didn't think he was expressing negative thoughts about me personally.

Henry said, "Gruesome."

The door opened directly into the living room, with just a waterproof mat and bentwood coat rack to mark the entryway, the mat carefully placed to receive wet shoes. Mrs. Rollins shooed Park and me into the living room, where two men were standing.

"This is Henry's daddy. You must have met him at the reunion. And this is Henry's brother."

"Good afternoon," Park and I mumbled together, while I wondered, don't they have names of their own?

"And—let's see—I told you I'm Henry's mama, of course." The woman uttered in a social voice. "Let's all sit down, shall we?"

I crossed the room toward a straight-backed dark wooden chair that would give me some height. "Ah-ah-ah!" Mrs. Rollins said, "Henry's chair," and she waved me away from it, ushering Ollie and me to a brown velvet sofa. The sofa fabric wasn't as soft as it looked. Its velvet fibers stood up straight and coarse and bristly and stuck right through my thin pants fabric into my thighs. The armrests were oil darkened where hands had rested. The floor showed a track of worn nap in the beige wall-to-wall carpeting. A flattened path went in a circle all the way around a brown ottoman that stood in the very middle of the floor, too isolated from the other furniture to be a footrest for the sofa or any of the four mismatched chairs. Everything looked as if it had been in the same spot for thirty years, and respectability lay over it all like a fine dust. Mrs. Rollins sat in a gray-pink upholstered chair. Henry sat in the wooden chair that Mrs. Rollins had kept clear. Two fat bars of light from the 9:00 A.M. sun came through the two east windows and unerringly picked out the shabbiest spots on the carpet to lay their bright trapezoids.

"So you've met our Henry," Mrs. Rollins said brightly.

"Yes," I said, bemused by Mrs. Rollins's ditzy manner. If she lived in my house she'd make me crazy in half a day. Didn't she realize this was a murder investigation? I said, "Your husband must have told you about what happened."

"Oh, he did. He did. How sad, that poor Dr. Schermerhorn being killed like that." Her pleasant face mimed sadness, not very successfully. After a couple of seconds it snapped back into a smile of social neutrality.

I said, "Did you like him?"

"Why, of *course* I liked him. That man was a healer."

"Did he heal your son?" I winced at the challenging way the question had come out. I hadn't meant it to be quite that confrontational, but I was getting more than a little impatient. From the tail of my eye, I saw Park shift uneasily.

"Why, Dr. Schermerhorn did the best he could. Autism is a terrible disease and a stubborn enemy."

"Uh. So you feel that when Henry left Hawthorne House he was better than when he entered it?"

Suddenly, Henry's father spoke. He was sitting almost invisibly still in a corner of the room and I jumped in surprise. "He *was* better. It cost us thousands of dollars, but it helped Henry."

The man's mouth slammed shut. He certainly hadn't been Mr. Conviviality at the mansion, either.

Ollie had that better-change-the-subject look on his face.

He said, "Henry, have you remembered anything happening in the night? Did you get up at all?"

"Um—um—" said Henry.

"Did you hear sounds? People arguing?"

"Arachnida, arachnida, duplication, duplication, duplication—"

"Five words, Mother!" Mr. Rollins said to Mrs. Rollins.

Henry hit his knees hard, first the right knee with the right fist, then the left knee with the left fist, in time with the syllables of his words. Neither of his parents asked him to stop.

"We don't want to upset Henry," Mrs. Rollins explained.

"Did *you* hear anything, Mr. Rollins?"

"Already told you. We were both asleep."

Park said, "You might have half waked. You might have heard something and thought you dreamed it. People quite often remember things later that they never consciously noticed. You know—when there isn't so much pressure. At the time, everyone was quite shocked by what had happened. So you might have thought of something since. On reflection." He was overexplaining, of course, but being less abrupt than I would have been.

Mr. Rollins said nothing, just shook his head.

I asked, "So you spent a lot of money on Henry's treatment?"

"Not that we couldn't accept Henry the way he was, you understand," Mrs. Rollins said, as Henry went on hitting himself. "God only gives you what you can bear."

"But still, Henry was autistic?"

"Well, of course. It was very sad. But he was the task God gave us. Our privilege. We are better people for having Henry. We all know how grateful we should be that we ourselves don't have a mental problem to bear. For instance, William is a better person than he would have been if Henry had been perfectly healthy."

William? Who is William? I realized that he must be the

brother, sitting in a low olive-colored chair, quietly watching us. His hands were folded in his lap.

I studied the room while pretending to give my attention to the four Rollinses, and noticed that there was nothing breakable here. No pottery bowls or china birds or glass tables or vases of flowers. The chairs and the coffee table had thick, solid legs and the sofa, so far as I could see, was virtually legless. The lamps were brass or some kind of gold-colored metal, although of course the lightbulbs would be glass. Other than the lightbulbs and the window panes, there was nothing fragile in this room. There were four photographs on the end table. One of two boys at a very young age—preschool maybe—the other three of Henry alone. None of the photos was glass covered.

At Hawthorne House, Henry had thrown a chair into a wall.

"We have all given a bit of ourselves to Henry," his mother said. "That is our blessing. Fortunately, William has never caused us a moment's trouble."

"Are you the younger or older brother, William?"

Mrs. Rollins said, "Older. One year older. From the moment that we realized there was a problem with Henry—that was when Henry was about two and William was three—William has always been there for Henry. Even when Henry broke William's toys. William was patient with a wisdom beyond his years. Someday, when we're gone, William will carry on for us."

"Is that right, William?"

William smiled and nodded.

Apparently trying to distract Henry from hitting himself, Mrs. Rollins said, "Henry, would you like some ice cream? I have rocky road."

Henry didn't answer.

"I would," said William.

"It's too early in the morning," his mother said.

William nodded. "Yes, that's true." Henry stopped muttering and hitting his own thighs. He jumped up, pounced forward and struck the ottoman several blows with his right hand.
I could see dust motes fly up into the rays of bright sunlight.

"We need to keep Henry fed, you see," Mrs. Rollins said,
"because he gets irritated when he's hungry. And he only likes
just certain foods."

"Sweet food," Mr. Rollins said.

"Lavish," said Henry.

Henry hit the ottoman a vigorous blow with both big hands
interlocked into one huge fist like a bowling ball. Satisfied
with the *whump,* he stood up straight, held his arms at his
sides toy-soldier fashion, and marched around the ottoman

"He has so few things to enjoy," his father said.

Mrs. Rollins paid no attention to Henry's marching, which
settled down to a steady "Babes in Toyland" metronomic
tramp, round and round and round, knees lifted high.

"Can we go back to the night of the murder?" I asked. "Are
you sure Henry wasn't up in the night?"

"Absolutely certain."

"But you wouldn't know, if you were asleep, would you?"

"Why would he get up?" Mr. Rollins asked huffily.

"Well, to go to the bathroom, maybe."

"Oh. Well."

"Does he wake you to take him usually, or go by himself?"

Mrs. Rollins said, "My son can go to the bathroom by himself *perfectly well*!"

"But in a strange place—"

"Not so strange," Mr. Rollins said. "He had lived there, you
know."

*I do know. That's exactly my point. And not a point on
Henry's side. This Rollins guy is just argumentative, it seems.*
"So if he got up, Mr. Rollins, and you were sleeping, he could
leave the room without your knowing."

"But *I* was in a strange place," Rollins said, as if pouncing on my argument, "and therefore I slept lightly and I would have heard him."

"Are you sure? You did imply that you were sound asleep." I saw a brief glance pass between Mr. Rollins and Mrs. Rollins, but neither changed facial expression.

"Of course I'm sure. And if you have any idea that he was skulking around killing that doctor, you're absolutely wrong."

Mrs. Rollins uttered a little squeak.

That doctor. Hmmm.

Henry marched around the ottoman, his big feet clumping on the worn carpet. Around and around. And around and around.

I said, "Henry, did you get up in the night?"

"Duplication," he said loudly, not looking at me or the Rollinses.

Henry marched right through our conversation, right between me and the other three Rollinses. If you had a clown juggling meat cleavers in the middle of the room, it could hardly have been more distracting. I felt my temper simmering. I told myself Henry was not trying to bother me personally. He wasn't capable of understanding how rude he was. *No, he doesn't care how rude he is. He doesn't give a rip about the rest of us, his parents included. God only knows what they've done for him over the years, and he just plain doesn't care.*

I almost screamed "Sit down!" at him. He was a big, grown man, and if he couldn't control himself, he needed to get out of the way. Then I thought, maybe I'm the one who ought to control myself. My hands had closed to fists and I unclenched them.

Okay, okay. Get on with it. Be professional.

I asked the parents a dozen questions: How had they heard of Hawthorne House? What had their earlier doctors told them about Henry's condition? What medication was he taking now? What did they expect him to get out of the reunion?

What had he said about it when he got home? My questions were all over the board, but with cautious, conservative people who hide their feelings, sometimes the best way to get a handle on them is to probe a little bit all over. None of the answers gave me any sense of Henry specifically and what he might be capable of. I believed Henry might be violent if he were provoked, but I didn't know what kinds of things provoked him, except maybe not having ice cream, and ice cream had been served Friday night. I'd seen the menu.

I was getting desperate for understanding when Henry broke my train of thought by shouting, "Awaaaay!" and then running out the front door. William got up immediately and went after him. Both Rollinses sat still, unperturbed, so although I worried that Henry might run into traffic, I sat still, too. I took very great care not to sigh audibly with my relief that he was gone.

"Since Henry has left," I said, "is there anything more that you can tell me about his condition? Anything you'd feel uncomfortable saying in front of him?"

"No," said Mr. Rollins.

Mrs. Rollins said, "Well, yes. We're well aware he acts very strange. People stare at him, you know. Even more so now that he's older. When he does something sudden, like yelling or suddenly running. Flapping his arms. You expect children to behave impulsively, but not adults."

"Does it bother you when they stare?"

"Oh, no. We have to take responsibility. It's partly my fault."

"What is?"

"Henry's condition."

"Why? Do you mean there was something you did while you were pregnant, or—?"

"Dr. Schermerhorn explained that when Henry was born we already had William. And I must have resented having to take care of a second child. Two so close together. It's true, you know, that we had planned to have one and then wait a couple of years and then decide whether we wanted another. But Henry happened. So I must have resented it, and I withheld love. We weren't aware of it. It was," she lowered her voice, "subconscious."

"But surely you've heard since then that there's a physical cause for autism."

"I *have* heard that. But what causes the physical cause? When he was just a toddler, he would arch his back and turn away from me and scream, and I *did* resent it. I know I did!"

"But by then he was already showing that he was autistic."

Mrs. Rollins folded her arms. "I don't want to talk about this anymore. It wouldn't be right for me to try to get rid of my burden. We resented having to take care of a second child and we neglected him. Emotionally. We didn't know we were doing it, but we must have. And we resented that he was difficult. But we've overcome all that now."

Mr. Rollins said, "We're righting the balance, you see. Caring for him with unconditional love."

"Fortunately, it's all been for the best," Mrs. Rollins said. "For all of us. William has been just as good as gold. Never a complaint. Even as a child, never a complaint."

Park and I thanked the Rollinses and left. I drew a deep breath as the front door closed behind me. Outside on the lawn, Henry marched around a big copper beech tree, hitting it with a stick. William stood guard.

Henry said, "Fagus sylvatica." I remembered it phonetically, and just on a whim looked up the Latin name for copper beech on the Net later. Henry was absolutely right.

"Well, it was nice to meet you, William," I said.

"I hope you find out who killed Dr. Schermerhorn, Detective. He was a good man."

"Did you know him?"

"No. Never met him. He didn't like relatives to visit Hawthorne House."

Henry said, "Fagus sylvatica."

"Didn't your parents ever visit Henry there?"

"A very few times. They were allowed to bring him home a few times. Twice a year, actually."

"Your dad seemed a little more willing to talk just now than he was back at Hawthorne House."

"Oh, it probably wasn't Hawthorne House. He doesn't talk so much around Henry."

"Is he worried that talking about him in front of him is rude?"

"I don't think that's it. I think he feels funny about talking a lot when Henry can't talk much at all. We try not to do things Henry can't do."

"Like—"

"Movies, restaurants, like that."

"So what is your work, William?"

"I'm a cab driver."

"That's great. Chicago has a great cab system, or so they keep telling me. Medallions are getting pretty costly though, aren't they?"

"Oh, unbelievably expensive. Plus these new tourist trolleys are really killing our downtown business."

"I have a friend who drives a cab," Park said, "and he says he has to work a twelve-hour day to make ends meet. He's got two kids to raise."

"I don't have kids. It would be hard for me to get married, what with Henry to take care of. Mostly I work nights because my folks work days and somebody has to be here with Henry all the time."

"You seem to have given up a lot to help him," I said.

"Oh, absolutely not! Not comparatively! Look at what he's lost. Or not lost, exactly. Never had. He has no friends, no job, no hobbies even. He can scarcely talk in a sensible way. How would it be for somebody as blessed as I am to turn his back on his brother?"

"But you didn't cause his problem."

"That's not the point. He has so little and I have so much. Aren't we obligated to help the less fortunate? And how much more so when the unfortunate person is your own brother?"

"It's very nice to hear that you love your brother."

"He's my hero. Look what he's had to bear. Nobody understands how hard it is to be Henry."

I YELPED AS I lowered myself gingerly into the roasting-hot car seat. The heat burned right through my thin slacks. After about thirty teeth-gritting seconds of getting myself accustomed to the pain, I asked, "What did you think of the Rollins family?"

"I sure don't think Henry killed Schermerhorn," Park said. "Not unless Schermerhorn was pounded to death. Not so sure his father wouldn't do it, though."

"What about that? Let's take it seriously. Say a couple of the parents saw this reunion as their chance to make Schermerhorn pay. Say Bettelby and Rollins Sr. get together, maybe even with Helene Tausche. Bettelby lets them in the front door. They go to Schermerhorn's room, knock him out and take him to the basement."

"So Mr. Rollins is wearing Henry's shoes and gets blood on one of them? That doesn't make sense."

"He wore Henry's shoes by mistake? They were in the same room, in the dark. Or he thought it didn't matter, since Henry is too autistic to be suspected."

"Mmm. How'd the blood get on April's sleeve?"

"Helene Tausche had some blood on her she wasn't aware of. She went to April's room to check on her. Remember they've never been apart in fifteen years. She inadvertently got blood on April's shirt."

"And Ben Goodspeed? Of course, his mother."

"Yes. But did Jeffrey Clifford go with them, or did his father slip into Hawthorne House, too?"

Ollie said, "I can't say the idea is impossible. Makes for a lot of coming and going in the night, though."

"Well, somebody sure came and went in the night."

Ollie took out his cell phone, flipped it open, punched in two numbers, held his finger over the third number, then flipped the phone closed, cutting off the call. I watched and said nothing.

I turned on the ignition. When Park still didn't offer to explain his actions, I said, "But what did you think of Henry himself? How did you feel about him?"

"How did I *feel* about him? You've been hanging around with shrinks too much."

"Undoubtedly. But tell me anyway."

"He was pissing me off."

"Jeez, me too. I was furious at him."

"Me too."

"And what I was thinking, we were only there maybe thirty minutes. His parents have to put up with it twenty-four/seven."

Park said, "That's true. And his brother."

"How do they do it?"

"Love."

"Right. Love and guilt."

I put the car in gear. Park turned on the radio. There was the tail end of an ad for mattresses, which would be at your door within twelve hours of your call. Plus they'd take away your old mattress, completely free of charge. Then the news came on.

"The figures are still being compiled on the number of dead from the city's most severe heat wave in recorded history. Mayor Daley is taking issue with the numbers given out by Chief Medical Examiner Donoghue. In a statement at a news conference this morning the mayor said—" There was a brief moment of dead air. Then a hum. Audiotape rolled, the sound quality poorer than the announcer's studio voice, the mayor's Chicago accent and tortured syntax immediately recognizable. "We have to look at the statistics that people die every day in Chicago. You cannot claim that everybody who has died in the last eight or nine days dies of heat. Then everybody that dies in the summer dies of heat."

Park said, "Jeez! He just doesn't get it, does he?"

"No, and I'll bet the announcer isn't going to point that out."

The announcer didn't, but he read a remark from the medical examiner, Donoghue. "The mayor is entitled to raise questions. We would be delighted to have the figures checked."

Park punched the radio off.

"It's the excess deaths," I said. "It's not everybody who dies during a heat wave. It's how many *extra* people died during the heat wave."

"No shit, Sherlock."

"I suppose he thinks that a city that has four hundred heat deaths will look a lot better run than one that has seven hundred heat deaths."

"Like that's what to focus on. Time like this."

I said, "I'm glad we aren't going to be called to one of those today. Dead body in a hot room for a week. Jeez!"

"Yeah. It'd be silly putty."

"Gross, Ollie." I handed him a folder. "Here. Find me April Tausche's home address. It's in Evanston someplace."

"Okay."

I said, "You want to make notes on the Rollins interview while I drive?" He pulled out a pad of paper. "Where's your laptop?"

"It's on the brink."

"You mean it's on the blink."

"Right. I'm gonna see if Jason can fix it for me."

CHAPTER 29

THE HEAVY DOOR to the corridor that led to the secretary's sanctum that led to the anteroom that led to the office of the mayor closed behind Gordon Fassbinder and Superintendent of Police Elmer Ramirez. Fassbinder was sweating, even though the air-conditioning in these suites was state-of-the-art.

"Laughingstock!" Fassbinder grumbled. "People don't actually use that word anymore, do they?"

"It doesn't matter. Chicago is not a laughingstock," said Ramirez. As Fassbinder brightened slightly, he said, "Chicago is an object of pity."

"Whatever. Get onto it."

"I know."

"I don't understand why Donoghue can't reclassify some of the causes of death. I mean, how can he be so sure?"

Superintendent Ramirez said, "He's the ME. That's how he can be sure."

"This couldn't come at a worse time. The urban beautification project. The City that Works project."

"Not a good time for the people who died, either."

Fassbinder shot him a sour look. "Get started."

Police Superintendent Ramirez, who had been called to the mayor's office for the early morning meeting, went back to his own office and sent for his chief of detectives south, Polly Kelly.

In Chicago, the police department does not issue a "Forthwith!" as does New York. The boss ordinarily says something like, "My office immediately."

Kelly was there immediately, which from her office to his, two floors up in the same building, was four minutes.

"Kelly! I've just come from the mayor."

"Yes, boss," she said grimly. Under these circumstances, she could well imagine Da Mare. Da Horror. In 1979, the city had been hit by a smothering blizzard. The mayor at the time, Michael Bilandic, well liked until then, failed to get the snow cleared as fast as Chicagoans thought he should. He was out in the next election, losing to a previous underdog, Jane Byrne.

"So what do we do?" Polly Kelly asked.

"He wants other news to, ah, rise to the top. You've got the highest-profile murder in years right now in the Second."

"Dr. Schermerhorn?"

"Exactly. Solve it. Get the story into the press fast."

She winced. "From what I've seen, there's not a lot of evidence—"

"Well, look harder! Do it now!"

"Yes, boss."

She went to her office and sent a "my office immediately" to Area Commander Tommy Hasseen.

I TOOK ONTARIO west to the feeder ramp onto the Kennedy Expressway. For some reason, you have to be in the right lane to get the ramp going left, which is south on the expressway, and the left lane to go right, which is north. I've studied the land around the road for years, trying to figure out why IDOT—the Illinois Department of Transportation, not IDIOT—thought this would be a reasonable way to design the road. Never have found out why.

My elderly car was chugging a bit. When winter came

again, this poor old Jeep was not likely to survive. I didn't care about its looks, but any car I owned had to start every time.

The sun was in the east, behind me so that I wasn't blinded, and in fact as I turned north the hot rays mostly hit Park, who was riding in the passenger seat. Even so, sweat trickled from my hairline into my eyes. The sweat itched and made me feel unclean.

"Ollie, what's the matter?"

"Nothing's the matter."

I negotiated my way past two taxis amusing themselves by running side by side.

"Ollie, there *is* something bothering you."

"Leave it alone. I'll tell you when—when I'm ready."

"Jeez! Ollie, don't do this macho thing on me. We've been partners forever. It's Jason, isn't it? What's he done now?"

"It's not Jason!"

I slammed my hand down on the wheel. "You make me so damn mad!"

"Watch where you're going! You nearly sideswiped that Nissan. I could ask you the same thing, you know. What's the matter with you?"

"Me?"

"Yeah. You walked out of there like you wanted to dice 'em and fry them."

"Henry was making me crazy. We just talked about that. He was making you crazy, too."

"I said 'them.' You were mad at the family, Emily."

I brushed my hand across my eyelids, where some of the sweat had accumulated. "Okay," I said. "I admit it. I'm mad at the whole damned lot of them."

"I feel sorry for them."

"Well, bully for you. But just look at the situation. They've got a child, a grown-up child, who's got a mental problem. Or a brain problem. Whatever the hell autism is, it's here, it's a *given* in their lives, right? What the parents have done with it is cripple the entire family. Their whole lives revolve around dealing with it. They can't sit peacefully in their living room. When they go to work, the older child stays home to watch his brother. When he goes to work, they're home. Between the three of them, they have three jobs, but you can't see the income in the house or the furniture or their clothing. They're being bled financially by Henry's expenses for whatever—"

"His medication is probably covered by insurance."

"We both know insurance never covers everything. Doesn't cover baby-sitting him. Probably doesn't cover all his therapy. And it surely doesn't cover hours of the family's labor. But say the parents want to do the caregiving, or feel they have to. They've roped poor William into the work too."

"He obviously wants to help."

"You can't tell one way or the other. You can't really tell whether he's just being goody-goody or really feels that way. He's probably never in his whole life been allowed to express any resentment of Henry."

"Maybe."

"He doesn't know any better. He's been brought *up* to want to help, goddamn it!"

"In a way, that's very nice, isn't it? Does his soul good. Don't we get a kind of blessing from doing good for the less fortunate?"

"I can't believe you! Would you want your Jason to be tied to the care of a younger brother *for the rest of his life*?"

"Well, I wouldn't want him to, no. But what if it had happened? Maybe *he* would want to."

"William is acting this way, all willingly self-sacrificing, out of guilt. He's healthy and Henry isn't, so he feels he has to make up for the imbalance. It's grotesque, and if his parents brainwashed him into this, it's wrong."

"It may not be for the rest of his life."

"If things go as they usually do, the parents will die first and William will be left with the full care of Henry. William already has no wife, no family, and probably not even the job he might have wanted if he didn't need to be home all the damn time."

"That's true."

"I'm just saying that he hasn't been given a choice in this. He's stuck. If he walks away today and starts a different life—like, say, moves to California, marries, has four lovely children, and works in TV production—he's still always going to know his parents back home are saddled with Henry. If he's a sincere man who loves his parents, that's going to gnaw at him."

"They could put Henry in some sort of group home, I suppose."

"Sure. I don't know how disabled the patient has to be and how much is paid for by the state, though. In fact, I think there's some sort of scale based on the parent's income. As a matter of fact, we ought to find out."

"Why?"

"It may relate to how resentful these parents are of Schermerhorn, if Schermerhorn took their money and didn't help their child and now they have to go on paying for more treatment. But my point is that Henry's parents are dumping on William."

"Well, they may have to," Ollie said. "They may not have the money for private institutional care. And Henry's their *child,* after all. They probably love him and want to take care of him."

"It's not fair to William."

"Life isn't fair."

"I *hate* when people say that. Most of the time they're trying to excuse the present system or get out of thinking of answers to hard questions. Don't interrupt," I said as Park started to huff and puff. "I don't mean you specifically. Okay. Just tell me this. Does Henry appreciate all this self-sacrifice?"

Park was silent for several seconds. "Well, you can't really know for sure."

"Damn right you can't. Because you have no idea what Henry is thinking. One thing is clear, though. He's not thinking like the rest of us. You can't really be sure he even cares."

Park sighed and leaned against the car door, putting the back of his head toward the sun. "Do I believe Henry appreciates it? He's surely one of the more seriously affected autistics we've seen. No, I guess I really don't think he does. He doesn't understand what life outside his family is all about."

"And the way everybody's life is mortgaged to his life makes me hopping mad."

"In that case, you'd better let me do the talking when we get to the Tausches' place."

IT WAS A PILLOWY APARTMENT. The Tausches' address turned out to be a three-flat, one on each floor, with the words "TAUSCHE SECOND FLOOR" written in curly letters in dark blue ink on a pink card next to a bell on the front porch.

The house was typically Evanston, built around 1900 of narrow wooden siding, with a big wraparound porch. The steps leading up to the front door were wooden too, once painted dark green, now badly worn by foot traffic and scraped from snow shoveling in winter, so that in many places the underlying boards showed through. Except for the worndown green steps, the house was painted white.

As Chicago grew during the 1860s, the first suburb north was Evanston, a refuge to which a great many of the rich fled to escape the noise and crowding downtown. The Tausche place was certainly not a mansion, but apparently had been a good-size middle-class home before being broken up into apartments.

I had called ahead. April's mother was expecting us and came down to open the front door. She led us back up the creaking stairs. A round-bodied woman who looked about sixty, wearing a flower-sprigged white dress, she gave the impression of a pillow, soft and yielding.

"Detective Oliver Park and Detective Emily Folkestone, ma'am," Park said.

"Come in, please," she said, even though we were already inside. "I'm Mrs. Helene Tausche, of course. I'm terribly sorry I missed seeing you when I picked up April yesterday. You two sit right there. I'll just get the cake and coffee."

Ollie and I exchanged a glance, but said nothing. Mrs. Tausche resembled April so closely that when April came in from the kitchen, I had the strange sensation of Mrs. Tausche returning, having just stepped into the kitchen to shed twenty years. We knew April was forty-one years old, despite her unformed, childlike quality. A cream-color cat followed her in, making figure eights around her ankles.

Park said to April, "Hello, Ms. Tausche."

April swung around, looking for the person Park was addressing.

"I mean you, April."

"Oh, April. Me."

"How are you?"

In a monotone, she answered, "Very well, thank you. And how are you?"

"I'm fine."

"This is Matilda." The cat, I now saw, was cream with a hint of cinnamon. She had no tail, and the back legs appeared longer than the front legs, making the rump a bit higher than the front of the cat, kind of like a jacked-up car. Her head was broader than most cats', but despite her distinctive appearance, I thought she was a truly beautiful animal. Her fur was extremely dense, and looked as if an outer coat of coarse hair lay over an inner coat of downy hair.

"She must be hot in this weather," I commented, but April either didn't hear or didn't care to answer. Instead, she turned slowly around and around.

Park continued to chat with April as she turned. She spoke now and then, although after her first preprogrammed responses, she was at a loss for content, responding in monosyllables, and he carried most of the conversation. I was free to study the apartment. One of the reasons I had insisted on these home interviews is that homes reveal people as little else can. The overstuffed chairs were upholstered in flower prints, with ruffled skirts. Ruffled white Priscilla curtains, drawn back with ruffled swags, hung over the windows. An air conditioner sighed ineffectually in one of the windows, stirring the fabric slightly. White puffy lampshades sat like barristers' wigs on fat-bellied china lamps. Big white ruffled pillows reclined on the sofa. On the whole, I thought, it was like finding yourself dropped into a whipped-cream pie.

And it irritates the hell out of me!

It was just as well that Oliver was doing the interview.

Mrs. Tausche entered with a girlish giggle and a tray of little plates, cups, and saucers, a larger plate with a crumb-topped coffee cake, another similar plate with another cake that looked identical to the first, a coffee pot, a little cream pitcher, a sugar bowl and a bowl of—heavens above! I thought—whipped cream. No, two bowls of whipped cream. Park jumped up, took the heavily laden tray from the woman, and set it on the coffee table.

"This sure looks delicious, Mrs. Tausche!" Oliver said, smiling cheerily.

April came and plumped herself down on a chair near me.

I studied April closely but saw no sign that the woman was uneasy in the presence of cops. *Is it possible she doesn't understand who we are?* April gazed avidly at the food, ignoring me and Ollie. For all my hard-won experience in assessing suspects, I was at a loss. I could not read April's facial expression, which was a completely vague look upon a soft, moon-shaped face, occasionally altered by a fleeting grimace. Her body language showed no nervousness. I had no sense of April's inner life. If April had lashed out at Dr. Schermerhorn, stabbing him to death, would she feel guilty now? If she felt guilty, would she show it in the ways other people might? If she had as little sense of social proprieties as it seemed, was there any point in watching for nonverbal cues the way I usually did? There probably was no point in asking the usual questions in the usual way.

What do I do now? This is no way to conduct an interview.

April grabbed at the coffee cake nearest her with her hand, breaking off a chunk. Her mother appeared not to notice, but bent over and cut three huge pieces from the other cake, slipped them quickly onto plates, and handed one to me, one to Ollie, and placed one on the table in front of a puffy footstool.

By now April had taken up a spoon and was scooping whipped cream out of one of the bowls into her mouth. Her mother placed a large spoon in the second bowl and passed it to me. "For your cake. Or your coffee, if you like. In Austria, they call it coffee *mit schlagobers.*"

Mrs. Tausche settled softly onto the puffy footstool near the coffee table, casting a glance at April, who now broke off another piece of coffee cake with her fingers.

"Of course, we know you weren't at Hawthorne House Saturday night, Mrs. Tausche," Park said. "But we hoped you might have talked with April about it. So that you could help us, uh, understand—"

"Understand what she may have seen but can't tell you, Detective Park?"

"Well, uh. Yes."

"I'm sorry. I didn't mean to interrupt you." Her round cheeks bunched up in a smile. Although very similar to her daughter, her hair was thinner and much lighter, leavened with white streaks, while April's was a pinkish tan. Mrs. Tausche's pale eyes were alive with intelligence. April's were avid but flitting.

"You want me to interpret for her, in other words, Detective Park. You don't have to beat about the bush, you know. Parents of autistic children are usually quite willing to talk about their problems. They deal with them every day, you see. As a matter of fact, most of the parents have spent quite a while at the beginning trying to get their pediatricians or teachers to realize there really *is* a problem. What I'm saying is I'm more likely to tell you all about her, to the point where you don't want to hear any more, than to be upset because you hint at the fact that she's autistic." She smiled again, cocked her head at the plates, saw that Oliver had eaten half of his cake and immediately gave him a second piece.

I looked back at April, whose hands were covered with cake crumbs. April had stopped eating. As I watched she dipped a finger into her whipped cream and lowered it near the floor, where the cat licked it off.

April in fact had actually finished only part of the first chunk of cake she'd taken, and had eaten only a bite of the second. I saw April reach her sticky hand for the other cake, the one her mother had been serving us from. Her mother deftly moved the hand away.

April burst into tears.

Mrs. Tausche said, "April, I'm not going to pay attention to that crying." Then she turned back to Park. "What do you need to know?"

Ollie said, "April's room was near Dr. Schermerhorn's. If the doctor was attacked there, we think there must have been some noises she might have heard."

"That makes sense. She hasn't mentioned any, though."

"Does April sleep soundly?"

April was still crying, but less snuffily. Her mother said, "No."

"Can you ask her what she heard?"

"Not exactly. Put it another way—I can ask her, but she doesn't necessarily—oh, well, let me try. April, did you hear any noises from Dr. S's room in the night?"

"No cake. Wouldn't give me cake."

"Me, April?"

"Dr. S."

"But that was years ago. To teach you. Or was it two nights ago?"

April just shook her head. I said, "They had ice cream, not cake, Friday night." April rubbed at the tears on her cheeks, smearing cake crumbs into the moisture on her pale eyelashes. Her mother patted her shoulder, reassuringly.

"Tie his hands," April said.

A shiver ran down my spine. "Tie whose hands?" I asked.

April didn't answer.

"I think she means back when she was a resident there," Mrs. Tausche said blandly. "There was a boy there at one time who—well, they had to use restraints. He was a danger to the others. He left very soon after that, of course. I'm sorry, but you see how it is; I can't really get specific answers to questions. When she speaks, it's in fragments usually. Her focus is kind of split up. What may sound like a sentence could have two parts that refer to two different things, if you see what I mean."

"Does she mind us talking about her when she's right here?" Park asked.

"No."

"You're very sure."

"When April *doesn't* like something, you can be *very* sure about it."

"I see."

"And I can tell you that if she had heard anything that frightened her in the night, she would have told me. April is very good at complaining."

Park went on. "Was she at all distressed when you brought her home?"

"Not really. She was tensed up and stimming a lot. It had been quite an experience for her, being out on her own."

"Does April get up and wander around in the night?"

"Never. She's mildly afraid of the dark. Cautious of the dark, I might say."

Park questioned Mrs. Tausche, as he and I had agreed, without me intruding. Since I was familiar with his style of interrogation, I recognized the thoroughness under the charm. It was not a one-sided match; Mrs. Tausche was alert and careful. I had the sense of a polite duel going on. A serious, deadly real but slow-motion duel, with soft blows, as if two people were beating each other with loaves of bread.

Park said, "It wasn't really dark. The halls at Hawthorne House were lighted that night. They didn't want anybody falling down the stairs."

"Well, it was a strange place for her," Mrs. Tausche said.

"Of course, not entirely strange. April had lived there for several years."

Mrs. Tausche smiled again. "That was many years ago. No, I don't think she would have gotten up. Not unless she had to go to the bathroom, and even that's unlikely. When she was very little, we taught her not to drink lots of fluids after dinner, because she was wetting her bed every night back then."

"When you say 'we' taught her—is Mr. Tausche around?"

"Well, he's around. But he's not around here. We separated many years ago."

"I'm sorry to hear that."

"It's all right." The woman was smiling *again,* I noticed, surprised. She smiled at quite inappropriate times. "There was a problem we couldn't resolve."

"Would you care to tell me what it was, Mrs. Tausche?"

"We had two other girls, younger than April. My husband

thought I was spending too much time taking care of April—
this was after she left Hawthorne House. He thought I was ne-
glecting Alice and Adele. So he took them, and I kept April."
Another brief smile.

"I see. I have just one or two more questions."

Deflecting this, she said, "Try a little more whipped cream
in your coffee, Detective Park and Miss Folkestone." Before
we could object, she plopped a fat dollop in each cup.

I said, "April, whose hands were tied?"

"Not Matilda," April said. Park and I exchanged a look of
defeat. "Matilda has paws."

Park said to the mother, "Did April like Dr. Schermerhorn?"

Mrs. Tausche said, "Of course she did," at the very moment
April said, "No."

"You didn't, April?" Park asked.

"Yes, you did," said Mrs. Tausche.

"No, no, no," said April. "No, no, no, no, no, no, no, no, no,
no, no." She sprang to her feet and ran away down the hall,
muttering "No, no, no," all the way. They heard a door slam.

"Now see what you did," Mrs. Tausche said. "You upset her."

Park said, "I didn't mean to. We really do have to ask questions, you know, Mrs. Tausche."

"I suppose."

"How long was she in treatment with Dr. Schermerhorn?"

"Seven years."

"Was she better afterward?"

"Of course," said Mrs. Tausche.

I finally spoke. "Mrs. Tausche? Where were you Saturday
night?"

The pale eyes turned toward me. "Right here. Worrying.
Except for the time she was in treatment, April and I have
never spent one single night apart."

CHAPTER 30

"NOT ONE SINGLE NIGHT APART," I said, as we got back into the stifling car. "What are the chances that she dropped in during the night to see how April was doing?"

I can't see anything else in your life, Mrs. Tausche. And if you went back, would you have run into Dr. Schermerhorn, challenged him, been berated and dismissed, and killed him? Was April with you when you killed him?

Ollie said, "Yeah. Let's remember that the back door was unlocked."

"Or April could have let her mother in the front. They could have planned it."

"Can April keep to a plan like that?" Ollie asked. "I don't know."

Very doubtful.

I was not going to jump to conclusions, and I knew only too well we had almost no proof of April's involvement, beyond a very small amount of blood on her sleeve.

I was not a naive, fresh police cadet. I had put in my training time. I had gone through the police academy, with no special allowance made for the fact that I was a woman. I had to carry the same weight as men a foot taller and fifty pounds heavier, run the same distance, climb the same flights of stairs in the same time as the men. I had to qualify with my weapon of choice, and fortunately had the sense to choose a heavy firearm. A lot of women pick a light sidearm not realizing that it's less accurate and they might fail to qualify.

After seven years as a patrol cop, I took the detectives' exam, passed, and was promoted. So far, so good. I loved the idea of actually solving crimes, although there had been quite a lot of that in patrol. Even murders.

As a detective I had been, if I had to say it myself, a real success. I had three commendations in my personnel jacket and was once mentioned by the mayor after an incident when I had killed a man and saved Park's life. I was considered a rising star, although an older cop had told me to be careful. "Old saying," he cautioned me. "Pass them on the way up, pass them on the way down."

"What does that mean? Don't rise too fast?"

"Yup."

However, I believe you can't possibly do too well. Partly, I had done well because I was hardworking. But in my own opinion, it was mainly because I was perfectionistic. So, our inability to pin down what several of our nearest witnesses may have seen was driving me nuts.

"Ollie, you know what? We can't tell from the facial expressions of any of the autistics what they're thinking."

"Well, duh!"

"And we can't tell from their words what they mean. Or even whether they're responding to the question we asked. Look at April Tausche. I am convinced that she saw Dr. Schermerhorn tied to ropes in the basement."

"I think so too."

"But we'll never get a clear usable story from her."

"Duh to that, too. Although some of them are more articulate than others. Jeffrey Clifford, for instance."

"Even he won't be any use at a trial. No lawyer is going to put one of the autistics on the stand. Suppose one of them saw the killer and told us so. They'd still get totally creamed by the defense counsel. And anyhow, you wouldn't be able to be sure that they would confirm what they said before."

"I just hope we get as far as a trial. I'd settle for finding the killer and worrying about the prosecution later."

"Don't let the state's attorney hear you say that."

Ollie said, "They have their problems, we have ours. We've got two hours before we have to be at the Cliffords'," Oliver said. "And it's only twenty minutes away."

"And therefore?"

"Therefore, let's find someplace to get an early lunch."

"Someplace air-conditioned," I added. But what I thought was, *You want to make a call, and you can't do it in the car because I'd hear.*

CHAPTER **31**

HELENE TAUSCHE HAD WALKED the two police detectives down to the front door and then wearily climbed the stairs back to the second floor. From her front window, looking out through the sheer fabric of the Priscilla curtains, she could see the two officers unlock their car, which appeared a bit old and dilapidated. Why lock that kind of car in a quiet neighborhood like this? she wondered. And then she decided that police officers probably locked their cars wherever they were. Habit, or maybe the police rules told them to.

The woman officer, Folkestone, gazed back at the house for half a minute or so while she stood in the street and kept the door open, waiting for the car to cool a little. Mrs. Tausche could not tell whether she could be seen behind the gauzy fabric, but she held still and Folkestone eventually got into the car.

As the car pulled away down Colfax and turned onto Ridge, Helene Tausche sighed. She knew they suspected April. She was well aware of having given mixed signals to the detectives. Part of that was in an intentional effort to present things the way she wanted them to seem. But part was just life itself. Nobody was just one sort of person, all the way through. Life was full of mixed signals, wasn't it? In fact, life was mixed, period, and you often didn't know whether something was a good thing or a bad thing. Not at the time and often not even years later.

Helene was also well aware that she appeared to people to be vague. The little plump, stupid lady who cooks all the time. But she wasn't stupid. She was desperate. And the only way she could keep herself going in this life was to seek comfort. Comfort. A little comfort food and some soft pillows and overstuffed furniture. It was little enough to ask. She had wondered for decades why she couldn't have a normal life like other people. What had she ever done that was so wrong? Why did she deserve this?

When they had placed April in Hawthorne House, with such great hopes for a cure, April was seven and a half. Alice was just two, and a year later Adele would be born. Helene had been sad when Dr. Schermerhorn decreed that they couldn't visit April very often. He only let them take her home two weekends a year, and they could come to Hawthorne House four times a year to take her "out" for the day. That was it, and Helene missed her so. It was sad.

But not an unmixed sadness.

Helene felt a great relief at home, not having to worry about April's tantrums. She no longer had to be on the alert for April getting angry at little Alice and pushing her down. Helene didn't have to be on guard every minute. It was an absolute delight to play with Alice and have Alice hug her and look right into her eyes. Adele, too—even as a tiny infant, Adele was more responsive than April had ever been.

Adele and Alice were just so much more *fun*.

Adele and Alice were wonderful!

That was why Helene knew that Dr. Schermerhorn was correct—she had resented April. The disruption April had caused in their lives made her sick and afraid. April didn't cuddle, didn't respond. She hit the other girls. She turned every holiday or birthday party into a horrible mess, because she didn't want anything to be different. What was an exciting celebration to the other girls was some sort of attack on April. Yes, Helene was angry, just as Dr. Schermerhorn said. The first child often is poorly raised, he said, because the parents aren't ready for it. They resent the change in their previously easy lives and they wish the child would vanish. So maybe she *had* caused April's problems. She was relieved not to have to deal with her own child!

And then after nearly eight years, April came back.

They picked her up at Hawthorne House when she turned fifteen.

It was supposed to be such a happy time. Helene and Jimmy had left Adele and Alice with Jimmy's mother for the day. At Hawthorne House they stopped to chat with Dr. Schermerhorn.

"Don't expect miracles," he snapped at them.

"But you said she was a lot better," Jimmy said.

"Better isn't perfect. Try not to screw her up again."

Helene gasped. Jimmy put his hand on Helene's arm. "But you said—but how should we deal with her? How do we handle her?"

"A little firmness should go a long way," Schermerhorn growled, and he turned his back and went into his office.

The counselor, a young woman named Beth, who had been standing by to help, said to the Tausches, "Let's go to her room and get her suitcase and things."

April was in her room on the second floor, sitting on the bed, which had been stripped. Blue-striped white mattress ticking made the bed look naked. "Hi, honey," Jimmy said.

April didn't answer.

Helene felt dread. She knew April didn't like change.

Jimmy bent down to pick up April's suitcase. Other than that, there was just one cardboard box. So little to show for so many years. "April, sweetheart. It'll be nice to have you home," Helene said. "Shall we get going?"

April leaped to her feet, grabbed the suitcase and threw it at the window. Jimmy deflected it just before it hit the glass, but it glanced off Beth's arm. She said, "Ow!"

"April, honey!" Helene said. "Aren't you glad to be coming home?"

"No, no. No, no, no, no, no," April yelled.

Helene said, "Are you all right, Beth?"

"Oh, yes. We're used to this."

Jimmy said, "We have to go to the car."

Beth said, "April, isn't it wonderful to be going home at last? With Mommy and Daddy?"

"No, no, no, no, no, no, no."

"But honey, you can't stay!" Helene begged, hearing the whine in her own voice.

April had not been home, in any permanent sense, in years. And even though April knew it was technically home, it didn't feel like home to her. She was scared, Helene knew. And Helene was even more scared.

It had taken two hours and the promise of hot dogs and potato chips to get April into the car. As they pulled away from the curb, Helene Tausche looked back and saw Dr. Schermerhorn standing at his office window, staring after them, expressionless.

※※

ALICE AND ADELE SCARCELY remembered April. To them she'd been a person who behaved peculiarly and came to stay for a few days a couple of times a year. Alice didn't remember the time when April had actually lived at home. Adele had not even been born then. But April was here now, and everybody was disrupted.

Helene very quickly realized that there was a difference between a small child having a tantrum and a full-grown near-adult of fifteen kicking, screaming, and throwing things. A child in a tantrum was almost cute. A big person throwing a tantrum was frightening. When April was thwarted, she was furious.

Alice was ten and Adele eight when April came home. The Tausches lived in a small house. They had spent virtually all of Helene's substantial inheritance from her deceased mother on April's care at Hawthorne House. Adele and Alice had to move into one bedroom, Adele giving up her small bedroom to April, and she was angry about it.

"I don't see why I have to!"

"She's your sister, sweetheart."

"I don't care. Can't she just go back to the—wherever she came from?"

Helene had actually lifted her hand to slap Adele, something she had never done before, but she caught herself in time. She was furiously angry, though. And self-aware enough to realize her anger was made worse by the fact that she felt the same way Adele did.

After a few weeks she noticed that Alice and Adele were not bringing friends home after school anymore. She was ashamed to realize it had taken her that long to catch on to it. She asked why cautiously, because she knew the answer.

"I can't bring friends home," Adele said. "I don't want them to see April."

"April has an illness. You can tell them that."

"She makes funny noises. And she doesn't say hello, and even when she talks—"

And when she did talk, her voice was peculiar, loud and monotonous. "Adele, I want you to bring friends over."

"I won't."

"It's not fair to April to make her the bad guy, Adele. She's the way she is. She's not trying to hurt you."

Adele backed up and crossed her arms.

"Adele, I'm talking to you!"

"I don't want to bring any friends over. Ever."

"Tomorrow after school I want you to bring Peggy over. She hasn't been here in a month, and you've been over at her house almost every day. What will her mother think?"

"I don't care. I don't want to."

"Tomorrow, Adele. Right after school."

Adele closed her eyes. "You can make me do it, but you can't make me happy."

No, she couldn't make Adele happy. She also couldn't make Alice happy, or Jimmy happy, for that matter, because he had to react to everybody else's unhappiness. And she wasn't making April happy, either.

When April smashed Adele's dollhouse, it was the last straw. Adele simply would not play at home. She stayed at friends' homes after school and only returned in time for dinner. If nobody was available to play with, she came home and went to her room to read or listen to music. Alice got onto an after-school soccer team and stayed out as long as she could. When the weather got too cold for soccer, Alice went out for basketball, even though she complained that "nobody cared" about girls' basketball. "Just the boys' games. The dads come and cheer for the boys and everything. We just play. Nobody comes to watch."

Helene took April to one of the games. She'd never do *that* again.

It was about that time that the fights with Jimmy started. They were horrible, screaming battles, where he accused her of favoring April.

"I'm not! April just needs more help."

"You do everything for her and nothing for Adele and Alice."

"I don't have to tie their shoes! They know how! I don't have to button their coats! How can you be so cruel to April? You know she needs me."

"You don't have any time for the other two."

"Jimmy, be fair. By the time I've gone for groceries, and taken April with me because she can't stay here alone, it'd be dangerous—and she's so slow! She stops and looks at her feet all the way along the sidewalk, and even in the store. By the time I get home, what with the cooking and the laundry, then there's April's lessons. I take her to therapy twice a week and do her lessons here with her every night—"

"Lessons. They haven't done much good, have they?"

"I don't *know*. Dammit, Jimmy! How am I supposed to know what April can and can't do? Or wouldn't be doing if we weren't working with her? She's got to the point where if somebody speaks to her she knows enough to say, 'Hello. How are you?' "

"Well, that's just great. That's going to help our other children just a real big bunch, isn't it?"

The kids cried when she and Jimmy fought. Well, April cried. Adele hid in the bedroom and Alice pretended she didn't hear. The fighting went on until about Christmas, when Jimmy asked his mother to come over and baby-sit. He took Helene out to a coffee shop and told her he wanted her to put April in a state home. Have her declared a ward of the state.

Helene was horrified. "I won't do it."

"She'd get care. Plus then Alice and Adele would get some care."

"That's not *fair*."

"Helene, our whole lives aren't fair. It's not fair that this has happened to us. And before you say it, I know life hasn't been fair to April, either. But we have to play the cards we've been dealt."

Helene began to cry. "I can't do it. They won't help her, I know they won't. It'll be like—"

"Like Hawthorne House?"

"I—no. Hawthorne House helped April."

"Really?"

"She's more stable. She has a lot fewer tantrums."

"That's because she's older. You're comparing a fifteen-year-old to a seven-year-old. You and I have done enough reading to know that most autistics get a little less angry and less frustrated as they get older."

Helene could not bring herself to think that the years of not having April with her family, the years at Hawthorne House, and, yes, the amount of money they'd spent keeping her there, had all been for nothing. She refused to address the question. "April's our daughter, Jimmy. I can't just put her away. A school was one thing. But warehousing her is different."

It was two weeks later that Jimmy asked her to choose. Either April went into care or he wanted a divorce. They didn't have enough money for two houses. If she wanted April, he would take Alice and Adele, sell the house, and they would both have to get apartments. But at least he and the two younger girls would have some peace.

For several days, Helene couldn't eat or sleep. She was afraid her father would find out what a failure she was. Her husband wanted a divorce! She could lose her children. The real choice was, if she didn't give one child up, she would lose two.

By the time the end of January had come and gone, she realized that, yes, she was fearful of telling her father that Jimmy wanted a divorce, sad about the horrible choice she would have to make about the children—it reminded her of that story in the Bible where Solomon threatened to cut the baby in half—but with all that, she was not fearful or sad about losing Jimmy.

Jimmy did not see the world the way she did. It was completely obvious that, while he loved April in his way, he did not think of her as quite a person. Not a complete human being. And Helene did. It was that simple. She agreed to the divorce. Jimmy and she agreed on days when she would have Alice and Adele visit. And that was that.

And now—oh, God. Now it was now. And the question wasn't just where has the time gone; where did the years go? *Where has my life gone? Everybody my age feels that way,* Helen thought. Alice was thirty-three now and had two children. One of them had some kind of learning disability, and she kept saying that she understood what her mother had gone through, but she didn't. Having a child in regular classes who just needed remedial language exercises wasn't the same. And Adele—Adele was past thirty. They had celebrated her birthday two months ago. Helene had wanted them all to go out for dinner, but Adele had wanted to have the party at her house, and Helene knew, even if nobody said so, that it was because Adele didn't want to go to a restaurant with April. Adele had twins who were healthy and—oh, Lord!—normal. She was expecting a new baby in five months.

So this was her bargain, a life with April. The other girls had turned out all right. Maybe not as happy as if . . . well, there was no point in thinking about that. And now here she was, in a small apartment with a child who was a grown woman who would never grow up. Insurance had never covered April, although Medicare paid for her medications. However, the state had a program now where they gave you a certain amount to take care of your own disabled child. She knew it was cheaper for the government than if she had put April into a state institution. Jimmy had helped her apply for it, and after a long waiting period, the benefits had come in. So here she was.

And she was happier this way. Wasn't she? No fighting? Helene had never been a people person, so maybe she was all right here with April. Had she made the right decision?

Had it been a horrible mistake to let April go the reunion? Helene had feared from the moment the invitation came that it was a bad idea and would only stir up bad memories. But the therapist had been so sure. "She should revisit her childhood. Express her anger. It might give her perspective on a confusing time in her life."

Confusing? Tuesday was confusing to April. So was morning. And bath time. And shoes. And the concept of yesterday.

And what about Helene? Did anybody care what was confusing to her? Or whether she had anger that had not ever really been expressed?

CHAPTER *32*

I TOYED WITH my iced tea, smearing condensate water around the tabletop. Oliver was in the men's room, and although he hadn't said so, I knew he was making a phone call.

The waitress came toward me with a pitcher of tea. I waved her away because I didn't want my view of the men's room door blocked. I was afraid of what news he was getting over the phone, even though I had no idea what the trouble was. I wanted to see Oliver the moment he came out. The rest room doors were around the side of the diner's counter area, just barely within view as it was, with the cash register partly in the way.

I sat in the booth, waiting.

When he stepped out, I took one look at his face, threw five dollars on the table, and walked him to the door. Outside, I opened the car doors to let the car cool and then sat him down on one of the many benches the town of Wilmette had placed along Green Bay Road.

"What?" I said.

Ollie was drawn and tense. "Give me a minute. I'll explain."

"You're going to put me off again."

"It's kind of a medical thing."

"It's not kind of a medical thing, you dummy. It's a medical thing. Tell me."

"I'd been having a sore throat. Then last week, Monday, I coughed and—this is gross, but I coughed out some blood."

"You never smoked—" I began.

"Yeah. That was the first thing I thought of, too. Lung cancer. So Tuesday, my internist set up chest X-rays and all that stuff, but he already had an idea what it was."

"What?"

"There was this, ah, sort of mass in my throat. Near the left tonsil." When I gasped, he added, "It wasn't so huge, or I'd have felt it. So anyway, my doctor sends me to a head and neck surgeon last Wednesday, and he, first he looks way down my throat with a scope, extremely unpleasant. Then he biopsies the, ah, mass."

I held my breath.

"So that was Wednesday, right? Thursday they don't have the results back. Friday they don't have the results back. Saturday they're not in the office and of course the pathologist isn't either. Ditto Sunday. This morning I'm on the phone yelling at the office staff, if it were surgery, they'd get results in twenty minutes. Like that helped! Anyhow, I go five days without knowing."

"Oh, God. That's terrible. And now what?"

"Ah . . ."

"The news is bad?"

"It's bad in a way. They still don't know. They didn't get enough tissue. Can you believe it? Apparently they got some clotted blood and serum and products of infection—by that I guess they mean pus but don't want to call it that. So now he tells me he wants me in as soon as I can get there. I gotta go and have them do *the whole goddamn thing all over again!*"

.⋈⋉⋊⋋.

"OKAY," I SAID. "NOW come into my office." I ushered him to the car.

Ollie chuckled somewhat grimly. Cops were used to the car being their living room, office, dining room, sometimes nap place.

"What would this mass be if it . . ."

"If it's malignant? Something called a squamous-cell carcinoma of the tonsil."

"Where does a thing like that come from? What causes it?"

"Smoking. And alcohol. Those are the risk factors."

"You don't smoke. And you don't really drink a whole lot, either." I knew this kind of talk was just a sort of bargaining, a way of saying "It can't be!"

"And being male. More men get it than women. It's a fairly common thing, turns out. Who knew?"

"If it is, what do they do next?"

"Surgery. Extensive surgery."

I pictured extensive surgery of the neck and throat. Would they go down the throat or in through the neck? I shuddered.

"If it isn't malignant, what is it?"

"Some kind of infection. Like an ulcer I guess."

"And if it is malignant and they do the surgery?"

"The five-year survival rate is fifty percent."

I felt as if my body had been hollowed out. This was impossible. Oliver was young and strong and—goddamn it—a good person.

Right. And life is fair. And if I try hard enough I can make the world sensible and righteous and rational.

I put my arms around Oliver and leaned my face into his chest. "Oh, Ollie. This shouldn't be happening to you."

I felt him hug me back.

We sat like that for several minutes, until I was aware of

sweat gathering between us, and still longer. It made me ache, what was happening to him now. Finally I pulled away.

"Call the surgeon, schedule the rebiopsy for this afternoon. When you go in, tell him that this time he's gotta get the results back ASAP. He damn well owes it to you."

"Okay, Emily. You're right."

"Take a taxi from here back downtown. You don't need to interview Jeffrey Clifford with me."

"Thanks."

"And if you want me to yell at the doctor to move it along quicker this time, let me know. I'm good at yelling. I'm already hopping mad, and I've only known about it for ten minutes."

CHAPTER **33**

THE OFFICE WAS just eight by ten feet. It was painted a dark moss green, which made it look even smaller. There was no window, and the lack of a view made it seem like a cave. No paintings or photographs hung on the walls, although there was a six-foot-wide corkboard on the wall behind Jeffrey, where he couldn't see it unless he chose to. No distractions. Jeffrey preferred it this way.

Jeffrey pretty well liked talking on the phone; he didn't have to see people and didn't have to constantly remind himself to look in their eyes. It was much better than talking in person. He liked e-mail even better. You had time to consider what to say in reply without the other person wondering why you were leaving a patch of silence. That had been a hard thing for Jeffrey to learn, that people wanted you to respond immediately after they spoke. With the normals, if they didn't know what to say right away, they said "Um," or "Well," or even "I don't know; let me think about it." This seemed foolish and unnecessary to Jeffrey, but he had learned that he'd better do it, or they'd think he was weird. In fact, he had practiced for six months with Dr. Spofford's assistant, just trying to remember to say "Um" at reasonable points in a conversation. It should be after about three seconds of silence, unless the other person had said something like "Let me think a minute," in which case you kept quiet.

Even the telephone, which was voice-activated, was out of sight behind a fabric screen. Its ringer was turned off; if a call came in, a dim panel on the wall glowed. When Jeffrey was working he had only the monitor screen and the keyboard in his visual field.

Now he said, "Hang up," and the phone system clicked off. He thought about the call for a few seconds. That detective, Folkestone, was going to come to the office to interview him. Why more interviews? Why here? He wasn't afraid, exactly, but he didn't like it, either. And it would certainly break his concentration on his work. He wouldn't get anything done for the whole rest of the day.

A light went on over the closed door. Jeffrey jumped. Not nearly as much as he would have at a noise. He quickly overrode the reaction. The imipramine he took every day helped a lot. Jeffrey said, "Come in."

Jim Huang entered softly and closed the door softly. He smiled at Jeffrey, making no particular effort to catch his eye. "Ah, the palatial office," he said.

"Hello, Jim."

Jim was one of Jeffrey's three partners. Although, if asked, Jeffrey always said he "worked at" CCCH Systems, in fact he and three friends from college, Jim, John Cruscinszki, and Mario Calucci had founded and built it. Early into computer interface systems, they had a nice sideline in games as well.

Most of the company offices had large windows facing a

grove of trees or the broad landscaped lawn that ran from the front of the building to the street. The building itself was a white circular structure. The four young men called it the Flying Saucer or the White Frisbee, an attempt to pretend that they weren't as proud of it as in fact they were. They had spent several years working in a set of grim offices in an uninspired "industrial complex" facing the Edens Expressway. This building was only four blocks from the first, light-years away in elegance and convenience. The Flying Saucer was medium size but was the height of magnificence by comparison and was the physical embodiment of the success they'd achieved.

Jim liked Jeffrey and Jeffrey liked Jim. Jim found emotions easier to express than Jeffrey did, but that was okay with Jim. He admired Jeffrey exactly the way he was. He just went ahead and jollied Jeffrey when he thought it appropriate. Right now he carried two mugs of a hot-coffee with chocolate syrup mixture, Jeffrey's with three marshmallows on top. He handed Jeffrey his.

"I heard about the mess at the reunion," Jim said.

"Yes. It was difficult for many persons."

"Told you—you can't go home again. The past may be prologue, but it sure ain't the present."

Jeffrey smiled, and then reminded himself to look at Jim. "You were right." He flicked his fingers a couple of times. "Home is where the heart is. Home is the hunter. Home on the range. Home away from home. Home sweet home—"

"Hey!" Jim said firmly, accustomed to Jeffrey's behavior. "Pinch yourself!"

Jeffrey did.

Jim said, "Is there anything you need? Can I help you with anything? That business with Dr. Schermerhorn has got to have been very major unpleasantness."

"Not really."

"Why not?"

"I do not miss him."

"Well, okay. I guess I can understand that."

"Look," Jeffrey said, pointing at his monitor. On the screen was a short sequence for a fantasy game the company was developing. Ordinarily, Jeffrey worked on more serious programs. Jim's eyebrows went up a bit in surprise that Jeffrey should be spending time on this. Jeffrey was creative in his work, but he wasn't especially playful.

Jeffrey said, "We had them wielding. A mace and a spear. That was awkward. This is better."

On the screen a hulking fur-clad figure swung a mace, a clublike implement with a nail-studded head, and his smaller opponent, dressed in a leather jerkin, fell back a few steps, since his weapon was much shorter. Then the smaller man lunged in under the mace and stabbed quickly, with a slender poniard, once, twice, multiple times.

"You're a police officer, Ms. Folkestone," said Dr. Carol Hansen. "Maybe you can give me your expert opinion on whether a crime has been committed in a case I'm reviewing."

I nodded politely, hiding the fact that I was anxious to get to the questions I wanted to ask, not to answer somebody else's. Giving the interviewee time to relax and get friendly was good investigative technique, but sometimes it's really annoying, and I hadn't learned it easily. Giving the interviewee time to interview the detective—well, we'll just see about *that*. I put my notepad on my lap and held my pen in my left hand, taking no notes. I resisted the urge to flip my pen back and forth between finger and thumb. At least Dr. Hansen's office was very well air-conditioned. In this weather, that could make me pretty happy to let her talk. I had over an hour before my appointment with Jeffrey Clifford.

"All right," Dr. Hansen said, adjusting her long legs. "This concerns a colleague of mine. A psychiatrist. His patient is a teenaged girl."

"I see," I said, thinking I sounded like a shrink myself. I waited for a chance to ask, "How did that make you feel?"

"She was sixteen when she first came to my colleague for help. Her parents are rich; her father's a manufacturer. They have nannies and all that good stuff. The father told my colleague that the girl had symptoms of depression. She also argued with her father a lot, which I think maybe pissed him off more than the depressed mood."

"So it was his idea, not hers, for her to see a shrink."

"Insightful of you. Yes, it was. The girl herself is an independent type and probably wouldn't have looked for help."

"And you don't blame her?"

"I'm not in this business to boss people around. To continue . . ." She paused, apparently thinking I might interrupt and challenge her on this, but when I didn't, she said, "The family is friendly with a husband and wife they've been close to for ages. The girl—this is cumbersome, calling her 'the girl.' I'll call her Ida."

"Fine with me."

"Ida and her parents see a lot of this other family. Ida sometimes baby-sits for the other couple's two children. The whole lot of them sometimes spend time at the other couple's summer place."

"Uh-huh," I said, on a rising note.

"A few years ago, when Ida was fourteen, the husband— maybe I'll call the couple the Smiths—when they were at Mr. Smith's office, Mr. Smith grabbed Ida and kissed her and made some sexual suggestions."

"She was fourteen? Sure, I'll give my opinion. That's a crime. And your colleague needs to report it. As a doctor treating a minor, he's a 'mandated reporter.' Just like a nurse or a teacher. They have to report child sexual abuse, and they can get into trouble if they fail to. You must know this, too, unless you don't work with children."

"As a matter of fact, I don't. I only treat adults."

"So has anything been done about this?"

"Let me go on and you'll see. After that incident, Ida objected to spending time at the lake with the Smiths."

"Small wonder! Does she say why she didn't report this sexual advance herself? I take it she didn't."

"Pressure from her father, I believe."

"The father knew?"

"Wait. There's more. The father is having an affair with Mrs. Smith and seems to think that if his daughter keeps Mr. Smith busy, it will be easier for him to carry on the affair."

"Oh, good heavens! Ida should go to a school counselor or the police. Immediately."

"There's still more. When she was sixteen, Mr. Smith took Ida for a walk along the lake and made an explicit verbal request to her for sex. She slapped his face."

"Good for her. I have to ask—is it possible Ida has imagined all this?"

"No. Ida's father seems to have told my colleague that it's all true. In fact, both families seem to know all about it."

"What steps is your colleague taking to deal with this?"

"He has advised Ida to ask Mr. Smith to get a divorce and marry her."

"What?"

"No kidding. That's his advice. However, Ida hates Smith. She's having bad dreams."

"Small wonder to that, too."

"She dreams about things burning. And her father rescuing her."

"She wishes he would."

"No doubt. No doubt. Little as I credit labored interpretation of dreams, this one is pretty obvious. And appropriate. She thinks her father should rescue her from this situation."

"What does your colleague say to that? I assume by now he's helping her to resist Mr. Smith's pressures and find some strength to build a life without her parents' help."

"Not exactly. He still says she should marry Mr. Smith. Also, he tells her she actually has sexual desires for him, my colleague, because he smokes and her dreams of things burning are actually disguised wishes that he kiss her."

"Good God, who is this idiot?"

"Sigmund Freud."

For several seconds, I didn't speak. Didn't feel like speaking. Hansen took the opportunity to add, "It was his first published case history. In his paper he called his patient, Ida Bauer, Dora. It's probably his most famous case. Around this time, he came under pressure from the medical establishment. They were horrified that Freud claimed adults could have sexual feelings for children. So he turned around and decided that Ida had fantasized the whole thing. And therefore her claims of disgust at Smith's advances meant that she really subconsciously *wanted* Mr. Smith to have sex with her. And also, he said, she wanted sex with her father. And with Mrs. Smith."

"But you said—"

"That everybody involved really knew Ida was right about the facts. Yes. Freud himself knew it at the beginning. He knew the father was using the girl for his own purposes. The father told Freud that he wanted the girl talked out of all her complaints about Smith. Ida was frantic that her father didn't believe her about Smith's advances. *Claimed* not to believe her."

"That would be the most painful thing of all, I would think. Not to be believed."

"And when Ida stuck to her story, Freud blamed her obstinacy on bad experiences at the breast as an infant."

"Ugh."

"It gets even better. The father had syphilis and had infected Ida's mother with it years before."

"And Freud knew this, too?"

"Absolutely."

I thought a bit about the tale, wondering just how the police or the schools would handle the girl's complaint today, but my mind kept going around in circles of outrage. "I want to say that she should see a therapist, but she *was* seeing a therapist."

"Exactly."

Finally, I said, "Well, we know more about child abuse today—"

"They knew enough then. A lot of Freud's fellow psychiatrists were horrified by the story. You know, in all his career, Freud only had about fifteen patients in psychoanalysis. Actually he claimed eighteen at one time and thirteen at another time."

"Really? I thought he spent decades working on his theories, working tirelessly with patients."

"Nope. He spent years working on his public image. And to be fair, working on his writing. He wrote beautiful prose, give the devil his due."

I smiled. "I take it you're an anti-Freudian."

"You've got that right."

"Why are you telling me this?"

"Because it relates to Schermerhorn."

"Dr. Schermerhorn was a Freudian, wasn't he?"

"An ultra-Freudian. But that's not the only thing. He was very much like Freud in a lot of ways. He was an uncommonly good writer. He made most of his money from his books, not from Hawthorne House or therapy. In his writing he could give that Freudian there's-a-mystery-here feeling and engage the reader. Did you know that Freud liked detective novels? Many people have remarked that Freud approached his patients as if they were mysteries. Freud viewed people as something like puff pastries, to be opened layer by layer. He commented on Ida's case by saying something like 'the lock has yielded to my pick,' meaning that he'd unlocked the mystery of her psyche. I have no idea whether he realized how Freudian he was being when he said that. He was a good writer; he should have written detective stories instead of being a bad psychotherapist. He would have done a lot less harm."

"But he's famous."

"Oh, yes. Famous. I'm sure he was pleased; he always wanted to be famous. But he was a crappy shrink. Remember the thirteen or eighteen patients I told you about? By 1897, well before he wrote most of his major books, virtually all of those patients had left him, and he hadn't cured any of them, and he knew it. None of them got better."

"None?"

"Not that anybody has ever been able to prove. In every case where a follow-up has been doable, that patient was not helped. Freud was using them primarily for case history illustrations anyway. Just like Schermerhorn. And he was willing to fudge his results. Just like Schermerhorn. He and Schermerhorn were cursed, in a sense, by being able to tell a good story. It led them to embellish their stories. They *made them come out right*."

"They gave their stories happy endings."

"Exactly. And neat plots. Certain behaviors were caused by certain symbolic antecedents. All neat and tied up. Real life isn't like that. When you solve a murder, Detective Folkestone, do you end up with every piece of the puzzle accounted for and fitting in neatly?"

"I live in hope. But it's never happened yet." I said, "So when you claim Schermerhorn, like Freud, fudged his results, what exactly did he do?"

Hansen gave me a sharp glance. "And who might hate him for it enough to kill him? I'll tell you what he did. The term 'charlatan' was invented for the likes of Jay Schermerhorn."

"Go on."

"For starters, Schermerhorn was not a psychiatrist."

"What? Of course he was."

"He was an M.D. At least he didn't lie about that. He claimed to have been in analysis with two of the great psychiatrists in this country and to have worked with them. But he hadn't. He had no advanced training in psychiatry, beyond a psych rotation during med school. In those days you didn't need an advanced degree to practice specialties. Actually, in some specialties you still don't. An internist can perform surgery if he wants, for instance. He doesn't have to be an FACS. So in a sense Schermerhorn didn't exactly lie.

"Anyway, Schermerhorn had a degree in what we would now call family practice. I imagine he decided he'd never get famous by treating strep throats and urinary tract infections." She paused and looked out her window, letting me see her for a moment from the side.

I was struck again by Dr. Hansen's incredible beauty. Whether in profile or full face, that perfect bone structure was evident. Dr. Hansen's white-blond hair was cut blunt, just to her chin, and swung silkily as she moved or talked. Bright blue eyes gleamed with intelligence. She was beautiful at her present age of forty-five. Even when she became very old, she would still have that lovely bone structure and when her pale gold hair turned white, she would appear very little changed. I always feel unstylish and undistinguished, and I envied her for what to me seemed to be effortless elegance.

"Schermerhorn also claimed to be a Korean war hero. In fact, he worked at Fort Hood as a medical staff member. He never left the States."

I made a note on my pad of paper.

"He was a champion fund-raiser, though," Hansen said. "He'd go to university or corporate dinners and speak of 'his kids' and how much progress they were making, and bemoan how expensive it was. He'd always have a few new, adorable anecdotes. Except if you worked at Hawthorne House, you couldn't quite remember the incidents ever happening, and if you asked around, nobody else remembered them either."

"Making the story come out right."

"Exactly. I'll give you another example, and then I have to get back to work."

Well! Have to get back to work, indeed! Dr. Hansen was a suspect in a murder investigation. But I bided my time and did not correct her. We would finish with my work before I let Hansen get back to hers.

"Schermerhorn got some of the drawings his 'autistic kids' had done into a major national magazine once. Drawing and painting were a form of therapy at Hawthorne House, you know. Pretty impressive stuff. You'd see this drawing a child had made, with some stick figures and over them huge ugly scribbles of black, so thick you had to look closely to see that there were human figures underneath at all. Then a second drawing done a few months later, with some figures including a child and swirls of brown and blue and stuff, but the figures not entirely obscured. Then a third drawing of a more complete-looking child outdoors with a fuzzy yellow sun blob in the sky."

"Wow."

"Right, wow. Problem was, not only had they not been done in that order, but the same child had not done all three."

"No kidding!"

Her whole account was making me angry. If Dr. Hansen could be believed, Schermerhorn was either self-deluded or self-aggrandizing, and maybe the people who worked there had been, too. "So the counselors knew this was a misrepresentation?"

"Some did. A very few, I think. You have to realize that Dr. S was the only person who saw the whole picture—pardon the pun—through the years. Unless a particular counselor had personally seen all three drawings done by three different children, she wouldn't know."

"But they would know whether the children were getting better or not."

"No. Not many counselors were there for more than two or three years straight, because they were young people going on to other jobs, so they could always rationalize to themselves that a particular child got better after they left, or had been worse before they came. Also, high-functioning autistics tend to improve as they get older, so the staff would see some legitimate improvement. To top it off, despite what Schermerhorn said, most of the children he accepted were not autistic in the first place. You'd get a hint of that from the fact that we had about half girls and half boys. The incidence of autism in the population is at least four boys to every girl. Some researchers think it's more like ten to one. So it would have been a very strange selection process to get half and half. The gender difference, by the way, is one of the reasons the men who first described autism and Asperger's syndrome, Kanner and Asperger, thought it was biological, not the result of bad parenting."

"So let me get this straight. Schermerhorn has this school for autistic children, many of whom are probably not autistic. He's getting money from various sources by claiming more success than he's really having, and by writing books about his success."

"Yes."

"Most of his staff think they're doing the children good. But some, like you, don't. What did you do about it?"

"Not enough. But you have to realize, Detective, that awareness comes over you gradually. You begin to wonder whether you're making progress with little Johnny. But you have only a few cases, and that's not an adequate sample. Meanwhile, what you see of the parents—and remember Schermerhorn didn't let the parents come around much—doesn't seem so bad. So you wonder if they really caused the problem, like Schermerhorn thinks they did. But in my case it started with a slowly growing doubt about Freudian psychology. Schermerhorn was *talking* with the children, trying to find out what early traumas damaged them. It was usually the mother's fault, in his mind. Cold mothering. The refrigerator mother. The bad breast."

"But Freud is still highly respected. He came up with the idea of the unconscious, for instance."

"Look, Freud had some useful insights. The unconscious— no. He acted as if he'd thought of it. Not so. People had been talking about unconscious processes the whole nineteenth century. By 1870 or so it was the trendy notion. Freud was born in 1856. He could have picked it up in any café in Vienna. And it wasn't original even then. Nietzsche was big on the idea that unconscious forces affect the way we act. I suppose we have to admire Freud for passing off the notion that he invented it. Probably most people you'd talk to today believe he did. But shrinks today mostly think Freud is just plain bullshit. He's considered a funny old curiosity by most people in my profession. Even while he was still practicing, his closest disciples were leaving him and going off in other directions. His stuff just didn't *work*."

"But you still hear about ego and superego and all that."

"Of course. 'Ego' has become part of the language. Nobody's ever seen an ego, or a superego, or an id. The psychoanalysts have a wonderful defense system taught to them by Freud. Anybody who disagrees with them is 'resisting.' In other words, if you don't believe in Freud, you're sick. Schermerhorn was just like that."

"So you're an anti-Freudian, but you're still a psychoanalyst."

"God, no!"

"You're not? But people told me—"

"They would have told you I'm a psychiatrist. That's an M.D. with an advanced degree in psychiatry. A psycho*analyst* may or may not be an M.D. But he's done extensive training and engages in talk therapy—you know, like the bearded Freudian savant in a chair with a notepad and the patient lying on the couch relating his dreams, free associating, while the psychoanalyst is on the alert for resistance and transference and all that rot."

"Uh-huh. So if you're not a psychoanalyst, what do you do? Counseling?"

"I'm a psychopharmacologist. I specialize in psychotropic drugs—antidepressants, antipsychotics, sedatives, and so on. I decide what kind of specific medication will help with a patient's specific psychological distress."

"Dr. Emerson is a Freudian."

"Oh, that poor chump Emerson!"

"He's a very well respected man. It's not a field I know anything about, but several people have told me he's very prominent, and I've done some backgrounding on him. He has published major articles in journals, he's got a thriving practice, and he's a full professor at Chicago—"

"He's stuck. Of course he has to be a Freud apologist. He's sixty-two years old and it's too late for him to make a change. I mean, what's he supposed to do, say, 'Oh, gee. I've been telling you for thirty years that Freud was a god and all your troubles are the result of infantile sexual desires for your mother, and now, gee, I guess I've changed my mind'? What does a person like him do? Give back all the money his patients paid in for therapy?"

"So Emerson is a charlatan too?"

"No, I don't think so. He's a genuinely kind man. He really wants to benefit his patients. He was charmed by Schermerhorn at a turning point in his—Emerson's—career and guided in the wrong direction. A person can be so committed that he sees successes where there really aren't any. You've probably heard the observation that no matter what kind of talk therapy you do, one-third of the patients get better, one-third get worse, and one-third stay the same."

"Yes, I've heard that."

"Well, the reality is even more . . . mm . . . unpromising. After a while some who got better get worse again, and some of the worse get better. In fact, psychoanalysts don't even talk about curing patients, they talk about managing patients. I'm not saying that you can't have cases where a not-very-insightful person learns things about himself that help him. But it's hardly a science and it's certainly not reliable."

" 'If they don't get better they didn't *want* to get better.' That has always bothered me."

"Right. The burden is on the patient. The therapist tells him he needs to work to get better and if he doesn't improve he hasn't done his work. And nothing the patient believes about himself or his motives is ever true; it has to be turned on its head by the therapist. You say you loved your mother, that means you hated her. It's been a very seductive fantasy for a hundred years. And very lucrative for the therapists. Most analyses last for years."

"Well, how did you get out, then? I've asked around. People tell me you wrote articles favorable to Dr. Schermerhorn's theories at first, like Dr. Emerson."

Dr. Hansen wasn't pleased with this. "I simply made the break. Regretfully, I wrote off maybe eleven early articles I'd published. You hope your written work helps you in your career, but I just walked away from those articles and started over. How could I do that when Emerson couldn't? For one thing, I'm about fifteen years younger than he is. Maybe that helped. Or maybe I've got more guts than Emerson."

"But you didn't worry about changing your opinion in print. You suggest that Emerson did."

"Look, I'm not responsible for Emerson's thinking. He may be sincerely convinced he's helping his patients. If he has ever come to doubt Freud and Schermerhorn, it was much later in life than I. I can tell you this, when I saw that one Prozac once a day wiped out a depression that Schermerhorn would have sworn was the result of bad toilet training, I had the humility to say the theories I had believed up to then were wrong."

"But Schermerhorn went on—"

"Exactly. Went on blaming the parents."

"And hurting the parents?"

"Of course. He had no solid data to justify blaming them in the first place. It was cruel."

"How does that make you feel?"

Hansen burst out laughing, then settled down to the first sincere-looking smile that I had seen her produce. "Well, you're pretty sharp, Detective."

"What was he like? Around the school? I've felt all along that finding out who he really was would lead me to whoever killed him, but I can't get a handle on him."

"Formal. He would be jolly with the children most of the time."

"Most of the time?"

"Sometimes he would take them in his office and yell at them."

"About what?"

"Not behaving the way he wanted. Being stubborn. Not improving."

"How did he behave toward the staff?"

"Dominating. He was the god of the mansion."

"I see. What about Dr. Schermerhorn's personal habits?"

"Like what?"

"Did he work hard? Use good table manners? Whatever you can think of."

"He was extremely hardworking, in the sense that he was there all the time, either talking with the children or working on his books and articles. Yes, he had good table manners. He was always well dressed, suit and tie, polished shoes, that sort of thing."

"Were you angry at Schermerhorn?"

"Of course."

"Were you even more angry because you had previously believed in him?"

"Of course. There's nothing as painful as betrayal. He'd sucked me into his view of the world and of the cause of the children's problems. He was good at that. He was very convincing."

"Very seductive?"

"If you mean what I think you mean, I did not have a sexual relationship with him."

"You protest strongly. You were a young, unmarried woman. And beautiful. He was a handsome, successful older man. You were thrown together in the same house working on the same project for several years."

"If I had had a relationship, I wouldn't tell you."

"So I'll put you down as having been seduced and abandoned in a purely intellectual sense?"

"I didn't kill him. And if I had, of course I wouldn't tell you."

⋈

"GO RIGHT ON IN."

The radio call had told me to "call my office." The office had said to go to the big cop shop: "Chief Kelly's office immediately." I had had to call Jeffrey and tell him I'd be delayed.

These things are never good news. The bosses absolutely never tell you to hurry up to come get a commendation. When I entered the office and found both Chief Kelly and Tommy Hasseen, my commander, I knew I was in trouble.

"Folkestone." That was all Hasseen said.

It was Kelly's office after all, and she was the one who said, "Sit down, Detective Folkestone."

I sat. Kelly nodded at Hasseen to begin. Kelly did not look happy.

"Where is Detective Park?" Hasseen demanded. "Why isn't he answering his call?"

"He's having a biopsy, boss. The radios don't work well in hospitals." *Take that, boss.*

Hasseen had the grace to give it a moment of silence, but just a short moment.

I noticed that Chief Kelly looked more than unhappy. She looked uneasy, like a person whose underwear is too tight, and Kelly was never less than in perfect control. Hasseen went on.

"We need an arrest in the Schermerhorn murder, Folkestone."

"Yes, boss. I'm working on it."

"Is Park able to help? Maybe I should replace him. Has his illness held you back?"

"No, sir. Absolutely not. It's just a test of some kind. He should be out in an hour."

"Good. Because I expect you to arrest that handicapped person, that Jeffrey Clifford person, today."

"We've been over your case file, Folkestone," Kelly said. "You have good evidence against him."

"But, boss, it's not enough. He may have stepped in the blood after somebody else—"

"Innocent people don't walk around in blood near a dead body and then not tell somebody. He killed the doctor."

"Autistics," I said, "aren't exactly like other people."

"The mayor wants an arrest, Folkestone," Hasseen said.

Now I got it. I said, "To take the heat off the heat wave."

They both kept silent, but Hasseen's face told me I was edging close to being sent back to patrol. I said, "Commander Hasseen, Chief Kelly, I'm really not convinced he did it. I'm going out to interview him where he works right now. Then I want to see his home too."

Hasseen said, "He'll lie to you. How is that going to help?"

"Autistics aren't very good at lying, boss."

"Now you're a shrink."

"Autistics are different. They aren't very social and they don't care very much what other people think, so they don't lie much. I don't think they're very good at planning, either." I knew I sounded flustered. "They want to be left alone and do the same thing day after day. They don't like changes and loud noises. They aren't killers."

"Hey, loud noises," Hasseen said. "There you got it. A day or two in Cook County Jail, all the clanging and banging and people screaming twenty-four/seven, and he'd confess."

"Please, boss, give me a couple of days. We're not gonna look good if we make an arrest and then have to let him go because it turns out some other guy did it."

They exchanged glances. Was it possible they wanted an arrest whether Jeffrey did it or not? Sure, it was possible. Hasseen certainly seemed not to care about evidence. But Kelly had a good rep as an honest cop, and didn't much like this rush to judgment. She made the decision.

"Take a day, Folkestone. But just one day."

CHAPTER 34

WHEN I GOT to my appointment with Jeffrey, I was still trembling inside, even though my hands had stopped shaking. Hasseen and Kelly could not have noticed, I hoped, but their attack hit me right where I live. Eleven years of my life had gone into being a cop, and the one thing I prided myself on was doing the job right. Doing the job to perfection. How dare they think I would arrest a man just to keep the heat off! How dare they!

I did not doubt that the mayor was humiliated by the horrible number of heat deaths. The present estimate was five hundred people dead and climbing. This was like five commuter trains carrying a hundred people each crashing in the Loop one after another with all onboard killed. What made it worse was that the dead were disproportionately poor, old, and black. Chicago politicians had criticized the mayor for ignoring precisely that part of the citizenry.

If the mayor, with his immense power, had come down hard on the police department to produce good news, the shock wave would surely reach Chief Kelly. The mayor had the power to fire the superintendent on a whim if he wanted to. He could certainly get rid of a chief of detectives. A direct order from the mayor to Superintendent Ramirez to Chief Kelly would account for her looking as if she had eaten worms.

But I had to be the picture of confidence in the upcoming interview with Jeffrey.

I was going in there knowing I could do my career a lot of good by arresting Jeffrey. The subtext in Commander Hasseen's part of the interview was "Show us you're a team player."

I hated this.

Well, it was now late Monday. I had at least until late Tuesday afternoon to give them a killer.

I pulled into the parking lot at CCCH Systems and was interested to see that the company occupied the entire building. It was two stories high, round as a pizza, and quite impressive. Double glass front doors led into a lobby located in an open atrium in the center of the building. Potted palm trees were artfully clumped to one side of the receptionist's desk. The ceiling over the central lobby went up the full two stories overhead, with a skylight directly in the center. Offices ringed the open space on the first and second floors, and a stairway to my right led to the second floor in a gentle curve. To my left, on the main floor, was a glass elevator and glass-walled office space. I could see through to a large room in which about a dozen desks were assembled, with chest-high dividers between them and about a dozen men and women sitting at workstations. To my right on the first floor were oak-paneled walls and doors with staffers' names on them or designations like "Conference One."

I wondered what Jeffrey Clifford did for CCCH. Whatever it was, it was nice of them to hire him, with all of his handicaps.

A dark-haired woman receptionist clad in a power-red suit said, "Good afternoon. I'm Shira Modello. May I help you?" While it was now about 4:00 P.M., her makeup and hair was as fresh as morning. How do they do it? I was hot, wrinkled, rumpled, and tired.

"Yes, thanks. I'm here to see Jeffrey Clifford."

"Do you have an appointment?"

"Emily Folkestone."

"Oh, yes. Just a minute, Ms. Folkestone." She touched a button, and said, "Chloris? Mr. Clifford's appointment is here."

Hmm. Mr. Clifford. Also nice of them. Very egalitarian.

Chloris arrived, wearing magenta that clashed fiercely with Shira's tomato red. "Will you come with me, please?"

We tripped along past the first-floor offices with the names on the doors. Oddly enough, these turned out to be the low-rent district, because we arrived at the back of the first floor, where there was an alcove with a small Turkish rug in the center, a small table against one wall, a vase of zinnias on the table, and four raised-panel oak doors leading off from the space. The names on the doors were "John Cruscinszki," "Mario Calucci," "Jeffrey Clifford," and "Jim Huang."

Cruscinszki, Calucci, Clifford, and Huang? CCCH? Us trained detectives pick up on these kinds of things ever so fast. And how did Jeffrey Clifford get into this high-powered group?

Instead of knocking, Chloris touched a button next to Clifford's door. I didn't hear any bell or buzzer inside, but in about thirty seconds, Jeffrey Clifford appeared.

He was wearing old Levi's and that same horrible old leather vest over an old green shirt. He had his elbows tucked next to his body. He looked past my ear instead of into my eyes. But he didn't look incompetent—odd, yes, but not incompetent.

"Come in," he said.

⊰⊱

HE EXPLAINED IN HIS oddly phrased sentences that these four offices had been built with two rooms each, an anteroom and a real office, but he used the anteroom. "Because it does not possess a window."

"We don't have to use this room if you'd rather not," I said as he led me past his tiny, dark office and into a much larger "real office" space, carpeted in a warm green, filled with file cabinets, three keyboards, three monitors, several printers, workstation chairs, and two big leather easy chairs with a low table between them. A bank of windows looked out onto a broad lawn.

"It is all right as long. As I sit here," he said, taking the chair that faced away from the window wall. Chloris had followed us in.

"Coffee, Mr. Clifford?" she said.

Not looking at me, he asked, "Would you wish coffee?"

I was almost going to say no, but how often do I say no to coffee? And besides, I wanted to see him in the role of host. This was a major change in my perception of Jeffrey Clifford, so I'd better get the full whammy.

They must have had a coffeemaker within yards of the office, because Chloris was back in two minutes with fresh fragrant brew, cream and sugar in pewter servers, and a plate of sugar cookies half-coated with chocolate.

"I'd like to live here," I said.

"Well, of course, we do not have bedrooms—" He caught himself and I could just about see him thinking that people like me often made jokes that seemed stupid to people like him. "Yes, it would be nice," he said. After another few seconds, he even remembered to smile.

I FOUND I LIKED HIM. Jeffrey Clifford was an attractive man. He was even courteous, in a somewhat preprogrammed manner. And he had coped all his life with a very difficult hand dealt him by fate. That was all well and good. The problem was, I was looking at a man who probably tortured Dr. Schermerhorn to death.

The fact that he had led a hard life and probably had a hard time at Hawthorne House as a child didn't excuse murder.

There may have been blood on April Tausche's sleeve and Henry Rollins's shoe and Ben Goodspeed's bedroom wall. But all of that blood—which was actually a small amount even added together—might have been from Henry's scalp injury at the sherry reception. I should have the lab results by tomorrow morning. Jeffrey was the only person who was directly connected to the murder scene, his shoe print in the blood.

One nice thing about Jeffrey that wasn't true of April, for instance, and was even less true of the minimally verbal Henry—he actually seemed to try to answer questions. With April, who was so fragmented in her own speech, I probably wouldn't even have gone at a question from different angles. But I thought I'd swing Jeffrey around a little, moving unpredictably from subject to subject. It's what we do with suspects who are resisting us, hitting them from one side and then an apparently unrelated other direction.

But first—

"Mr. Clifford. Before I ask you questions, you know you don't need to answer them. You're potentially a suspect. You have the right to remain silent. Anything you say can be used against you in a court of law. You have the right to speak to an attorney and to have an attorney present during questioning, and if you cannot afford an attorney, one can be provided to you at government expense."

I was protecting myself, and any future prosecutor, by covering the bases. You can arrest a person without Mirandizing him as long as you don't ask him anything beyond his name, address, and social security number, but you have to caution any serious suspect if you're going to question him. We have a slightly longer form of Miranda we use when we go a step further, detaining a suspect. We have a printed form which we ask him to sign. If he won't, we video ourselves giving the warning to him verbally.

He said, "I do not object."

Well, okay. I took a sip of the coffee. It was extremely good.

"Mr. Clifford, I have been told a dozen times that it's hard for autistics to make changes in their daily routines. If so, why did they come to the weekend at Hawthorne House?"

He thought for well over a full minute, a long time in a personal conversation, but had hastily inserted "Hmm" at about the thirty-second point. Finally, he said, "Not many came."

Damn. He was kind of right. "You mean out of all the children who had been treated by Dr. Schermerhorn?"

"Seven came. Perhaps four were autistic. Not Jane. Not Cameron."

He was right about that, too. Cameron appeared to have some other sort of problem. There was Deemer, of course, but he hadn't exactly come to the reunion. He'd been at the mansion all along.

"But why did those seven come?"

Again he thought just as long as he damn well wanted to. Half a minute. A "Hmm." A minute. I was about to repeat myself when he said, "They confronted their demons."

This was a different Jeffrey, different from the one I had imagined to exist; clearly he thought about other people. He had easily enough smarts to plan the murder of Jay Schermer-horn. Maybe even to involve other people in it. I was about to follow up when a light blinked over the door. Damn.

Jeffrey said, "Come in."

A man in his thirties stepped in the far door, took a couple of paces past the smaller office, then saw me and stopped. "I'm sorry, Jeffrey. I didn't know you were busy."

"That is perfectly all right."

The other man glanced at Jeffrey and I suspect decided that Jeffrey had not failed to introduce us because he didn't want to, but because he had forgotten you were supposed to do so in situations like this. "Jim Huang," he said, holding his hand out.

"Emily Folkestone." I didn't tell him I was a cop. There wasn't any need, and you don't have to embarrass the inter-viewee if there's no reason.

"Uh—Jeffrey, I was just going to ask whether you'd gotten around to that sales interface. But I can come back later."

Jeffrey said, "I should have told you. It is completed. I have been doing it. In off hours. And I believe I can run. Graphics. And the sales interface on most machines on the Internet now. Either MACs or PCs. I have built an object-oriented language."

"Oh, man! If this works we are truly golden! Get me the de-tails, okay?"

"Yes."

"Nice to have met you, Ms. Folkestone."

"You too, Mr. Huang."

During this exchange it was obvious to me from his glances back and forth that Huang wondered what I was doing talking with Jeffrey and what our relationship was. This knowledge of what someone else is thinking is hard to explain, but we all have it and we know it when we see it. Except not Jeffrey. It was equally obvious from the straight, simple answers Jeffrey gave that he did not realize Jim might even think about this. He probably did not notice Jim's glances at all.

It was also very interesting to see somebody defer to Jeffrey this way.

Jim closed the door behind him as he went out. "Why do you have a light instead of letting people knock on the door?" I asked Jeffrey.

"Sudden sounds distress me."

"Even just knocking?"

"Yes."

"Did you kill Dr. Schermerhorn?"

"No."

I swear there was no more emotion in the "no" than in the "yes" that preceded it.

"Did you like him?"

"No. He was a noxious person."

"In what way?"

"Dishonest. Opportunistic. Insensitive. Cruel."

"Cruel to you in particular?"

"Dr. S was cruel to everyone who. Did not behave exactly as he wished."

"How did he wish you would behave?"

"Normally."

Oh, dear. "Jeffrey, did you stab Dr. Schermerhorn thirty-seven times?"

"Thirty-seven times?" he asked, and immediately there was a lift of interest in his voice. I knew he liked numbers.

"That's right."

"No, I did not."

"We found your footprint in blood near his body."

He did not respond.

"That's a question, Jeffrey."

"No, a question is phrased—"

"Never mind that! Why would we have found your footprint in blood near the body?"

"I do not know."

"Do you know how it got there?"

"No."

If you hit a wall of denial, switch fast and try to shake them up.

I said, "What do high-functioning autistics think of low-functioning autistics?"

His eyes opened wide and for a second stared *directly* into mine. I could have sworn amusement had swamped his usual odd behaviors. He smiled. "You mean," he said slowly, "do high-functioning autistics. Look down on low-functioning autistics. The way normals. Look down on all autistics?"

I felt a flush creep up my neck and face. I felt like a worm. How could I have been so insensitive?

I said, "I'm sorry."

He looked puzzled. "You are sorry about what?"

"I was rude. I guess I'm sorry about the question because—ah—I'm sorry about how the, uh, normals treat autistics."

"Why are you sorry? You did not create the problem."

He was perfectly serious. He actually didn't understand why I would be sorry about something that was not especially my fault. People do feel guilty about things that are not their fault, of course. Normals do. And how normal is that?

"What happened to you when you were a child at Hawthorne House?"

"I was fed. Dr. Schermerhorn talked with me. It was his plan. To find out what thoughts made me behave as I did. It would have been more therapeutic. If he had given me lessons in how to talk like other people. I have a doctor now who has shown me a. Game called Mr. Face which they play with young. Children who are autistic. It has different mouths. And eyes. And noses. And eyebrows. And when you play it somebody says make a happy face. And you have to pick the correct elements. To put on the face to make it happy. Or angry. Sad. Surprised. And the children learn. How to tell what faces mean. When they are carefully taught, some of them learn to do it almost as. Automatically as normals."

This was very sad. "So you're learning faces that way?"

"No. It is too late to develop that part of my brain. My therapist is showing me. Movies with the sound off and then he asks me. Questions about what emotion the actors are showing. And what the faces mean. We especially use soap operas. I am learning. But as for instinctive perception of faces, it is too late for me."

"So you spent the years you could have been learning this being talked to by Dr. Schermerhorn?"

"Yes."

I noticed he was flicking his thumb and two fingers against each other in a repetitive snapping movement. "Why do you do that?"

"Autistic people need to reduce input. Too much coming in makes us. Go on overload. I now have here the windows, a visitor, and coffee. It is too much."

"But doesn't snapping your fingers add to the input?"

"No. I have never. Determined exactly why not. It is like humming when you do not wish to hear something. Even normals do that. I assume we autistics concentrate on the stimming and. Blank out the other input."

"Like I close my eyes when I want to think hard."

"That is precisely right."

"But you're a very high-functioning autistic."

"I am an Asperger's."

I was thinking that high functioning meant that he could plan a murder, but I said, "You speak and respond quite norm—quite like everybody else."

"I am much better than I used to be."

His face looked unusually pensive, so I asked, "What are you thinking about?"

"My work. I am writing code. In my head. A computer is forgiving. It is an extension of the brain. Made perfect. No emotions."

"Is that good?"

"None of the defects. I can write code. Which is perfect. Perfect code is beautiful. Complete and whole, like a flower. The computer does not know that I am pausing to think. It does not ask, 'What? What!' "

I could have cried.

He said, "I can not multitask. You may have observed. That I do not drink this coffee unless there is a moment when we are not talking."

"I'm sorry. I didn't notice. Shall we stop a minute and let you have coffee?"

"There is no necessity. Because I can not multitask, I can not drive a car. My sister drives me to work. She picks me up after work. Occasionally Jim. Huang drives me home."

"I can see that a car involves an extreme amount of multi-tasking."

"I cannot walk and whistle." He smiled. "I can make furniture. It is one piece at a time. I can hold with. My left hand. But not manipulate. I can not tie shoes. My current thinking is that tying shoes requires. Two hands doing two different things. Simultaneously. I want to, but I can not do it."

"That's awful." And it was. I looked at his feet. He wore loafers.

"I can not form friendships."

"What about Mr. Huang?"

"What about Mr. Huang," he repeated.

"I mean, isn't he a friend?"

"He made friends with me first. I sincerely hope that my friendship. For him is the same as the friendship he has for me, but I. Do not know. How do normals know that?"

"As a matter of fact, they're often wrong."

Seriously, but without particular emphasis, he said, "Every day of my life I have thought about it. Why is this me? Why am I this?"

～❦～

YOU MAKE UP YOUR mind before you have the facts. We all do. That's called prejudice. Two days ago I had decided after a few minutes' acquaintance that Jeffrey was stupid. Stupid and resentful, and now I had detected neither stupidity nor resentment. He was incomprehensible, sure. Certainly not dumb and apparently *less* angry than what he called a normal would be in his situation.

I was ashamed of my hasty judgment, but really I should cut myself a little slack. You make up your mind before you have the facts because you have to; there is no way in the world to know everything, and you do have to get on with life. The important thing is to be open enough to let the new facts, as you find them, change your mind. And to try to find those facts.

I still thought Jeffrey was a murderer.

CHAPTER 35

CCCH SYSTEMS WAS LOCATED in Northbrook, which is a northern suburb some twenty miles from the center of Chicago, but right on the Kennedy/ Edens Expressway, so leaving CCCH I hopped easily back onto the highway. Skokie, where Henry Rollins's father ran a small dry cleaning business, was just fifteen minutes south. *Henry Rollins's father!* Now I was doing it, leaving out his name and describing him as a satellite of Henry. The man's name was Archie. Use it!

In his own place, Archie Rollins looked entirely different.

He looked three inches taller, brighter of eye, quicker of movement. He said, "Detective Folkestone," cautiously, and he wasn't thrilled to see me, but he neither blustered nor cringed. I had sort of expected him to be abrasive after the meeting at his home yesterday.

The dry cleaning shop smelled like they all do. Located in a well-maintained strip mall, it was scrupulously clean and apparently profitable. The circulating hanger rack was packed full of finished, bagged garments. A young woman customer was leaving when I arrived and an older woman employee was carrying the just-left pile of cleaning toward a labeling table on the far side.

"Do you want to talk here?" I asked Archie.

"Let's step outside. I can keep an eye on the business from there."

We stood in the drenching heat of late afternoon. The long narrow parking lot, with diagonal spaces painted onto the blacktop, was roasting hot. My feet sank slowly into the tar. I checked out Mr. Rollins's feet. Average men's size, I would guess about nine. He couldn't have kept Henry's shoes on his feet if he'd tried. Therefore, he had not worn Henry's shoes and trod the shoe in Dr. Schermerhorn's blood. But had Henry worn them that night?

"Mr. Rollins," I said, "I imagine you're a good, law-abiding citizen."

"I like to think so."

"You probably don't approve of people who obstruct justice."

"No. Of course not."

"I'm sure you've seen news clips on TV of people who knew things about murder cases and didn't tell the police. Things that could have helped find a killer."

"My son did not kill that doctor."

"Mr. Rollins, I don't think he killed Dr. Schermerhorn, either. But I know he was out of your room for a while that night. He may have seen something important." I didn't know for sure, of course, but I strongly suspected it. Rollins said nothing.

"Mr. Rollins?"

He sighed. "I was sound asleep all night. It had been a stressful evening."

"But—"

"All right. I think he got up to go to the bathroom."

"What makes you think so, if you were asleep?"

"Henry is very methodical. He wants everything the same always. He wants his shoes left next to his bed with the toes pointing out so he can sit on his bed and put them on in the morning. They're slip-ons, to make it easy for him."

Yes, they had been slip-ons. Very large loafers. Impossible to keep on average-size feet like Mr. Rollins's.

I said, "And?"

"It was perfectly innocent, I'm sure. That he got up, I mean. I put the shoes next to the bed when I got him into bed after the dinner. I was half-asleep when I realized I hadn't bothered to point them toe out. I'd pretty much just dropped them there. Stress, I guess.'

"Go on."

"Well, you can guess what I'm going to say. When I woke up in the morning, they were toe out."

———

FROM CCCH IN NORTHBROOK, I had gone down the Edens Expressway to Skokie. The Edens feeds into the Kennedy—which is coming in from O'Hare and points west and north—for the rest of the run into downtown.

Since the Cliffords lived in Chicago, I knew Jeffrey must make this run every day, up to Northbrook in the morning and back at night. It's quite a commute, although the fact that he would be countering the larger rush-hour traffic, which was into Chicago in the morning and back out to the burbs at night, would have helped. He had said his sister usually drove him. That argued an unusually helpful and devoted sister.

It was late rush hour now, and just a little less busy in the southbound lanes than the northbound. I hoped Jeffrey was home from work.

The house was clad in gray stucco and squatted like a gray cinder block on a flat lot. Despite the uninspired shape, white trim and a blue–gray roof made it modestly attractive. The path that led to the front door was in keeping, straight as a ruler, and edged with white petunias.

The time was 7:00 P.M., probably the Clifford's dinner hour, still light out and just as hot as it had been at noon. I pulled into the driveway, then noticed two cars there. If either of them wanted to leave, I'd be blocking them in. I backed out and parked in the street. There was just one small space left, right in front of the house next door.

Which gave me a diagonal view into the Clifford's backyard.

I was looking at four people loosely grouped around a smoking barbecue grill. Jeffrey was obviously Jeffrey, even seen from the back and at a distance. His elbows were held awkwardly near his body, the forearms parallel to the ground. He was staring away from the group, toward the mass of green trees and bushes that framed or fenced the yard, and I could just imagine him reducing his sensory overload by not watching the other figures or the grill. Probably trying not to listen, either.

A man of Jeffrey's age or a little older paced back and forth, while a man in his late fifties peered at the grill. A young woman, whose hair was blond like Jeffrey's, must just have emerged from the house when I first saw them. She had a stack of plates balanced on her left arm and was taking napkins that had been piled on the plates, placing them at intervals on a picnic table.

I felt awkward, but I had got myself into this intentionally. Dinnertime had seemed a chance to meet as many Cliffords as possible. It was really good luck to find four of them together.

Go to the doorbell and ring it, or walk around the back? Why be coy?

They saw me coming. The older man, who had to be Jeffrey's father, since he had the same build and facial structure but darker hair, held a barbecue fork. The woman, Jeffrey's sister I supposed, put the plates down. They didn't move, and seemed in their silence to close ranks.

Jeffrey had not picked up on the change in their mood. He didn't turn around.

"Hello. Mr. Clifford? I'm Detective Emily Folkestone. I'm in charge of the investigation into the death of Dr. Jay Schermerhorn."

At this Jeffrey turned around and noticed me. I swear I could not see the least sign of guilt or fear on his face. It bothered me a lot that he was so difficult to read.

"Edward Clifford," said the older man, coming forward as if to intercept me, shaking my hand. "And this is my older son, Anthony, and my daughter, Catherine." His voice was measured.

Catherine shook my hand but didn't say anything.

I said, "I think I saw you at Hawthorne House yesterday, Ms. Clifford. I was inside and we didn't get a chance to talk."

She looked as if she didn't particularly regret our lost opportunity to talk. She was courteous, though. "I went over to pick up my brother," she said.

Anthony nodded at me politely enough without coming forward.

"We spoke on the phone, Detective Folkestone," Edward said.

"Yes. Saturday." And he'd been crabby, too.

He remembered. "I'm sorry I was unpleasant. I was worried about Jeffrey and I took it out on you."

Well, when somebody goes out of his way to apologize, all you can do is accept gracefully. I glanced at the barbecue preparations. Nothing on the fire yet, a platter of raw steaks on a folding table near the grill, a bowl of green stuff with plastic wrap over it on the picnic table, and coals in the grill sending up a lot of smoke. Dinner wasn't ready.

Facing Edward Clifford, I said, "I would like to ask you all some questions. I've talked with Jeffrey." Turning directly to him, I asked, "Do you mind if I talk with your family about what happened, and our conversation? Police interviews aren't confidential, you know, but I'd prefer not feeling I was broadcasting your remarks." I had Mirandized him earlier and he should know his rights.

Jeffrey looked up at the trees. "Anything I have said. Has left my mouth. I do not own it any longer."

I took that as "Okay."

"It probably won't surprise you all to hear that Mr. Clifford— Jeffrey—is among the suspects in Dr. Schermerhorn's murder."

"That's not right," Catherine said.

"He didn't do it," said the eldest Mr. Clifford.

Anthony said, "Jeez!"

I said, "He wasn't the only person at the reunion who didn't like the doctor. I'm beginning to find out there were quite a few, in fact. You could help me if you gave me a better idea of Dr. Schermerhorn, what he was like, how he handled the patients there—"

"Handled!" Catherine said.

"I suppose I'm interrupting your dinner—"

"The coals aren't ready yet," Edward said.

"All right. Can we sit down somewhere? Can you talk to me? Is Jeffrey's mother coming out, too? I'd like to get the fullest picture I can."

There was utter dead silence. I felt like even the birds in the trees quit singing, because for a few seconds I was so focused on their faces. They looked as if they had all turned into wax people.

Then Jeffrey hummed. Flicking his fingers, he hummed and hummed and hummed.

Edward Clifford said, "I think I had better speak to the detective by myself."

"Jeffrey and I will take a walk," Catherine said in a strangled voice.

"You go with them, Anthony," Edward said to his elder son, who shrugged and started around the side of the house to the front walk. Catherine and Jeffrey followed, Catherine holding Jeffrey's arm companionably.

"My wife is dead," Edward said.

CHAPTER **36**

"SHE DIED DURING Jeffrey's sixth year at Hawthorne House," he told me a few minutes later, as we sat indoors, in their living room. "She committed suicide. There. In the kitchen." He pointed at the blue-and-white room we had just walked through, where a package of dinner rolls lay on a white enameled kitchen table.

"I was at work. Both children—Anthony and Catherine, I mean—were at a two-week summer camp in Wisconsin. You see, she would not have done it in a situation where the children could have walked in and found her. She loved her children. *All* her children."

He stopped. I couldn't speak. There was something fluttering under my ribs. I knew I wasn't going to like what came next.

"Jeffrey had been home for three days the weekend before. Catherine and Anthony were about to leave for camp. Jeffrey was very unhappy. He hid in his room all the time as if Nancy or I would hurt him. Schermerhorn allowed him home only two weekends a year, you know. Allowed all the children home only two weekends a year."

I nodded. Still didn't want to speak.

"Autistics don't like change. 'Visiting' his own home was a change to him, since he spent three hundred and fifty-nine/three hundred sixty-fifths of the year at Hawthorne House." I was reminded by this that Edward was a mathematician and physicist, which explained this numbers thing. But I also remembered someone had said that the close relatives of autistics often had autisticlike characteristics. Edward was precise. He spoke pedantically. "When we took him back that Sunday evening, he was more withdrawn than when we had picked him up. He was humming and stimming and squeezing his eyes closed so that he wouldn't have to look at anything. Dr. Schermerhorn met us at the door, and he said, 'See? See what you do to this child?' "

I crossed my arms over my chest and hugged my elbows.

"Of course Schermerhorn had been telling us for years that it was our toxic child-raising that had caused Jeffrey's problems. But Schermerhorn blamed Jeffrey's mother especially. The 'refrigerator mother.' The bad-breast mother. The mother who secretly wanted to destroy her child."

Evening sun came through the kitchen windows and made a bright spot in the center of the white floor.

"So my wife packed the other two children off to camp and made preparations. She went to her doctor and got sleeping pills. They weren't quite as careful with prescriptions in those days, but he was our family doctor, and he trusted her, and I think would have believed her even today. She came home, poured herself a glass of water, sat at the kitchen table and took them all. Then she poured a small glass of scotch and drank that. She rarely drank alcohol, so a little bit must have made her sleepy. Or numb. And she just sat there and fell asleep forever."

He stopped speaking. I could not begin to think of any words of comfort. I waited and waited and when it got too awkward, I said, "But Catherine and Anthony are healthy, apparently well-brought-up people. Why did your wife *believe* Dr. Schermerhorn, if she knew she had raised him the same way? If she knew she had taken good care of him?"

"Does any mother ever believe she has raised a child perfectly?"

SEVERAL MINUTES PASSED. Mr. Clifford rose, went to the kitchen, and poured two glasses of lemonade, one for him and one for me. As he did it, I stared fixedly at the trapezoid of pale orange sunlight on the kitchen floor. I was mesmerized, of course, by the vision of Jeffrey's mother slowly falling from the chair and lying in that box of sunlight, dead.

"Besides," he said, sitting back down, "you believe people in authority, people who have training. And medical degrees. You respect people other people respect. You assume there's a reason for it."

"Yes, that's true."

"And an autistic child isn't easy to raise. One time, when Anthony was about ten and a teacher asked how many children there were in his family, he said two. When we went in for parent-teacher conferences, she mentioned our 'two' children, so we knew Anthony had left Jeffrey out. We explained, of course. Nancy and I didn't know whether he had forgotten Jeffrey because Jeffrey was away so much, or whether he wanted to forget about him. When Jeffrey was home, he was difficult and took up a lot of Nancy's time."

"What did Jeffrey think about all this?"

"Who knows what Jeffrey thinks? We've asked him and he says things like, it couldn't be helped or it's all over now. He's very verbal. It isn't that. He talks but he doesn't talk about feelings. I suppose it's a blessing that he's very bright. Nearly half of all autistics never talk at all."

"He runs a business."

"Yes. And makes really good money at it. He has a specific talent he applies, though. It doesn't really involve explaining to people how he feels. Or chatting with people. Or making sales."

"Did he believe what Dr. Schermerhorn was telling him?"

"About his mother being to blame? Maybe. Maybe not. Certainly he'd have been hearing that explanation from the kids at Hawthorne House. It was the explanation they were all given. Did you know the toilets at Hawthorne House kept getting stopped up?"

This sounded out of left field. "Somebody mentioned that."

"Did they mention why?"

"Why? No, I thought maybe old plumbing."

"No. They got stopped up because, the parents, poor things, were separated from their children most of the year, so they sent photos. 'Remember us. Love us.' Or they'd give the kids pictures to take back to school after a visit home."

"I see."

"But Schermerhorn had so thoroughly convinced the children that their parents had hurt them, that the kids tore the photos up and flushed them down the toilet."

Oy.

WE HEARD HIS CHILDREN coming up the sidewalk out in front of the house. "I made chocolate cake, Anthony. Your favorite," Catherine said.

They must have turned in to the path next to the house, because the voice sounded closer when Anthony said, "Jeffrey's favorite, too."

I glanced at Edward. He knew right away I was thinking

that Anthony felt the cake had been made for Jeffrey. "It's not that Anthony is jealous of Jeffrey," he said. "After all, Jeffrey can't do many of the things Anthony likes most. Drive a car. Play baseball. Anthony is dating a wonderful young woman right now. Jeffrey doesn't even know *how* to date. But Anthony is angry about the effect of Jeffrey on the family."

"Very understandable."

"Unavoidable, I suppose. It's ironic that with all the things Jeffrey can't do, he's making more money than Anthony. I don't mean to suggest Anthony is jealous of that, either. His anger has always been at the situation, and it started years ago. Long before Jeffrey got into CCCH."

I nodded. "Do you think that Dr. Schermerhorn supplanted you as the father in Jeffrey's life?"

"I certainly think he did everything he could to achieve that."

He paused, then said, "When I snapped at you on the phone Saturday," Edward said, "it was partly that I'm not especially a people-person, either. But it was also guilt. When Jeffrey's therapist first suggested he go to the Hawthorne House reunion, I was uneasy. Then I decided maybe it would be good for him. When I heard about the murder, it brought all my doubts back. It was my fault for sending him, or if not exactly sending, not trying to dissuade him."

"It's no problem. I get snapped at a lot in my job."

The three kids—grown kids—came in the kitchen door, having found nobody in the backyard tending the grill. "Hi, both," Catherine said lightly, peering into the living room. Her gaze scanned us carefully. Apparently she found no lurking threat. She relaxed her shoulders.

"You'll want to get your steaks on the grill," I said, rising.

"You'll stay for dinner, won't you?" Catherine asked.

"Yes. We've got plenty," Edward said. Jeffrey, now standing behind Catherine, was absently feeling the blue-and-white gauze curtain on the window in the kitchen door.

"No, I'm sorry. It just—ah—isn't a good idea. Thank you, though."

"Really, we won't embarrass you with any discussion of your job," Edward said, seeming as best I could tell to mean the invitation quite sincerely. If I had this much trouble reading his facial expression, and spent this much mental energy decoding his tone of voice, how did Jeffrey ever cope, with no effective input from either?

"We saw a dog with a new puppy," Jeffrey said to the curtain.

Anthony shrugged at me, a gesture just short of rolling his eyes at Jeffrey's irrelevancies.

"Well, okay. I feel a little—well, thank you. I'll stay."

People may say I'll do anything for potatoes. I did *not* accept simply because Catherine had just removed a huge bowl of my favorite food, potato salad, from the refrigerator. But I admit my reasons were mixed. And mostly, I think, bad. This verged on unethical behavior, accepting dinner from a family when at least three out of four of them had excellent reasons to kill Jay Schermerhorn. Even Anthony must have hated the guy. Add in Jeffrey's footprints in blood and *what was I thinking*?

Partly I was hoping to get a better read on these people. Partly I wanted to see Jeffrey in situ. Partly it was instinct, which I hoped wasn't leading me astray.

※※

STEAKS SIZZLED ON THE grill. The wonderful aroma made the oppressive heat of the day seem jolly and desirable. Holding a glass of lemonade, I sat at the big picnic table and relaxed. Somewhat. Edward had offered me a beer, or, he said, "I mix a good martini."

"No, I'm driving. But thanks."

※※

I KEPT MY EYE on Catherine Clifford. She and Jeffrey resembled each other very closely—soft blond hair, slender bodies, and open blue eyes. I had noticed earlier that Jeffrey looked a lot like Brad Pitt. Catherine did too, but in a feminine way. There are women who look soft but in fact are resolute and strong, who look yielding but are persistent and dependable. From the way Catherine made sure that the condiments were on the table, that her father had lemonade, that Anthony had a beer, and did it without being bossy, I thought she was exactly such a person. She looked after Jeffrey, occasionally patting his arm as she passed. And this I noticed, too: that whenever she patted his arm, she made sure he saw her coming. She never did it from behind. Avoiding surprises.

Jeffrey and Catherine looked alike and Anthony and Edward looked alike, darker than the other two and more heavily built, though not fat. In seeing Catherine, then, I thought I might be seeing her mother, Nancy, twenty-five years earlier, when Jeffrey was at Hawthorne House. Not just that her appearance would be similar. Nancy would have been reliable and helpful to her son. Perhaps persistent in trying to find him help. She would have searched for advice. And then she got him help—the wrong help?

Quite often the girl in a motherless family becomes the little mother. That experience must have changed Catherine, made her tougher, but I'd bet that basically she was a lot like the mother she had lost.

We sat around the big picnic table and passed dishes. Edward took Anthony's steak off the grill first because he apparently liked very rare meat.

I noticed there were two bowls of potato salad, one much larger than the other. "Shall I pass both of these?" I said, since they were in front of me. "Or is this one extra?"

"The big one has celery in it," Catherine said. "The other one doesn't."

Jeffrey said, "Celery is noisy."

Catherine said, "It's true. If I'm eating celery, I can't hear what anybody else is saying."

Edward gestured at the smaller bowl. "Catherine makes the potato salad and takes this portion out before she mixes in the celery for the rest of us. But of course you're welcome to either one."

"If you are tired of hearing us talk," Jeffrey said, "you can eat celery."

I was just thinking, by gosh, Jeffrey made a joke, when Catherine said, "Jeffrey made a joke."

"A nonautistic joke," Edward said, smiling.

"What's a nonautistic joke?" I asked.

"One you can understand," said Jeffrey, and the whole family laughed, even Anthony.

The Cliffords treated Jeffrey as an adult member of the family. I was tempted to think "normal adult," which was actually how they did treat him. As an adult with a specific, but not shameful, disability. It was interesting that they and he all referred to autism and its problems completely frankly. There was no whispering behind his back, for instance. I liked this about them. They were dealing with it in what in my opinion was the right way.

I had been uneasily aware that sometimes I thought of Jeffrey as an overgrown child. Other times I realized he was a full-grown adult. I just hoped I didn't convey any condescension to him.

I also realized that, when I first met Jeffrey at Hawthorne House, I saw him as a collection of symptoms—the awkward movements, the pedantic way of talking, his constantly looking over my shoulder instead of into my face. This got in the way of thinking of him as a person. It was a bias, of course, but it was laziness, as any bias is. The attempt to categorize quickly was the result of a lack of effort on my part, an unwillingness to take the time and put out the mental energy to study him and try to see the world from his point of view.

Still, I was here to find out a few things, after all, not to be polite. And besides, the Cliffords were frank enough, so I said, "Who paid for sending Jeffrey to Hawthorne House School?"

Edward said, "I did. Although there was some state copayment as well. With the one or two really needy students, the state paid all the cost."

"I see."

Catherine said, "You realize that most of the students there were from really wealthy families."

"I didn't at first, but I'm picking up on that."

"*Really* rich families. A couple of them had autistic children in the Hawthorne House School and paid the fees and donated heavily to the school as well."

"Including to Dr. Schermerhorn's salary?"

"Well, of course."

"So, ah, so how much did it cost to go to Hawthorne House School?" As a college professor, Clifford would not have been rich. His house was nice, but not lavish.

Edward said, "In 1995 dollars it would be—well, no, let me recalibrate. We figured out at the time that a year at Hawthorne House was almost exactly three times room, board, and tuition cost at an Ivy League college."

"Whoa!" I was breathless. "Wow."

"You're paying for room and board and tutors and live-in counselors and three-times-a-week therapy by a psychiatrist. There was a ratio of one live-in counselor to every two students."

"Wow," I said again.

"That was the reason Hawthorne House School eventually closed. It got just too expensive to run."

Everybody was dead silent. Jeffrey, the least affected, took a roll from the bread basket, carefully avoiding the crisp garlic flatbread. Noisy, I supposed.

Giving that much money every year to Hawthorne House

must have seriously crippled this family. Probably everything that would have gone into savings, or retirement funds, went into Jeffrey's treatment. I wondered how seriously this cut into Anthony and Catherine's lives and schooling.

After half a minute, Anthony chuckled mirthlessly.

"What?" I asked him.

"I can read your mind."

"Okay. What was I thinking?"

"You're thinking, 'Was it worth it?' "

"Yes, I had the thought." That he could ask me this, knowing that Jeffrey's going to Hawthorne House had led directly or indirectly to their mother's death, seemed taking frankness awfully far. Still, they had had more than twenty years to adjust to the suicide. If Anthony's question made them uncomfortable, it wasn't my fault. Poor Edward; he thought he would be saving Jeffrey's life and instead the result was his wife's death.

"What was Dr. Schermerhorn like?" I asked.

When nobody else answered, Catherine said, "I never spoke to him. I saw him a couple of times, but I never spoke to him. Not even once."

"Neither did I," Anthony said.

I glanced at Jeffrey, but he was staring at the top of an oak tree in the backyard next door. Then he said, "Doctor. Doctor. Is there a doctor in the house? What the doctor ordered. Apple a day keeps the doctor away."

"Hold it, Jeffrey," his father said.

Catherine said, "Pinch yourself."

Anthony said, "He could stop if he wanted to."

Jeffrey did pinch himself, and he stopped running riffs on "doctor" but he began cocking his index and middle finger against his thumb and flicking them out fast and hard. He wandered a few feet away.

"Schermerhorn was a zealot," Edward said. "He was so sure he was right that he rode right over anybody else. His counselors hung on every word. He was a little god. Schermerhorn loved to turn a good phrase, and when he did, he made sure people heard it. He was a dictator. While Jeffrey was in Hawthorne House we hardly ever saw him."

"It was horrible for him not to develop a relationship with his own parents," Catherine said.

"I went to a couple of Schermerhorn's college lectures, just to see what was going on," Edward said. "What he most loved to do was cite examples of what his patients told him about their fears or dreams and then relate them back to some event in their early lives. Very early lives, like under two years old. He made some connections that sounded brilliant. Nobody quite realized that they were all a sort of fiction. You could make up any early trauma you wanted, and use it to explain a later fear. It might never have happened, but it sounded great."

"He was a fake," Catherine said.

Edward said, "I don't know. He certainly made things mean what he wanted them to mean. But he was dazzling in the way he did it."

Anthony said, "That asshole should have kept Jeffrey or he should have fixed him."

There was one steak left when we finished dinner. They had been perfectly honest when they said there was plenty for me. I helped them carry the dishes back to the kitchen. Catherine served chocolate cake and watermelon. Jeffrey took cake and no watermelon. I suppose cake is quieter.

After a while, Catherine said, "Would you like coffee?"

"No, thanks. I'd better get going." It wasn't dark yet, but there were some stops I planned to make on the way home. I got up. "Thank you very much for your hospitality—Catherine, Anthony, Jeffrey, Mr. Clifford. I'm sorry I had to meet you under such awkward circumstances."

They got up, too.

Anthony said, "I'm leaving, too. I have an early day tomorrow."

Maybe I had a surprised expression on my face, because Anthony said, "I don't live here, Detective. I have my own place."

Well, I suppose he would. He was thirty-five or so. It was unlikely that all the Clifford children would live permanently at home. Anthony waved at his family, nodded at me, and walked around the side of the house to the street. In a few seconds I heard a car start up.

"I wish you well in the investigation, sort of," Edward said.

Then I almost said, "Mr. Clifford, may I talk privately with your son?" Stupid! I had done it again, mentally treating Jeffrey like a child. He was an adult, an accomplished adult, in fact, and could decide for himself whether he wanted to talk with me privately.

"Jeffrey, can we chat a couple of minutes before I leave?"

He didn't quite get that. "We are talking now," he said, but his father got it. So did Catherine.

"Look, Detective Folkestone," she said. "I don't think it's right for you to try to surprise my brother into some—some unguarded statement. He didn't kill that disgusting man. Leave him alone."

"It's murder," her father said. "No matter who was killed, it's still murder. She has to ask questions."

"She already did."

"I have just a few more."

"You're harassing him."

"I hope not, Ms. Clifford. It's not my intention—"

By now Jeffrey understood what I had asked. He got up from the picnic table. "We will walk," he said.

JEFFREY LED THE WAY down the lawn into the part of the backyard farthest from the house. There was an old swing set still in place, rusting a bit. Some late peonies, probably falling behind their June-blooming brethren because they were in shade, dropped their last rosy petals into the grass.

The extreme heat of the day had moderated only a little. Orange light from the low sun made the top branches of the trees brassy. The shadows here by contrast were deep blue. Sun had cooked the soil all day and the warmth soaked through the soles of my shoes.

I wanted Jeffrey to talk with me, *with* me. I looked at him but he was staring at the slide attached to the swing set, and flicking his fingers.

"Can't you *stop* that?" I said.

He froze, stopped flicking for a couple of seconds, then started back to it faster. I was embarrassed, trying to figure out how to apologize.

He said, "No."

The word hung in the air. I lowered my head and looked away from him. "Jeffrey, I'm sorry."

"It is not a problem."

"Yes, it is. I'm frustrated with the investigation, but I shouldn't take it out on you." He didn't respond. "I have to admit, though, I'm frustrated with you, too."

"People become frustrated with. Me quite frequently."

"Jeffrey, this is serious. It's not a matter of gestures or behavior. I believe you know more about Dr. Schermerhorn's murder than you're telling me. I found blood on your shoe and your shoeprint in blood was near Dr. Schermerhorn's body. You and I both know that virtually proves you were there."

No answer.

"You were there while the blood was wet."

"I can not tell you. Anything about how that happened. I can not tell you anything about. The murder of Dr. S."

I frowned. Jeffrey was virtually expressionless, although he at least looked in the general direction of my face.

He was a handsome man. Actually he was rather beautiful, with good-looking bone structure and that light corn-silk hair, which picked up all sorts of gold and copper highlights from the low sun. He was smart, too, despite the difficulty he had in expressing his ideas in a casual way. And I would guess that he was generally a kind person. There wasn't anything self-seeking about him, no bragging, never an attempt to one-up other people, like his brother, Anthony, maybe would. He had an otherworldly lack of emotion.

All this didn't mean he was placid. He could have flown into a rage and killed Dr. Schermerhorn. Well, no, the murder was planned, not the result of sudden rage. Would he have planned such a killing? It was clear now that he was smart enough to plan and to plan it well. Careful, perfectionistic, able to structure a long string of computer code to reach a desired end. And one more thing—killing didn't really require a lot of people skills.

Back and forth. When I thought of the evidence I thought he did it. When I thought of him, I hoped he hadn't.

"Did you believe it, when Schermerhorn blamed your parents for your autism?"

"Yes. I was seven years old. What did I know. How I got this way?"

"Jeffrey, you reacted when I mentioned that Schermerhorn had thirty-seven stab wounds. Why did you notice that especially?"

"Do you not know?"

"Don't be like Ollie! Sorry. Forget I said that. I have a partner who likes to tantalize me when he gives me news. No, I don't know."

"Over the years, Hawthorne House treated thirty-seven children."

Oh, ye gods! I should have noticed. Was it possible? He could well be right. One painful wound for each child—

Abruptly, Jeffrey said, "What does one person owe to another person, if shielding. The other person. Could be harmful to oneself?"

I was startled and puzzled. "I guess if the other person has done something wrong, he or she shouldn't be shielded."

"But then, of course, the. Question is what is wrong. And what is right?"

"Yes. That certainly is a major question."

"Right and wrong is difficult." He paused, and I waited, wondering whether he knew who killed Dr. Schermerhorn. He could have come on the scene, stepped in the blood, and left.

He said, "And I also wonder, what is love?"

Out of left field! Was he thinking about love in a general way? Was he talking about falling in love with me? Had I made more emotional connection with Jeffrey than I intended? I realized I found him attractive, however complicated any relationship with him could be, and I had been thinking about that at the very second he asked the question. Was he attracted to me? Obviously, with the investigation ongoing, we were not going out on a hot date. Let alone I didn't know how to deal with all his problems. Well, that wasn't quite fair, either. We all have our problems and I was beginning to think that his were not the worst I'd ever seen. He was neither selfish nor cruel.

Cruel? My mind's eye produced the unwanted picture of Dr. Schermerhorn lying on his back in a sea of his own blood, punctured thirty-seven times.

I wondered whether Jeffrey was saying that someone he loved committed the murder. His sister? Did he suspect Catherine had done it? His father? Or possibly a patient or counselor he had loved as a teenager back in Hawthorne House? If he had loved a fellow patient, and the patient had hated Dr. Schermerhorn all these years and seized on the reunion as a chance for revenge, would Jeffrey have sympathized? I suspect he would have. If so, he might have been asking me what loyalty such love required.

"Love is as much of a puzzle as good and bad, in my opinion," I said. "Why do you ask?"

He said, "Because I want to know."

Uncomfortable, I started walking back to the barbecue and he followed.

⚔

STARTING UP THE CAR, I paused with my foot on the brake to look at the Clifford house.

Edward Clifford must realize how big a motive his wife's suicide gave Jeffrey to kill Dr. Schermerhorn. Well, of course he did. He wasn't stupid. He was a physicist who'd been teaching at the University of Chicago for twenty years or more. Not only wasn't he stupid but you deal with students that long and you're not likely to be naive, either.

So why had he told me about his wife? The Clifford family could just as well have said a few polite words, let me see they were getting ready for dinner, answered whatever questions I asked, maybe even given me a drink of lemonade, and I would have left when their dinner was ready. So why? The obvious answer was that he figured I'd soon find out about his wife and laying it right out in the open would make it look like it had been—what, exactly?—accepted, maybe, long ago. Still—I might only have found out that his wife was dead. If I looked into it more deeply, I might have found out that she had killed herself. But I might never have discovered why if they hadn't told me.

Another explanation was that it didn't matter because he knew Jeffrey had not killed Schermerhorn and he thought either I couldn't prove Jeffrey had, or would soon discover who really had.

Had he known Jeffrey was innocent because he himself had slipped into Hawthorne House that night and killed the doctor?

But then, I wondered about Catherine too. If she blamed the death of her mother on Jay Schermerhorn, she probably hated him beyond measure. Her remarks suggested that she did. Was she here at home all Friday night?

Had Edward Clifford been provably home Friday night or early Saturday morning when Dr. S was being murdered? He lived with Catherine, but surely she didn't check on him in the small hours. It was no more than half an hour's drive to Hawthorne House at that time of night. Possibly he had the best motive of all. He had found the body of his wife on the kitchen floor. How horrible that must have been, and how much he must have hated Dr. Schermerhorn! His children would go on to live their lives, but maybe he hadn't, in any real sense. He had not remarried. Who knew what depths of remorse and emptiness his matter-of-fact manner might be covering?

Anthony, too, had been damaged. He clearly resented the attention his brother had received and doubted whether Jeffrey was as impaired as everyone else thought. I know how that felt; Jeffrey looked so normal. Anthony had to have been terribly hurt by his mother's death. But how much he blamed Dr. Schermerhorn was a question. Or did he blame Jeffrey?

I remembered the hideousness of Schermerhorn's torture. Jay Schermerhorn had taken an hour to die, according to Dr. Choudhary. I wondered whether each of those thirty-seven cuts represented a quick stab or a knife pushed in slowly. Slowly, probably. Hatred, hatred, hatred.

CHAPTER *37*

OLLIE SAID, "Want some lemonade?"

"Lemonade! Everybody keeps giving me lemonade. Doesn't anybody drink beer anymore?"

"Whoa. Sorry."

"No, no. I'm sorry," I said.

"Are we in a bad frame of mind?"

"I've just had a long day. I could have *one* beer, you know. I'm driving, but it's the only alcohol I've had all day."

Ollie handed me a beer, grabbed himself one as well, and we sagged down into his ugly but comfortable, tweedy, over-stuffed sofa. There were newspapers piled on the coffee table, with several coffee cups and pop cans set unsteadily on them. A shirt hung over the back of a chair. It was 10:00 P.M. and still hot. We both rolled the cold cans over our foreheads at the same instant, and then laughed.

Ollie said, "My air conditioner isn't going to last if this heat goes on. Right now it's barely able to bring the temperature down ten degrees."

"From ninety-five to eighty-five?"

"I have news. We got the blood work back. They subtyped the Henry Rollins bloodstain from the ballroom floor."

"And? Ollie, don't make me wait!"

"The subtypes don't match Dr. Schermerhorn. The subtypes of the blood on Jeffrey Clifford's shoe, April Tausche's sleeve, Ben Goodspeed's bedroom wall, and Henry Rollins's shoe do match Schermerhorn's blood."

"Oh. Oh, now, that puts a different light on things." This was hard to take. "I was so sure those four couldn't possibly work together, but . . ." I just shook my head.

I worried. Ollie sipped beer.

He didn't mention his biopsy. Since he would have had it performed today but would not know the results, I didn't nag him for details.

He said, "You're reacting kind of funny to this. Is something wrong?"

"I got called in to the chief of detectives' office. And Hasseen was there."

"*What!* Tell me."

I told him.

"Oh, God," he said. "They gave us one day? One day? We're in big trouble."

"Well, that gives us to tomorrow afternoon."

"Right. Like I said, we're in big trouble." He thought a little while, and added, "Why didn't I hear the call?"

"Hospitals have a lot of electronic interference."

"What did they say when I didn't show?"

"I told them you were being biopsied and I'd get with you right away."

"Oh, damn. My name's gonna be mush."

"Mud. No, they accepted it. They want us to arrest Jeffrey Clifford."

"You know, Emily, Jeffrey probably did it. Going by the evidence."

"It's not proof."

"Tell me what you found out today."

"Well, Henry was up in the night, even though his father had claimed he wasn't."

"Henry admits it?"

"He can't really. But his father believes he was. He found Henry's shoes in a different position in the morning. And the blood didn't get there by Archie Rollins wearing the shoes. The father's feet are way too small."

"Okay. I just can't imagine Henry doing much more than going to the bathroom and coming back, though. He isn't very, mm, capable."

"No. There's a lot we don't understand yet about that. Jeffrey Clifford, however, is quite capable. I went to his place of work, CCCH Systems? Well, it's not just his place of work. He's not a low-level employee. He and three friends own it, founded it, and are making serious money from it."

"No shit!"

"But, Ollie, he wasn't in any sense pretending to be stupid when we talked to him at Hawthorne House. I just assumed it. The way he talked when I interviewed him is the same clunky way he always talks. Even at home. He's physically awkward and not very good at social phrases and gestures."

"I'm still amazed."

"Yeah, I know. And before you say it, I know it seems more possible that he could have planned the killing ahead."

"He's the only person we've got solid evidence against."

"I know. I know."

"I'll summarize. He's smart. He was there. And he stepped in the blood."

"I know."

"You don't sound pleased."

"I would hate to think he did it. He just doesn't have the anger level."

"How do you know that?"

"Well, I went by his house—his father's house—at dinnertime. In fact, I had dinner there."

"What! Are you nuts?"

"Oh, come on, I'm being honest about it."

"Honest is good. Stupid isn't."

"They're a nice family, Ollie. They're straightforward about Jeffrey's autism. They're not so obviously wounded as April's mother. Except—"

"Except what?"

I told him about Jeffrey's mother's suicide. He stared at me as if I'd lost my mind. He said, "*Nice family?* Sure, they may be nice. They're a nice family with an f-ing *huge* motive. Huger than I thought. Now we've got that he's smart, he was there, he stepped in the blood, and he has the *world's biggest motive*. Schermerhorn screwed with his head!"

"There's something about him that's gentle. He doesn't have a lot of anger. It's more like he's puzzled by how irrational normal people are. He likes playing around with lines of computer code and making them perfect." Ollie stared at me. "I'm not so sure about his father, though."

"Jeffrey is the one who was definitely on the scene that

night. He was bullied by Dr. S for many years. His mother committed suicide. It's his shoe that stepped in the blood. I don't suppose you think his father snuck into Hawthorne House in the middle of the night and then stole Jeffrey's shoes to wear while he offed the doctor."

"No. But tell me this, Ollie. If Jeffrey's smart and careful enough to wear garbage bags over his feet, how could he be careless enough to take them off and step in the blood?"

"Killers are stupid."

"People always say that."

"It's true."

"It's usually true. But it doesn't apply to all killers. Most people make mistakes, but the whole signature of this particular crime is planning and careful execution. Taking the bags off his feet and stomping in the blood is just way out of character for the rest of the crime."

"You seem, uh, a little partisan."

Ollie hits the nail on the head sometimes. I was partisan. I liked Jeffrey and his family, even Anthony, whom I sympathized with a lot. Anthony surely had not done anything to deserve the disruption his brother had caused the family. Nor did he deserve the horror that had rained down on their house. Jeffrey had caused that, but he had not meant to cause it. He wasn't to blame. I was feeling pressed, sad, and very worried.

"Ollie, you may be wondering why I came by here this late tonight."

"You mean you didn't just want to see me?"

I couldn't tell whether he was joking or serious. Anyway, I wasn't going to turn back at this point. "The Cliffords made me think about families. You've given me the impression lately that you were having some problems with Jason."

Ollie put down his beer. "It's not exactly problems. It's more like he goes out and doesn't tell me where he's been when he comes in."

"You're worried that he's doing something wrong?"

"No. He's a good kid. The trouble is that he doesn't share his life with me much. We don't exactly talk."

"Why do you think that is?"

"The divorce. When he's with his mother in Memphis, it's like I don't care enough to be there with him, and when he's with me here for the summer, it's like she doesn't care enough to be here. So we both don't care enough."

"Have you told him you think this?"

"Not really."

"Which means no. When you say he doesn't tell you about his life, do you tell him about your life?"

"Not really."

"One thing that impressed me about the Cliffords tonight was that they were very open about Jeffrey's autism and the mother's suicide. That may be one of the reasons they all seemed pretty healthy."

"Maybe. It's easier said than done. Where does a person start?"

"Ollie, I assume you actually had the biopsy today."

"I did. If they don't get it right this time, I'm gonna shoot somebody."

"This whole thing has been going on while Jason was home here with you. Have you told him?"

"No."

"Finding out that his dad is mortal is a growing-up experience. It's real. You're going to be all right, but you shouldn't have to go through the waiting all alone. And he has a right to stand by you."

"I don't want—I would feel funny bringing it up. I mean, what am I going to say? 'Guess what, Jason? This doctor is going to call me tomorrow and tell me whether I get to live or die?' "

"You'll find a way. You need to tell him."

"It'll just worry him."

"He has a right to be worried, and he doesn't deserve to be deceived."

"I'm not *deceiving* him. I'm just delaying telling him until I know more."

"You're hiding an important matter from him, and that's not right."

"Emily, if I tell him, I'm not sure what that'll do to our relationship. We may never get back to where we were before."

"Exactly!"

JASON ARRIVED HOME about fifteen minutes later. He let himself in with his key and found me and Ollie sitting together on the couch. Jason was wearing earphones, which he took off but left hanging around his neck so he wouldn't miss much of the music. I could hear it from where I sat.

"You remember Detective Folkestone, Jason?"

"Oh, sure, Dad." The tone plus eyebrow lifting meant he didn't think I was a detective, but rather some other sort of female, probably one leading his father astray.

I said, "We all went to the CPD baseball and picnic thing two years ago in Grant Park."

"Ah, mm, right," said Jason, reconsidering. "Whatever." He was a teenager, all right. Unimpressed, skinny, all elbows, not exactly sullen but definitely not giving away much.

"Where you been?" Ollie asked.

"Just out."

Before we could engage in any other childish where-did-you-go? Out. What-did-you-do banter, banter time-honored by far too many generations now, I got up. "I have to get going. Long day."

"Good night, Emily."

" 'Night, Ollie. 'Night, Jason."

Jason, relenting, said, "G'night, Ms. Folkestone."

"And Ollie, you'll follow through on that matter, right?"

"Right."

"Right now."

"Right. Jeez, Emily."

I let myself out the door, but was pleased as I sloooowwwly closed it to hear Ollie say to Jason, "Something I've got to tell you about."

Five

He that has eyes to see and ears to hear may convince himself that no mortal can keep a secret. If his lips are silent, he chatters with his fingertips; betrayal oozes out of him at every pore.

—SIGMUND FREUD

CHAPTER 38

Tuesday, July 18, 1995

I SWUNG BY OLLIE'S at eight-thirty Tuesday morning. He was expecting me and came out the door as soon as he saw my car pull up, saving me from having to turn the car off and go ring his bell. Surprisingly, Jason came out of the house after him. A teenager awake at eight-thirty in the morning in the summertime? What's wrong with this picture?

Even more surprising, as Ollie got in the front, Jason got in the back.

I pulled away from the curb. "Where can I drop you, Jason?"

"Um, see—" Ollie said.

"I'm coming with you guys," Jason said.

"Well, yeah, but we're going to a murder victim's house to officially gather evidence." I hoped we'd find evidence. There had been way too little up to now.

"I know. I'm coming anyway," Jason said.

I looked over at Ollie. My eyebrows asked, "What?"

Ollie said, "Well, it's not exactly forbidden. It's not the scene of the crime."

I got it now, and it almost made me weep. The kid wasn't letting his dad out of his sight. At least there wasn't any need to ask Ollie if he'd told him about the biopsy.

What would this do to the chain of custody of any evidence we found? Not much, really. It felt awkward because it was a victim's house, but you search for evidence in offices all the time with people working in the offices next to them. You search on the street with passersby tromping past. Still, if a defense attorney got wind of it, I was sure he'd find some damn thing to say about how unprofessional it was.

Yeah, and I didn't have the heart to turn the kid down.

Should I ask Ollie to take the morning off and do something with Jason?

No, I suspected Ollie needed to work.

Against my better judgment—after all the kid was only fifteen—I said, "Okay, Jason, but you'll have to stay in the living room. *All* the time."

JASON MADE A SPOT for himself on the stiff, brocade sofa in Schermerhorn's living room. His earphones were blaring loudly enough for me to hear. And it was something that actually sounded good. I had to engage in hand gestures to get him to pull the earphones off long enough to hear my question about what it was.

" 'Screamin' the Blues.' "

OLLIE AND I SETTLED in for some serious work in Dr. Schermerhorn's office. Serious and, given the time pressure, desperate.

While the office was extremely well organized, it was daunting because it contained the accumulation of at least forty years of work. Four four-drawer filing cabinets were banked along one wall. The facing wall was dark oak shelving packed with books and rank on rank of tall shelved cases with shallow drawers. The drawers were like those used to store photographic slides, but instead held minicassette tapes. Each drawer was categorized by year only, no descriptions. I opened the one labeled "June–Nov. 1979" and counted five rows about forty tapes deep, at least two hundred minicassette tapes in just this drawer. I pulled out a small handful. Each had a name marked on it and a date. Of the five I held, I recognized a name on one, "Jane Macy 8/19/79."

"This drawer alone would take us a hundred hours to listen to."

Ollie said, "A sombering thought!"

And it was.

ON SUNDAY OLLIE AND I had sorted the papers on Dr. Schermerhorn's desk. There weren't very many of them. I had riffled through the patient files, too, but hurriedly.

"We'd better check his files for any recent letters," Ollie said.

There was a doctor's bill, part of which had already been paid by insurance. "Dr. Schermerhorn was pretty healthy for a man his age," I said, studying his blood work and urinalysis.

"Except for being dead, of course."

"Ollie!"

His HDL-to-LDL cholesterol ratio was fine, everything else within normal limits, but his PSA was high. The doctor had scribbled in the margin that he wanted to "take a closer look at the prostate."

There was a note from a house painter to the effect that his bill for painting an upstairs bedroom had been what they agreed upon and not at all high for the work involved, including "all the mullions."

With so little on the desk, I paged through his files, checking the most recent stuff first. Since he filed in the way I considered proper, with the oldest stuff always to the back of a folder and the newer stuff to the front, it was easy. The Hawthorne House files were broken down into many subcategories, including "Hawthorne House Reunion," which contained some estimates of costs, a letter to the civic-minded group that owned the building hoping to spread the loss if the reunion failed to get enough people to meet its break-even point, a copy of a query from Schermerhorn to his lawyer, asking whether he could be held accountable for additional costs if the reunion was a net loss, a letter from Dr. Emerson originally suggesting the project to Schermerhorn, a letter from Schermerhorn to NBC suggesting filming the reunion for posterity (an idea that apparently hadn't come off, even though they had filmed the opening reception), and a draft of the invitation letter. Most interesting was the full list of names to whom the invitation would be sent. It added up to a hundred seventy people, including thirty-two of the thirty-seven former patients and fifty-eight of their parents. The rest were staff—counselors, psychiatrists, cook staff, cleaning people, nurses, and so on. So the actual group that came was just a fraction of the total list.

Ollie and I at least skimmed every piece of paper that had come in during the last year, and Ollie did a thorough search of Schermerhorn's correspondence file for the previous two years. "Nobody wrote him threatening letters," Ollie said. "Pity."

I had kept an eye on Ollie, worried about him. He was going through a terrible experience which I didn't know how to help with. Plus he didn't seem to want any help.

"What happens today, Ollie? Do you call your doctor?"

"No. He's going to call me." He patted his pocket. "I have my cell phone." Suddenly uneasy, he took it out, punched power and listened. It must have been working, because he put it back in his pocket.

We went on with the search. But there was no smoking gun. There wasn't even an ominous lurking shadow. We heard Jason cough in the living room. The kid was being wonderful, though, minding his own business and not coming in every five minutes to ask whether Ollie had heard anything. None of that are-we-there-yet? thing that kids do so well. Jason, I decided, was growing up.

Ollie's phone rang. He jumped. I tried not to. At a time like this, you convey optimism, no matter how scared you feel.

I heard footsteps in the hall, and Jason burst into the room. The little devil had apparently turned off his music and just hung out on the sofa for the last hour, quiet as a mouse, listening for the phone.

"Yes?" Ollie said into the phone. "Hello, Dr. Beecham." There was a pause. Jason and I held our breaths. "Well, what do we do now?"

He looked more cheerful, but what did that mean exactly? Then he said, "I'll stop by your office this afternoon. Thanks." He thumbed the phone off. Jason sucked in a breath.

"Not malignant," Ollie said.

Eloquently, Jason said, "Um, gee, Dad."

"It's an infection. I'm supposed to go by his office and get a prescription."

Jason stepped over to his dad and put one arm over his father's shoulder. A two-armed hug might be too much mushy stuff, I guessed.

"Tell you what," I said. "Why don't you two go out and get a late breakfast? I'll carry on here. Take my car."

CHAPTER 39

I HAD BROUGHT a player for the minicassette tapes. Why Schermerhorn didn't have one was a mystery. Or maybe he did, but kept it stored in some closet whose depths we hadn't plumbed. Anyway, the one I brought was dependable. I pulled out the boxes of tapes, grateful that they were dated and named, and rummaged for the people I wanted to hear.

My behavior was utterly impermissible, of course. To read patient files we should get a court order. If the patient was dead, we probably could read them without that. But if the doctor is dead and the patient alive, the patient retains a privacy right in the files.

I pulled out all of the ones of Jeffrey Clifford during his first year at Hawthorne House. There were forty-seven of them. So Schermerhorn was having a session with Jeffrey about once a week, allowing for Jeffrey's two home visits and probably a vacation for Schermerhorn or sickness on the part of Jeffrey or the doctor. I wasn't going to spend forty-eight hours listening. An idea of what went on would be enough.

And would be entirely wrong. I was rudely violating Jeffrey's privacy.

※※

OLLIE CAME BACK after a bit more than an hour.

"Where's Jason?"

"Dropped him off at some friends."

"So—how's he feeling?"

"Good." Ollie paused and almost blushed. Actually I think he really did blush. "He's going to a movie with me tonight."

"Oh, Ollie. That's great!"

"Well, you know, he'll go with me but it's his choice of movie," Ollie said modestly. "*Bad Boys* with Will Smith and Tea Leoni."

"You gonna miss The Brady Bunch movie?"

"Hey! Don't diss it! I've heard that's really funny. But Jason's a Tea Leoni fan."

"And why not?" I hugged Ollie, embarrassing him even more.

"What have you been finding while you're doing my work and yours both?"

"Come in here and listen to this."

"You know, they gave us one day. That's today."

"The end of today."

"I'VE LISTENED TO three sessions," I said. "Fortunately, they're each a bit less than half an hour. Schermerhorn must have figured that a fifty-minute psychiatric hour was too long for a child's attention span."

Ollie probably heard a serious tone in my voice, because he gave me a close look. Then he sat down in the other office chair, and I punched on the tape.

A man's voice:

"Well, young Jeffrey. You've been here two weeks now. Are you settling in well?"

"Mm-bbs." Unintelligible mumble.

"Jeffrey, you must speak up."

"I would like. To go. Home."

"You can't go home. You must stay here and learn how to behave."

Silence.

"Your room looks very nice. How do you like your room-mate?"

No answer.

"They tell me you like mashed potatoes." This was said in a jolly voice.

"Yes."

"But that you won't eat potato chips. Why is that, Jeffrey?"

"Mmm."

"Do they frighten you, Jeffrey? Is it because when you eat them you have to break them?"

"Mmmm. Nnnn."

"Do things that break frighten you, Jeffrey? Do you think that you might break easily?"

The dialogue, if you could call it that, continued, the rumbly, insinuating, fatherly man's voice doing almost all the talking. I tried to put the child's voice—so light, so tentative—together with the voice of Jeffrey as I knew him now. There was no similarity in pitch, and not so much of this hesitancy left in Jeffrey today, but there was something about the phrasing that I would know anywhere. As I had noticed over the past few days, Jeffrey did not break up a string of words the way other people did. I might have said, "I-would-like-to-go *home,*" with the first part of the sentence spoken rather quickly, and emphasizing the word "home."

I had already heard the tape, but the feeling came over me again—the boy's fragile voice, the man's so smooth, so ingratiating, and so paternal. My feeling was one of fear at the extreme disproportion of power between the two.

"Now, young Jeffrey. I want you to pay close attention to everything we tell you here. You have failed at many schools. This is your last chance, you see."

"Chance. Take a chance. Chances are. Chance—"

"Stop that!" Schermerhorn bellowed. I saw Ollie jump.

The Jeffrey child said nothing.

The man's voice went on. "Jeffrey, while you are here, you will try to remember your dreams. And you will keep them in your mind to tell me later. Do you understand?"

Jeffrey must have nodded. Schermerhorn said, "Good. Did you dream last night, Jeffrey?"

Half a minute went by. I could even hear a fire or police siren on the tape, a 1974 siren going down a 1974 Prairie Avenue and fading away in the distance.

"Jeffrey!"

"Mommy."

"Mommy what?"

"I dreamed Mommy was here."

"You must give that up, Jeffrey. I am your father now. Your parents don't want you. They left you here because they can't stand you anymore."

Jeffrey began to cry. He cried and cried. Finally, I clicked off the tape.

Ollie said, "Oh, my God."

CHAPTER 40

PAPERWORK IS HARD. I had spent the whole day rummaging in Schermerhorn's files. My eyes felt as if they were made of sawdust. It was nearly midnight and Ollie had left at six for his date with his son. I didn't have anybody waiting at home, thank goodness. I was hot, despite the efforts of Schermerhorn's air conditioners. You could never quite retrofit these old houses to be really cool. Everything I wore was crumpled. But I'd finally got hold of the tail of the beast and I wasn't going to let go. The files I'd just found were the equivalent of keeping two sets of books.

I got a call on my cell at what would have been dinnertime, if I had been having dinner, from Commander Tommy Hasseen's aide.

"Hold for the commander."

He came on bellowing. "I told you what I wanted. I was perfectly clear!"

I said, "Yes, boss. Yes, boss," until he finally let me get a word in.

"I'm just collecting the rest of the evidence, boss."

More demands.

"I'll have a much more solid case, sir, if I put everything together. Yes, boss. Tomorrow early. Yes, sir!"

⊰⋈⊱

SCHERMERHORN MUST HAVE believed no one would ever see
these notes. And I suppose no one would have in the normal
course of events. Schermerhorn could have destroyed them if
his health had become bad, if he thought that he might die and
a biographer might find them. Why a person keeps things like
this I'm not sure. It's probably like Nixon keeping the Water-
gate tapes, a belief that everything he does is so important not
a scrap of it should be thrown away.

I held in my left hand the description of Jeffrey Clifford
dated September 28, 1974, the day he first arrived at
Hawthorne House, the one I had read on Sunday. It was what
Schermerhorn called an intake evaluation. I held in my right
hand a description of Jeffrey Clifford with no date, but labeled "intake evaluation." The paper was different, the typewriter font was different. And the evaluation was different.
The first said:

> Jeffrey Clifford presents as a seven-year-old male with a
> history of school problems and difficulties at home. His
> parents report many enrollments in public school and in
> schools for problem children, none successful.
>
> History of normal delivery and apparently normal de-
> velopment [pediatrician's report appended] until age three,
> when according to parents he began to withdraw. Parents
> report accelerated reading skills up to age five. During this
> period, Jeffrey did not make friends and withdrew further
> from family as well.
>
> Pt. has two siblings, m. nine and f. five. Father employed
> as professor, mother housewife.
>
> In first interview, pt. appears well nourished, and med-

ical report confirms good physical health. Pt. uncommunicative, refusing to make eye contact, flapping hands. Utters occasional nonsense words, but can speak sense when he wants.

Posture unconventional, elbows held close to sides. Gait awkward. Axis of body bent forward from waist.

Note to self: Father cold and perhaps resigned. Sits still and does not agitate or ask many questions. Mother attempts to show concern for J. but despite fidgeting wants to get rid of the child. Eager to have him enrolled at HH. Sat straighter and leaned forward ready to do combat whenever I suggested other possible approaches.

"Intake diagnosis: Autism consequent on maternal rejection."

In my right hand was:

Jeffrey Clifford presents as a seven-year-old male with a history of school problems including fighting and destroying other students' work and recalcitrance at home, including hiding in his room for days on end. His parents report many enrollments in public school and in schools for problem children. He was expelled from all of them for anger and fighting.

History of normal delivery and apparently normal development [pediatrician's report appended] until age three, when according to parents he began to withdraw. Parents report accelerated reading skills up to age five. During this period, Jeffrey did not make friends and withdrew further from family as well. Now does not speak normally at all.

Pt. has two siblings, m. nine and f. five. Father employed as professor, mother housewife.

In first interview, pt. appears well nourished, and medical report confirms good physical health. Pt. refuses to talk, refuses to make eye contact, flaps hands. Utters only nonsense words. Severe cluttering.

Posture extremely rigid, elbows held close to sides. Gait awkward. Axis of body bent forward from waist.

Note to self: Father cold and perhaps resigned. Sits still and does not agitate or ask many questions. Mother attempts to show concern for J. but despite fidgeting wants to get rid of the child. Eager to have him enrolled at HH. Sat straighter and leaned forward ready to do combat whenever I suggested other possible approaches.

"Intake diagnosis: Autism consequent on maternal rejection."

Where was the child who "could speak sense when he wants?"

I stuck sticky notes next to the changed sections and bracketed the sections in pencil on the notes. Although the sheet I called the second one was undated, I was sure it had been made up later, using the "first" as a basis. All the changes were in the direction of making Jeffrey seem sicker when he arrived than he really was. It was simply not credible that the alterations had gone in the other direction, eliminating his most serious symptoms at the beginning of "treatment." Everything that had been changed was setting things up so that Schermerhorn could say later, even if Jeffrey didn't in fact get any better, "See, when he came in he wasn't even talking and look how much better he is now."

I had no idea what "severe cluttering" could possibly mean, but after poking around Schermerhorn's office for a couple of minutes, I located a psychiatric dictionary. Cluttering turned out to be jerky, rushed speech with faulty phrasing. Confused phrasing was a feature of cluttering, as a clutterer might intend to say "I'll show you to a seat," and instead say, "I'll sew you to a sheet." The dictionary also stated that cluttering tended to persist throughout life. If Jeffrey was a clutterer, I hadn't noticed it, and if no cure had been developed by the time this very current dictionary had been printed, I hardly thought Schermerhorn had cured him in 1974.

Kurt Deemer's intake interview included many of the behaviors he had already told me about, but Schermerhorn also wrote "mother poss. IVDU, poss. heroin." IVDU I already knew meant intravenous drug user. The CPD had nothing in its files to the effect that Mrs. Deemer used anything other than the societally approved drug alcohol. I suspected Schermerhorn had "deduced" this on his own. There was a second sheet on Deemer as well, in which his truantism, petty crime, and attacks on horses were increased in severity. A thing called a Szondi test was in his file. This was probably what he meant when he told me Schermerhorn gave him a "soundy" test, where he had to pick pictures of two people he liked and two people he disliked from groups of eight. Apparently the test showed that his need for aggression and masculinity, the *s* factor, was unusually high. So was the need to exhibit emotions, the *hy* factor, and the narcissistic ego need, the *k* factor. The need for tender, feminine love, the *h* factor, was low. Either the test was accurate, or Deemer had figured out, as he claimed, what Dr. Schermerhorn wanted to hear.

April Tausche also had two intake sheets. In the one that I chose to believe was the original, it was clear that April even then had been worse off than Jeffrey. Her intelligence tests were lower, for one thing, and her speech was almost nonexistent. It got worse, of course, in the revised intake evaluation sheet. Schermerhorn gave April a new symptom in the second sheet—obstipatio paradoxa. Back to the psychiatric dictionary again. Wow. This term apparently meant paradoxical constipation in which the child holds the stool in. Sometimes, it said, the child passes little marblelike stools and holds them between the buttocks, irritating the skin there, often causing sores. Schermerhorn wrote "This is caused by an unconscious sexual phantasy, possibly exacerbated by repressed aggression."

April had also been administered something called the Arthur Point Scale test. All I could find out about it in the dictionary was that it was a kind of IQ test appropriate for children between seven and fourteen who did not have adequate language for other IQ tests. The dictionary didn't tell me how to assess the results, but it looked like Schermerhorn gave her a lower number on the "second" sheet. I would ask the department shrink what the score meant, but I'd ask him casually and carefully, since I had no right to have looked at the patient's record in the first place.

The fudging of records might have been a smoking gun if a parent had been trying to sue Schermerhorn. Or if a donor organization wanted to prove that he had not been entitled to the grant money he received. But this long after the fact, it didn't suggest a motive for murder.

❧

I STOOD UP, creaking with tiredness, and went out to Schermerhorn's kitchen. There was an automatic coffeemaker with beans already in the hopper. I wanted to use it, but we are so trained not to mess up anything that might be evidence, however far-fetched the idea that it was relevant to the crime, that I left it alone. Too bad. I wanted it *so much.* It was the one item in Schermerhorn's house that I might have enjoyed. Instead, I paced around and then did neck exercises for a while.

❧

ON THE TAPE, the young Henry Rollins said, "Ah-ah. Ack-ah."

Schermerhorn's voice said, "We've talked about the nuthouse, Henry. It's a bad place. Children who can't get along in the real world go to the nuthouse"

"Noooo—"

"In the nuthouse, you're locked inside all day every day. The food tastes terrible, because nobody cares about you, like we do here."

"Aaaaa—"

"Now, I want you to talk, Henry. You have to start talking. I know my name is hard to say, so we're going to start with yours. Henry. Say Henry."

"Aaaaa—"

"Henry. Henry. Henry."

"Reeee—"

"That's better. Say Hen."

"Aaaa—"

"Hen."

"Aaaa—"

Thwack! I heard a sharp sound that sounded like a slap. It couldn't be, could it?

"Hen."

"Aaaa—"

Thwack! Thwack!

Schermerhorn's voice said, "You make me hurt you to help you. Say Henry!"

Six

Woe to you, my Princess, when I come . . . you shall see who is the stronger, a gentle girl who doesn't eat enough or a big wild man who has cocaine in his body.

—SIGMUND FREUD

CHAPTER 41

WE WERE PARKED, talking cop style, the two cars side by side, mine facing north and his facing south so that his driver's-side window was next to mine. It's an odd sort of cop-car mating ritual, I guess.

I had told Ollie my promise to Commander Hasseen. He just rolled his eyes. The only thing we could do was keep on trucking. We decided to split up today's interviews, because Ollie had an idea about the locked-or-unlocked back door at Hawthorne House.

"I am going to beard Kurt Deemer in his den," Ollie said.

"Not going to tell me what makes you think he'd leave the door unlocked?"

"Nope. It's a deep psychological reason and we've both had all the psychology we can stand in the last four days."

"Well, he's a sneaky little monster. Keep an eye on him."

"Sure. I'll be my usual beagle-eyed self."

✧

OLLIE ARRIVED AT Hawthorne House at eight-fifteen. Deemer worked an eight-to-four day usually. Or at least he was there eight to four. How much work he did was another question.

Deemer was late, of course. Mrs. Kisilinski let Ollie in, and at the request for Kurt pursed her lips.

"If that hoodlum was involved in the murder, it would be extremely irresponsible of you not to warn me."

"We don't believe he was, ma'am," Ollie said in a soft tone.

"Because I'm here alone with him most days, and I don't like it."

"We don't believe he killed Schermerhorn, ma'am."

"It's quite wrong to leave me hanging like this."

"We don't think he killed Schermerhorn, ma'am."

"He's very odd. You have a responsibility to the public, you know."

Repressing the urge to make a scary face and hiss, Ollie sat in a chair and waited for her to go away.

When Deemer arrived, Mrs. Kisilinski sent him to Ollie.

"What do you cops want now?"

Glancing around to check that Mrs. Kisilinski was out of earshot, Ollie said, "I want to confirm that you unlocked the back door the morning of the murder."

"Why'm I gonna help you?"

"Why are you not?"

When Kurt just stared at him, Ollie said, "I have a really great idea. For once in your life, do something just because it's honest. Just because it's the right thing to do."

Kurt stared at him as if he were nuts, but in a mesmerized voice said, "I got a key, you know. I punched the unlock button on the back door because I hadda make a way where somebody else coulda got in. Otherwise the whole goddamn thing would for sure be blamed on me."

IF NOT JEFFREY—

Who hated Schermerhorn? I asked myself.

Dr. Carol Hansen.

Hansen lived in an apartment fairly far north on Lake Shore Drive. This is Chicago's Gold Coast, a neighborhood four miles long and half a block wide, bordered by Lake Michigan on one side, the non-lake-view apartments on the other, and held aloft by a lot of money.

Her apartment on the Gold Coast was about ten miles north of the Hyde Park area near the University of Chicago where Hawthorne House was located. It was near enough that Carol Hansen could have attended the reunion and the symposium by day and gone home at night. And yet it was far enough so that it made some sense to stay. I couldn't argue that her staying overnight necessarily meant she wanted to be there to kill him.

I would have really liked it if one piece of information in this !$^*&#! case pointed unmistakably to somebody's guilt. I'd had it with ambiguity!

Oh, blast. Of course. There was one piece of information. Jeffrey's bloody footprint next to Schermerhorn's body. In Schermerhorn's blood.

※⊯⊱

I GOT STUCK ON the northbound Dan Ryan Expressway for half an hour because of a truck carrying pipe, plumbing pipe that looked about an inch in diameter and maybe eight feet long. The driver—this I got from my scanner—had "failed to secure the rig" so that when he passed a car and swerved right to get back in lane, the whole load rolled into the expressway. Hundreds upon hundreds of long lengths of one-inch pipe. Several cars had skated on the pipe, piling into each other. When I made it through the mess of crumpled cars, there was just one lane open and workers were still rolling pipe onto the shoulder into big drifts.

Is this a great city or what?

※⊯⊱

OLLIE CAUGHT ME ON the cell phone just as I was pulling in to the curb at Hansen's. My police ID might not get me through jammed cars bumper to bumper on the highway but it could let me park in a No Parking spot.

"Emily? I've talked with Deemer and just left Mr. Bettleby."

"And?" He explained what he'd got from Kurt Deemer. He'd gone from there to Mr. Bettleby's office. Since Bettleby had come to the Hawthorne House reunion by himself, his son and wife having refused to set foot in the place, he probably resented Schermerhorn a lot. I had been interested in him because, unlike any of the other parents, he had been alone in his room, free to come and go at any hour of the night. He could have got out, killed Schermerhorn, and gone back to bed with no one the wiser.

"He's not the killer, Emily."

"Just like that? How do you know?"

"He's got a neurological condition. It's a disease that causes the nerves in the hands and feet to progressively lose sensitivity."

"He was walking around well enough." I should have noticed if there was something that seriously wrong with him. *I can't be that sloppy.*

"Did you see that he was wearing ankle-high boots? They hold his feet rigid, I guess. But the point is, Emily, he can't close his hands fully. He can hold a glass to drink and he can wedge a fork or spoon between two fingers, but he can't close his hands enough to hold a pencil."

"Or wield a knife, I suppose?"

"Right. Even if he held the knife, he wouldn't have been able to put any strength into stabbing with it."

"Well, hell, let's see if we can eliminate *all* the suspects. The mayor will love that!"

"Emily, you haven't eliminated all the suspects. We both know who we still have. Sorry."

⚔️

"DR. HANSEN?" I SAID to the doorman. He called up to Hansen's apartment and apparently she said come up. The doorman gestured at an elevator that was all white carpet and mirrors. White carpet? What about Chicago winters? They must replace it constantly!

It was 10:00 A.M. Carol Hansen opened her door wearing lounging pajamas the color of whipped cream.

"Am I too early?" I asked, because of the pajamas. In fact, I was later than we had arranged.

"No. It's okay. Come on in."

As I crossed the foyer, which was paneled in some kind of pale wood, a man stepped out of an archway into the left side of the living room ahead of me. He was dressed, if I may call it that, in a pale green towel wrapped around his waist. Nothing else. He carried a large steaming mug in his hand.

"I left the coffee on the—oh, sorry," he said.

He was a hunk. I personally am far too sensible to be swayed by broad shoulders, a chiseled profile, lush black hair curling over the forehead, a high brow, and eyes the color of melting caramel. But when he said, "I'll leave you two alone," I was sorry to see him go.

He looked about twenty-four. She was forty-four. In a perfect world, this should not get anybody's attention. We don't have a perfect world.

Carol Hansen was unabashed. She grinned at his departing back, then she sat in a big leather chair and gestured at a chair facing hers for me. I obeyed. Seeing people's homes—you always learn something.

He came back. "Does this mean you don't want me to make brunch right now?" he asked.

"Not right yet," she murmured. He left again. She said,

"He's adorable. You can't expect him to be smart, too. Can't have everything."

"Yeah," I said. "Reality is a bummer sometimes. Don't you just hate it?"

"So what did you want to talk with me about?" she asked.

"Sex—"

Inadvertently I glanced at the hall, where the gorgeous young man had vanished. Carol Hansen burst into laughter. I did, too.

"—at Hawthorne House," I said. And had to stop to giggle some more. This merriment was hardly professional on my part.

"Look," I said, more sternly. "There were potential sexual undercurrents at Hawthorne House that nobody talks about."

"No kidding."

"Well, we need to talk about them. First, that school had to have been an explosive environment, sexually speaking. Say you had fifteen or so students there at any given time. Probably over a third of them were teenagers. Of both sexes. Say five or six students between thirteen and eighteen, just the age when their hormones are like little volcanoes."

"True."

"Well, help me out here. How did you deal with that?"

"Poorly."

"Come on. Please?"

"Well, yes, there were problems." She twiddled her thumbs, apparently not aware she was doing it.

I wanted her to talk about Schermerhorn and reveal stuff about her time there. But I was focused as much on her as on what she was talking about. To put it another way, when I pushed her to tell me who could have hated him and why, I was asking for reasons she might have hated him.

"There were a couple of incidents where teenagers— patients—got into the room we called the linen closet and got naked on a pile of sheets and pillowcases. There was even a

case of a male counselor having an affair with a female counselor, pretty much under everybody's nose, and nobody
knew."

"Anybody get pregnant?"

"One young woman. A counselor, not a patient."

"What about Schermerhorn?"

She paused, nodded to herself. Her thumbs stopped circling
each other.

"Schermerhorn," she said, "was a toucher. He'd pat women.
We didn't know in those days that it was inappropriate behavior. Little 'harmless' assaults on women in the workplace
were common."

"Did he touch you?"

"Of course. I laughed and moved away."

"Did he touch students?"

"Yes. He'd pat the girls. Did you know there were no
shower curtains in the students' bathrooms? He'd check the
girls and boys out while they were showering."

"Didn't anybody complain?"

"Sure they did. The girls especially. But they were *patients*.
They had no power."

"That was—why would he want no shower curtains?"

"Schermerhorn had some Freudian-based idea that the children should be comfortable in their own sexuality. Naturally,
he didn't shower in curtainless showers. But the children had
to. He encouraged the boys to masturbate and then talk about
it afterward."

"Talk with him?"

"With him. With each other. Again in the interest of open-
ness."

"What about Schermerhorn himself? Could he have had an
affair with one of the counselors?"

"He could have. I don't believe he did. If he did, it was kept
very, very secret. Hawthorne House wasn't an environment

where secrets could be kept for long. Even the two counselors' thing only lasted four or five weeks."

"Well, then. Could one of the counselors have *wished* he had made love to her? Could one of them feel rejected?"

She looked at me with her head cocked slightly.

"Ms. Folkestone, how could I possibly guess whether some woman secretly wanted Dr. S to seduce her and then secretly hated him for *not* doing it? I'm not a mind reader. My job would be a lot easier if I were."

"Mine too," I mumbled.

She was studying me so closely that I thought she knew I suspected her. She went on.

"To Schermerhorn, like Freud, everything was sexual if you looked deeply enough. From my observation, autistics vary a lot in their need for sex. Some are quite embarrassing, because they don't have any idea about what's socially acceptable. They'll masturbate at the grocery store, for example. And others seem to have no interest in sex at all.

"If you ask me, and I guess you are, I don't think sex explains the horrible way he was killed. And I especially don't think it's enough reason for a murder fifteen years later."

"People brood about wrongs done to them."

"This goes beyond brooding. The person who killed Dr. S *hated* him."

"I know." I said, "Hatred like you have for somebody who owed you something and wasn't there for you. Like you would hate a father who betrayed you."

"Like the children, you mean. Schermerhorn became effectively their father."

"Yes. Or somebody who didn't have adequate fathering himself or herself. And—is it 'transferred' you psychiatrists say?—transferred their feelings to Schermerhorn."

"Yes." She smiled. "And I assure you my father was, and is, a lovely man who is also a wonderful father."

She had the grace not to grin at me triumphantly.

"Dr. Hansen, you didn't tell me that Schermerhorn hit children."

"Where did you learn that? Never mind. You're right, but he didn't just hit them. He slugged them. He pulled one girl out of the shower and slapped her so hard she fell back in. When he slapped them he claimed he was the children's superego and he had to externalize the superego so that later they could internalize it."

The sneer in her voice could have etched stainless steel.

"I mean," she said, "he used Freudian theory to justify doing whatever the hell he bloody well wanted. Which is awfully easy to do with Freudian theory. We were hearing authoritarian idiocy from him. And eating it up. Sandboxes represented defecation. Swimming pools represented urination."

"Yuck."

"If a child wanted to take swimming lessons we were to be alert to how he had been toilet trained and the sexual conflicts that came from it. Can you imagine? The problem is that if childhood sexual conflicts explain everything then they explain nothing. It's like saying everything is caused by air. Every girl has penis envy? Well, it sure doesn't bother most of them. Most little girls think penises are silly. It's boys who think they're great."

I nodded.

She smiled. "But that isn't what you came here for, is it?"

"Who do you think killed Schermerhorn?"

"Somebody from outside, who came in during the night."

"The front door wouldn't open without a key and the back door was locked."

"You came here to decide whether I killed Dr. S, didn't you? Maybe I'm soured by life and want revenge on Dr. S? Well, no. Sorry. Don't make me out to be a victim of life. I'm happy with my life and happy with my career."

"You probably went into psychiatry thinking you would cure the mentally ill."

"And didn't? You're right if you think I'm at the age when people realize their dreams were unrealistic. That they can't change the world."

"You don't have children, do you?"

"Oh, poor me, no. I'm not crushed about that, either. People my age, who have children now in their teens or twenties, are beginning to realize they can't mold their children into exactly the people they wanted. The wise ones decide to want what they have, of course. Some others are very angry that they've spent their youth raising children who are unpleasant or ungrateful."

"So you're happy."

"I believed, like all young people, that the psychiatrists before me just hadn't been doing it quite right. I could cure everyone. I found out I couldn't. But by God, these days I'm coming close. I do good in the world. Genuine good. I make people better. You bring me a schizophrenic, hearing voices, bedeviled with commands in his head that tell him to set fire to his house or kill his dog because it's Satan in disguise. I give him medication and in two weeks, no more voices! Ms. Folkestone, I've got something that *works*!"

CHAPTER 42

"DR. EMERSON," I SAID, "I'm very deeply troubled." Erik Emerson raised his white eyebrows and simply nodded. Maybe he didn't want to say "Go on," because it would sound too shrinklike.

"The only solid evidence I have points to Jeffrey Clifford having murdered Dr. Schermerhorn. I'm under pressure to arrest him. I feel sympathetic toward him, and I don't really think he did it. Am I being swayed by feelings of sympathy?"

"I don't know. My guess is that you're too experienced an investigator for that." Emerson settled back in his chair. "We all have our emotions, but when we're aware of them they don't usually distort our perceptions. Much."

Emerson looked tired and sad. And unwell. He looked more exhausted than he had on Saturday, just after he had found Schermerhorn's body. This office of his was quite warm, in spite of the air conditioner. I could see the setting on it from where I sat, and he had it on midrange, not cold. A line of tiny ants snaked up the wall near the air conditioner's cord, maybe attracted by its moisture.

I said, "*Could* he have done it, Dr. Emerson?"

"People can fool you. Thirty years in this business and I still get taken completely off guard by something a patient will do."

His office was paneled in a warm wood, cherry, I thought. Against the wall behind me was the psychoanalyst's couch, which he had pointed out with a smile when I entered. Then he'd seated us in two very comfortable leather chairs near the window. An open door led into another room filled with books, and diagonally I could see a slice of a small room and a white porcelain sink. A bathroom must be part of the suite.

"You have two offices, Dr. Emerson? This is almost as big as my apartment," I said.

"I practically live here. This is my office for seeing patients. My writing office and reference books and so on are in there." He gestured at the second room.

"Does your family object to that?"

"No. No family. I'm all alone in the world." He smiled, taking the pathos out of the words.

In fact, I knew he was unmarried. I had done my research, just as I had with Dr. Hansen. "Sounds like a lonely life."

"Not at all. My work is my life."

"But surely you have relatives. Parents? Siblings?"

"I was brought up by my grandmother."

"I suspect there's a sad story behind that statement."

"My parents were killed in an automobile accident. On New Year's Eve. They weren't drunk. The other driver was."

I sighed. "How old were you?"

"Three." Dr. Emerson was suddenly much less chatty. I changed topics.

"If the autistics are unlikely killers, what kind of person *would* kill Dr. Schermerhorn?"

"Oh, dear. Do you want me to produce a profile?"

"Not really. Profiles work, when they work at all, on serial killers where the victims are more or less randomly chosen. But in this case the victim is clearly the mainspring. Schermerhorn was killed because he was Schermerhorn, not because he was handy."

"He was a wonderful man. He was like a father to me."

"Not all of his former patients love him."

"Dr. Schermerhorn could be authoritarian—"

"That's an understatement. He hit children when they didn't live up to his demands."

Emerson drooped.

"Didn't he, Doctor? If they didn't do what he wanted, he slapped them and punched them."

"No, not the way you think. But—" Emerson sighed. "Yes, he did. But he thought of himself as their father. He punished them as a father might. I don't condone it. I don't condone it when a real father strikes a child, either, but he saw himself that way."

"And so did the children?"

"Yes, so did the children. They had left their families behind, you see, and he was the only parent they really knew."

"He wanted to be everybody's father."

"Yes. I suppose so."

"So the killer might have the mind of an angry child, killing his father?"

"Possibly."

"Killing the person who had become his father when his father was no longer available."

"Possibly."

"Killing the father who betrayed him?"

"Possibly."

"The father who betrayed him as Schermerhorn betrayed you?"

TIME PASSED.

"How did you know?" Dr. Emerson finally asked.

I hadn't known. "I wondered why you let us think Schermerhorn suggested the reunion. Actually, you suggested it to him. But mainly, I think, because of all the people I had met, you were closest to him. You were the one who really *cared*. And he wasn't the person you thought he was."

Emerson closed his eyes.

"You trusted Schermerhorn more than any child did. They may have adopted him as a second father. You gave him your entire life. You did everything he wanted—you even *thought* the way he told you to."

Emerson dropped his forearms onto his thighs and turned his hands palm upward, a gesture of giving up. "He seemed to understand humanity. He understood the children. Or pretended to. He seemed so wise."

"Why did you believe him?"

"He was teaching at the university. He was running a school. Oh, God, I thought he had the credentials. Other people believed him, too. It wasn't just me. Everybody believed him."

"But you must have seen what he was doing to those children's parents."

He wrapped his arms across his chest as if he were cold.

I said, "I can understand laymen believing him, but you?"

"We only have our own perceptions of the world to go on, you know. Ever. You never can look at anything without preconceptions. Without the emotional colors you paint it with. He was so wonderfully convincing. I *saw* children getting better."

"But were they?"

"I realize now they were only getting older. Of the whole group, I know *now* there were only a couple who really improved enough to lead a normal life. At least five went into institutions and have never come out. The rest just survived, pretty much unchanged."

"But you believed—"

"Ms. Folkestone, have you ever met a discarded lover some years later and asked yourself how could you ever have kissed those lips? He or she is the same person, but he or she is now repellent, because you see him differently."

"True."

"It was all sham. He gave himself out to be a Korean War hero. I was there, in Korea. I was at the Battle of Kumsong River. Thirty thousand Americans died in that war. Think of that from today's perspective. But he never left the United States. He just traded on it. I didn't know that until quite recently.

"Jay didn't actually know anything about psychiatry. He wasn't even *trained*. *He made it all up.* I realized it decades later, when I was fifty-five years old and it was too late to change. It was like, I don't know, like biting into a hamburger and finding worms."

I said, "If it were me, I would have wanted never to see him again, instead of staging a reunion."

"Perhaps. I certainly should have felt that way. I know it now."

"Why did you suggest the reunion? Did you stage the whole thing just to have a chance to kill him?"

"No!"

"You set it up so that there would be lots of people around who hated him. Lots of suspects."

"No! It was a test! I wanted to find out what he really was. I hadn't seen Jay in several years. I thought, exactly like Carol Hansen, I'd see whether he was sorry."

"Was he?"

"Oh, not at all! He was proud of himself. To this day I don't know whether he ever believed in Freudianism or in what he told those poor parents, that they had damaged their children. But I knew Friday night, it didn't matter whether he believed it."

"What do you mean?"

"He didn't care! He had used those children as fodder. For his international reputation. As little stories for his books."

"Yes?"

"He was proud of his books, so I picked up one and hit him with it."

Maybe Emerson was making an argument that it was an impulse killing, not premeditated. If you don't bring a weapon, that argument works sometimes. Or maybe he was sincere.

"Just like that?" I asked. "Was there a trigger that set you off?"

"Yes! Yes! And I'll tell you what it was. You know Ben Goodspeed?"

"Of course. He came to the reunion with his mother? Yes."

"Dear little Ben. He's the nicest person. He smiles, but he doesn't talk. Jay said—what he said was that I shouldn't have invited Ben because he wasn't a good advertisement for Jay's books!"

I could imagine Schermerhorn saying that. And I might have slugged him myself.

"Are you trying to tell me it wasn't premeditated? To come here last weekend and kill him?"

Any smart suspect is going to say he didn't plan to kill. Premeditated murder is far more severely punished than impulse killing. But I believed that Dr. Emerson right now was beyond being self-protective.

"Maybe. Subconsciously. I had a feeling I was giving him a last chance, but I hadn't told myself what I would do if he failed the test."

"Still, why now? You've known what Schermerhorn was for years. Why kill him now?"

Emerson rubbed his eyes. He started to say, "I didn't intend—" Then he sighed wearily. "I give up. Maybe I did intend to kill him. I'm sick. I have congestive heart failure. I'm not dying, or at least not right now. But it's been progressing faster than I hoped. I'm tired all the time now. My meds are gradually failing to give an effective response. My doctor knows perfectly well I'm an MD, but he fiddles along, increasing dosages as if we were getting somewhere."

I sat still. I remembered him coughing occasionally. Was that from fluid in the lungs? And he had been up late Saturday night. He had told me he couldn't sleep. People with congestive heart failure, I believed, had a hard time breathing lying down. I wanted to say I was sorry about his illness, but he was a murderer and he must realize that I would have to arrest him.

It was at least a minute before he went on.

"Maybe I did. Maybe I thought I would only get more tired

and weak and then if I didn't do it now I would never be able to do it at all."

There was one thing I thought was true, a kind of compliment I could give him. "Doctor, I honestly believe that in your *medical* life you were trying to do the right thing for your patients."

He studied me and decided I was telling him what I really thought.

He said, "When I first realized that the whole Freudian approach was just stupid, I was—I was—can you possibly imagine what that was like? Everything I thought I knew! I wasn't professionally naive. I had tried the early tranquilizers on some of my patients, things like Miltown, but they didn't work very well and the side effects were unacceptable. You could stupefy patients but not really fix them. They didn't impact my belief that the real, honest approach to mental problems was through the psyche. But the first time I tried Prozac and it worked, I can't express how I felt—happy for the patient, but it was a horror for me, I'm ashamed to say."

"Tell me."

"Prozac was released for public use in 1988. I first prescribed it in 1990. I remember it as if it were yesterday. The patient had been in treatment for four years, four days a week. An airline pilot who was depressed and angry a lot of the time. You see anger in depression quite a bit. He'd gotten into a couple of screaming arguments with supervisors at work and it looked like another one might cost him his job. His father had been horribly critical of his children. Nothing this man did, as a boy or as a man, ever pleased his father. He'd come to understand during our sessions how that had hurt him, but he wasn't getting better. So I gave him an antidepressant, thinking of it as a crutch. Within two weeks, he was smiling and relaxed. I *saw* the depression slowly lift. So I asked him what he planned to do about his anger at his father, and he said, 'Oh, I just have to get over that.' Casually. What we had been working on for four years! God."

"I understand."

"Do you? I doubt it. I asked myself—where did all that Oedipal terror *go*?"

I kept silent.

"I felt like up till then I had been a witch doctor, making gestures over my patients. We psych students who wanted to go into psychoanalysis—we were told by our training analysts we were artists of the soul, because no two sadnesses were the same. We had to wrestle and probe for explanations and save the psyche. And then Prozac came along and all the sadnesses were the same. A serotonin deficiency.

"My whole *life*! The work I did. All those years. Suppose you worked a quarter century thinking you were helping people and then decided all you'd done is hurt them!"

"Do you use antidepressants in your practice now?"

"Of course. I have to. For my patients' sakes I have to. I'm not a monster, Detective Folkestone."

At the word "monster" he may have recalled the horrible way he killed Schermerhorn. I know I was thinking about it right then.

"You were going to let me arrest Jeffrey Clifford."

He said, "No!"

"You started to tell me you couldn't predict what a patient might do."

"No! I'd never have let anybody else take the blame for Jay's death. Never! In all my life I only did one intentionally cruel deed. It was cruel beyond anything I could have imagined before I did it."

I watched as several expressions passed over his face— horror, fear, anger, and some that puzzled me as much as they would puzzle an autistic.

He finally said, "And I don't think I'm sorry."

I gave him half a minute to gather his emotions. "Why," I

asked, "didn't you ever change your public stance? Why didn't you repudiate Freud and Schermerhorn if you found out they were wrong?"

"Cowardice," he said. He rubbed his forehead up and down with the palms of both hands.

"Dr. Hansen changed her mind in print."

He seemed not to have heard me. "My last articles came out five years ago. I've published nothing since. I have never defended Freudian psychoanalysis in print since I found out it was tripe."

"But during the weekend at Hawthorne House you challenged Dr. Hansen."

"I did that—"

"To cover up your change of heart. To cover up so that you could kill Schermerhorn and get away with it."

"No."

"Doctor, you wanted it to look like you were his biggest fan!"

"Noooo."

I changed topics. "How do you treat your patients now? Since your epiphany?"

"Like all honest psychoanalysts, I treat my patients who have big trouble, like major depression and schizophrenia, with drugs. If they have especially difficult symptomatologies, I refer them to psychopharmacologists."

"And you use psychoanalysis for what?"

"Like most psychoanalysts, I'm reduced to treating whiny neurotics."

Before I arrested him, I cautioned him, but he didn't pay much attention to my words.

He said, "All those children! All those children! All those years!"

CHAPTER 43

THE GARAGE AT the Clifford house was double length. The part nearer the street looked newer and there was a car inside. The back part must have been the original garage, remodeled as a small woodshop. I could see lights on in the back through a very small window in a side door. It was still full summer daylight at 6:00 P.M., but no doubt the window didn't provide enough light for woodworking.

Edward Clifford stood in the kitchen door of the main house, watching me. I had explained to him we'd made an arrest, and that I'd like to tell Jeffrey myself. Jeffrey was woodworking. When Jeffrey was a child, his father said, he kept smoothing things with his hands. Many years later, after Jeffrey had left Hawthorne House, his father remembered that and thought, maybe Jeffrey would like to sandpaper wood. Maybe he would make things. Now he made handcrafted furniture.

There was no sound of power tools as I stepped inside. I closed the door softly behind me.

Jeffrey bent over a carpet-topped workbench, drawing a strange tool toward himself. I said, "Jeffrey?"

He stood straight.

"Detective Folkestone."

"Would you call me Emily, please?"

"Yes."

"What is that?" The tool he held was a blade about a foot long, with perpendicular handles at both ends. He had a hand on each of the handles. The sharp side of the blade was toward him. Strangest knife I'd ever seen.

"It is a drawknife," he said. "Both hands do the same thing."

He drew it toward himself again, peeling a wafer-thin strip of wood from a long curved piece held in place by cloth-padded clamps. He picked up a similar piece of wood, grace-fully curved, tapering from a couple of inches wide at the top to just an inch at the bottom.

"Solid cherry," he said. "For a taboret table."

"You don't use power tools?"

"No."

Two of the legs were finished—not sanded or varnished, but fully carved. One stick of cherry remained untouched.

"It will be like this. But not exactly." Jeffrey took me to a closed-off boxy area lined with plastic sheeting in the corner of the garage where a small table stood. It was a beautiful lit-tle thing, legs gently curving, the round top made of cherry also, with an inlaid design on the tabletop, a chrysanthemum blossom of light wood edged symmetrically with tendrils and tiny leaves.

"This is a place. To varnish dust-free," Jeffrey said.

I realized I didn't hear Jeffrey as speaking strangely any longer. I didn't hear his pauses or his monotone. I was hearing what he said, not how he said it. And I had not noticed his awk-ward posture since I walked in, either. When had this change taken place? He had become simply a human being.

"I came to tell you we made an arrest. You're not under sus-picion any longer."

"That is good."

"Aren't you going to ask me who killed Schermerhorn?"

"No. I know. Who it is."

"You know?"

"I surmise it was Dr. E."

"You're right. Jeffrey, tell me what happened the night Schermerhorn died."

JEFFREY WAS NOT PARTICULARLY good at narrative, but he was very good at noticing and remembering detail. What he had done was perfectly clear. And it was important to him to make it clear to me:

Jeffrey woke up abruptly and sat up in bed so suddenly he felt dizzy. He was not in his familiar room at home. That was bad. Familiarity was comforting. Also it took much more energy to cope with a place he didn't know well.

He knew where he was, though, and it scared him. It was because he was in Hawthorne House that he woke up. There was sweat on his forehead, right at the hairline. When he brushed at it, the moisture felt cool on his hot face.

Jeffrey had waked with a jolt because he was terrified that Dr. S had come in his room and was standing at the foot of the bed.

Bed check. Dr. S did a surprise bed check every couple of weeks to make sure the kids had their lights out and weren't reading or joking around. Now, as an adult, Jeffrey was able to wonder why a man with a home and a wife of his own would wait around until late at night just to pounce into bedrooms and catch children being a little bit disobedient. At the time he had never asked himself that question. Dr. S wanted to be scary. He *was* scary. Springing at you in the night through your unlockable door was just one more way to be terrifying.

But this door had a bolt.

Jeffrey slipped out of bed to check the bolt, knowing he was behaving foolishly. There was a perfectly clear memory in his mind of pushing that bolt home before he went to bed. Indeed, there was a memory of being greatly satisfied at bolting the door.

It was bolted.

Jeffrey started to return to his bed, but his fingers began to flick against his thumb, almost without his mind being aware of it. He was nervous, keyed up by his sudden terrified awakening. His wristwatch was still on his wrist. Last evening he had thought it would be consoling to leave it there, something he was familiar with, and it squeezed his wrist gently, which he liked. He clicked on his room light, looked at his watch, and discovered it was three-thirty in the morning. His shoulders itched. His feet were cramped even though he was barefoot. He'd never get back to sleep this way.

He pulled his bathrobe over his pajamas, put on his shoes, and, unbolting his door, went out into the hall.

There was a light burning at the top of the stairs.

He picked his way down, in no danger of tripping because the light, even though low wattage, was well placed, and another bulb burned on the second-floor landing.

Maybe if he got something to eat he would be less nervous. There had to be leftovers in the refrigerators, or loaves of bread left out. A folded-bread sandwich would help. From earliest childhood, he had eaten folded-bread sandwiches, wouldn't eat them any other way, and had what his mother called snit-fits if anybody inadvertently cut his bread.

On the second floor, Jeffrey decided to detour into the ballroom. The miracle of the big chrysanthemum on the floor drew him in. A small work light burned over the entry doors, but most of the room was quite dark.

It was enough light for Jeffrey. He walked directly to the center of the room, where the petals of the huge flower all met. In the very center were inset rounds of a beautiful fruitwood representing flower stamens. Jeffrey stood right on them, in the very middle of the flower, in the very middle of the room, savoring the completeness. Quietly, he knelt and felt the marquetry, felt the join of the petals, the perfect matching of the shape of the circles to the holes in the wood around them. Even now, a hundred years after the wood had been set in place, his fingertips could hardly feel any seam between the two, so well had they been inlaid. Jeffrey stroked the wood, petting it, congratulating it. It was sound and happy, perfect.

Then he stood and walked out the door and took the stairs down.

In the basement kitchens there was evidence of the evening's reception and dinner, the pots and pans stacked on the counters along with the large caterer's cylinders containing knives, forks, and spoons. They were all clean and ready for the new day. One of the ovens was on its automatic-clean cycle. The counters had been scrubbed. The refrigerators were tightly closed. Trash and garbage appeared to have been taken outside.

Which made it all the stranger that there was a meaty smell.

Actually, Jeffrey thought, it was a raw-meat smell, richly bloody. Other out-of-place odors came to him now. Feces and urine. Possibly a toilet down here in the basement had overflowed. All the odors were coming from the basement corridor.

Surely it was wrong to leave raw meat stored anywhere near a flooded bathroom. A reputable caterer wouldn't do that, would he? Jeffrey pulled the string that turned on the nearest overhead light in the basement corridor and followed the smells.

Meat and bay rum. How very peculiar.

The smells grew stronger. There was no problem following them. The problem was finding the strings that pulled on the overhead lightbulbs. The bulbs themselves were dim and turning one on was not much help in finding the next. The string of one touched his face like a cobweb. Some of the bulbs were burned out.

All the smells were coming from up ahead, around the corner. Jeffrey could think of no reasonable explanation for that. He followed the scent to a doorway. He reached out and pulled the string to a ceiling bulb right inside the room.

And saw what lay on the floor.

⚅

HE TAPPED AS LIGHTLY as he could on the paneled oak door on the second floor. Nothing happened. He tapped again. Jeffrey knew April was in this room. Jeffrey knew every room in the place.

The door opened with no warning. Jeffrey nearly fell inside.

"What? What?" April asked. She wore a pink bathrobe, but otherwise looked just the same she had during the day—no makeup, her face pink, too, and naked seeming. She showed no sign of being surprised to see Jeffrey here in the middle of the night.

"Got to show you something."

"Something bad?"

"Something good. Let us get Henry."

"No, no."

"Why not?"

"His father."

"That is true." Jeffrey stared down at his shoes. "Let us try anyway. We will just open his door and see."

April went into her room again and emerged with a daytime shirt pulled on over her pajamas. Jeffrey thought it looked very strange, but it must made her feel dressed.

Henry was lying wide awake and his father was sound asleep, snoring. Henry came when Jeffrey beckoned.

Several minutes later, Jeffrey trooped downstairs, followed by April, Henry, and Ben. As he went, he said a little rhyme that he remembered from his time here as a child. Dr. S had told his mother during one of the few times she had been allowed to come and take him away for a weekend, "He's playing better with other children, Mrs. Clifford. As you know, autistics will play next to other children, but not with them. It's very rare for them to share."

Jeffrey for years after would repeat to himself, "Rare to share. Rare to share. Rare to share."

Now as he led his band down the stairs to the basement to share his discovery with them, he said under his breath, "Rare to share. Rare to share. Rare to share. Rare to share."

Jeffrey led the way, followed by April, then Henry, then Ben. None of them asked any questions or made any remarks to any other, and none spoke, except Jeffrey, who started a new rhyme as they passed through the kitchen. "Rare to share," he mumbled. "Shows you care. Rare to share. Shows you care."

They walked very softly through the kitchen and into the cellars, misty with spiderwebs and dim bulbs.

In fact it was only fifty feet down the cement-and-brick corridor to the doorway Jeffrey was seeking. It seemed farther because they moved slowly, overawed by the surroundings.

Dim light spilled from the room ahead. And the odor. Jeffrey could tell the other three noticed it; he could hear them sniff at it, trying to identify it.

Then he stopped at the doorway to the room. The three behind him clumped close without bumping him. He edged forward just a bit.

On the floor lay the naked body of Dr. Schermerhorn.

Jeffrey stepped inside, two paces nearer to the corpse, letting the others see. April came into the room. Henry came after her, slipping quietly but unhesitatingly closer to the body. He crouched, reached into the trail of blood that had run from Schermerhorn's punctured abdomen. Slowly, slowly, he reached out his hand and with his index finger touched the blood.

"True," he said. "Dead." He wiped his finger on his shoe.

"Yes, he's dead," Jeffrey said.

April turned toward the other three, looking into their faces in turn. Into their eyes. Jeffrey thought, looking into their beings.

April and Ben smiled in delight.

Henry said, "Lavish."

CHAPTER 44

JEFFREY ASKED ME, "Did you guess? When you came to Hawthorne House. That first day. That Dr. E had killed Dr. S?"

I said, "I should have. Henry was trying to tell us. He had gotten up in the night, or at least looked out of his door, and had seen Emerson carrying Schermerhorn down the hall and into the ballroom."

Jeffrey said nothing. I went on. "He saw four legs and four arms, which he described as being like a spider. Eight legs."

Jeffrey said, "Arachnida. Spider. Indeed, yes."

"And two white-haired heads."

"Duplication. Indeed. I understand now. But I did not understand it. When he said it." After a moment he added, "But Henry was not. Trying to tell us."

"No?"

"He was just speaking. He does not wish to communicate."

"Jeffrey, I've decided you were being literally truthful when you told me you didn't know how your footprint got next to Schermerhorn's body."

"I did not. Know I had trod on blood."

"Yes, but you knew from the first that Dr. Emerson had killed Schermerhorn."

Jeffrey did not hear this as a question. I said, "I mean, did you know immediately that he had?"

"Actually, I just now understood. That you were asking a question. Despite the fact that it was not. Phrased as a question should be. It takes me a moment to decode that, however."

I waited. He said, "Yes. I did believe quite soon. That Dr. E.

Had killed Dr. S. When Dr. E passed near me Saturday morning at breakfast. And again in the ballroom. He smelled of bay rum. Dr. S always smelled of bay rum,"

"But he spent some time with Schermerhorn Friday evening."

"In my estimation, it would require. Very close contact. To retain a scent twelve hours later. Dr. E also smelled of blood."

"I can't believe you could smell it. He would have showered."

"Why?"

"Wouldn't you take a long shower if you'd killed somebody?"

"I would not kill."

"But he must have showered and that would wash the scent off his body."

"A short shower. Perhaps. To take a long shower at three A.M. Might wake somebody up. And make them suspicious."

"You're right. But any shower would wash off the scent."

"I would surmise the bay rum scent. Would be in the suit pants of Dr. E. Or his shirt."

"You're right. Again. Emerson would have carried the inert body to the dumbwaiter and the scent would get on his clothes." The fact that he'd worn the plastic bags over his clothes later for the killing process would only hold in the scent, because it got on him before the killing in the basement.

"Still, Jeffrey, why didn't you tell me?"

"I perhaps should have done so. However, I was grateful to Dr. E. He had been. Kind to us. When we were children. He was not like Dr. S. He had no need to dominate. I had scarcely remembered how kind he. Was until I met him again."

"I see."

"I was conflicted." He smiled as he said the word.

"Whatever. You could have saved me a lot of trouble if you'd told me." But would I have believed him then?

Jeffrey said, "I think gratitude such as I have. To Dr. E. Is very much like love."

"Yes," I said.

"I would like," he said, "to make. An experiment."

"What kind of experiment?"

"I would like. You and me. To go to lunch in a restaurant."

Seven

The doctor should be opaque to his patients and,
like a mirror, should show them nothing
but what is shown to him.

—SIGMUND FREUD

IT WAS HIGH NOON and Jeffrey was in the process of amazing himself. He was eating lunch at a restaurant and was not nervous. In fact, he felt good, even though he had never done anything exactly like this before. Emily Folkestone sat across from him. He noticed that there were ink stains on the middle finger of her right hand, slightly smudged, as if she had tried to wash it off but couldn't get it all. She smelled of lemons, which he assumed was the scent of her shampoo.

"This is kind of amusing," Emily Folkestone said to him. "Whenever I find a seat in a restaurant, I always try to get one where I can see the windows and doors. It's a cop thing, wanting to know if there's a terrorist with a gun coming in."

Jeffrey said, "And I wish to face away. From the doors and windows and people."

They were in a pancake house on Chestnut Street. They had both ordered the apple pancakes. Pancakes were quiet food. The restaurant was quiet, too, much less busy at lunch than in the morning. Jeffrey had feared eating out would be difficult, and he wondered all morning whether he had made a mistake, but he went ahead. After all, what was the worst that could happen? He might have a fit of nerves and start to spin out word associations. He had brought some medication just in case.

"You look different, Jeffrey," Emily said.

"Oh. Actually, I look the same. But my clothing. Is different." It was looser and not so nice in feel, he thought, but he could stand it. "My sister picked it out for me. To wear to eat in a restaurant."

"You're guileless, Jeffrey."

"Is that bad?"

Emily said, "No. I think it's good."

"Thank you."

He was startled when Emily Folkestone touched his hand. In addition to the lemons, she smelled like flowers. Perfume, maybe? Had she worn perfume to please him? He thought he would ask what kind of flowers, and then he thought he shouldn't. That was probably a too-personal remark. She said, "I think your going to Hawthorne House for the weekend, after everything that happened to you there, was an act of great courage." She took her hand back.

"Thank you." Jeffrey wondered what all this meant. Pictures went through his mind. He had read a great deal about sex at one time, many years ago, as a teenager, but he didn't think he'd like it. Kissing appeared particularly unsanitary. Why should it be a good thing to exchange saliva?

"I want to be. Thought of as human," he said, carefully adding, "Emily," as she had asked him to do.

"I should hope so," she said.

"But I don't think I want to have a romance."

CHAPTER 46

OLLIE AND I WERE trying to identify a body. The man had been found dead in an SRO hotel three days before, ten days dead, and still no one had come forward to claim him. He was one of seventy-five heat death victims unidentified and unclaimed. No one had missed him, no friend, no relative, no church, no job. Most of the unclaimed dead were men, as were most of the heat deaths, for that matter. Most of the dead were elderly. Most elderly people were women. But most of the people dead from heat were men.

Old women have more relationships than old men.

Our man had been about seventy-five. He had lived in this building on South Michigan for four years. They had a name for him, Willie Larsen, and he paid his rent in cash. The desk men had seen him go out to the store and come back with a small bag of groceries every Tuesday and Friday for years. Some of them would say, "Hello, Willie." Sometimes he answered.

"Never saw him go out on weekends. Or after three in the afternoon. Scared of the teenagers, probably."

In his room were Alka-Seltzer, aspirin, Tylenol, Pepto-Bismol, and some creams for dry skin, all in a little plastic carry case, since the bathroom was down the hall and shared by everybody on his floor. No prescription medication. He had a tiny refrigerator. The only things in it were four packages of bologna and a stick of margarine.

His wallet held no driver's license, no insurance cards. He was getting money from somewhere, but there was no bank information and no social security card.

Since on the Tuesdays and Fridays he went out he never stayed longer than two hours, we hit every bank within a one-hour walk. No luck. We talked with every resident of the SRO. No luck.

It was beyond belief that any person could live with so little contact with the rest of the world, and yet there were seventy-five such cases among the heat deaths in Chicago. Unidentified people. Nonpersons. There had to be many more people like them, without contacts, among the living.

Ollie and I finally sank onto a bench in a bus stop shelter near the SRO. The weather was still hot, eighty-five instead of a hundred, and the shelter was hotter than outside because it acted like a solar oven. But I think we were so disheartened about Willie Larsen that we didn't care.

Sure enough, the media gave the heat disaster scant coverage after a few days passed. Suburban newspapers had scarcely paid attention in the first place, and suburban editions of downtown papers quickly cut back, possibly thinking the deaths were dreary reading, without any countering excitement. After July twentieth, even city editions were letting the stories fall to the back pages. Seven hundred and thirty-nine people had died in that week, beyond the expected natural mortality. But the media were already producing stories questioning the medical examiner's findings. Columnists asked whether the heat wave had been real or a "media event."

A commission was established to study what had happened.

The arrest of Dr. Emerson for Dr. Schermerhorn's murder preempted the heat wave story on the major television news shows the day of his arrest. The story ran above the heat wave in the papers, too. It was a big deal on the TV news, and in magazines like *People* and the *Enquirer*-style papers, where one of them headlined "Shrink Sinks Shrink." A more moderate paper had it as "Disciple Kills Beloved Doctor." The media didn't have a clue about Dr. Emerson's motive for killing Schermerhorn. He wasn't saying. I loomed large in most reports as lead investigator, but I didn't give them anything beyond the basic fact of Emerson's arrest and confession. If he didn't want to talk about why he killed Schermerhorn, that was his business. So they all spun it as Emerson's envy of his more popular, much more successful mentor.

I was sad about that.

Ollie said, "Maybe Willie Larsen *wanted* to lose himself."

I nodded. A short period of silence followed. Cars drove past, kicking up hot dust.

We had gone to Dr. Erik Emerson's home as soon as he was booked and had called his lawyer. He lived in a small apartment on Pearson. The building was about thirty years old, pleasant but undistinguished, many of the tenants being Northwestern Medical School students living three to a room and a few of them law school students as well.

While a lot of the students, the super said, had small one-room studios with a railroad kitchen, Emerson had two rooms and a real kitchen. That was about all the difference. Ollie and I stood amazed when we walked in. There was a single bed with a striped cotton bedspread. Two Goodwill-quality nightstands flanked it. A landscape print hung on the wall over the bed. The kitchen held a few aluminum pots and pans. The living room was most discouraging of all, just a purplish worn sofa, a floor lamp of the type that holds its own round table, a floor lamp with a bullet-shaped shade, a melamine coffee table, and cheap bookcases filled with high school and college texts. It was the apartment of a student. A 1960s student.

There were half a dozen bookcases, storing books from as far back as 1960, many of them textbooks. On a bottom shelf, more than a dozen books were turned backwards, their cut-page side to the room, the spine with title to the wall. I pulled one out. It was upside down, as well. Turning it up I found one of Dr. Jay Schermerhorn's early works. All the other turned-to-the-wall books were his as well. "Ollie," I said, pointing at the shelf.

"Oh."

What was even sadder, I thought, was that Dr. Emerson had repudiated them but he hadn't been able to throw them out.

If we had seen this days ago, would we have suspected Emerson right away.

The lab found traces of cement dust on Emerson's clothes. It matched the very old cement in the bag that had been tied to Schermerhorn's foot. The lab could connect Emerson to the killing pretty well. Not that Emerson was fighting the charge.

But that was done now. We sat in the shelter of the bus stop, exhausted.

Ollie said, "You like this Jeffrey Clifford."

"Yeah."

"He's a person kind of stripped down to the essence. You'd like that."

I was surprised at Ollie's perception, although I shouldn't have been. "Yes. No front. No social face. No dressing up the outside and thinking it affects the inside."

More silence.

I said, "I thought I was quite a bit like him. I thought I'd established something like little beachheads into his thinking. And I had. But not really enough. He's right to say nobody understands him. I like him, though."

"You gonna go out with him more?"

"I might have dinner with him sometimes." I turned and looked square at Ollie. "It's not a romance, Ollie. He's not—he doesn't have a romantic bone in his body."

"He's a nice guy."

"You're a nice guy, too."

"You want to come to dinner with Jason and me tonight? We might go out for a pizza."

"Place with air-conditioning?"

"Fussy, fussy, fussy."

"I'd like to bring my nephew Petey, if that's okay. I think he needs a change of scene."

Acknowledgments

A LOT OF PEOPLE HELPED by providing information and expertise. Any mistakes in this book are entirely their fault.

There. I always wanted to say that. However, it's not true. Any mistakes, worse luck, are mine.

My thanks to:

Dennis M. Banahan, novelist and retired Chicago police officer, for help on when it is permissible to search suspects.

Veteran state's attorney Robert F. Cleary for much advice.

Doug Cummings, WGN Radio, for his knowledge about reporters and reporting.

Jeanne Dams for writing advice and wisdom.

Alzina Stone Dale for her expertise on all things Chicago, in this case especially the Hyde Park area.

Michael Allen Dymmoch for several insights about autism.

The book *Lost Chicago* by David Lowe, for wonderful pictures of old Chicago mansions, gone forever. Everybody should own this book.

Rod Hathaway, professional insurance agent. He had numerous suggestions about alternatives for parents with children who need ongoing medical care.

Henry Kanar, D.D.S., M.S., emeritus associate professor, University of Michigan, for his expertise on avulsed teeth.

Mark Zubro for input and wisdom achieved in a lifetime of teaching young people.

The heat wave of 1995 was, unfortunately, real. For a full account, see the fascinating book *Heat Wave* by Eric Klinenberg.

Dr. Carol Hansen is fictional, but Carol Hansen is real. She won a role in this book in an auction of objects and opportunities in support of Writers' Theatre, which mounts wonderful productions at 325 Tudor Court, Glencoe, Illinois. I want to thank her for her support of live theater, which always needs friends, and hope she enjoys being a psychiatrist for a while.

A READER WHO IS FAMILIAR with Bruno Bettelheim and his Orthogenic School will see many similarities between Bettelheim and Dr. Schermerhorn. There are also big differences. But it will be obvious that I developed Schermerhorn to explore some of the problems of Bettelheim's approach to treating children. Since Bruno Bettelheim's death in 1990, more and more criticisms of his treatment have appeared in the press, written both by psychologists and by former patients. I am particularly outraged when a person like Bettelheim uses his position of authority to cast blame, as Bettelheim did, at the parents of the children he had in his care. How cruel to tell a parent that he or she secretly wanted the child dead, that parental coldness had caused his autism. And how doubly cruel to tell that to the children.

There are many, many interesting books available about Bettelheim, or autism. They take various positions on Bettelheim, on Freud, on the training of psychiatrists, and so on. A very few of them from a rich list are these:

For words from Bruno Bettelheim himself, there is *The Empty Fortress: Infantile Autism and the Birth of the Self* (The Free Press paperback edition, 1972 [text first copyrighted in 1967]). Here Bettelheim declares: "Throughout this book I state my belief that the precipitating factor in infantile autism is the parent's wish that the child should not exist."

And *The Uses of Enchantment: The Meaning and Importance of Fairy Tales*, by Bruno Bettelheim (Vintage Books, 1977).

Written by the brother of a patient, an important exposé of Bruno Bettelheim is *The Creation of Dr. B,* by Richard Pollak (Touchstone [Simon & Schuster], 1997).

Written by a patient who spent thirteen years in the Orthogenic School, and largely supportive of Bettelheim, is *Not the Thing I Was,* by Stephen Eliot (St. Martin's Press, 2003).

A fine book explaining Asperger's syndrome is *Asperger's Syndrome: A Guide for Parents and Professionals,* by Tony Attwood (Jessica Kingsley Publishers, 1998).

One of the most difficult aspects of dealing with autism, and one often very difficult to talk about, is the impact of the condition on siblings. This is sensitively explored in the book *The Normal One: Life with a Difficult or Damaged Sibling,* by Jeanne Safer, Ph.D. (The Free Press, 2002).

The training of a psychiatry student and socialization of a psychiatrist into the psychiatric community and into either the biomedical or psychotherapeutic camp is described in *Of Two Minds: The Growing Disorder in American Psychiatry,* by T. M. Luhrmann (Knopf, 2000).

A well-known critic of Freud is Jeffrey Moussaieff Masson. In his book *Against Therapy* (Common Courage Press, 1994), he argues against not just Freudian analysis but all psychotherapy.

Another opinion of Freud can be found in *Seductive Mirage: An Exploration of the Work of Sigmund Freud,* by Allen Esterson (Open Court Publishing Company, 1993).

The Memory Wars: Freud's Legacy in Dispute, by Frederick Crews et al. (New York Review of Books, 1995), contains Crews's opinion of Freud with rejoinders from other psychiatrists.

Autism from an autistic person's point of view can be found in *Emergence: Labeled Autistic,* by Temple Grandin and Margaret M. Scariano (Warner Books, 1996).

Grandin has written several other books on her experiences as an autistic person.